AN UNREASONABLE MAN

Arthur Boyne seemed to most people to be an amiable eccentric, a man whose career in the Indian Civil Service had not progressed as far as he deserved, who was prone to cynicism and hypochondria, and who entertained socially reckless notions of atheism and socialism. But to his wife and family he was an unreasonable man. His misanthropy, his shortcomings as father, husband and breadwinner drove his wife deeper and deeper into a bitter neurosis and two suicide attempts, and they were linked inextricably with his chronic hypochondria. Whenever any unpleasant obligation or confrontation loomed he took to his bed. He probably spent half his life there.

In this remarkable study of hypochondria and a marriage of nerves Henrie Mayne describes the effects of Arthur Boyne's strange condition – on his own life and on the lives of those around him. His remoteness, cynicism and obstinacy seem all the more extraordinary for their depiction in this long and magnificently readable novel against a background of social manners and international upheaval from the colonial heyday of the Raj in the 1890s to the traumatic austerity and confusion of the Second World War and its aftermath.

Henrie Mayne, who received a B.Sc. from the London School of Economics, is a lecturer on the history of architecture. She has written short stories and has made translations, but this is her first novel.

AN UNREASONABLE MAN

HENRIE MAYNE

QUARTET BOOKS   LONDON

First published by Quartet Books Limited 1976
A member of the Namara Group
27 Goodge Street, London W1P 1FD

Copyright © 1976 by Henrie Mayne

ISBN 0 704 32117 3

Typesetting by Bedford Typesetters Ltd

Printed in Great Britain by litho by
The Anchor Press Ltd Tiptree, Essex

To Hilary

'The reasonable man adapts himself to the world; the unreasonable one persists in trying to adapt the world to himself. Therefore all progress depends on the unreasonable man'
– George Bernard Shaw, *Man and Superman*,
'Maxims for Revolutionaries'

AN UNREASONABLE MAN

Prologue

The Cedars,
Victoria Avenue,
Byculla,
Bombay,

23rd March, 1949

My dear Nephew,

It is with a heart bowed down with grief that I write to inform you of the death of my revered friend, Mr Arthur Boyne, late of the Indian Civil Service, at the Provincial Hospital at Port Elizabeth, Africa. The *Times of India* apprised me of this melancholy event at my breakfast table, since when I have been unable to partake of morsel of food or sup of drink. All men are mortal and we should be prepared for death to cut the cord in the twinkling of an eye. Alas! I was not so prepared and my distress is unbounded, the more so as the solid gold tea-set (engraved with his initials and carved with roses, lotuses, big games and other suitable emblems) which I had intended to dispatch to him in celebration of our half-century of friendship, is only now nearing completion. It shall be dispatched instead to his widow, to whom it may prove to be some small consolation as a token of my high esteem, but that is not at all the same thing.

It is scarcely necessary for me to remind you that the late lamented is the father of our fortunes and the protector of our house. Were it not for the government contract that he bestowed upon us to the astonishment of our rivals and the discomfiture of our enemies, we would not hold the position of respected affluence that is indubitably ours today. That was close on fifty years ago but it was from this seed that our great fortune grew and, like the elephant, I do not forget.

1

Many a time in the course of those years have I begged the late lamented to accept a token in acknowledgement of my gratitude – a motor car perhaps or a cheque to assist in the education of his progeny, and always he replied: 'Still trying to bribe me, you old devil . . .' (he used the term as one of affectionate familiarity you understand). 'Think of Clive!' he would say. 'Remember Warren Hastings!' After his retirement, when such jests were no longer applicable, I succeeded in getting him to accept one or two small trifles to culminate in the gift already mentioned and now never to be delivered to him – a gift inspired by the memory of his propensity for the beverage, tea.

I now come to the purpose of this missive. The suggestion has been made by your aunt, good woman that she is, that I should honour my esteemed friend's memory by the laying of a wreath on his tomb. 'And how am I to do that in Cape Province, Africa, when I am in Bombay, India, woman?' I cried in my dismay. It was then that she thought of you, our nephew in Nairobi, Kenya. 'Bairamji will do it on your behalf. He is in the same continent,' she shrewdly pointed out to me in my grief. So, my nephew, you will take the train to this Port Elizabeth, inquire at the hospital where is the late lamented's resting-place and lay upon it the finest and largest wreath that money will buy. Please arrange for a photograph of the same that I may have suitably framed in a silver frame, *in memoriam*.

Your expenses will be defrayed when you submit the account. It is some time since I received your news and I trust that your business prospers and that your wife and children (how many are there now – eight? nine?) and other dependants are all in good health, by the grace of God. Please hasten in the dispatch of my melancholy tribute to my honoured friend and doubt not that it shall be remembered in your favour when the day of reckoning comes. Your aunt, cousins, nephews and nieces send you their greetings.

Ever your affectionate uncle,
Jamshedji Doongaji

The Cedars,
Victoria Avenue,
Byculla,
Bombay.

3rd April, 1949.

My dear Nephew,

Your letter anxiously awaited has caused me grave vexation. It is fitting to think that the ashes of my esteemed friend should repose in the bosom of the Indian Ocean, but, on reflection, this is a matter that you might perhaps have had the foresight to ascertain by telephone before making the fruitless journey to Port Elizabeth. Do not refer again to great distances. In India, too, we have great distances. (It would have been more prudent also to purchase the wreath after acquiring the relevant information.) However, I am nothing daunted. It was perseverance that succeeded in building our great fortune and it is by perseverance that I shall succeed in my present ambition to honour the memory of the dear defunct, Mr Arthur Boyne, I.C.S. You shall therefore charter an aeroplane to fly over the nearest portion of the Indian Ocean and deposit upon the billows a wreath as described in my letter of the 23rd ult. I shall require a photograph of the wreath floating, and though this may be more difficult to achieve than on *terra firma*, it is not beyond the scope of air photography.

The speed with which you dispatch my mission will count in your favour, rest assured.

Your affectionate uncle,
Jamshedji Doongaji

'Remember Boyne?'

'No, I don't think so.'

'He was a chap I knew in Delhi in '96, '95 it might have been . . . Went out about the same time I did. He was on the Viceroy's council once. Statistician or something . . . Rum chap. They thought a lot of him when he first came out. Never got anywhere though.'

3

'What about him?'

'He's dead, that's all. It says here he died in Port Elizabeth. Wonder what he was doing there . . . Queer fellow. Never made the grade. Didn't get on with him myself. Well, that's another of us gone – '

'Have a drink.'

'I think perhaps I will.'

'Lucy? Hullo? Is that you Lucy?'

'Hullo, Mother.'

'Lucy, I've just had a cable, from Dickie. It says – where are my glasses – it says, are you there Lucy . . . it says, "Father died suddenly Port Elizabeth Hospital. Writing. Love. Dickie." '

'Oh, *Mother* . . .'

'But Lucy, I didn't know he was ill!'

'No.'

'I'd no idea – '

'It said "suddenly", didn't it?'

'Yes. Thank goodness. He could never have stood a lingering illness. I've had such a shock – '

'I'll be over presently, Mother.'

'No, no, you're busy. Such a shock. The boy just walked in with a telegram. I was – '

'I'll be over presently. Goodbye for now.'

The child Frances, doing her homework on the floor in front of the fire, straightened up suddenly.

'What's the matter with Granny?'

'Nothing.'

'Why're are you going over there?'

'Only about some business. Have you finished your homework?'

'But Mummy, what's "suddenly"? You said "suddenly".'

'Did I? Look darling, it's time for your bath. You go and turn it on and I'll put away your books for you.'

'But *Mummy* – '

'Oh well . . . Look here darling, it's bad news I'm afraid. Ganfer's dead.'

There was no sound for a moment as the child rose slowly to her feet, the colour ebbing from her face. 'No!' she said suddenly,

'No! No!' as she rushed from the room slamming the door behind her. The bathroom became noisy with her lamentations. Here was grief indeed.

1

Arthur John Boyne was born in a dismal street in the vicinity of Paddington Station. His father was the younger son of an Irish peer; his mother, whose origins were humble, came from Liverpool. He was the eldest of five children whose legitimacy was never in question until their father's death. This took place in a singularly grievous way. One foggy evening in November, Arthur, poring over his Latin, was ordered by his taciturn and often harsh-tempered father to come for a walk. The suggestion was unusual and the weather repellent, so the boy hesitated, but only for a moment, noting the look on his father's face. The walk led through the cold gas-lit streets to a church as cold and dim and empty as the streets outside. Arthur was surprised, as he had never before seen his father in a church (he himself at fourteen was entering on a fleeting, pious phase in his life), but he knew better than to ask questions. His father marched him to the altar, ordered him to kneel and repeat after him, 'I Arthur John Boyne, swear by Almighty God to look after my mother, brothers and sister in the event of anything happening to my father.' The walk home was in silence. When, half an hour later, his mother sent him upstairs to call his father to supper, he found that he had cut his throat with a razor.

Of that calamitous time, only one other scene remained vividly in the boy's memory. Among his father's papers establishing his real identity – the commission he had held in the Indian Army, his marriage lines to a compatriot of high degree and similar items – was a letter from the Duke of Suffolk, dated nearly twenty years before.

My dear Algernon,

I am appalled at this terrible news. All comment is superfluous. I know that it is fashionable to abuse you and to sympathize with your wife, but I for one am with you, whatever you may or may not have done. If at any time, in any way, I can be of service, please call upon your most sincere friend,
Suffolk.

This letter the 'widow' in her desperation and under pressure from Liverpool relatives sent to the rich and influential duke, 'that prominent member of court circles' as he was commonly styled in the press.

A few days later, a carriage drew up at the Boynes' door from which alighted two gentlemen – the duke's agent and attorney. After a short session with Mrs Boyne, Arthur (hastily scrubbed and changed) was driven away to meet his benefactor at the attorney's office in Holborn. Here the duke, handsome, unsmiling, distant, took a long look at the awkward spectacled boy, remarked as if to himself, 'So you're Algy's son . . .' and soon left the room. Arthur never saw him again. It was then explained to him that His Grace, in memory of his close friendship with his father, had undertaken to help his unfortunate dependants . . . a small annuity for the widow . . . a gentleman's education for one of the sons . . . The one condition was that none of them were ever to approach His Grace. They never did.

Fortunately, the boy selected for the duke's beneficence was clever. At the public school to which he was now sent he was wretched, but highly successful in class. Clumsy and short-sighted, he was miserably bad at games. While lacking social graces and unwilling to comply with the prevailing form, he started by being bullied and ended unpopular – but scholastically he triumphed. He left school with a major scholarship to Cambridge and several minor exhibitions. As his public school years were the most miserable of his life, his Cambridge ones were the happiest. It was here that he tasted freedom, companionship, the intoxication of new ideas – and here that he fell in love.

Arthur's rooms were at the top of the staircase. On the ground floor in magnificently panelled rooms facing the court lived Archie Burnett – a blood. Archie was high-spirited and convivial. He was work-shy, a gifted mimic, and in an age when all cultivated circles aspired to produce their own music in the home, he liked nothing better than to entertain with an inexhaustible series of songs, largely Neapolitan and Spanish, accompanied by his own guitar and sung with a ferocious command of accent. These talents, combined with liberal hospitality, soon made him the centre of an admiring circle. Arthur, starved of affection and friendship at home and at school, hero-worshipped from afar, approached a little nearer and to his surprise and joy soon found himself an accepted member of this magic circle. Not that he allowed himself to go in for nightly junkettings. He was a scholar with certain standards to keep up. But once or possibly twice a week he luxuriated in this stimulating company.

Myopic and lacking in ordinary powers of observation, it was a long time before he noticed the photograph. It stood on the piano in an expensive frame. It showed a young girl scarcely more than a child leaning over a photographer's rustic gate against a backcloth of a lake and trees. She had a fringe and long, gently waving fair hair, a pointed chin, delicate features and a rapturous expression in her eyes. Arthur's gaze was riveted. Never had he seen such beauty – not even that night at the Alhambra. And the innocence. . . . As he gazed, listening to the languorous southern love-songs, he found himself burning to know more. At last the opportunity came when he could ask Archie, casually, 'Who's that?'

'That's my little sister Isabelle. Be, ee, double-el, ee . . . she's very particular about the spelling. That's our Huguenot ancestry,' he guffawed.

Isabelle . . . Isabelle . . . how sweet the name was . . . Isabelle . . . And Arthur as he went dreamily up the staircase to his rooms knew he was in love.

Mrs Boyne was in slightly easier circumstances. Her younger sons

8

were apprenticed in the City and Arthur largely paid for. The suicide had in fact left some small savings, and there was the duke's annuity. They had moved therefore from the dismal house near the terminus to a little house in a row, one street away from the park. Directly facing the park was a row of tall, imposing houses backed by long narrow gardens, at the end of which was a row of coach houses, each serving the mansion in front of it. It was facing this row of coach houses that the Boynes now lived. Arthur discovered that by an extraordinary coincidence the Burnetts lived in the row on the park almost exactly opposite and was invited by Archie to call. This he did precipitately.

As the parlourmaid showed him upstairs to a drawing-room on the first floor, he could hear the faint tinkling of a piano. It was the massacre of a Chopin nocturne, but to Arthur it was the music of the spheres. Then he saw her, seated at the piano, wearing a white blouse with bulky sleeves and a dark skirt – the dress of a schoolgirl. The delicious hair was up. The photograph had by no means exaggerated her prettiness. The soulful look was less in evidence, but this only made her the more approachable. Arthur's heart was hammering. He found that he could not utter, but Isabelle seemed not to notice and prattled artlessly until Archie and the formidable Mrs Burnett made their appearance.

Arthur's recollection of that tea was of upsetting his cup and knocking over the cakestand. Though a friend at Cambridge, he was socially ineligible for the grandeur of the Burnett circle. Isabelle's father, a man of good family and considerable ability, had amassed a fortune by various means. He had managed to acquire a seat in Parliament, where he held the distinction of never having spoken in any debate, though his constituency was the richer for his bounty. He divided his time between his many interests, his club and bouts of chronic bronchitis, leaving his children and home to the rule of his able but despotic wife. The social gulf between Burnetts and Boynes was not one that could be bridged, neither would Arthur have wished it. Though his family sometimes coarsely referred to his friends 'the toffs opposite' and wanted to know when they were going to be asked over, they would have been thrown into trepidation had any invitation come. Neither was Arthur asked again. This did not worry him at all. His love was the stuff of dreams. It was enough for him to live within a stone's throw of this exquisite little creature, to loiter in the park as if by accident to bow to the carriage as she drove past with her mother, to see her sometimes returning from school followed by a housemaid carrying her books; above all, to be able to see the light at the back of the big house from his own bedroom window, to imagine her retiring for the night; though here his thoughts stopped short at a rosy vision in white, brushing her shining hair before a looking-glass.

Dreams . . . then work. For he was never so besotted with love that he could not switch off his dreams and lose himself equally in study. He had inherited a mathematical gift from his father who, after his mysterious disgrace, had supported his second family in precarious poverty by becoming a maths coach at a crammer's. But while the father hated the subject as abysmal drudgery, the son loved it. It was to him as music to the musician or painting to the painter: a mysterious universe where few could enter, always to hand as an escape from the burdensome realities of living. And so it remained all his life.

There came a day when Isabelle and her mother were to visit Archie at Cambridge. A river party was planned, a picnic at Grantchester, a return to his rooms to tea afterwards. Arthur found himself included and sheer joy kept him humming tunelessly for days on end in happy anticipation. All depended on the weather. For a whole week before, the sun shone in cloudless skies and little breezes played along the river. Would it, could it last? It did. The morning dawned in a pearly haze that promised heat to come. Light spilled into the courtyards in great golden shafts piercing geometrical patterns of blue shadow, shafts of light in which the motes danced. The air was still, awaiting the arrival of a goddess. At last she came. She wore a flowered dress of gossamer material, a huge white hat with rosebuds on the brim, and she carried a parasol. When she turned her smile which combined shyness with coquetry on Arthur, he felt his limbs turn to water. But yes, he could walk, or was he floating? His legs encased in white flannels, his straw boater at an unusual angle, he followed in the rear of the procession to the river. Here he found himself seated in the second punt (for he was no adept with a punt pole). But the first punt was near enough for him

10

to see the tendrils escaping under the great hat, one hand trailing in the water, the other manipulating a little fan to keep off midges, near enough to hear the high-pitched school-girlish laugh that drifted back at intervals. This slow gliding over the muddy stream with the sunlit meadows slipping by and all that loveliness just ahead, this surely was paradise. On the homeward journey, he found himself miraculously in the same punt – at the other end of it. Afterwards, in his room, he tried to remember the conversation and found he could not. Only in the final approach to the landing-stage, when a race developed between the two puntsmen and he found himself splashed from behind, with trickles of water down his neck and his spectacles' bespattered, Isabelle's reproachful giggling – 'Oh poor Arthur . . . look how you've splashed him again' – made the experience infinitely enjoyable.

Later, in Archie's rooms, a derogatory remark was made about the young ladies of Girton, 'blue stockings and suffragettes', and Isabelle unexpectedly sprang to their defence.

'But you don't mean to tell us you want to be one of them?'

'Of course I do. And I shall, you'll see.'

A feminist cried Arthur's heart. *My love's a feminist. Beauty and brains allied. I am going to marry her one day.* But this was a secret he kept to himself for another two years.

11

2

Arthur's final examinations were a triumph. A Wrangler and then third in the Indian Civil Service, at that time the highest competitive examination in the world.

A number of careers were now open, but he had set his heart on India. His father had never spoken of India, though his thoughts often returned bitterly to the world, from which he had severed himself, of frontier fights, dusty cantonments, balls in hill stations, pig-sticking. . . . Arthur's thoughts were inspired by the Victorian dream of Empire, of benevolent despotism over backward peoples, years of solitary toil in bad climates, with glittering prizes at the end for those who stayed the course.

'Arthur, the world's your oyster,' Archie said. 'Don't let us down, old boy. We shall follow your career with interest. "I knew the Viceroy in his salad days," I'll be saying . . .'

'They don't choose the Viceroy from the men on the spot, ass.' Arthur was smiling fatuously.

'Well, the Governor then. Sir Arthur Boyne, K.C.V.O., K.C.M.G., etc. . . . What! Thank God the pater's been provident enough to see to it that I don't *have* to work. Good luck, old boy.'

In the midst of his preparations for departure, Arthur received an invitation from the Burnetts to spend a week at Barmouth, where they had taken a house for the summer holidays. Arthur's undoubted success in the scholastic field had raised him in Mrs

Burnett's eyes. Now the pain of leave-taking was to be sweetened by a whole week spent in the company of the beloved girl. Now at last he could propose marriage in person and not by letter, of which he had already made a score of unsatisfactory drafts. His joy on arriving at Barmouth, where Archie met him with a pony and trap, was a little dashed at finding that he was not alone among Archie's friends to be invited. There, already installed, were Richmond, who extemporized brilliantly on the piano, Quentin, Archie's intimate from his school days, and Harrington, whose lively wit and pleasing manners made him a favourite with Isabelle's mother. So Arthur was more on the circumference than at the centre. But this was what he was used to.

Isabelle had left school and was to start at Bedford College in the autumn. A pioneer in higher education for women, she had elected to read science. She took herself very seriously, and it was a bold man who dared tease her now, but these academic pretensions combined with her prettiness gave her a piquant charm. Arthur's love soared to ever greater heights.

On the day before his return to London, when he had given up all hope of ever being alone with her and had started mentally re-drafting his proposal, Arthur suddenly found that he *was* alone with her, on the sea's edge. He found himself staring at Isabelle's pink toes, now submerged by a miniature wave, now revealed on the wet brown sand as the water sucked past them. She was paddling, her white dress held up in both her hands to reveal a pair of ankles that he found unbearably moving.

'Isabelle,' he cried without preamble, all his well-rehearsed phrases abandoning him, 'Isabelle, will you marry me?' She stared down without answering and he had to say it again to make sure that she had heard.

'Oh *Arthur!* . . .' Laughing, blushing and confused, she clasped her hands, and in doing so released her skirts which were engulfed by the incoming wavelets. 'Oh Arthur, *look* what you've done now!' and she fled to the dry sand, uttering little shrieks of dismay as the wet skirts flapped against her ankles and Arthur followed in pursuit. When, at last, she stopped, he wanted to fling himself on his knees before her, but the sands were far from empty and he was afraid of making her conspicuous and himself

13

ridiculous. If only they could have found themselves in one of those woodland glades in which he sometimes saw her in his dreams. However, realizing that this public isolation was the best he could hope for, he began to press his suit, telling her how he had loved her from the moment he had seen her, from the very first moment he had seen her picture even. Switching suddenly to the practical, he explained his circumstances (refraining only from mentioning his promise to his father), assuring her of the wonderful life he could now offer her, the promotions that lay ahead. 'So, if you'll only say "yes", Isabelle. . . .' He was about to add that she would make him the happiest of men when a shout from Archie, still distant but bearing down upon them with a small white sand-shoe in either hand, made him pause.

Isabelle had said nothing, but she was blushing in a most promising way. Her eyes were cast down.

'Please, Isabelle, please . . .'

After a pause, during which Archie seemed to approach by leaps and bounds, Isabelle spoke: 'Oh Arthur, no.'

Arthur's spirits dropped. Then he had an idea. 'Of course, I know I ought to have gone to your father first. I will as soon as . . .'

'No, it isn't that . . .'

'What then? Isabelle, is it – is it – someone else?'

'No, Arthur. But you know I'm going to college. I'm going to study science.'

Arthur's spirits rose again. While he favoured higher education for women in theory, he could not regard it as serious competition. 'Of course, I understand. I'll wait. I'll wait as long as you wish. Isabelle, may I write to you?'

'Yes.'

'And will you write to me? Sometimes?'

She hesitated. 'Er yes, sometimes.'

'Oh thank you, dearest Belle. I love you. I'll wait for you. I love you so. I'll wait for years.'

And he did.

3

Nothing Arthur had read or heard prepared him for his first taste of India. Everything was larger than life. The light was more blinding, the filth more indescribable, the smells worse, the beauty more breathtaking, the riches richer, the poverty more abysmal than a European could picture from travellers' tales. Above all was the sense of power that the grovelling servility of a host of menials gave to a young man who found himself overnight a member of the governing class. It was a heady draught offset by a nagging sense of exile. To counteract the loneliness and considerable hardships, the English cherished their club life. Here, over a game of cards or billiards (tennis and golf when the climate allowed), over successive rounds of whiskies, they made and renewed contacts which gave relief from the burden of the day. Here protocol reigned unchallenged. The arbitrary power of the Commissioner's lady could make or break you, and the wife of the Public Works Department (Drains and Sewers) knew her place. Arthur did not understand these niceties and was quite unwilling to master them. He was shy and tactless with his superiors, gauche with the ladies, and, while wanting to be friendly with his equals, would not conform to their recognized standards. He would have liked to make friends with the Indians with whom his work brought him into contact, but the disapproval and condemnation even of his fellows, the warnings against familiarity, the all too obvious familiarity itself, inseparable from touchiness and tedious misunderstandings – these were formidable obstacles. When he ventured into Indian homes, where invisible women whispered behind a screen while the host conducted prolonged courtesies, Arthur fidgetted, ill-at-ease until he could beat a retreat.

Work was everything – work and Isabelle's letters. She wrote sparingly, little snippets of news every two or three months ending 'your affectionate friend Isabelle'. These artless notes were his chief joy. The most trivial item of gossip, the poignant spelling mistakes, brought Isabelle to him with startling reality. He would have liked to wear the letters next to his heart and to sleep with them under his pillow, but the temperature dissuaded him. For his part, he wrote by every mail painting a future for his dearest Belle in glowing terms, ending with protests of undying devotion. He never doubted that she would one day be his.

Arthur's first post was in the Finance Department at the provincial headquarters, then Bombay. He delighted in the work and soon impressed himself on his superiors as promising. He lived in what was referred to as a Chummery, sharing a household with four or five other unattached young men with whom he was friendly but not intimate. His time was spent in long working hours at the office, daily lessons in the vernacular and avid reading – a mixed diet of John Stuart Mill, Herbert Spenser, Karl Marx, H. G. Wells and Bernard Shaw, Huxley and Darwin – literary fare which made him rather despise the simple recreations of his fellows. He was becoming opinionated.

As the second hot weather approached with the devastating heat that sapped the vitality of the white-skinned, Arthur had a sudden lucky break. The adviser to the Accountant General was on leave, his successor ill, and Arthur was sent for to fill the gap. It was the chance of a lifetime. New Delhi was not yet built, and the Government of India still yearly transferred to the refreshing joys of Simla during the worst months of the year. Here he found himself suddenly attached to the Viceroy's Council at the age of twenty-four in a world in which Arthur Boyne apparently counted – a cool world of startling beauty where you could lift up your eyes to the everlasting snows, while a pageant of delicious creatures swept past in their rickshaws in the deodars' shade. 'It would be truly perfect, dearest Belle, if only you were here,' he wrote, and Isabelle, shrinking from the task of dissecting frogs in the private house in Baker Street which was all her college boasted for premises, thought seriously for the first time of a life in India.

Arthur never knew what caused his set-back. It is certain that he suffered an attack of dysentery which was slow to clear up. Later, when he had formed the habit of attributing all disappointments and reverses to ill health, he was sure it was the dysentery that did it. Yet, at the time, he had perplexing doubts. Though shy and reserved, he was curiously lacking in the natural deference due from a subordinate to his superiors. This he condemned as fawning and scorned as the basest flattery. He was a poor mixer in a society where it was important to mix with a crowd that conformed to certain social conventions. He had emerged from his voracious reading an agnostic and a socialist, neither very good things to be in Simla at that time. He refused to attend divine service on the queen's birthday, and he sported a conspicuously red tie. All told, rather a queer fish.

After a protracted local sick leave, when it was at last clear that the illness had left him and he was able to work again, he found himself sent to the Central Provinces. Here a very different life awaited him. This vast tract of country, the ancient Massif Central of the peninsula lying roughly halfway between Bombay and Calcutta, inhabited largely by the most backward tribes and interspersed with independent principalities, was administered by a mere handful of Englishmen. After some months in the local capital, he was given a chance to deputize in a lonely outlying district.

It was the size of Yorkshire, a mixture of jungle and arid plain with here and there outcrops of rock and sudden ravines with two wide rivers, sometimes shrunk to a mere trickle and in the habit of drying altogether when the rains failed. The villages were small and poor, scratching a precarious living.

Arthur reached his destination (after many hours of jolting on a bullock wagon over unspeakable roads) tired, aching, filthy but exhilarated. He was monarch of all he surveyed. What he surveyed was a large house with lofty rooms and some thirty retainers disposed on the steps waiting to do him honour. 'My heavens, I'd like a bath,' he exclaimed when he had acknowledged their obeisances.

'As the Presence orders,' responded his new butler gravely. 'Step this way, Protector of the poor.' Rather more than a monarch, Arthur thought . . . something of a god.

Looking back on those years of great loneliness and heavy responsibility, his memories were, curiously enough, of happiness and satisfaction. There was no time to feel bored. After a long day maintaining law and order, settling disputes between landlord and peasant, peasant and money-lender, inspecting schools, hospitals, prisons, roads, irrigation schemes, conducting court cases, working through dispatch boxes – in fact, keeping the wheels of government running smoothly, there was no time to foster a spirit of discontent. In addition he had the respect, and, more than the respect, the adulation of the people surrounding him. At sunrise he would be in the saddle setting forth in the exquisite dew-soaked dawn to take a look at his world: the mud-walled villages with their temples, the fields of sugar cane, maize, lentils, barley, the water buffaloes being driven to the water-holes by naked boys, the scenes of land disputes, religious disputes, robberies – his world that he ruled with unflagging zeal and benevolence.

But better still was to come: the cold weather that brought the idyllic camping season. After the paralysing heat of the hot weather and the discomforts of the rainy season, October came in cool and dry and Arthur set forth to visit his domain. Thirty camels transported tents, stores and staff, divided into two groups so that one half pitched the encampment while the other half moved on to pitch the next encampment some ten to fifteen miles or a morning's ride ahead. It was camping in style – office tent, sleeping-tent, dining-tent, bathroom tent and lavatory tent with freshly dug sanitation. The cavalcade of servants included, in addition to the usual staff, the camel-men, grass-cutters and the grooms. Arthur would spend two or three nights at each stage: the day spent in dispensing justice and the late afternoon and evening in strolling out with a gun to bring back something for the pot.

'It's pure *Jungle Book*, dearest Belle,' Arthur wrote. 'I keep expecting to meet Mowgli.'

4

One of the things that Arthur liked best was
the freedom from pecuniary worries. He had never known what
it was not to be hard up. Until now, if his boots leaked it had
been because he needed the money for books. A new suit had
meant that he must forgo all forms of entertainment for a year.
Now he had in addition to a fine house and lots of servants his
own carriage and horses, a very good income and the certainty
of a handsome pension to come. Living in an outlying district
he was able to save, setting aside a monthly sum known as 'For
honeymoon at Saint Moritz', for that was where Isabelle had
once said honeymoons should be spent. Sitting on his verandah
in an easy chair at the end of the day, sipping a cool weak whisky-
peg and watching the bats wheeling against the stars, he sighed
with satisfaction as he reflected gratefully on the inestimable
benefit of freedom from money worries.

It was short-lived.

One morning with his office mail was a letter from his mother.
Seeing an English stamp, his heart leapt in the hope of a letter
from Isabelle, but it was his mother's angular sloping hand and
he set it aside to be read after the morning's work. Mrs Boyne
wrote that Harold, the youngest brother, had a chance of a
position with an engineering firm with good connexions abroad,
but there was a two-year course of apprenticeship to be paid for

first, and how could that be done? Almost he could hear his mother's grumbling, complaining tones. 'It's all very well for you, Arthur. You've had all the luck and you don't know how it feels for poor Harold to have to give up his chance because there's no one to help him . . . If only his father had provided for us . . .'

Arthur did not hesitate. He cabled and sent a banker's order. His savings were gone. But it was nothing to be worried about. He was in a position to borrow if necessary, and he would be able to save again. The honeymoon was not immediate. It was nothing to be worried about. He ought to be feeling a noble joy in being privileged to help. If only his mother had asked him frankly instead of whining and hinting. If only he liked Harold. If it had been that dear fellow Bertie now, who had a gay, friendly charm unknown to the other Boynes; but Bertie was a low-grade clerk in a city firm where his mediocre attainments needed no boosting. Harold, self-seeking and egoistic from boyhood, had always been his mother's favourite, and she resented that he could not have been the one singled out for the duke's preferment.

Anyway, it was paid now – that first instalment on a solemn vow made at the age of fourteen to a half-crazed father. In another year's time, when Harold's apprenticeship was paid for, he should be able to start saving again.

That night Arthur wakened feeling an unaccustomed chill. He had dreamt that he was back in the little house in the mews and the snow was falling in large flakes through the open window. He was just about to spring up and close the window when he woke in his large familiar room in the tropic night. But the sensation of chill persisted, accompanied by a vague malaise. He did not lie awake long, for he was gifted with the ability to sleep in almost any circumstances, but in the morning he felt listless and depressed. The next night he awakened with the ague. It was his first attack of malaria. The fearful fits of shivering were succeeded by a mounting temperature when the sweat ran from him in streams. In his fevered imaginings his recent reverse began to assume catastrophic proportions. The servants nursed him devotedly (while the little crowd of petitioners bearing their gifts waited patiently on the verandah and grew in number daily) and the doctor was sent for from a distance. He was a cheerful bachelor, a Scotsman, with many years experience of the country, who tended to make light of the affliction.

'Y're over it now. A drop of what you fancy'll do you good. I'll pour you a whisky.'

'Couldn't touch it.'

'Och, come on man. It'll cheer you up.'

'No. I feel too ill.'

'Well, that's the way with malaria. But you're over it now. Your temperature's down. Come on. Doctor's orders.'

'A very weak one then,' said Arthur in a dying voice.

'There, that's better. Drink up. You'll be as right as rain in a day or two.' He stumped round the room, puffing on a small foul pipe and relating anecdotes of Arthur's predecessors in the bungalow. Arthur, lying with his eyes closed, listening to the buzzing in his ears, hardly heard him. After a time he said:

'I thought I was going to die.'

Dr Quinn laughed. 'Not you, man. I don't deny it makes you feel sickish, but thank God the worst's over.'

'I don't believe in God.'

'Och, well now! I'm a Presbyterian myself, but I don't suppose it makes much odds. You can't be worse off than these poor heathen in the matter of religion,' and he embarked on a further series of anecdotes, dealing this time with death and disease, that Arthur found himself listening to with a gruesome relish.

The next morning very early Dr Quinn departed.

'Goodbye old man. You'll be all right now. Cut down on the quinine and cut out some of the irrigation is my advice. Those tanks now are a breeding-ground for mosquitoes. So long.'

As after the dysentery, Arthur was slow to get well. He was sunk in brooding over his sickness and the zest for work was gone. At last a long-awaited letter from Isabelle restored his spirits.

5

That year the rains failed. For many weeks the ground had been like concrete, awaiting the rain which never came. It was famine.

Famine organization was part of the normal work of a district officer. This was Arthur's first experience of the calamity and, from the moment the order came that the Famine Code was to be put into operation to the time when the danger was past, he found himself working as never before on behalf of his people. Work had to be provided for every able-bodied man who would in a normal year have been tilling the soil – work on reservoirs, granaries, wells, roads . . . work to prevent future famines – and grain to buy with their wages, free grain for the dependants, the old and the sick. In the grain distribution rascality often flourished abominably. Arthur grudged the time spent punishing a fat store-keeper or grain-dealer who, unmoved by the emaciated wretches claiming their ration, gave short weight or overcharged. He despaired when the caste system prevented a starving man from accepting food unless prepared in the prescribed way by a member of the right caste; or a Brahmin from working at all in contact with a common coolie.

'It would be simpler to let them starve . . . why do they need to make it so difficult for me . . . as if I hadn't enough to do . . .'

But he knew that nothing could deflect him from the huge, heart-rending endeavour to save their lives.

Each day the sky was like a leaden dome, pressing down on the cracked earth with searing heat. The dying, crawling skeletons, whose bones seemed about to pierce the skin, presented a ghastly spectacle along the roadside. The days turned to weeks, the weeks to months and Arthur lost count of time. Even Isabelle receded to the back of his consciousness. Work at a frenzied pace, snatched sleep, work, a few hours' unconsciousness and then back in the fearful reality – check on new administrative staff in neighbouring village . . . see if children of coolies working on new dam are fed . . . check dam itself . . . check on store of seed saved for planting . . . set aside strongest bullocks for survival – dispose of rest . . . send in figures for mounting death-rate . . . for remission of taxes . . . get new government horses *urgent* –

'Sahib! Sahib!'

'What is it?'

It was Fazil Khan, his favourite and privileged bearer – a gigantic Pathan whose red beard proclaimed a successful pilgrimage to Mecca in his youth. He was faithful, loveable, and a sworn enemy of the munshi, his superior, who was taking dictation at the moment. The dislike was mutual.

'Sahib, I swear by the prophet our troubles are ended! The rain comes. By the pricking in my beard I know –'

'Get out.'

'Assuredly, your honour. I thought to give your honour pleasure –'

'Get out.'

Arthur had never before spoken discourteously to his trusted servant. It was an indication of the nervous strain under which he lived. The big man withdrew with a dignified bow while the munshi tittered with pleasure and Arthur swore under his breath.

That night, the rain fell in cataracts. The new dam burst under the wall of water and many of his other new constructions were washed away. By morning the roads were a foot deep in mud and the familiar landscape was a scene of devastation. The famine was over.

Not so the troubles, for cholera followed fast. Now Dr Quinn was everywhere, innoculating all he could lay hands on and at

24

the same time vaccinating against the ever dreaded smallpox. The anguish continued and it seemed to Arthur that the scourge that followed was worse than the famine itself, but a day came at last when the epidemic had abated and the land, with its sprouting corn, wore a look of hope.

'You ought to put in for a spot of leave, old man,' said Dr Quinn, who had called on him one evening to report progress at the hospital. 'You've had a hard time of it. Ask and ye shall receive. Taking India as a whole though, it's a funny thing how local it's been.'

'Funny? Ha! Ha!'

'Och well. Ye know what I mean.'

'I suppose so. D'you really think I'd get leave? I'm not due for another year nearly.'

'I'm sure you would. I'd back you up. Tell me do you have a young lady at home?'

'Yes.'

'Well then that's all the more reason.'

'Yes.'

'Is she the pretty lass in the picture by your bed?'

'You've guessed.'

'I didna think it was your mother.'

To his unbounded joy, Arthur was granted six months immediate home leave after his famine duties. Four years had passed since he had arrived, a callow young man. Now, after a fearful ordeal, he was returning to his beloved. He landed at Tilbury on a bleak March day. When he at last reached Bayswater, darkness was falling in a steady drizzle of rain but Arthur felt his spirits could never be damped by rain again. Only he must get a warm overcoat – heavens, how cold it was! The Boynes greeted him unemotionally as was their way, though, in their way, they were quite pleased to have him home. With the exception of Bertie (dear fellow), they were more interested in their own affairs than to hear about an Indian famine. They sat in the parlour – a concession in honour of his homecoming – having a pot of tea before going to bed. Arthur would have prefered the relative warmth of the kitchen. He was longing for news of the Burnetts, but could not bring himself to ask openly when suddenly Kate, his sister, a rather gaunt red-haired young woman of twenty, exclaimed:

'Well you won't have heard about the funeral and all. I mean to say you couldn't, could you, being on the sea?'

Arthur's heart stopped beating. A black void yawned before his eyes. From a throat suddenly dry and constricted he managed to croak, 'Whose?...'

'Why, Mr Burnett's, of course. You knew he was ill, didn't you?'

'No.'

'It was the pneumonia. Ever so sudden, really.'

'You know, Arthur, he used to get those bronical attacks in the winter.' Mrs Boyne had taken up the tale. Arthur usually winced at her verbal inaccuracies and longed for her recitals to end, but he scarcely heard her now. . . . 'Took a sudden turn for the worse . . . two nurses he had and several doctors . . . one of the nurses told me – and you know he wouldn't have anyone come near him but his wife and daughter so they had to wait till he was unconscious-like to get the nurses . . . funeral was last week here . . . it was a proper big affair . . . they buried him after in Kensal Green . . . it seems they have a family vault there . . .'

'And I must say,' added Kate with unusual generosity, 'your Isabelle did look ever so pretty all in black.'

Arthur pushed away his cup and stood up suddenly. 'Where are they now?'

'Who?'

'Isabelle and her mother, of course.'

'Judging by the time, I should think they're going to bed –'

'Are they still there, I mean?'

'Yes, but they're leaving. Packing up already I heard the coachman saying.'

'I'm going over there –'

'What! At this time of night! Arthur, you can't! It's not decent . . .' The chorus of protests restrained his impulsiveness. He left the room and went up to his bedroom in a daze.

'You don't tell me he's still sweet on that stuck-up girl,' remarked Harold in the silence that followed Arthur's exit, and added coarsely, 'Wouldn't you think he'd have got over lusting after her with all the chances he must have had to slake his thirst among countless Oriental beauties. I know if I'd had his opportunities – '

'You know I don't like to hear you talk like that Harold,' said his mother fondly.

'Darling, darling Isabelle . . . Oh my dearest, my dearest love, don't cry . . .'

He was in the big drawing-room overlooking the park, and Isabelle was in his arms, but only for a moment, for she pushed him away fiercely – 'Don't Arthur, I can't bear it.'

Arthur's heart overflowed with the burden of her grief. How often in his loneliness he had imagined their reunion, but not like this, never at all like this. The unrestrained weeping, the savage rejection of his comforting love, of his longing to protect and console dumbfounded him. Unexpectedly, he found an ally in Mrs Burnett who entered the drawing-room at that moment, greeted him kindly, accepted his condolences with dignity and sent Isabelle to get on her things for a morning drive in the park with Arthur. 'It will do you good' – the command was authoritative and Isabelle submissively went upstairs. Arthur found himself appreciating his future mother-in-law. He learned that Archie had left just before his father's fatal illness for a world tour and was at present in South America, that they had already bought a smaller house in a neighbouring street and were to move there very soon. Mrs Burnett further put him at his ease by questioning him graciously about his life in India.

The drive in the park in the fitful morning spring sunshine was good for Arthur as well. He kept glancing at the beloved girl at his side, pale and pretty in her mourning, and was filled with tenderness. Isabelle's abandoned grief had passed as suddenly as it had come. There were no further references to the recent tragic happening.

After two or three days of this calm, Arthur felt encouraged to renew his proposal of marriage. Although he had told himself for seven long years that Isabelle would one day be his, he was almost surprised to find that no obstacle now stood in his way.

27

Mrs Burnett, incredibly, favoured him as a suitor for her daughter's hand. If she found him rather gauche, and his background not what one would have wished, he was doing well in a splendid service (it was not as if he were in trade, after all), his prospects were excellent and there was no doubt that he had been faithful and assiduous for a long time. She gave her consent to an engagement. She had been shocked to learn from the lawyer, after the funeral, that her husband, that impulsive benefactor, had not left her nearly as well off as might have been expected. Isabelle was twenty-three and there were no other presentable suitors on the carpet. She stipulated that the marriage should take place after Mr Burnett had been dead a year.

Isabelle was not in love with Arthur so much as in love with love. Her enthusiasm for her studies had waned. She was still an ardent feminist at heart, and would wax vocal on the subjects of equality, votes for women and higher education, but she secretly found science rather dreary and the application was lacking. She had been bridesmaid to several cousins and rather fancied the role of bride. Arthur's devotion was flattering and touching. She was fond of him. Other young gentlemen had been attentive at times. She had indulged in several minor flirtations which had banished Arthur from her thoughts. (She had never set herself to discover why the possible suitors had faded away: it was in alarm at her earnestness – those very blue-stocking qualities that Arthur appreciated.) But Arthur, separated from her by distance and time, had remained faithful, unswerving in his dog-like devotion. She had it in her power to reward this devotion with the gift of herself, but she, too, had a stipulation.

'Arthur, I *will* marry you, only . . . oh, it's so difficult.'

'What is, dearest?'

'I don't know how to say it – '

Arthur, who had hold of both her hands, proceeded to kiss them gently. She could feel the tickling of his moustache.

'I *don't* know how to say it,' she repeated in a stricken voice.

After a pause during which he held on to her hands tightly Arthur said: 'But you must help me, my love. I must know what's worrying you.'

'Well, Arthur, I don't want any of *that*. I don't want to have children, oh, can't you see?' The words came breathlessly, almost in a whisper. In the pause that followed Arthur relinquished her hands. He was thrown into a confusion. Suddenly Isabelle buried her face in her hands and burst into sobs. Through the sobs he heard incoherent sentences: 'I couldn't bear it . . . I don't want to be like Mrs Porter . . . it's disgusting . . . I couldn't bear it . . . I couldn't . . . oh it's horrible . . . it's disgusting . . . I couldn't *bear* it, don't you see . . .'

Arthur could only see his love's distress, which melted his heart with pity. He was overwhelmed with the desire to soothe, comfort and console his little frightened darling. As he stroked the shining hair and murmured endearments, he made promises: 'It shall be as you wish, my dearest. Whatever you say, always. Only let me be with you and look after you. Let me care for you, Isabelle . . .' At last the sobbing subsided, she smiled through her tears and he kissed her gently on the forehead. The dreadful scene was past. Isabelle returned abruptly to her light-hearted, endearing ways.

Presently Arthur asked, 'Who's Mrs Porter?'

'She's our charwoman. She's horrible. Oh don't . . .'

Mrs Porter came in the mornings to do the front steps and the basement floors for the cook. She was a shapeless, toothless creature who always looked to be in an advanced stage of pregnancy. Over a mid-morning cup of tea, she loved to tell the maids of her husband's ill-usage of her. With twelve screaming children, a thirteenth on the way and a husband frequently out of work, she was indeed pitiable. Isabelle could not repress an involuntary shudder whenever she encountered her, and scurried down the front steps as if someone were after her if Mrs Porter were there, sprawling on her knees in the thankless act of 'whitening'.

On leaving the house Arthur went straight to Spinks, and after examining a number of rings he settled for a magnificent one of three fine diamonds which cost a great deal more than he could afford. 'Well, one doesn't get engaged every day,' he told himself as he boarded the omnibus back to Bayswater.

Isabelle was enchanted. Mrs Burnett was impressed. The only fly in his ointment came at home.

'I don't grudge you your happiness, Arthur, you mustn't think that,' said Mrs Boyne when the congratulations were over, 'there's little enough of it in life to my way of thinking, so you must make the most of it and I'm sure I hope you're going to be very happy, but, of course, it *is* hard on Katie, there's no denying.'

'I don't understand you, Mother?'

'Well, I suppose it's natural enough for you to forget all about your own flesh and blood when you're in love.'

'Sorry, Mother, enlighten me,' said Arthur good-humouredly.

'You must enlighten him,' cried his sister in mocking tones. 'Oh, let him alone, Mother. I don't want to go anyway.'

'Be quiet, Kate. Look, Arthur, if you hadn't been going to get married, it would have been natural enough for Katie to go out to India to keep house for you, where she'd have had plenty of chances she can't get here. I've had it in my mind to ask you for a long time. What chances can I ever give her, I'd like to know? She's a nice-looking girl and I don't want her to end on the shelf. Who does she ever meet here?'

'Len Baker,' observed Harold, 'that's who.'

'Oh, shut up!' cried his sister fiercely, and ran from the room, slamming the door behind her.

Arthur was contrite. It was true that his own great happiness was blinding him to the lot of others. Kate might not strictly belong to the underprivileged depressed class who had his sympathy as a Fabian socialist, but she was nevertheless one of the unlucky ones whose narrow life offered no scope. It was in his power to widen her horizons, even probably provide her with a new life, and she was his own sister. It was selfish of him not to have thought of it himself.

'But of course, Mother! Kate must come to us. Only give us a year or so to get settled into our new life and she must come and stay with us for as long as she likes. It will be company for Isabelle,' he added, warming to his subject. 'That's all settled. Now I want to bring Isabelle to tea on Sunday to meet you all. Mrs Burnett has her sister and the admiral staying, so just Isabelle.' If he had qualms concerning Kate, he soon dismissed them. It was a long way off still.

Isabelle never forgot her introductory tea-party with the Boynes. She came within an ace of breaking the engagement. Arthur, with his Cambridge voice and quiet ways, had not prepared her for the sheer vulgarity of his family background. She was miserably ill at ease, a fact which escaped his attention altogether, so proud was he of his treasure. Later, when he had escorted her home, he found the Boynes loud in her praise. He realized suddenly that his mother might have broached the subject of Katie's visit to India, which would have been inopportune, and he was grateful to her for leaving it to him. It all seemed to have gone very well, he thought.

But Isabelle was wretched. When they retired for the night she went into her mother's room and wept.

'Oh, it was awful. Really awful. His mother was such a shock to me. I never imagined – '

'What's the matter with Mrs Boyne?'

'She's so common, Mother. So dreadfully *common*.'

'Then it's all the more to Arthur's credit that he is such a presentable, honourable young man. Many great men have sprung from lowly origins.'

'I know, Mother, and I'm very fond of Arthur, but I couldn't bear to have those people for my in-laws.'

But Mrs Burnett's common sense prevailed.

'Then you must count yourself lucky that they don't live in India, dear child. You won't see very much of them after you're married, you know. My little goose must learn to look on the bright side.'

6

On her way to be married in Bombay the following spring, Isabelle had suffered torments of sea-sickness in the Bay of Biscay, but had revived in the Mediterranean to enjoy the delights of life aboard an ocean liner. When the ship arrived at Bombay, there was Arthur in the tender to meet her. He had been given a week's leave for his wedding, and a senior official and his wife had offered to have Isabelle to stay with them before the long journey back to his station.

The evening after her arrival, her hosts gave a little dinner-party for her. Isabelle wore one of her new trousseau gowns and sparkled with excitement at her host's right hand. Arthur, at the other end of the table, was more than usually inattentive to his hostess, so intent was he on Isabelle's triumphs, which reached a peak later in the evening when she was urged to sing. Her thin clear soprano dispatched a cycle by Liza Lehmann and launched into some Tosti ballads, ending with 'Goodbye' which brought a tear to every eye. Arthur's joy and pride knew no bounds as Isabelle slid from the piano-stool and dropped a pretty curtsey to show the performance was at an end. But they would not let her go and clamoured for more, and as her repertoire was by no means exhausted she was quite willing to oblige. A little French lullaby, a German *Lied*, '*Mi chiamono Mimi*' . . . She received an ovation.

*

Arthur didn't really enjoy his wedding, owing to the stag party given in his honour the night before. Isabelle, longing suddenly for the comforting presence of her own family, felt lonely and nervous in the great echoing cathedral with only a handful of strangers in the empty seats and Arthur beside her as much a stranger as any. After the wedding breakfast, they were given a send-off at the station and the long journey up-country began. They took with them a Goanese half-caste ayah whom Isabelle had selected for her maid from a number of applicants on account of her knowledge of English. Agnes, the Goanese, was a bad traveller and her lamentations soon made Isabelle repent her choice. She travelled in another part of the train, but at every station came to the carriage with new complaints. Isabelle gazed from the window at the India that was to be her home, the swarming crowds jostling on the platform, the mud villages with their temples, the women with waterpots on their heads, the naked children, the oxen turning the water wheels, the feathery date palms, the endless cultivation. Exciting at first in its novelty, the immensity and sameness soon began to depress her. At evening, as the sky flamed into a magnificent sunset, they attacked a splendid picnic hamper. After a second glass of champagne, cooled from ice in a thermos flask, Isabelle's spirits revived.

'Tell me about the bungalow, Arthur. You've never described it to me.'

'Well you're going to see it soon enough. Oh dearest, I still can't believe – '

'Yes, but what's it like? I want to know exactly what to expect.'

But Arthur was no good at description.

'Tell me about our neighbours.'

'You know there aren't any, dear – at least, not very near.'

'Well, but the Indians.'

'The natives? Let me see, there's the local Rajah. He's no trouble. There's the Mohammedan doctor at the hospital, quite a nice chap in his way. There's the circuit judge – he's a Bengali. He spits quite a lot.'

'Oh Arthur, you are funny.'

They decided to make an early night of it in view of the long day to follow. At the next stop, Arthur kissed his bride tenderly on the brow and retired behind his curtain, leaving her to the ministrations of Agnes. He was asleep in a matter of seconds.

'They are very bad common pipples, mistress. They make a lot of noises and they take too much rooms.'

A glass of champagne placated her and she departed giggling. Isabelle lay awake for hours listening to the bumping of the wheels, twisting the broad band on her wedding finger (that Arthur had had made from gold found in his river) and trying to calm her madly racing thoughts. When she had given up all hope of sleep, she found herself slipping into a dream. She was walking in a tunnel and in the light at the far end could see her father standing. As she began to run towards him, there was an explosion. It was a cork from the champagne bottle that the thrifty Goanese had managed to squeeze in, dislodged by the vibration. Arthur did not stir. Isabelle could just see his faint outline. She decided to rouse him for comfort, thought better of it and wept.

It was afternoon of the next long day when they changed from the express to the local line, and evening when the last stage, the hard drive over the terrible road, began. This time the bullock tonga took their luggage and Arthur had his own horses and carriage waiting for him. The coachman hung garlands of marigolds round their necks. The drive seemed interminable – the choking clouds of dust that rose from the horses' hooves, the pungent smell of the marigolds, the gleaming eyes of countless wild animals in the darkness, the wails and shrieks of Agnes on the box as the carriage bumped over the potholes – but at last it was over as the carriage left the road and launched down the drive. A series of triumphal arches constructed of bamboos and lavishly decorated with brilliantly coloured paper pennants, illumined by scores of torches, led to the porch, where, in letters of gold a yard high, the word MELCOWE extended a greeting to the new mistress. The sleepy servitors grouped on the steps sprang to wakefulness. All the pariah dogs of the neighbourhood roused themselves in chorus. Arthur gathered his bride in his arms and lurched up the steps to carry her over the threshold, a ceremony he had often rehearsed mentally.

The cook had prepared a gala dinner, but they were too tired to attempt it.

Arthur had given orders that his big room was to be made ready for the memsahib and he would occupy an adjoining one, but he noticed it had been prepared as a nuptial chamber. Hastily ordering his things to be moved, he went to inquire of any developments during his absence. When he returned, Isabelle, exhausted, was already asleep.

7

It was mid morning when she woke. In the shuttered gloom of the big room, she saw Agnes seated in front of the dressing-table trying on her rings. The Goanese, unabashed, came towards her.

'Mistress, I wait for you to waken up. Master, he gone out long time ago. He come back two o'clock. Mistress, I do not like my room. At the mission I have nice chest of drawers. Here is packing cases. It is not good. The servants are not nice pipples. They are jealous because I am a European . . .'

'I want my breakfast, Agnes.'

'Good, I fetch it. After Mistress will see . . .'

'Later, Agnes.'

When Arthur returned from his morning's inspection, his bride had finished exploring her new home. The smiling obeisances of the servants delighted her, but she was irked by her inability to make even the simplest remark that they would understand. She determined to learn Hindustani without delay. Conversation with Agnes tended to pall.

In the large dining-room, sparsely furnished with camp-type furniture, they sat down to a luncheon consisting of flannelly fish, rubbery chicken (curried) and mango-fool, the whole washed down by bottled beer. Arthur wolfed it appreciatively, while Isabelle picked. A turbaned, white-robed servant stood behind each chair. It made Isabelle unaccountably shy, for she knew well that they could not understand what she said. His hunger assuaged, Arthur asked: 'D'you like it Isabelle? It's your home now.'

'Oh yes.'

'You really do?'

'Of course. I'm afraid Agnes doesn't.'

'She'll settle down.'

'Well I don't know – '

'Then she'll have to go. It's quite simple. You must tell me later any changes you want made. From now on, you give the orders.'

'Oh Arthur, if only I could! It's so awful not knowing a word.'

'We'll soon remedy that. I'll arrange for the munshi to give you an hour's Hindustani lesson every morning. It's an easy language to pick up.'

'Oh good. What are we going to do this afternoon?'

'Well, I've got to go over to the Court – a lot of cases held over from last week. I'm in arrears, you see. I must have been away getting married, that's what it is.' He led his wife from the room, giving her a playful tweak on the ear.

'*Pas devant les domestiques.* Arthur, how long do you think you'll be? What shall I do this afternoon? Is there anywhere to walk to?'

'It's too hot for you to walk at this time of day. We might do a little stroll in the evening when I get back.'

'When?'

'Dearest, I'm not quite sure. I'll be as quick as I can. You have a rest in the meantime.'

'I don't want to rest. I didn't wake up till after ten.'

'How about writing some letters home? The mail goes to-morrow.'

'Very well.'

'Now I'm going to have ten minutes' nap. It wouldn't do to fall asleep in court. Wazir Ali, see that I am called in ten minutes' time. You'll excuse me, dearest,' and his bedroom door closed behind him.

*

37

My dear Mother,

I have been here one day, no not a whole day yet and I don't know how I am going to stand it.

Isabelle tore the sheet of paper into very small pieces, ran into her bedroom for a handkerchief and wept. When she came back, Wazir Ali, smiling, was waiting to attend to her needs – in case she wanted the chair moved a few inches nearer to the desk, for example. She waved to him to go, but he moved only as far as the door and remained there impassive.

My dear Mother,

This is a fearfully lonely place. There are no neighbours and nobody speaks English except the ayah and I don't like her. I have nothing whatever to do while Arthur is at work all day.

After a long pause, Isabelle stared at the sheet of paper, blinking back her tears. Then she slowly tore it up also and slowly started again.

My dear Mother,

I will begin at the end and then afterwards tell you all about the wedding and the journey here. You must imagine your daughter mistress of a large white single-storeyed house, surrounded by deep verandahs and a fine garden. There are innumerable servants, I haven't counted them yet and it will take me a long time to learn all their names . . .

She continued in this strain, page after page, in her neat orderly hand. This letter set the pattern for the future. For the outsider (and her mother was now on the outside of her life) it was to be bluff and dissimulation. Only to Arthur, who was after all responsible for her, could her sufferings be made abundantly clear. But that would come later.

That evening she played and sang at Arthur's request. He had had a piano sent all the way from Calcutta for her and Isabelle was touched when she learned of it. The black mood was forgotten. Arthur saw the lamplight falling on her bare arms and fair hair and listened to the clear voice singing the songs he loved. It was all just as he had dreamed it a hundred times in his solitude. When she had finished, he went and knelt beside her, lifted her fingers from the keys and kissed them gently. 'I'm the luckiest man alive,' he murmured humbly.

'Oh Arthur . . .' To check his caresses she asked: 'How long d'you think the heavy luggage will be? I want to get all my things unpacked – the linen and so on and my pictures and photographs. And the bicycle. I'm longing for my bicycle.'

'I'll get after it tomorrow. See if I can hurry it along. As for bicycling, there's only the one road. But we can do better than that. Isabelle, I've got a surprise coming.'

'Oh, tell me!'

'Then it wouldn't be a surprise.'

'You must tell me. I don't *like* having surprises and shocks.' But Arthur was suddenly obdurate.

'What shall we do now, then?'

'I think it's bedtime. I have a long day tomorrow.'

'But it's not yet ten. At home I never go to bed before eleven at the earliest.'

'Sorry, dearest. I have to get up at five-thirty. Tell you what, I'll take time off tomorrow after tea and drive over to Chowalgarh. I haven't been for some time and I want to keep the new fellow there up to the mark. We'll drive through some fine jungle. You'll like that.'

'Right, Arthur.'

'Good night then, dearest. One kiss.'

'Just one then. Good night.'

'It's not what one expects,' Agnes remarked to Fazil Khan a few days later. 'I suppose your master is a eunuch.'

'Shut your mouth, woman.'

'He's not been near her yet and there's no good reason for it – as I should know.'

'Shut your mouth, polluter of the atmosphere, or I swear by Allah you'll live to regret it!'

'Moslem dog,' remarked Agnes scornfully and moved on about her business.

But Agnes was under a cloud. A new fleecy blanket was missing from Isabelle's shelves, and her mourning brooch, made from her father's pearl dress studs and greatly treasured, was nowhere to be found. Isabelle, still hoping that the brooch would turn up, hated suspecting Agnes and didn't know quite what to do. It added to her feeling of oppression.

The 'surprise' turned out to be a lovely chestnut gelding, Phoebus. Arthur was overjoyed at Isabelle's obvious pleasure in the creature. She loved the feel of his strong, satiny neck against her cheek, the soft lips nuzzling the palm of her hand for a lump of sugar, the lively, intelligent eye. Her early-morning ride, with the syce on his pony at a respectful distance behind, became the one delightful portion of the day. It was the rest of the day, with Phoebus safely in his stall and the remorseless sun driving her indoors, where there was nothing to do after her hour's Hindustani lesson but study her vocabulary and put in a little desultory piano practice – nothing whatever to do – that was intolerable. She had arranged her books, which were few and mostly old favourites from school-room days, arranged and rearranged her photographs, hung Aunt Fanny's watercolours, and what remained for her? Letter-writing? She had already written to her mother, brother, friends and relations. There was nothing to do but wait for Arthur to come home, tired and hungry. It wasn't fair that he should always be so busy and she have nothing to occupy her days. A small flame of resentment burned in her.

'How's the Hindustani going?' They were in the drawing-room after dinner and Arthur had already suppressed a yawn.

'All right, I think.'

'Have you started trying it out on Fateh Mohammed yet?' (Fateh Mohammed was the cook, a cheerful obliging fellow, given to unfortunate bouts of drinking. Arthur loved him.)

'Not yet.'

'That reminds me. Always keep the tantalus locked. It's his

weakness. He's so sorry afterwards it nearly breaks your heart. Besides, it's against his religion.'

'But Arthur, d'you mean to say he drinks? How horrible! He seems so nice – '

'He is. He's a good chap. Don't worry, he doesn't often. I'll deal with him if it ever happens again.'

'But . . .'

'Tell me, Belle, I want to know. Is the munshi a good teacher?'

'I think so. . . . It's his breath I can't stand. He smells horrid.'

'Well, can't do much about that, I'm afraid. It's what they eat that does it.'

After a pause, Isabelle began, 'Arthur – '

'Yes.'

'Oh Arthur, I hate to say it, but I think Agnes has been stealing my things.'

'Stealing, you think? I shouldn't wonder. These mission products are generally bad types. What have you missed?'

'My brooch that Mother had made from Father's pearl dress studs. I can't find it anywhere. And there's a lovely new blanket gone . . . But perhaps it isn't Agnes.'

'Probably is. I never had anything stolen before.'

'But you just told me Fateh Mohammed steals your drinks.'

'Oh well, I don't call that stealing. If I'm so stupid as to leave them unlocked, he helps himself.'

'But Arthur, I'd like to know what that is if it isn't stealing!'

'That's just his weakness. He cooks the books too. The way he looks at it, it's his duty. Custom of the country. When he gets too exorbitant, I deduct something and we start over again. No hard feelings on either side.'

'Well, I think it's perfectly horrid.'

'Custom of the country dear, that's all. It's their prime duty to feather their nests to the best of their ability and provide for their dependants.'

'But it's terribly dishonest.'

'Depends how you look at it. They're all the same in that and I try to see their point of view. When a horse is claimed to be eating enough for two elephants, or when the gardener charges for enough seed to sow a public park, I start drawing the line. They expect it. They're as honest a crowd as you could wish to find and I'd trust my life in their hands – with the possible exception of the munshi. I dare say he'd be tempted to sell me to the highest bidder, if occasion arose.'

'Arthur, it isn't funny. Please be serious.'

'Sorry, dear. You're worried over losing these things. Naturally. And I'm not going to stand for that. Must be that Goanese. Fazil Khan doesn't think much of her and he's a sound chap. I'll have her room searched first thing in the morning.' He began to write on the back of an old envelope: Memo: Ayah's room to be searched. Items missing: pearl brooch, blanket.

'Anything else missing, d'you think?'

Isabelle did not answer.

'Is there anything else – ' to his consternation she burst into tears. 'Don't cry, dearest Belle. Don't cry. There's a very good chance we'll get your things back. Oh please don't cry . . .' She was turned away from him, groping for her handkerchief. Arthur, longing to comfort, remembered another passionate storm of weeping and restrained himself to patting her shoulder. He was deeply disturbed.

When the weeping subsided, her incoherent cries resolved themselves into 'I can't bear it,' repeated again and again.

'What, my love? What is upsetting you? What is it you can't bear?'

'Everything . . . this place . . . you . . . everything . . .' She turned to face him. 'Can't you see how miserable I am?'

Physical symptoms prevented him from answering. He was shot through by an acute internal pain – like that time he got a kick in the stomach on the football field. There was a pounding in his head and his throat went suddenly dry. He stared at Isabelle. Like a maltreated dog, his dejection was total and abject. After several moments, he looked away still unable to speak.

'Can't you see?' she repeated.

Arthur shook his head. 'No,' he said at last. 'I didn't know.'

'I'm shut up in this house with nothing to do. Nothing whatever to do. Oh *can't* you understand?'

'One week . . .'

'What?'

'I said one week,' he repeated slowly.

42

'Yes, I've been here one week,' Isabelle cried, working herself up to a near frenzy, 'and it's driven me nearly desperate already. What are you going to do about it? There's nothing whatever for me to do after my early-morning ride and my lesson – nothing. What d'you expect me to do? Sit and twiddle my thumbs?'

She paused dramatically, expecting a reply, and Arthur made an effort to collect his scattered wits.

'What do you do at home?' he asked. 'I mean, what did you do before?'

'At home? There were always a hundred things to do. If it wasn't lectures and work, there were lots of people to see. I could go to Mudie's or William Whiteleys . . . I could visit my cousins or friends. I could go for a walk in the park. Whereas here' – she grew shrilly eloquent – 'I can't go out! Oh dear me no, I'm confined within these four walls like a prisoner. As for ever seeing anyone – the loneliness, Arthur, is simply unbearable. You're away at your work all day long. Sometimes you haven't been home for luncheon even. You come home in the evening tired out and want to go to bed. It's not fair. I can't stand it. If there was something for me to *do* it would be different. I can't even move a chair. I'm not allowed to do a thing. . . . Can't you find something for me to do? Why can't I help you with your work?'

'I'm afraid that wouldn't do,' Arthur said slowly, and his voice sounded strange to him.

'There you are, you see! You don't want me to do anything!'

'I'm fearfully sorry, Belle. I didn't realize it was so lonely for you. It was stupid of me. I didn't think. I really am dreadfully sorry to have been so thoughtless, Belle.'

As Isabelle looked like dissolving into tears again he went on hurriedly: 'But it won't always be so quiet and lonely for you. The Rajah wants to pay his respects, I know, and one or two others. They've only been holding off because they thought you were busy settling in . . . I've got Dr Quinn coming over in a day or two and he'll be staying the night. You'll like him, I know. Then there's the Chief Commissioner's visit at the end of the month. He brings two A.D.C.s with him and you'll be busy entertaining them. It won't be so bad Belle – you'll see.'

Isabelle smiled, blinking the tears away.

'Oh, Arthur, I'm sorry, but – '

'I'm the one who should be sorry, dearest. Forgive me and I'll try to do better in future – make a better life for you. Though I can't forgive myself for being so thoughtless.'

She sighed: 'I think I'll go to bed. I've got rather a headache.'

'Have you, dear? Let me get a whisky and soda.'

'No thank you.'

'Just a small one. A chota peg. It'll do your head good.' As he busied himself with the drinks he had an idea. 'Can you play backgammon?'

'No.'

'Or chess?'

'No.'

'Come on. I'll teach you backgammon. It's a good game. You'll like it. I've often wanted someone to play it with when I was alone.'

After nearly an hour of the game, Isabelle suddenly said: 'You know, Arthur, this sofa's really very shabby and these chair covers are rather worn, aren't they?'

'Are they, dear? I daresay they are. I took them over from my predecessor and they weren't new then.' Arthur was not one for noticing.

'Would you like me to get them re-covered?'

'Splendid idea! You can choose some stuff in the bazaar and the dhirzi can run them up for you on the verandah. Or there are catalogues from Bombay and Calcutta, if you'd like to send away for the stuff?'

'I'd rather try the bazaar first.'

'Good. I'll get Fazil Khan to take you in the morning.'

'What are your favourite colours, Arthur?'

'I'll leave that to you, dear. I'm sure to like whatever you choose. Is your head better now?'

'Yes, thank you.'

The atrocious scene lay buried.

Next morning when Isabelle wakened she clapped her hands as she had learned to do for a signal for the servant stationed out-

44

side her door to summon the ayah. She was surprised when Fazil Khan entered, smiling, with her tea. He was followed by Arthur bearing the stolen items. The culprit had been apprehended and dispatched while Isabelle still slept.

'You were perfectly right about Agnes, dear. I've sent her back to Bombay. You're well rid of her. Now you won't have any more trouble. I've sent out word that we're in need of an ayah and there'll be some lined up for us to have a look at in a day or two. I must fly now. I'm hours late . . . I'll see you this evening, dear. Oh, and Fazil Khan will be waiting to take you to the bazaar when you're ready.'

Among the applicants ranged on the verandah was a dark youngish woman, graceful in her sari, with a glittering caste-mark on her forehead. She knew a few words of English, having served as ayah with a family recently retired. Arthur had met them at the local hill station and had heard them lamenting losing her and wondering how they could manage in England with four unruly children who responded only to the ayah.

'You were with the Rivers-Garnetts?' he asked.

'Yes, Sahib,' and the dark eyes filled with tears as at a poignant memory.

'She seems devoted,' Arthur said. 'Are you married?'

'Yes, Sahib.'

'What's your husband's name?'

'He Sanmogun. He good man, Sahib.'

'What does he do, this son-of-a-gun?'

'He do nothing, Sahib. He very good man – '

'You mean he wants a job?'

'Yes Sahib. He very – '

'Good man. Yes, I know. Well, we'll see about that. How old are you?'

'I forty-five, Sahib.'

'She's worn well,' Arthur said. 'I shouldn't give her a day over thirty. Less.'

'What's your name?' Isabelle asked.

'I Manikum ayah, Mum. I Amma, Mum.'

'You mean you're called Amma?'

45

'Esmissy Trivassy Garanat, she say me Amma, Mum.'

'I see. What's your religion, Amma?'

'I heathen, Mum.'

'Oh, let's have her,' Arthur said. Amma smiled shyly, revealing a fine set of teeth stained crimson by betul-juice. This was the beginning of a tender, unswerving devotion that was to last for nearly twenty years.

8

'Arthur, what's today?'

'Wednesday.' They were sitting in the drawing-room after dinner. The stifling heat on the verandah had not yet succumbed to the blessed cool of night.

'But what's the date today?'

'Twenty-seventh. Let me see, that's right. Twenty-seventh. I was thinking this morning, there's twelve weeks to go before we can hope for the monsoon. Ten weeks and we can expect the first signs with any luck. We've got to have good rains this year to make up for last year's famine. Stocks are still dangerously low.'

'Arthur, doesn't the twenty-seventh mean anything to you?'

'How d'you mean?'

'It's our mensiversary.'

'Our what?'

'Arthur, don't be dense. You know what an anniversary is. Well, it's a month ago today since our wedding.'

'Is it really, by jove? Seems more than a month ago, doesn't it?' he added tactlessly.

'What do you mean by that?'

'Nothing. I mean a lot seems to have happened for one month. I mean, before you came the months seemed very much the same and just slipped by monotonously.'

Isabelle, partially pacified, changed the subject.

'You wouldn't have thought that upholstery was so hot to sit on. These cane chairs are much cooler, aren't they?'

'Yes, I know. But I like what you've done to the drawing-room, Belle. It's brightened the place up. The dhirzi did a good job.'

'Well, I don't think they fit very well.'

'Dear, I was thinking. These coming weeks – months – are going to be very trying for you. I don't mind telling you I'm a bit worried. If the rains are late, we're in for it. We've not had a chance to get over last year.'

'I know.'

'Anyway, you aren't used to great heat, and with the thermometer standing at over a hundred degrees in the shade all the time, it can be very disagreeable. How would you like to go to Pachmarhi for the hot weather? It's not very far and quite high enough to be pleasant. The hotel's nice – it's run by a retired sergeant-major and his wife. Plenty of people to take you about and give you a nice time. Golf and tennis at the club. There's lots going on.'

Isabelle had listened in silence. Now she spoke with emphasis.

'No, Arthur.'

'No? Why not, dear? It really would do you good.'

'I don't want to be done good to. Certainly not.'

'But I don't quite understand – it's just for the worst of the hot weather . . .'

'I refuse to go.'

'Why, Belle?'

'A wife's place is with her husband. I married you for better, for worse. The hot weather's 'the worse'. I'm not the sort of wife who goes gallivanting off to hill stations, leaving her husband sweltering and toiling in the plains.'

'It's very noble of you, Belle. I can assure you most wives are only too glad of the opportunity. The plains in the hot weather are no place for a white woman.'

'What's the difference? If you can stand it, I can.'

'I have to. I can't pretend I like the hot weather very much. And the rainy season, Belle, that's often even worse. It's so steamy and thick and slimy – unpleasant in unexpected ways,

48

too. D'you know, I've seen plants come out of the walls that grow three or four feet in the course of a night. You go to sleep and there's nothing there and you wake up and see a blooming great bush – white and fleshy. Beastly things. And as for the fauna – '

'Arthur, spare me! It'll be bad enough when the time comes. Don't try and persuade me to go any more. Anyone would think you want to get rid of me.'

'It's only your good I'm thinking of.'

'Well, my mind's quite made up.'

Arthur felt embarrassed and apprehensive. He lit his pipe in silence. He knew that he should express his gratitude for Isabelle's unselfish determination to stay with him through the hot weather, but he was not given to eloquence. After several minutes' silence Isabelle said:

'A strange thing happened today. I couldn't understand it.'

'What, dear?'

'I went to the Rajah's Zenana this morning to pay a call on the women. I want to get behind this purdah and get to know Indian women and help them if I can. Well, we were getting on quite well I thought. They were chattering away and I was airing my few sentences of Hindustani when someone brought in the newest infant. I admired him for all I was worth – not that I really thought he was pretty (I don't think any babies are pretty when they're very young, whatever their colour), but I was just trying to do the polite. Suddenly the mother snatched the baby up and bolted. Then the others went as well and I was left with two of the oldest wives and they didn't seem to have anything more to say, so I came home. It was all very abrupt and rather rude, I thought. I even had the feeling they were glad to see me go. I've been wondering ever since what was the matter with them.'

'I can tell you the answer to that one. If you praise a child, a jealous god might overhear and decide to make away with him. The best thing is to say, "That's a puny little wretch: he won't last long," and leave it at that. Then everyone feels safe.'

'Good gracious!'

'It's true. You see, they live in terror of their gods; or they might think you've got the evil eye.'

'Arthur, how can you!'

'You never know. Or they might think you wanted the baby for yourself. You see, generally speaking, if you admire anything they present you with it straight away.'

'Oh dear, oh dear . . .'

'Cheer up, Belle. If he lasts over the first couple of years I don't suppose they'll hold you responsible.'

'Arthur, stop it! It's not funny. I'm very upset. Here I go with the best of intentions meaning to be kind and all I do is put my foot in it. I do think you might have warned me. How could I possibly know?'

'I'm sorry, dear. Didn't think of it. Fact is, there's so much to learn. I've been in this country about eight years now and I don't know the half of it. I've got trouble coming to me next month for example. It's a religious procession that's held every year and it always means a riot. Gaol overflows every time because I haven't found the right way to deal with it.'

But Isabelle was not to be diverted from her mortification.

'I do think it's horrid when you set out to be nice and friendly and things go against you. It wasn't my fault. How was I to know I was offending them?'

'Of course not, dear. One lives and learns, that's all.'

'You ought to have *told* me those things. Can't you explain it was a mistake?'

'Me? I'm not even allowed to see the ladies in question.'

'Explain to the Rajah, I mean.'

'No really, dear. No good at all. Best leave it alone. Anyway, I don't think you're losing much. I can't imagine you'd have much in common with the purdah ladies.'

But Isabelle was vexed. She was a bad loser. Arthur had already learned that if she wasn't made to win at least every other time at backgammon, she grew irritable and disgusted with the game.

After a moment he asked: 'How's Phoebus doing?'

'He's lovely. But Arthur, I'm afraid I bring him home in a terrible lather. It's cool when we set out, but by the time we finish our ride, it's sweltering even at that hour.'

'I know. I should try to come back by Gokul Das's. That mile of pipuls I planted my first year here gives some shade.'

50

'I never go past Gokul Das's house.' (He was a landowner of some local consequence.)

'Why ever not?'

'He's got a dog I can't stand.'

'That little fox-terrier bitch?'

'Yes. Horrible.'

'Why? Does she run out at Phoebus?'

'No.'

'She's not maltreated, I can assure you. He's awfully proud of his English dog. My predecessor gave it him as a pup.'

'She's just awful. I can't bear to look at her. She ought to be put to sleep.'

The animal in question had known a rapid succession of litters. She was a fat, friendly, noisy little creature whose dugs flapped from side to side as she waddled and nearly scraped the ground. Isabelle was deeply revolted. It reminded her of Mrs Porter.

Arthur decided not to pursue the matter of Gokul Das's dog. He realized suddenly that he wasn't feeling well – hadn't been all day. 'I think if you don't mind dear, I'll turn in. I'm feeling awfully tired.'

'You generally are,' she said derisively.

Again that terrible internal pain and the hard pressure in his chest. Isabelle's mood was dangerous. Arthur realized suddenly that there was going to be a scene. The yawn died in his throat. His face assumed the beaten-dog look. He swallowed with difficulty and said apologetically, 'I'm sorry, dear. There's a lot of work at the moment. . . . It's the heat as well . . .'

'I'm sorry too, Arthur. I know you work very hard and I don't want to be unfair. But you're at it all day and in the evening you just want to go to bed. What about me, I'd like to know?'

'It must be very dull for you Belle.'

'Dull! It's simply murderous. I've got to do something, Arthur, d'you hear? I've got to have an occupation. I'm an active, healthy young woman condemned to inactivity. It's practically solitary confinement. I'm so bored, bored, bored, I could scream.'

Arthur was aghast. He could think of nothing to say.

'It's not that I'm pining for a gay social life,' she went on. 'I knew there weren't many Europeans here, but I never realized, and neither did Mother, that there was absolutely no one. You

51

didn't tell us that, Arthur. Well, when I'd realized that, I decided to make the best of it. I thought I'd get to know some of those poor ignorant Indian women who've never had any opportunities. Teach them English, perhaps. Show them how we do things. Have a sort of study circle. And look what happens the first time I try to do anything. How was I to know of such pitfalls? Oh, it's all so beastly. Well, say something can't you?' She was drumming angrily on the arms of her chair. Goaded, Arthur seemed deprived of speech. He saw now that he'd taken what seemed to him a small thing too lightly.

'How about reading?' he suggested feebly.

'*Reading!* You talk as if I could just run round to the circulating library for a nice book!'

'There are some good books in my room. I found Mansell's *Theory of the Leisure Class* quite fascinating.'

But Isabelle was not listening. After the exasperated, pent-up flow that resulted from her brooding came the inevitable tears. It was a cycle that Arthur was to recognize.

'I'm so miserable,' she sobbed. 'I'm so miserable . . . so . . . wretched . . . oh . . . so . . .'

'Don't cry, Belle. Please don't cry. I can't bear to see you cry.'

'You don't care what becomes of me – '

'Ah, Belle – '

'Go away. Don't touch me! Go away, can't you . . . go away . . . go away . . .'

Arthur slowly left the room, like a man under orders. He was aware that this dreadful thing between them was not buried, not even dead. There had been no reconciliation at the end this time. He turned to go back to her and halted, for a host of sensations had invaded his consciousness: the unmistakable signs and symptoms of an attack of fever. He was ill. He could do no more. Suddenly some part of him embraced the thought joyfully. With an anticipatory shiver, he began to pile the blankets on his bed.

Isabelle was filled with remorse. She had never seen a man with the ague. To hear his teeth chattering with uncontrollable shaking when she herself was burning with oppressive heat was terrifying enough. Later, when his temperature soared and there seemed times when he scarcely knew her, she remembered her father's last illness and was sure that Arthur also was dying. In an agony of fear, she stroked his hands, sponged his forehead and murmured unfamiliar endearments. Arthur smiled at her. Oh, twice-blessed illness that had shown him a way out of hell and then led him to the tender and loving girl of his dreams. The smile wrung Isabelle's heart. Just so, her father had smiled before lapsing into final unconsciousness. Poor Arthur – how good he was, how patient. . . . How she had tormented him that evening. But how was she to know that he was ill? He had only said he was tired, he said that all the time . . . Arthur felt a kiss light as a butterfly on his cheek. It was followed by a tear. He smiled again from pure happiness. Isabelle, overcome, ran from the room into the comforting arms of Amma waiting in her room.

'The doctor. We must send someone for Dr Quinn at once.'

'It is fever, Mum. Fever go away arter.'

'I want the doctor.'

'It is bad fever, Mum. Arter fever go.'

'You think he'll get better, Amma?'

'Sahib get better, Mum. Fever go away.'

'Oh Amma . . .' White and brown arms interlaced, their tears flowed together.

The bridge built by Arthur's illness over the gulf that yawned between them was too fragile to bear the heavy traffic of daily life. Isabelle was not cured of her discontent, but the terrible scenes were latent, incipient only, rather than boiling into active irruption. She had started to write articles: 'An Englishwoman's First Experience of India', which occupied some of her time. At Arthur's suggestion, she had taken up photography as a hobby and spent many evening hours tramping through the jungle with Wazir Ali at her heels bearing camera and tripod. Meanwhile Arthur, listless for a long time after his attack of malaria, was seriously worried. If the rains failed a second year running. . . . At last it was clear that they had.

From the moment the district was declared a famine area, Isabelle found plenty to occupy her. Work at the hospital, the

53

schools, work among the old, the infants, checking the grain distribution . . . The dreadful spectacle of the starving, with limbs like sticks, distended bellies and listless eyes that held no gleam of hope filled her with revulsion, but she was excited and happy to be useful and occupied. During the long hours when to venture out might mean sunstroke, Arthur let her check over lists of figures, overlooking her inaccuracies. She wrote long letters home describing her experiences, and embarked on 'An English-woman's Impressions of an Indian Famine'. The *Times of India* had accepted one of her articles. The *Madras Mail* another. The long hours of fruitless brooding were no more. She stood up to the terrible heat better than she had anticipated, and evening found her as exhausted and ready for bed as Arthur was. Arthur, grimly tackling the outrageous tasks that faced him with a confidence born of his former experience, assumed a new authority in her eyes as the terrible weeks wore on.

'Arthur, oh Arthur, you've come at last! There's a dying man in the compound.'

'Is there, dear? There've been a lot of deaths at Narsinghpur today. I'm afraid it's only the beginning.'

'But, Arthur. It's too ghastly. I just found him lying in the compound when I went across to look at Phoebus. I nearly fell over him.'

'I'll have him moved, dear.'

'But don't you understand, he's *starving!* I never saw anything like it. He's a skeleton. You can see his bones. I don't know how he got there – he must have crawled, dragged himself. Oh, it's so awful. I took him a bowl of rice. He won't touch it.'

'No, I don't suppose so.'

'He wouldn't take anything from Fateh Mohammed, either.'

'No, I'll see if I can find his caste.'

'Arthur, he can't speak. I tell you he's dying.'

'There, there, Belle, don't upset yourself. There's nothing you can do. I'll go and see to it.'

When he was gone, Isabelle gave way to a storm of weeping. When at last he returned, she was still moaning and rocking herself to and fro.

'Look here, Belle, I've been thinking about this for some little time. I want you to go up to Pachmarhi now. You've done a splendid job (great help to me) and I don't want you to crack up. The worst of the famine's probably over. If the rains came, we shouldn't be able to move! Anyway, I'm not going to have you here when the cholera starts and that's flat. I'm afraid it's no good arguing about it, dear.' Arthur's voice was authoritative. He expected opposition. As none came he continued: 'I've got Chapman coming through here tomorrow and he's on his way to Pachmarhi. He'll take you along and see you fixed up. He's a nice chap.'

Isabelle answered in a small child's voice: 'Well, if you really think it's right . . .'

'I do.'

'But I hate leaving you here alone, Arthur, in this awful, awful . . .'

'That's all right, Belle. I'll join you there when it's all over. Get some local leave, see. You'd better tell the ayah to start packing your things right away. He'll want to start early.'

'All right, Arthur,' Isabelle said in the small meek voice. There was a new admixture of gratitude, affection and admiration in her feelings towards him.

At the hill station Isabelle had a whale of a time: picnics, dances, riding, tennis, golf, concerts at which she sang with great acclaim. Besides, she was the heroine of a famine. There were times when she genuinely agonized over Arthur working in his stricken district, but they grew fewer. The life of a pretty young grass widow in a gay resort full of unattached gentlemen didn't allow much time for fretting. 'Major Rivers has been very attentive . . . I danced most of the evening with the Commissioner . . . Colonel Standish gave a party for me, at which I sang . . .' Arthur noted these remarks in her letters with satisfaction rather than jealousy. It was enough for him that the beloved girl was safe and happy. Indeed, there would have been no cause for jealousy, for Isabelle's vivacious exterior concealed a sexual frigidity that was extreme.

At last the long agony in the plains was ended and Arthur

arrived at the hill station, looking not unlike a famine specimen himself. Isabelle was solicitous and kind, though his dislike of the club and aversion to dancing put a brake on her activities.

After a short leave, the cold weather having started, they went into camp.

Isabelle took to camping with enthusiasm. In this nomadic, beautiful existence their brother-and-sister relationship seemed to have no sinister significance. It was the nearest approach in all their married life to a period of sustained happiness. Together they savoured the sheer joy of existence. The scenes were varied, full of interest and often of incredible beauty. The great Waingunga river, boiling over its marble rocks. The quiet pools where the jungle animals came stealthily to drink. The sharp loveliness of dawn as they ate cold bacon sandwiches and drank hot chocolate before setting forth, the horses standing by, stamping with cold. Evenings round the camp fire with the sparks flying and the stars burning overhead while Arthur played the gramophone – a little Gilbert and Sullivan, or some Offenbach, perhaps – and the servants squatted, huddled in a circle close to the burning logs, their wondering eyes fixed on the great horn. There was the occasion when Fateh Mohammed, who had blotted his copybook rather too often of late, redeemed his trespasses by quite literally saving Arthur's life, precipitating himself at a wounded tigress who was charging his master and thus diverting her attention and giving Arthur the split second necessary to fire the fatal shot. There was the occasion later when Isabelle bagged her first tiger (Arthur already had two to his credit). This was a man-eater that had long ravaged the district and Isabelle's triumph was a cause for general rejoicing.

9

The return to the bungalow was a return to hell. Isabelle's discontent rapidly assumed control. Arthur's life was a pattern of supressed nervous tension succeeded by illness. His attacks of malaria were alarmingly frequent. At each attack Isabelle was invariably kind, sympathetic and affectionate in her way, even when his slavish gratitude irked her. After each attack he remained as weak as a kitten, getting through his work lying down, moving only from his bed to a chaise-longue on the verandah. It was as if he could not face returning to the miseries of living. In the evenings, to escape from an intercourse full of pitfalls, he had formed the habit of reading aloud. Isabelle detested it and chafed inwardly. On the occasions when she chafed outwardly as well, she was smitten with remorse the following day, when Arthur was invariably worse. It was a situation that was rapidly becoming intolerable.

When, after several months, dysentery was added to the fever, it was clear that something had to be done. Dr Quinn called in consultants who agreed on the verdict. 'It's a year's sick leave for you, old man, possibly more, in a temperate climate. And then you must put in for another district – a healthier one.'

Arthur was shocked. In this prolonged illness he seemed to have lost his initiative. He listened in silence.

'Well now, it's all decided. You've nothing to worry about.

The chief'll be sending someone to take over in a day or so. You can make arrangements about the servants. They'll fix your passage at headquarters. I want you out of here as soon as possible. On a stretcher if need be.'

Arthur remained without speaking, slowly shaking his head from side to side. Noting his dejection, Dr Quinn exclaimed: 'Cheer up, old man! You'll feel fine when you're home in England.'

'But it's scarcely two years since I was home.'

'You were on furlough then. This is sick leave. Some people get all the luck.'

'You think I'll get sent somewhere else?'

'Certainly. Somewhere higher up, I expect. With a bit of company for your wife as well.'

'Isabelle doesn't like it here. As you see, she's lonely here.'

'It's no place for a woman on her own. Now if she had a young family growing up, it'd be different.'

Arthur was tempted to unburden his heart, but the effort was too great.

'I like it here,' he said finally.

'And you've done a splendid job. Famine two years running was a bit of bad luck. They won't forget what you've done for them. I bet there'll be loud lamentations when Boyne Sahib goes. You've made it hard for your successor.'

Arthur smiled. Then the worried look returned.

'I don't think Isabelle really likes this country, apart from the camping.'

'Ah, she'll get used to it. Just you wait till the first baby arrives. I'll come and take charge of that event, if I'm able, wherever you are.'

Again the opportunity to tell his troubles. But he only shook his head and sighed.

'Cheer up, old man. Things are never as bad as you think. Now, the married state is something I've no experience of at first hand, but I've heard tell the first two years are the wurrst.'

Arthur had a further blow in store. The mail from England brought a letter from Mrs Boyne announcing that Bertie had contracted tuberculosis. The doctors were sending patients at that time to the dry desert air of Egypt. A sanatorium at Heliopolis was recommended. But the *cost* . . . How could they possibly afford such a thing?

Within ten minutes of receiving the letter, and without waiting to discuss the matter with Isabelle, Arthur had dispatched a runner with a cable urging Bertie to proceed to Egypt without delay. With it went his savings. The thought of Bertie, the dear companionable brother, stricken with this terrible scourge was almost more than he could bear. As for himself, he would have to raise the money somehow for the expensive year that lay ahead, but what did money matter with Bertie's life at stake? . . .

On a gruelling May morning, Arthur was carried up the gang-plank at Bombay on a stretcher to the interest and concern of the other travellers, but it was with his usual buoyant step that he descended the gangplank at Tilbury a month later. They had passed the ship carrying Bertie to Egypt somewhere in the Mediterranean. No time had been lost there, and Arthur was full of hope. Bertie was showing remarkable powers of recovery. Isabelle, on the other hand, was nearing a breakdown. Under the strain of recent events she had developed insomnia. The doctor pronounced her to be suffering from 'nervous prostration', the recommended cure for which was 'change', which naturally did not exclude entertainment.

It was in the cab on the way back to the hotel in Cromwell Road, after an evening at the theatre spent with friends of Isabelle's, that Arthur broached the subject that was troubling him.

'We'll have to draw in our horns you know, dear. I can't afford to live at this rate for long.'

'Long? We've only been home a week tomorrow.'

'I know – '

'It's not as if you did the paying this evening!'

'I know, Belle, but next time I will, when we give a return party. I was only pointing out I can't afford it for long.'

Later, when they were in their private sitting-room, Isabelle returned to the subject. 'But I thought we had plenty of money, Arthur? You always said . . .'

'In India, yes dear, where most things are provided for example. It's quite a different kettle of fish here.'

59

'I see. I always thought we had plenty . . .'

'No, dear. In fact, at the moment, what with all this illness, I'm feeling the pinch a good deal. I'm on half-pay you see. I'll have to start seeing about raising something pretty soon.'

'Arthur! You don't mean the money-lenders.'

'Not yet, I hope. I must get some advice on the best way to set about borrowing.'

'Oh, how horrible!'

'Why, dear? It may be a painful process. There's nothing *horrible* about it.'

'But it is! It's dreadful. We'll be running into debt.'

'We'll be living for a time on borrowed money. All businesses are run on borrowed money. It's the way the capitalist system works. John Stuart Mill has a chapter . . .'

'But Arthur, how, how, how did we get to this stage? I always understood an Indian Civilian's pay was so good and nobody could call me extravagant.'

'Of course not, dear. You ask how? Now take the case of Bertie; his cure is going to run into a lot of money. It's a slow business, tuberculosis.'

'You mean to tell me you're paying for sending Bertie to Egypt?'

'Of course, dear. There's no one else. Mother has nothing to spare and Bertie hasn't a penny himself. Of course it's up to me – '

'I *can't* get over it. Why should you be the one who's responsible?'

'I suppose because I want to be, Belle – there's nothing I wouldn't do for Bertie – within reason. But quite apart from that, I'm under solemn oath' – and he proceeded with the story of his father's death and his own origins.

Isabelle listened with signs of growing agitation. At last she burst out: 'The wicked, shameless old man!'

'Who?'

'Your father.'

'He wasn't old, though I thought he was at the time. I don't suppose he was over fifty when he finished himself off.'

'I think it's disgraceful!'

'What, Belle?'

'Having all those children when he'd one family already.'

'Well, he was cut off from them, you see. Dead, as far as they were concerned.'

'It was *wicked* of him. And to leave them unprovided for. I can't get over it. The selfishness! – Then to think your name isn't Boyne at all! Then what's my real name now? Oh Arthur, tell me . . . I *have* to know! No! No, don't tell me . . . I couldn't bear to know and not be able to claim kinship. Oh dear, how horrible it all is . . . how very upsetting . . .' The dreaded tears fell fast. Presently she said: 'There's always my little bit of money.'

'I never thought of it. Oh Belle, that would be a great help. Help tide us over this bad spell.'

'That's all right, then.'

'I'll pay it back when I'm able.'

'Nonsense. What's mine is yours.'

'Oh Belle, you are good.'

'I'll go tomorrow and see how much there is. It's only a small sum for dress allowance. I haven't needed any clothes so I haven't touched it. You know I don't get my money that Father left till Mother, till Mother . . .'

'Dear, I was thinking, how would it be if we went abroad for a few months? We can live much more cheaply on the Continent than in London. What d'you think of a bicycle tour in the Black Forest? And we can end up at St Moritz and have our honeymoon there after all?'

Isabelle dried her eyes. 'Arthur that's a lovely idea! Do let's.' She was already finding that London without a home, without her mother and brother, was no longer the same. As for Arthur, an ardent Wagnerite, he was longing to see the castles of the Rhine. So it was settled.

The tour, on the whole, was a great success. They crossed to Calais and made their way slowly across the northern lands (by train and bicycle) in the cool northern summer to the Feldberg, where they spent several weeks pottering about the Black Forest. Isabelle was a Francophile, under the influence of her mother's proud French ancestry, and the many holidays spent in Paris and

Boulogne-sur-Mer with her parents and Archie. Now she began to share Arthur's romantic passion for the Germans, especially the friendly, courteous peasantry who stared without comment at her bloomers, in pleasant contrast to the ribald remarks these garments tended to invoke in the French.

Arthur had occasional returns of illness – a day or two spent in bed here and there when Isabelle ventured out sight-seeing on her own – but for the most part he was well. The constant change of scene, the vast scented pine forests, the romantic evidences of history, the gargantuan meals, the temperate summer, the simple charm of the natives – all combined to banish his troubles and give him the feeling of well-being that he associated with camp life.

When autumn came they sent for some trunks, dispatched their bicycles and proceeded by slow stages across Switzerland.

If Arthur had imagined that St Moritz, the honeymoon resort of his dreams, would of itself bring about a happier state of affairs in their married relations, he was doomed to disappointment. The hotel was nearly empty, as the season had not yet begun, and they felt conspicuous and self-conscious in the deserted public rooms. Adjoining single bedrooms had become an established rule that he dared not break. When the snow came and the hotel began to fill up, they took to bob-sleighing with enthusiasm and precipitated themselves down the Cresta run with many (fortunately minor) accidents. Arthur refused to venture on skis or skates, but took long invigorating walks while Isabelle skated with an assorted crowd of many nationalities. She was enjoying it and forgetting her 'nervous prostration'. She wrote to her mother, living now in Spain with Archie, and urged her to join them. Mrs Burnett arrived with her companion to spend Christmas. She had aged. The break-up of her home, the loss of husband and daughter, had been very unsettling for one who had led a sheltered, even pampered life. She had always been authoritative and often censorious, but the olympian calm had given way to a new petulance and irritability, due chiefly to the nightly bromide which she now found necessary to lull her wakefulness.

It occurred to Arthur, harassed as he was by shortage of money, that his mother-in-law had a good deal more than she needed. In due course, some of the money would go to her daughter.

She couldn't be getting more than 4 per cent on her investments while his bankers were charging him 12 per cent. A simple transaction whereby he paid her say 6 per cent on a loan of £2,000 would be a benefit to all concerned. Alternatively, she might prefer to give her daughter a certain sum outright, instead of waiting to die first . . . With singular lack of finesse, he decided to broach the subject one afternoon when he was having tea in her sitting-room. Isabelle was still on the skating-rink. He fidgeted awkwardly, rattling his cup in his saucer (a nervous habit which Mrs Burnett found excruciating), and after clearing his throat several times, laid his proposition before his mother-in-law.

Mrs Burnett had a Victorian's horror of debt. She was not ungenerous, but held it an almost sacred tenet to live prudently within one's means, setting aside yearly sums for the future. Borrowing means debt. The very word conjured up a picture of Arthur in a debtor's prison while her daughter begged her bread in the streets. She was outraged.

After a pained silence, Arthur, thinking he had perhaps not made himself very clear, began going over the ground again.

'So you lied to me.' The words came slowly and deliberately.

'What?'

'You lied to me.' It was spoken almost affably.

'I . . . I don't know what you – '

'I was given to understand that you were in a position to marry. I was given to understand that you were in a position to support my daughter.'

'So I was. I am, but – '

'On the contrary. After rather less than two years of marriage, you are asking me to support you both. Correct me if I'm mistaken, but I have the impression that you are asking me to lend or give you the sum of two thousand pounds.'

Arthur was dreadfully upset. But he had an even temper, slow to wrath and always ready and willing to see the other side of an argument. He realized dimly that he had played his cards badly and that in Mrs Burnett he had a formidable opponent.

'You took Isabelle to live in a place that's not fit for a white woman to live in, let alone a girl brought up as she has been. No, don't think that she has complained to me. She's far too loyal for that. But the fact remains that you deceived me again as to the life you were offering my daughter. I should never have allowed her to marry you had I known the true facts.'

Arthur was astounded. Somewhere at the back of his jangled emotions he could now feel the horrible approach of anger. He drove it back.

'But I can support Isabelle properly in India,' he said feebly. 'In India she has a house and servants and horses and . . . she's well looked after, I assure you. The first few years as a district officer's wife may not be quite the life you might have chosen for her, but I'll get promotion. In a few years she'll be a commissioner's wife, and then she'll have a fine life.'

'I want no more promises, thank you.'

'It's just for the moment that times are hard for us and I . . . I . . . just thought you might care to help, that's all.'

'What other commitments have you?'

'What d'you mean?'

'I mean, what other payments are you making in addition to supporting a wife? What are your debts?'

Arthur, ignoring the second question, told her of Bertie's plight.

'I'm sorry to hear this. It is indeed a misfortune.' After a pause she continued: 'I see. So you support your family as well. You didn't choose to tell me that before. Have they no sources of income beside yourself?'

'Very little. My two other brothers are supporting themselves.'

'So I should hope. Then what it really amounts to is this. You expect me to contribute towards your family.'

'No such thing!' He was angry at last.

'That is just as well.'

'I am sorry I ever raised the matter since you take it like this,' Arthur said. He got up to make for the door. He had tried to speak with dignity, but realized only too well his total inadequacy to deal with the situation.

'Sit down. Sit down, I said. And now listen to me. I will give you this two thousand pounds. I will not lend it because I don't believe in lending. I will give it to you on one condition. It is that Isabelle return to me until such time as you have cleared off your debts and are in a position to support a wife.'

64

'Isabelle to return to you?'

'That is what I said.'

'It's preposterous! She's my wife. We're married.'

'Are you?'

Arthur stared at his mother-in-law. It would not have surprised him to see her foam at the mouth and stick straws in her hair. She must be mad.

'Are you? *Then where is my grandchild?* I have observed that you occupy separate rooms?'

'It's none of your business.' Arthur was trembling.

'Keep a civil tongue in your head, young man, and understand this: everything that concerns my daughter *is* my business. Now you may go and think over what I have said. Send Isabelle to me when she comes in.'

At that moment the door opened and Isabelle entered, flushed from her exercise and humming the 'Blue Danube' waltz that had been played repeatedly at the skating-rink. Mrs Burnett lost no time in acquainting her with the situation. Isabelle was dumbfounded. She stared at her imperious mother, cold and haughty in her anger, and then at her husband, wretchedly worried, almost hang-dog.

'Oh, Mother, don't be angry!' and she threatened to burst into tears.

'Be quiet, Isabelle, and let me finish telling you what I have been telling Arthur. I am prepared to give him the sum of money he needs, provided you return to me for a year. We will take a small furnished house in London temporarily, until such time as he is able to support you decently – '

'Oh, but he does!'

'Nonsense, child. That dress you're wearing is one I had made for you before you married. It is evidently nothing to him that his wife should be shabby and out of fashion.'

'Mother, you're unfair! This dress is hardly worn. I haven't needed it in a hot place like – '

'I'm not prepared to argue, Isabelle. I am not satisfied at the way your marriage has turned out. Until Arthur can do better for you, I want you to return to me.'

'Mother, I can't possibly! I refuse! I married Arthur for better, for worse – '

'You refuse, Isabelle? Very well, I have nothing more to say.'

'Oh, Mother, please. You're being hateful – '

'To think that my own daughter should speak to me like that!'

'But it *is* hateful! Arthur only wanted you to invest some money in us instead of in some – '

'That will do, Isabelle. I have nothing further to say. Go now, both of you.'

Isabelle began to sob, and Arthur, consoled a little by her spirited defence of him, put an arm round his wife and guided her, still sobbing, from the room.

Mrs Burnett remained staring after them. Suddenly she called: 'Purdy! Purdy, come here.' The companion, who had missed nothing of what had occurred from the keyhole of the adjoining bedroom, entered timidly.

'You are to pack. Pack everything at once, do you hear? We are leaving this place. First you can run down to the reception desk and find out about trains. And then do the packing. And Purdy, bring me my sal volatile.'

Isabelle was prostrated. She finally ordered a little supper to be brought to her bed. Arthur had already taken to his and refused nourishment. In the morning, when they descended miserably to the dining-room, it was to learn that Mrs Burnett had left St Moritz.

It was Christmas Eve.

10

Isabelle had hoped for a reconciliation before she went back to India, but Mrs Burnett had returned to Archie in Spain. Archie eventually persuaded her to reply to Isabelle's letters, but a brief interchange of rather frigid notes was the nearest they ever came to a resumption of relations.

Meanwhile Arthur and Isabelle, depressed by the hotel festivities and having come to hate St Moritz, decided to move on. It was outrageously expensive anyway. A travel poster of the castle of Chillon, projecting romantically over still lake water, attracted them to Vevey, where they found a cheap, clean pension. Isabelle's spirits were low. Arthur kept counting the months that remained before he could return to India. Yet out of this unpromising state of affairs the eventual consummation of their marriage came about.

They were returning from a walk and paused to look at the sunset splendour reflected in the lake beneath them when Isabelle suddenly remarked in a matter-of-fact tone: 'If all Englishwomen refused to have babies, the British Empire would soon come to an end. Wouldn't it?' As Arthur didn't reply immediately, she continued: 'I've decided to be a wife to you, Arthur.'

Even to a mathematician and economist, the reason sounded inadequate. He began warily: 'Then you really mean, dearest – '

'Certainly I do. My mind's made up. So that's that.'

'Oh my darling – '

'You know that room with the double bed and a balcony over the lake they showed us? Well, it's still vacant. Let's go back and move our things.'

'Oh my love . . .'

'We may as well get it over with,' said Isabelle practically. Arthur hoped she referred to the process of moving rooms. They continued their descent.

It was certainly a revolting business, Isabelle decided, but at least it was quickly done. It was really a lot of fuss about nothing. So this was what being married meant. All the married women she knew must have gone through with it. But why had no one ever told her what to expect? Mother now – the thought of her mother brought back the tears. What principally disturbed her was that two separate identities seemed to inhabit Arthur's frame: the worshipping lover and the reserved almost diffident companion of the daylight hours, who was never so happy as when working out a problem in advanced mathematics on the back of an old envelope – a pursuit from which she was totally excluded. She approved the worshipping lover, particularly at a distance. She would have liked to spend the rest of her life on her pedestal. She could not understand how the ardent worshipper could in the course of the day show such astonishing impartiality as to her presence, even appearing to forget that she was there. She was often wounded, nettled by his seeming indifference, and this very fact escaped his attention. When, bewilderingly, he was ready to make love again, she reproached him and there were quarrels. If Arthur abased himself sufficiently, they were soon made up. There is no doubt that he was not a very good lover. His inexperience, the fact that he had got away to a bad start, his natural shyness and gaucherie all combined to hinder him from progressing in this field.

After some weeks Isabelle had a bilious attack. She dosed herself with castor oil, but the remedy proved ineffective. Arthur, worried at her continued ill health, sought out a doctor. A few simple questions, a cursory examination.

'*Mais Mme est enceinte. Zut alors! Je vous félicite.*'

In their ignorance they had not even thought of the simple explanation.

Arthur was overjoyed. Isabelle, alternately cross in the mornings and pleased by evening, was going to bear a son. She wrote the great news to her mother. Mrs Burnett replied with some condescension that she would be pleased to furnish the layette. Isabelle could choose it at Whiteleys on her return to London.

'No thank you,' said Arthur with rare resentment. 'I'd rather you used my account at the Army and Navy. They'll ship it all out.'

The breach remained. But Arthur was now as considerate as she could wish, all his waking hours. It was in this relatively happy relationship that their long leave at last drew to a close and they returned to India.

Arthur found himself posted as Deputy Commissioner to Bagra, one of the choicest stations in the Province. It was relatively high-lying (though not, of course, in the hills) and boasted a clubhouse and beautiful public gardens. There were six European officials in all – the Police Superintendent, the Forest Officer, the Education Officer, the doctor and Arthur's assistant – all of them married. The Deputy Commissioner's house was an almost palatial two-storeyed residence, built in the days of the East India Company when the officials did not expect to return to England before retirement. After the dismal solitude of her first station, Isabelle was enchanted with the place. Furthermore, she was the Burra Memsahib, a fact which pleased her inordinately. In addition, the uninhibited joy of Amma, Fazil Khan, Wazir Ali and Fateh Mohammed at being reunited with their master and mistress and at the dazzling prospect of the approaching happy event – all combined to produce a sense of general well-being. Fateh Mohammed, looking as if butter would not melt in his mouth, took an especial delight in his confections at the select weekly dinner parties, or the monthly burra Khanas that Isabelle gave, seating her guests solemnly in order of precedence. She did not make any close friends among the small group, but to her, all social intercourse, even if slightly antipathetic, was better than none.

Arthur's magisterial court and government offices (contemporary with the house and suitably grand) were half a mile away, approached by a great avenue. He tried not to venture further than this, so solicitous was he of Isabelle in her delicate condition. She had given up all strenuous exercise and walked in her garden, giving a few orders to the gardener and his coolies, well satisfied with the beauty of the scene. If only Arthur had waited, she thought, if only he had had the sense to bring me here, instead of to that dreadful place, that miserable quarrel would never have happened . . . It was a habit of thought that had already become ingrained in her – a ceaseless, senseless milling over the past.

As her time approached, Arthur's apprehensions grew. He took over one of the deep shady verandahs for his business so as to be on hand for the first twinge in order to send for Dr Quinn (at twelve hours' distance), so little confidence had he in his subordinate's power to save his wife's life. The nurse, an English midwife procured from headquarters, was a sensible body who had spent many years in the country. Arthur found her brisk 'Nothing to worry about' infinitely depressing. 'Have you decided on names?' she asked conversationally. Isabelle was all for Edmund after her father. Arthur was all for leaving it to Isabelle. Time dragged. At last Dr Quinn was sent for, rather prematurely. Isabelle's labour was long and at times hysterical. Arthur knew that she was dying. He kept thinking of their first two years of married life. Of course she had known that child-bearing would kill her. . . . Nearly demented, he sat on the verandah, listening to the whining voice that dragged interminably on: 'And now oh most gracious and lofty Presence, Protector of the Poor, judge I pray thee betwixt thy servant and this malefactor, this father of lies, this son of perdition, whose bullocks nightly trample my corn on their way to the water-hole, whose young oxen take a short cut through my field of lentils – '

'It's a girl!' Dr Quinn's hand was on his shoulder. 'Congratulations, man! You've a bonny daughter and your wife's doing fine.'

'Oh my darling, my love, never never again,' Arthur murmured in his wife's ear.

'No. Never again,' Isabelle repeated and intercepted a wink that the midwife directed at Dr Quinn. She decided to fire her as soon as she was stronger.

Arthur went to bed for a week.

11

Dr Quinn had expected a small celebration. When he found that Arthur's temperature and pulse were normal, he suggested going over to the clubhouse to drink the health of the new arrival, but Arthur remained prostrate in one of the downstairs spare bedrooms.

'Come on, old man. There's nothing wrong. You're feeling the after-effects, that's all. I thought at first you might be in for a go of fever. A bath and a burra peg'll soon put you right.'

Arthur lay with his eyes closed. He shook his head slowly as if the effort of speech were beyond him.

'What's up?'

There was no reply.

'Any pain? Sickness?'

'I feel ghastly.' Arthur spoke in a dying croak.

'Anywhere special?'

'Everywhere.'

'Anything you want?'

'No, thank you. I'm sorry, old man.'

'That's all right. I'll look after myself. See you later then. Have some sleep now.' When, some hours afterwards, the doctor reeled into the house, a little the worse for liquor, all his patients were sleeping soundly.

Very early next morning, Dr Quinn was off again.

'Feeling all right this morning?' he asked Arthur. 'I'm dashed if I do, but anyway you missed a fine party.'

'I feel ill. Too weak to move.'

Dr Quinn took his temperature and pulse again. 'Normal,' he snorted. 'You put me in mind of a tribe of savages where the custom is for the father to go to bed when the wife is in labour. Funny lot. Well, go up and see your womenfolk presently. Isabelle's expecting you. So long.'

Arthur couldn't diagnose his illness. An immense torpor invaded his limbs. All he wanted to do was to drift into unconsciousness. Fazil Khan remained within call, dispatched at long intervals for a pot of tea. The nurse, baffled by the situation, took messages to and from Isabelle. On the third day, when the station had called to pay their respects and the Rajah and other notabilities had sent gifts, Isabelle became impatient.

'Mrs Boyne's getting upset. She wants to know if you've got malaria. You're doing her no good lying here.' Nurse was forthright.

With Fazil Khan's help, he bathed, put on a dressing-gown and went very slowly up the stairs.

'I'm so sorry to leave you, dearest. I've been ill.'

'What with, Arthur?'

'I don't know. I couldn't move hand or foot.'

For once Isabelle was unsympathetic. She felt, understandably perhaps, that any sympathy going ought to be directed towards herself. They were neither of them baby-lovers and beyond satisfying themselves that the infant was not ailing, they were glad to leave it to the ministrations of the nurse and Amma.

It took Arthur several more days to return to his normal life. Never once as he lay in the downstairs room did he ask himself the reason for this strange distemper. He accepted it as it came and lay in a kind of stupor vaguely hoping for it to pass.

Isabelle was annoyed at forfeiting the Christmas camping, but it was agreed that the infant, Lucy, was too young for it and she clearly could not be left behind. Life at the station had resumed its normal round and Amma proudly pushed the baby about in a fine English perambulator tricked out with a frilled canopy. Christmas was celebrated by an annual service in the little church buried in the public gardens behind a screen of bamboos. It was conducted by a visiting missionary. Isabelle drove to it decked in her best. Arthur refused.

'But why won't you come? I think you ought.'

'No thanks, dear. That's one legend I don't hold with.'

'What are you talking about?'

'Christmas. I can't swallow this business of God being born at Bethlehem and all that. "To save us poor sinners he came from above" we used to sing at school – '

'Oh, don't start now, Arthur.' Isabelle was struggling into a pair of long kid gloves and frowning over a tiny button-hook. 'Do hurry and get dressed.'

'I've told you, dear, I'm not coming. It's against my principles to subscribe to superstition. "God and sinners reconciled." I ask you now – '

'But Arthur, you owe it to your position as Deputy Commissioner. It's a formal occasion.'

'I don't like formal occasions.'

'I don't care what you like. I still think you ought to go.'

'Sorry, dear, I've got a lot of letters to write. Anyway as you've got the whole lot coming to dinner, I'll be as formal as you like then. And it's not a bad idea to keep an eye on Fateh Mohammed before a dinner-party.'

'Oh, you can always think up excuses for doing what you want to . . .' Arthur could be very trying.

At the age of three months, the baby fell ill with a violent attack of dysentery. She grew pitifully thin and did not respond to treatment. Isabelle was frantic. 'It's so awful after all the care I've taken,' she wailed. 'I always see that the bottles are sterilized for Amma to give. I have everything boiled. How, how, how could this have happened?' For six weeks the baby's life hung in the balance. It was decided that the only hope was for Isabelle with Amma's help to take her to England. The hot weather was approaching. Arthur could not leave. He was consumed with anxiety. Preparations were under way for the journey. Would the baby stand the journey? . . . Two days before the departure was due, the infant made a remarkable recovery. She took nourish-

74

ment, appeared to smile, took some more and smiled unmistakably. At this point Amma, who had nursed her day and night throughout her illness, seemed to take leave of her senses. She broke into a curious dance, uttering piercing screams of thanksgiving, and fell to kissing the feet of her master and mistress. Later it transpired that Amma and the other Hindu servants had clubbed together for a goat to be offered in sacrifice at a neighbouring shrine dedicated to the goddess Kali, in a last-minute endeavour to avert her wrath. It was a miracle. Lucy at any rate never looked back.

'No sense in risking moving her now,' said the doctor, mopping his brow. 'She's unquestionably better. With any luck she's over the worst.' He had visited her twice daily for weeks and tried every known treatment without success. He had mentally more or less written her off. Within a fortnight, Lucy was restored to normal, though perhaps a little underweight. She did him great credit, he decided.

The spacious, well-built house was relatively cool even in the great heat, as the punkah-wallahs on the verandahs, prodded awake by zealous servants, kept the air circulating. Nevertheless a spell in the hills seemed essential for the baby's health and Isabelle departed with Amma and Lucy to Simla, where Arthur was to join them for a short spell when the hot season and rains were over.

It was a repetition of the gay life she had known at Pachmarhi, but gayer and grander owing to the sumptuous presence of Vice-regal Lodge presiding over all. Isabelle replenished her wardrobe and plunged happily into the festivities. She soon found herself in demand. By the time Arthur arrived, she had already taken part with success in gymkhanas and amateur theatricals and sung with éclat at several concerts. They sat on their balcony, gazing across the wooded hills at the glistening snow-capped peaks away to the north that tore a jagged line across the heavens.

'Did I tell you? There's a dance at Lady Palmer's tonight. Oh, Arthur, I am looking forward to dancing with you. You weren't well enough that time at Pachmarhi after the famine. Isn't it absurd to think that we've never danced together!'

'Not really. I don't dance.'

'Well, you're going to! You'll soon pick it up with me. I know – we'll roll up the rugs in the sitting-room and I'll show you a few steps now.'

'Oh no, thank you, Belle. You go – I'll enjoy seeing you setting forth in your war paint. By the way, were the new dresses a success?'

'Yes, I think they are. They cost a lot of money, but I had to have them to do you credit.'

'Of course. I'm sure my stock's risen considerably.' Arthur made as if to kiss his wife, but Isabelle warded him off.

'Arthur, you're not serious about not coming to Lady P's dance?'

'Deadly serious.'

'But Arthur, don't you want to dance with me? Everyone says what a good dancer I am.'

'I'm sure you are, dear.'

'Well then?'

'Well then what?'

'Arthur, don't be so maddening!'

'I'm sorry, Belle. I can't dance – never could and never will.'

'I think it's perfectly ridiculous!' said Isabelle hotly. 'You simply won't try.'

'I suppose not.'

'You don't want to please me.'

'Dearest, I do.'

'No, you don't. You write all those letters saying you love me and how you miss me and then when you come, the very first thing I ask you to do, you refuse.'

'I'm sorry, dear.'

'You're not! You're not sorry at all!'

'Oh, Belle, don't get angry. I'd do any number of things to please you, you know I would – only taking the dance floor is not one of them.'

'Why not? Why not, I'd like to know? I tell you people jump at the chance of dancing with me. My programme's always full. And then my own husband refuses – ' Isabelle was near to tears.

Arthur looked worried. 'I don't know that I can explain,' he said slowly. 'I *don't like dancing*. That's what it is. I find it rather unpleasant – so does my partner, I might add. To me it's funda-

76

mentally ludicrous. I suppose it's a personal matter. Let other people dance if they wish to. There is no doubt it fulfils a primitive instinct. Naked savages have always – '

'Oh, stop it!' Isabelle cried in exasperation and fled across the sitting-room, slamming the bedroom door behind her.

After a moment, Arthur followed gingerly. She was standing looking out of the window with unseeing eyes.

'Belle, I'm sorry. I'm such an oaf. I realize it must be very trying for you.'

'Oh, Arthur, that means you're coming then?'

'No, dear.'

Isabelle sighed and added emotionally, 'Here we are together again after months and months apart, and I thought it was going to be such fun to celebrate it.'

'Well, I thought of celebrating our reunion too. I thought a little dinner up here away from all those pairs of eyes in the dining-room. I ordered it to be sent up and a bottle of wine . . . But if you'd rather go to the dance, Belle, I'll turn in early. I'm tired anyway after the journey . . .'

'Arthur, don't you *mind* me dancing with others? Aren't you ever jealous to think of me in the arms of another man?'

'It hadn't occurred to me . . .'

'You're not human! Oh why, why do you have to be like this? Why can't you be more like other men? You won't ever go to the club at Bagra because you say it bores you, but here it's different. I suppose you're not going to take part in any of the social events.'

'I expect not.'

'You'll condescend to leave your card at Viceregal Lodge, I presume?'

'That's obligatory.'

There was a pause. Then Isabelle asked: 'Why do you hate your fellow beings?'

'I don't think I do.'

'Yes, you do. You despise them.'

'No. But I don't much like their conversation.'

'Why?'

'I'm afraid because it bores me. I find it inconceivably boring. It's because I've got no talent for that sort of thing. Then I find

77

myself involved in insincerities. Well, I'd rather read a book any day.'

'So you've come up here to read books?'

'No, dear. I've come to be with you.'

'But not to do any of the things I like?'

'Oh, Belle, I've thought of lots of things you'd like. There are some glorious walks, excursions I used to go on here before I went down with that go of dysentery. I thought I'd be able to show you. . . . But if you'd rather go on with the things you've been doing, I don't mind.'

'How could I? Everybody knows you're here. It would be terribly embarrassing for me. How could I explain?'

'Is an explanation necessary?'

'Oh, Arthur, you're hopeless!'

'Well, you could always say I'm ill . . .'

'And then you'd be seen striding round Jakko.'

'Dear, I can't see it matters greatly. If you're going to Lady Whatnot's dance, perhaps you'd better start getting changed.'

'I'm not going.'

'Not?'

'If you're not going, I won't.'

'Dearest, let's not go over that ground again.'

'No. As you've arranged a different sort of celebration, Arthur, I'll fall in with your wishes. Though I can't see why I should always be the one to give way.'

Mercifully Arthur did not think of the obvious answer until she had left the room.

Ennui returned at Bagra, whose charm had worn thin. Amma took complete charge of the child. There was nothing for Isabelle to do. She was back in a state of aching discontent.

The scenes that occurred were somehow less agonizing than in the early days. Repetition had staled the initial shock. Arthur had several attacks of malaria during which Isabelle inevitably reproached herself for unkindness.

The dreaded approach of the hot weather brought an unexpected stroke of luck. Isabelle was breakfasting on the verandah after her early-morning ride and was wondering dejectedly how

78

to spend the rest of the long day ahead when Arthur suddenly returned home, waving a bunch of letters.

'Wonderful news, Belle. I've been lent to Lahore for six months. Special duty. This means Simla for you and the baby, for the hot weather and rains, and I shall be able to run up occasionally. I get half as much pay again, and if I do well . . . Oh, and Belle, there's a letter from Bertie to say his last test is negative. That means he's over it. Isn't that absolutely splendid!'

Simla was not the same as last season. Isabelle found that her especial admirers had left, while by pure misfortune two ladies of whom she had fallen foul ('Cats, Arthur, spiteful, stupid cats they are') were firmly established in the hotel, sharing an adjacent table where, with lowered heads, they giggled together in a highly offensive manner. ('Considering one's in jute and the other tea, I can't see what business they have to be in this hotel at all . . .')

When Arthur arrived, Isabelle was surprisingly ready to fall in with his plans. He proposed a tour to Narkunda, riding and walking as the terrain allowed, with Amma and Lucy borne in a palanquin behind them. They were to sleep in government rest-houses. Isabelle little guessed that this expedition was partly planned to evade a dinner and dance invitation from Viceregal Lodge. She only learned of it on their return.

'Oh, what a shame! It just *would* come when we were away, and now you're off tomorrow.' As Arthur made no rejoinder, she added: 'That's one invitation you couldn't have refused.'

'Whose?'

'The Viceroy's, of course.'

'I couldn't have gone.'

'You'd have had to.'

'No uniform.'

'Why?'

'I don't know where it's got to. It's full of moth anyway.'

'Well, you must order a new one at once.'

'No fear.'

'Arthur, don't be so stupid. You have to have one for official occasions.'

'What! Spend £30 on something I might only wear once?

Rotten waste of money! I can always be ill. Probably would be, anyway . . .'

'Oh, Arthur . . .'

'Belle, I want to give you a present. I was looking at an emerald ring in that shop in the Mall this morning.'

'You can't afford it.'

'I can. Bertie's cured and I've just made £30 towards it on not ordering a uniform. Come and look at it, dear.'

On the trip to Narkunda they had travelled mainly along narrow tracks cut in the mountains with spectacular views across open valleys on the one hand and often precipitous walls of rock on the other. Sometimes they met trains of yaks laden with merchandise from Tibet, the men no less shaggy than the beasts, and Isabelle's heart was in her mouth as the sure-footed creatures negotiated the narrow passing spaces, ignoring the yawning gulfs with the nonchalance born of practice.

'It's a good thing they know the rule of the road,' Arthur had said.

Sometimes the way lay through forests of flowering rhododendron, sometimes pine, and always another towering range revealed itself before the still-distant snows.

What a splendid idea the trip to Narkunda had been, thought Arthur. Lucy, an aggressive red-head of two, needed companionship. Things had really been very difficult lately. Arthur, looking round for some token to mark his joy, had been delighted when his eye fell on the emerald ring.

That evening after dinner, Isabelle sat turning and admiring the beautiful ring on her finger.

'If only you hadn't to go tomorrow? I can't bear to think of you in the plains . . .'

'Only another three weeks and then we'll all be home in Bagra again, with the best time of the year beginning.'

'Arthur, there's just one thing that makes me feel miserable. If only . . .'

'What, dear?'

80

'It's that miserable quarrel with Mother. If only it hadn't happened. If only you could write and tell her you're sorry – sorry it ever happened . . .'

Arthur took a long time over lighting his pipe.

'Couldn't you please say you're sorry? Couldn't you, Arthur? If only you knew how unhappy it makes me . . .'

'You want me to write a letter of apology to your mother?'

'Oh yes, please, please. To make it all come right.'

'Very well, dearest, I'll write and tell her her daughter's married to a rotter who doesn't know how to look after her.'

'Oh, Arthur,' Isabelle wailed, 'don't try to be funny. This is deadly serious.'

'Sorry, dearest. I'll write and offer my sincere apologies for having caused her grave annoyance.'

'But you'll write sensibly? Not like a government memorandum?'

'Of course I'll write sensibly. I'll write the best and humblest apology ever penned. She won't be able to resist it. Belle, can you smile now? Say cheese, dearest.'

But Arthur's letter never reached Mrs Burnett. A few days later Isabelle received a cable from Archie in Paris: 'MOTHER SERIOUSLY ILL STOP VERY ANXIOUS.' It was followed the next day by one announcing her death. Isabelle was overwhelmed with grief. She could hardly wait to get away from Simla, the scene of her loneliness and sorrow, but she must stay till the rains ended. Daily she tormented herself, living over again the terrible quarrel. It would never have happened if Arthur hadn't . . . 'Too late, too late,' she would cry tragically as she faced again the awful finality of death. Amma, worried, brought Lucy to distract her, but Isabelle only sobbed, 'Too late,' for now her mother (already beatified in her daughter's remembrance) would never see her granddaughter, or the grandson who was to come.

'She was ill, dying, and I was not with her. I never knew. I was not told . . .' Isabelle was inconsolable. There were times when it seemed to Arthur, trying vainly to comfort her, that she held him in some way responsible for her mother's death.

The letter from the lawyer announced that Mrs Burnett had

left everything she had to her son. Isabelle was to receive £500 a year from her father's estate.

'I don't want it! I can't bear to benefit from Mother's death! I can't bear it!'

Arthur held his tongue.

12

Isabelle took so long to recover her composure after her mother's death, and was so full of the nervous fancies associated with pregnancy, that Arthur embarked on a new disease reckoned to be an abcess on the liver. His furlough was due in the autumn and it was arranged that he was to go to Carlsbad for a cure and be at hand for the birth of the baby which was to take place in France. Archie, disillusioned with Spain, had sold up after his mother's death and bought an old house in Brittany. It was a small château in a sadly decayed condition. While it was being put in order, he took a furnished house in the little town of St-Servan nearby and suggested that the Boynes share it during their leave. It was equipped with servants and a bathroom in the basement where, with due notice, a wood-burning stove was capable (except in the coldest weather) of raising the temperature in a cylinder that abutted on a tub. '*Tout à fait convenable, surtout pour une famille anglaise,*' as the house agent put it. The Boynes accepted gladly.

Amma left her homeland with some trepidation, but her devotion was so great that she would have followed her 'family' to the ends of the earth. She settled her marital problems by giving her little sister to the shiftless Sanmogan for wife, in her place. Having provided him with a son, Tumbi, as shiftless as himself, she had remained stubbornly barren. The arrangement seemed to suit everyone. After her first pangs of seasickness, (during which she recited 'I dying Mum' for twenty-four hours, until mercifully the ship ran out of the storm) she adapted herself wonderfully to foreign travel. Her smiling ways made her a favourite on board ship, while her gorgeous saris proclaimed her a princess to the Breton peasants who had never seen an ayah. Her diet presented some difficulty, the staple food being the forbidden veal, until Archie hit on the idea of calling it 'white mutton'.

Isabelle had looked forward to Archie's companionship. She was disappointed. Her brother had changed. Years of doing nothing had turned his gay insouciance into a grumbling, restless cynicism. Lacking an audience, he was often bored and moody. Worst of all, she had the suspicion that he was seriously attracted by a young Frenchwoman (a native of Corsica on holiday in the neighbourhood) of whom she violently disapproved as a scheming hussy. She was greatly disquieted and longed for Arthur to come and take his share of the burdens. He had followed two months later and gone straight to Carlsbad. Isabelle still had a month to go to the birth of her child.

At this point, Lucy got whooping-cough – violently, as she did everything. It was some time before the shattering cough which drove the household to distraction day and night was diagnosed. For Isabelle, the child was dying of croup, consumption – dying anyway. It was into this stricken household that Arthur arrived, wonderfully set up by his cure and to all appearances in robust health.

In due course Isabelle was safely delivered of a son. This happy event could have been an occasion for unrestrained thanksgiving, but inevitably Isabelle's grievances came to the fore: the tragic fact that her parents had not lived to see their grandson, the brooding over the bitter breach between her mother and her husband, the pricks of daily life in which the ineptitude of the French doctor and the standing quarrel between the English midwife and the French servants loomed large – all combined to make for fretfulness. When the agonizing sound of Lucy coughing across the landing gave pause, she could hear the tinkling of the piano in the drawing-room below which denoted the presence of the detested Corsican, practising her wiles on the helpless Archie. Naturally Arthur was not the slightest use. He had taken to his bed at the birth of his son. When, finally, he was prised out of it by his wrathful wife, when Lucy was seen to be recovering and Edmund acknowledged to be a flawless baby ('a Burnett to his finger-tips'), Isabelle tried to enlist her husband in the battle against the Corsican.

'You've got to *do* something about it, Arthur. There's not a moment to lose. You've got to speak to Archie.'

'Who, me?'

'Yes, you. You're one of his oldest friends.'

'Well, that doesn't necessarily give me the right to interfere in his affairs.'

'Arthur, don't be so obstinate. You know you can't stand her either. It's only because she flatters him so that Archie doesn't see through her.'

'I expect you're right.'

'Of course I am. She'd be a disaster. She's not even young!'

'She has a rather ripe style of beauty.'

'She's awful! Will you speak to him this evening?'

'No.'

'*Arthur!*'

'It's no good, Belle. It wouldn't do any good.'

'Why? Why wouldn't it?'

'Well, you're up against the demon Sex, you know. When a man's dead set on having a woman, and one can see he's absolutely potty about her, you can't just talk him out of it. He's not open to reason. It's a biological urge . . .'

'What a beastly way to speak! . . .' Isabelle was affronted. She was used to Arthur's strictures on religion, but this way of dismissing the love of a man for a woman was highly offensive to her. A biological urge . . . Perhaps that was how Arthur thought of his long, faithful attachment to her . . . How very beastly!

'Sorry, dear,' he was saying, 'it wouldn't do any good and might cause a lot of trouble. We've got to go on sharing this house for another two or three months.'

'But Arthur, you're not going to deny the noble and spiritual side of love? If Archie were in love, truly in love, with a woman

85

who was worthy of him, I would be glad. But this is a mere infatuation with someone totally unsuitable.'

'Looks like a bad bet to me, but I'm no judge. If I were *asked* for my opinion, now, I might venture to suggest . . . but there – I'm not likely to be.'

'If you saw a man standing in front of an express train, you wouldn't pull him back to safety?'

'Not if I knew he'd decided to commit suicide. I believe in the rights of man, the freedom of the individual . . . Tom Paine has a chapter that puts it far better than I can.'

'Arthur, you'll drive me mad.'

'Sorry, dear. I'm sorry you're so upset over Archie's paramour, but I'm afraid, as I see it, it's *his* funeral.'

'You're just no help. No help at all. You never are.' Isabelle played her last card. 'I suppose you realize she's a bigoted R.C.'

Arthur's face fell. 'It's a life sentence, then.'

'And she'll bring up his children as papists.'

'Pity. Tell you what, Belle. I'll write to him as soon as we've left and try as tactfully as I can to point out some of the pitfalls.'

'It'll be too late then! You're always too late . . .'

'Ah, Belle, don't cry . . .' Mercifully, Amma's entrance with the baby, Edmund, put a stop to the fruitless discussion.

The stay in Brittany ended without matters coming to a head. Isabelle was distracted to some extent from her brother's affairs by the visits of several old friends and relations. The only Boyne visitor was Arthur's sister, whose long-postponed visit to India was now arranged for the following cold weather. Isabelle could not be said to hit it off very well with her sister-in-law, but she was determined to 'do her duty' by her and display her in the marriage market. She gave a lot of time and thought to the clothes she would need, in the choosing of which it was essential that Mrs Boyne should not have a hand. Katie, she decided, was singularly unappreciative of all that was being done for her. It was not a happy augury.

Arthur posted his letter to Archie in Marseilles before the ship sailed. It was, as Isabelle had guessed, too late. Archie, scenting opposition, only waited for the Boynes' departure to press his suit. His letter announcing his forthcoming marriage followed by the next mailboat.

I'm sure you meant well, old boy, but you're all wrong. She's the girl for me and I'm madly happy. Unfortunately, Marie-Louise went through my pockets in a playful way and purloined your letter and read it! Her English is coming on fast! She's out for your blood now (that applies to Isabelle too) but she'll get over it in time. I'm afraid it was my fault, very careless of me, old boy, so blame me if you must, not her.

But Archie was underestimating his bride's Corsican blood. Marie-Louise Burnett never forgave the Boynes.

Arthur found himself posted to a district altogether less attractive than Bagra. As the other Europeans there were all married, offering no opportunities for Katie, it was decided that Isabelle should take a house in Pachmarhi for six months for the entertainment of her sister-in-law. It was better also for the children's health.

Katie arrived, stolidly Boyne, showing very little interest in the wonders of the Orient, none in her nephew and niece, and, worst of all, she seemed to shrink from social contacts. Isabelle made strenuous efforts on her behalf. She was longing for gratitude and appreciation, but none seemed forthcoming. 'I daresay Katie is shy,' Isabelle wrote to Arthur, 'and things will get better later on, but at present she seems to take no pleasure in the dances, picnics and so forth that I arrange. She has nothing to say for herself.' But things went from bad to worse. After the first few weeks, Katie couldn't be persuaded to join in anything. She pleaded a headache, complained of the heat and seemed to spend most of the day in her room, writing letters. She was roused from apathy only by Isabelle's suggestion to send for the doctor.

'What you need is a tonic.'

'Nonsense!'

Isabelle didn't care to be spoken to like this. 'Katie! You're very rude. After all I do for you . . .'

'Well, leave me alone, can't you!'

'I call that very rude.'

'Sorry. I don't feel well.'

'That's precisely why I should like you to see the doctor.' Isabelle looked at her sister-in-law. The girl did look ill.

'No. I don't want the doctor. I won't see him if you send for him. It's only the heat.'

'You'd find it cooler out of doors than shut up in this room all the evening.'

'Perhaps.'

'Of course you would. Come on now and sit out on the verandah. It's quite cool there.'

'All right.'

When they were reclining on the verandah with cool drinks in their hands, breathing in the heavy scent that rose from the waxen trumpets of the creeper that smothered the balustrade, Isabelle decided to try again with her sister-in-law.

'Katie, you haven't forgotten tomorrow night's the dance at Government House?' As there was no answer she continued: 'I want you to wear your white tulle.'

'I can't.'

'Why ever not.'

'I can't get into it. I tell you it's this heat makes me swell.'

'Well, the dhirzi will soon let it out for you. That's easily done.'

'All right,' said Katie desperately.

Arthur arrived from the plains for a long week-end. The brother and sister had very little to say to each other, Isabelle observed. How different from Archie and me . . . how I would tell him every little thing and he would do imitations of all the people he'd met and we'd laugh . . . Then she remembered that it hadn't been so much like that the last time with that hateful Marie-Louise there. She gave a despairing sigh.

'What is it, dear?' Arthur asked. He was already in bed. Isabelle sat before the dressing-table, brushing her hair.

'Oh . . . so many things . . . I was thinking of Archie and that creature.'

'My mother used to say, "What can't be cured must be endured." Not a bad precept for the individual. You have to distinguish though between what applies to the individual and what to the masses. Acting on that precept, there'd have been no French Revolution, no reforms – '

'Arthur, Katie's not well. How d'you think she's looking?'

He paused to consider: 'Looks a bit square to me. Funny, she used to be as thin as a rake. Must be putting on weight.'

'It's the heat.'

'Better get the doctor to her.'

'She won't have him. I've asked her.'

'Probably only needs dosing. That reminds me – has the syce got rid of Phoebus's worms yet?'

'I don't know.'

'I'll go into it in the morning.'

'Arthur, I'm worried about Katie. This visit isn't a success, you know.' She sighed again deeply.

'Give her time. She's probably just a slow starter. Belle, if I may make a suggestion, it is that you spend far too long brushing your hair. Come on, dearest.'

Not long after Arthur's departure, Amma came to her mistress one morning looking unusually solemn.

'What is it, Amma? Nothing wrong with the children?'

'Baba-log well, Mum. Esmissy Sahib no well.'

'What do you mean, Amma?'

'Esmissy Sahib no well, Mum. Esmissy Sahib have baby coming, Mum.'

Isabelle was stunned. The room seemed to revolve round her. When she could speak, she grasped Amma by the wrist and cried, 'When? When? Now?'

'No now, Mum. But baby come presently.'

A terrible revulsion filled Isabelle's mind. She remembered horrible stories of servant girls who got into trouble in Kensington Gardens, her early revulsion at the kissing to be seen in the park that in some unspecified way led to unwanted babies. Such things didn't happen to ladies. Without pausing to reflect, she flew to Katie's room where a scene of classic dimensions occurred. The terrified girl, ignorant of her condition, haunted by fearful suspicions and too frightened to seek advice, in the end confessed that her last night before sailing for India might have given rise to the trouble. Her seducer was none other than her childhood sweetheart to whom she was secretly pledged, who was waiting only for the moment when he could support a wife. 'I never wanted to come and he couldn't bear leaving me . . .' she sobbed. Isabelle, outraged, refused to listen further. Now was the time for action. She devised a cable from a sick mother recalling her daughter urgently, found that a P. & O. liner sailed from Bombay in three days' time and packed Katie off with all speed, having arranged by telegram for Arthur's agents to meet her at vital points along the journey and see her safely stowed on board. She left visiting cards on her sister-in-law's behalf at all the houses where she had received hospitality, receiving herself many expressions of sympathy, but always wondering if suspicions existed. . . . She wrote to Bertie (the letter would go overland from Marseilles and arrive a week before the ship docked) explaining the circumstances, telling him to meet his sister at Tilbury and exhorting him to arrange the marriage without delay. (This in fact took place on Katie's return and was the start of a long and reasonably happy union.)

Only Arthur's reactions gave her no satisfaction. He not only refrained from reproaching himself for the agonies to which he had subjected his wife (for, after all, he was responsible for the grievous visit), but made a further jocular reference to the 'demon Sex', to 'nature having its way . . .'.

'Thanks for making all the arrangements, Belle. She should never have come. I do feel, dear, that if he marries her, we must make them an allowance till things improve for him. He's really quite a decent chap.'

Isabelle felt that definitely she was not being appreciated. She tried to imagine how her mother would have taken it and wept bitterly.

13

As Arthur's district was considered unhealthy for young children (Lucy had had recurrences of dysentery), Isabelle spent six months of the year in Mussoorie, a hill station two days' distant, a beautiful mountain resort less grand than Simla. Arthur, when not having attacks of malaria, was absorbed in his work. There were no more famines. After three years spent in this way, Isabelle found herself expecting another child. She was glad. Only in child-bearing could she find relief from boredom. She had given up trying to write articles, to interest herself in the women of the country, to study something of the history, customs and sects of the east. She had adopted the Anglo-Indian woman's outlook of blasé indifference to those tiresome natives. Queening it in her expanding household, she was relatively contented.

'Are you sure, dear?' Arthur asked when the news was broken to him.

'Of course I'm sure.'

'If you're pleased, then I am. Very.'

'Certainly I am. I want another son, or two or three. With my money added to your pay we can afford it, I should hope.'

'My clever little wife,' Arthur said, unusually demonstrative.

'There's nothing clever about it. Any monkey can do the same. Any rabbit . . .'

'Clever little monkey then.'

'Arthur, who was it who wrote about the anodyne of child-bearing?'

'I don't know, dear. It seems a singularly inept phrase. I always understood it to be a painful process.'

'And so it is!' Isabelle still took Arthur's remarks *au grand sérieux*. 'I should just like to see *you* go through with it!'

'Poor Belle. Doomed to disappointment.'

As the hot weather drew on, Arthur added a grumbling appendix to his ailments. He was due for home leave in the autumn and it was decided that the new baby should be born in England and Arthur's appendix removed at the same time. On the recommendation of friends, they decided on Bournemouth as having the best winter climate. With Amma (now a seasoned traveller) in charge of the two children, they left Bombay again, Arthur once more carried on board with a last-minute attack of fever.

The new baby, a girl, was born as scheduled. Arthur took far longer to get over his operation than Isabelle the birth of her daughter. Nearly three months still remained before they could start the month's journey back to India, three English winter months stretching before them in intolerable dreariness. Arthur took to his bed for a number of reasons. Isabelle chafed that England held so little for her, her family gone and friends and relations largely scattered. Only Amma – happy wherever her loved ones were, whether pushing her baby and supervising the highly active elder children on the blustery chines or keeping them entertained in the depressing surroundings of a half-closed seaside hotel where the other guests were of advanced years, disliking noise – Amma was always smiling and contented. Visits to London were few. Even with Isabelle's income, Arthur found they were always living beyond their means.

'Why don't you take the children out for a little walk?'

'I'm just going to bed.'

'Why?'

'Warmer.'

'You'll soon get warm walking.'

'I prefer my hot-water bottle. You go, dear, if you feel like it.'

'I can't. I've got to attend to baby's bottle. You know I never leave that to Amma. It has to be done with scientific care and precision.'

'Right, I'll see you later then.'

'And Arthur, I've decided to talk French to Lucy and Eddie. Why, Archie and I were bi-lingual at that age! What good's Hindustani going to be to them later in life?'

'Well, my French accent's not going to be much good to them either. Still, it's an idea. You go ahead.'

'And don't you think it's high time Lucy learned to read and write? Why don't you start teaching her?'

Arthur thought for a moment. 'Why not? I might have thought of it myself. Let me see, how old's the child? Five, is it? Why, at her age, John Stuart Mill was starting on Greek, having pretty fluent Latin by that time, if I remember right. Is Lucy really five? Great Scott, there's not a moment to lose. I don't know why I haven't thought of it before. I'll give her her first lesson in bed.'

'You'd do much better sitting at a table.'

'Not necessary.'

It was the beginning of Arthur's interest in his children as entities. He had never tried talking to young children before. It hadn't occurred to him that communication was possible. As babies he had found them frankly rather repellant, but for stuffing the young inquiring mind with miscellaneous information, he had a kind of genius. His sustained patience in arousing a desire to learn, capturing a child's fleeting attention and encouraging it to master some subject, revealed a hitherto unsuspected talent in him that was to play a large part in his children's lives.

'There ith no God.' Lucy was having her writing lesson. She had progressed rapidly and was on to simple sentences. Eddie lisped the sentence after her and watched her laboriously penning it.

'Say *is*, Eddie. Not *ith*, *is*.'

'Ith!'

'It'll come in time. Finished, Lucy? Now what's the next one? Remember?'

'All Gods are man made.'

'Good. Now write it. You say it, Eddie.'

'All Godth are mamade.'

'Gods, Eddie. S again. Now say it very slowly.'

'How can I write with you talking?' Lucy complained. 'Chup*
a minute, can't you.'

Isabelle had entered the room.

'Lucy, you're not to speak like that.' She came and looked
over the child's shoulder.

'Arthur, what a horrid sentence! Why don't you start with the
cat sat on the mat?'

'Because I'm inculcating an important moral principle. Killing
two birds with one stone. You can't start too early. I want my
children's minds to be free of fear and base superstition from the
very first. I can remember when I was Lucy's age being badly
frightened of God. There was a sampler with an all-seeing eye
that frightened the daylights out of me. These children are going
to learn from the start that there's no such thing. There's a
chapter in Herbert Spencer's *Education* I'd like to read you this
evening – '

'Well, they've got to get to bed now as there's a long journey
tomorrow. The boat train leaves Liverpool Street at two you
said.'

'Good night then, children,' and he stooped to give them the
salutary kiss on the top of the head recommended by Herbert
Spencer.

Arthur's new district was again an unattractive one. He seemed
to be making no progress with the years of service. Isabelle set to
to make a home of the new bungalow. It was the usual curious
mixture of grandeur and simplicity, luxury and squalor, that she
had grown used to. After six months, however, Arthur found
himself promoted to the post of Commissioner of Customs and
Excise with a house at the provincial headquarters and another
at the hill station, Pachmarhi, for the hot weather. With his
increase in pay went a corresponding and apparently inevitable
increase in their scale of living. Nevertheless, there now seemed

* Hindustani for 'shut up'.

some prospect of slowly paying off those accumulated borrowings. The setback was not slow in coming, from the usual quarter. Mrs Boyne wrote a distracted letter.

I couldn't sleep a wink all night I'm so upset and then this morning I thought of you to help us in poor Harold's trouble so I'm hurrying out to post this letter. Well it seems that poor Harold met a girl on this ship coming back from Egypt. I've been looking forward ever so to his getting his leave and now of course this has to happen and spoil it all. Well he didn't mean any harm and I'm sure the poor boy didn't do anything wrong but this horrid girl says he asked her to marry him and Harold says he never did no such thing. Anyway it seems that now she's going to sue him for what's called Breach of Promise unless he gives her £250 at once and that just shows what a low class mean deceiving piece she is. Of course poor Harold hasn't got it, how could he, and he says that if this business comes to court he'll lose his job. I've been so worried since he told me. I haven't closed an eye. Then I thought that you being the rich one of the family would be ready and willing to help your own kith and kin and I felt a bit better after I remembered you but I shan't be easy in my mind till the money's paid over because you never know what such a mean spiteful hussy as this girl must be will do. When I think that Harold might lose his job because he's never been no more than a bit silly like everybody always is on a ship he says I can tell you Arthur I come over bad at the very thought . . .

Arthur groaned and let the letter fall. Isabelle, reading a catalogue from Calcutta, looked up.

'What's the matter?'

'Read,' said Arthur unwisely, handing her the letter. He began to chuckle softly to himself. Isabelle read it through frowning.

'Well, you're not going to pay for *that*, I hope!'

'Got to.'

'What d'you mean? Why?'

'*Ghost beneath swear.*'

'What?'

'Never mind. I'm afraid there's no help for it, dear. Poor old mother's half out of her mind with anxiety.'

'But why should *you* . . .'

'Because I have to. Because there's no one else.'

'Arthur!' Isabelle cried angrily, 'I won't have it! I won't have it, d'you hear!'

'I'm sorry, Belle. I feel pretty fed up about it myself. Harold's an ass. This'll be a lesson to him, I expect. Be that as it may, we can't have him losing his job. This girl probably is a bad lot, and I daresay he has been unlucky. All I know is I've got to help. I'll have the munshi send off a cable.'

'Arthur, you've no right to do it! How *dare* she say you're the rich one! Why, without my income you'd be very hard up. Arthur, that's half my income for a whole year. Half my income!'

'Belle, I'm fearfully sorry, I really am. But I've no choice, dear. I promised to help.'

'You mean that time you promised your father when you were still a child? All that "I swear by Almighty God . . ." Seeing you're an atheist . . .'

'A promise is a promise,' Arthur said solemnly, 'no matter in who's name it's made.'

'So you'd sacrifice your wife and children to keep a ridiculous promise that never ought to have been made?'

'Ah, Belle, not quite that . . .'

'And it's *my* money you're spending this way!'

'In so far as your money goes into the general pool and this will have to come out of the general pool, I suppose one must reckon that a proportion of it . . .'

Isabelle, on the verge of tears, had risen to her feet. 'I never thought the day would come when I should be *glad* Mother is dead,' she cried in a tragic tone.

'Ah come, Belle . . .'

'Glad, d'you hear! Glad she can never know the sort of thing you do. Glad she cannot see you paying no regard to my wishes and feelings. Glad, I tell you. *Glad!* . . .' Overcome by tears she ran from the room.

Arthur sent for the munshi.

*

As a commissioner's wife, Isabelle no longer found time hanging heavy, since there was a good deal of official entertaining that Arthur's position as head of a Department called for and in which he gave but little help. He was in any case compelled to work very hard at the new post. Isabelle spent much time and thought on her dinner parties, writing out the menus and the guests' names in her well-formed handwriting on little shiny tablets that could be washed clean with a sponge. These she framed in elaborate floral decorations. Arthur did no more than put in an appearance, if he could not think of a way out. He never accepted return invitations. It was a great strain for Isabelle, although she liked entertaining. Fateh Mohammed too had to be watched closely.

It was on the occasion of the biggest dinner in her career as hostess, when the Chief Commissioner and his lady were bringing visiting grandees on a tour of the country, that Fateh Mohammed's downfall came about. Isabelle, hastening round the gleaming table to give a finishing touch to the smilax that she had arranged earlier as a centrepiece, fell over his feet. Fateh Mohammed, overawed by the greatness of the occasion and the signal honour due to a Commissioner's cook, had retired to his private heaven. Isabelle's mortification was extreme. The frightened servants emerged to remove the inert form and receive the first arrivals simultaneously.

Eddie sat in his high chair on the verandah surrounded by a group of painted wooden animals while Amma plied him with spoonfuls of food. It was a long-drawn-out game of which Arthur disapproved.

'One for *baloo*. One for Eddie-baba.' The spoon hit its target. 'One for *mor*. One for Eddie-baba. One for *sona cutta*. One for Eddie-baba.'

'No, *thona cutta* want another one.'

'Nuther one for *sona cutta*. Now one for Eddie-baba.'

But Eddie pushed the spoon away. 'Where Fateh Mohammed gone?' he asked.

'He gone,' Amma said, and unexpectedly burst into tears.

'Where he gone?'

'I want Fatty,' Lucy said, and both children began to cry and shout 'Want Fatty', while Amma's lamentations rose to a wail.

Arthur strode out of his study, infuriated by the noise, his nerves on edge. Parting with the friend of many years who had saved his life had been deeply painful to him, but for once he agreed with Isabelle. There was nothing else for it. No use fighting the demon Drink.

'Stop that beastly noise this minute! All of you. Amma! I forbid you to play with those animals again at mealtimes. Eddie, you're to feed yourself in future. D'you hear me? Lucy, be quiet, or I shall beat you!'

Silence fell. The children had never seen their father angry before. Snivelling, Amma gathered up her charges and crept away from the scene of wrath.

Arthur stood with his pince-nez in his hand. He was not given to outbursts of emotion. As his anger cooled, he felt suddenly weary. He was aware of the passing of the years. Fateh Mohammed gone. Wazir Ali had left his service when they went to Bournemouth. Only Amma and Fazil Khan remained among the faithful.

'It's a bad business,' he said to himself as he returned to his desk. 'A bad business . . .'

14

Isabelle bore two more children in the next four years – a son and a daughter. An under-ayah was engaged to help Amma with the three youngest, and a French governess procured from Pondicherry for the two eldest. Isabelle thought that the French would progress better with a professional, and there were other lessons besides. She who had found time hang heavy, had never enough of it now – time that brought the inevitable crop of mishaps, diseases and accidents that come to a young family growing up, and which can, in the tropics, turn suddenly dangerous. The children had dogs, guinea-pigs, rabbits, a tame myna, a tame bulbul, mongooses and even deer for their pets. Each child as it grew old enough had a pony of its own which it rode uninhibitedly from the drawing-room to the golf links that lay just beneath the house which stood on a crag. Lucy and Edmund had for friends the sweeper's two sons, Cassiwa and Bhaiya Lal, a pair of nearly-naked rascals with whom they spent a large part of their time in the tops of trees, learning items of information that would have astonished their parents.

Arthur decided to invest in a motor-car for his tours of inspection of distilleries, customs houses, opium factories and so forth. It was one of the first to come to the province. It had a single-cylinder engine that made a noise dear to the natives' hearts and (always good for a laugh) a little squeaky voice pro-

99

duced by squeezing a rubber bulb. A door in the middle of the back, at the top of a flight of steps, led to seats inside, facing each other, as in a farmyard float. The driver sat up in front, exposed to the dust, wearing goggles and a bee-keeper's veil. On a good day; it could achieve a speed of twenty miles per hour.

Arthur's spirits always soared as he left headquarters behind. In the outlying districts, his motor-car was an object of ceaseless, awestruck wonder. He would pull out the electric coil and, handing it to the village elders to hold, switch on the current to give them a minor delicious shock, telling them how he had tamed a *shaitan* who spoke in *bijli* (Hindustani for 'devil and 'lightning' respectively) and imprisoned it within to do his bidding. It was considered a very good magic and was immensely popular. Arthur was never so happy as when taking his simple pleasures with the villagers or administering fines with affectionate good-humoured banter.

'Twelve sacks of lentils, you say? Then what's that sack doing over there?'

'There are twelve sacks, your Excellency.'

'Count, man, count.'

'There are but twelve . . .'

'What's in that sack?'

'I am a poor man, your Excellency. I have many mouths to support . . .'

'Don't waste my time.'

'Assuredly not, your Excellency. That is but grit.'

'Grit supplied for the roller? For the new road?'

'It is very like . . .'

'If you've been stealing the grit, I shall report you to the roads department.'

'Stealing? Your Excellency is joking! I am a poor man, Protector of the Poor, toiling to keep alive my dependants. If, at the end of a day's labour, I succeed in gathering up a handful of grit that has fallen by the roadside, is that stealing?'

'All right, all right, what's it for?'

'Your Excellency, Protector of the Poor, I will explain all. This year the lentils are *too* good. Never have I seen such lentils. They are fine and full and totally lacking in grit. This sack of grit is to mix with the twelve to make an average yield, lest the people complain next year when they are back to normal . . .'

Lucy and Edmund, soon known as a regular feature of Arthur's tours, were garlanded with marigolds and given sticky sweet-meats and tight-packed bouquets of flowers wherever they arrived, presented by the head man.

'This bunch's heavy,' Lucy said, 'feel, Eddie.'

'Terrible heavy.'

'Let's see what's inside.'

'I'll pull too.'

'Look, it's that ruby bangle again! It's the same one I had last time. Father, can I keep it now?'

'You cannot.'

'. . . five, six, seven, eight, nine, ten rubies! Isn't it a heavy one!'

Arthur took it from her and handed it ceremoniously to the head man.

'Ram Lal, when's your case coming up?'

'In next quarter sessions, your Excellency.'

'Don't imagine that you can sway the course of British justice by bribes. And don't go away thinking that if you'd coughed up one of double the value it would have been acceptable. The British raj has no price. Get that into your thick head if you can, you silly old man.'

Mademoiselle from Pondicherry had lady-like manners and an indigo complexion. She was fond of relating how an attack of typhoid in her infancy had turned her so dark that her own mother failed to recognize her. She could also be counted on for long and ardent descriptions of her countless admirers, a recital the children particularly enjoyed. She was given to fainting in moments of emotion, nicely timed for a gentleman at hand to be able to catch her. However, she spoke excellent convent-taught French.

*

101

There were guests to tiffin – the Chief Commissioner, a rather grumpy, taciturn man and his supercilious wife. She disapproved of many things, particularly of bringing up one's children in India, and had dispatched her own to England at an early age. Isabelle was nervous. The conversation hung fire.

'One of the grass-cutters,' Lucy remarked during a pause, and switched automatically to French which was the normal rule at table, '*a eu un bébé ce matin pendant qu'elle taillait l'herbe.*'

'*C'est une petite fille qu'elle a eu,*' Edmund added. '*Bhaiya Lal était là.*'

'*Pas vrai?*' Arthur was interested.

'*Elle a coupé la corde ellemême avec une grosse pierre,*' Lucy continued conversationally, sawing with her knife on a chicken bone by way of illustration.

'*Ram Bux a du l'aider.*'

'*Non, il est arrivé trop tard.*'

'*La prochaine fois j'y serai moi. Ça doit être très intéressant.*'

'*Plus que les lapins, je crois bien.*'

'*Elle est revenue avec le bébé sur le dos, endormi sur sa botte d'herbe.*'

'A clear case for bakhsheesh,' said Arthur.

'*Elle a expliqué, qu'elle n'avait pas pu tailler autant d'herbe que d'habitude, parcequ'elle s'est arrêté pour avoir le . . .*'

'Will you be quiet, children,' Isabelle hissed frantically. In view of their choice of subject matter she dared not remind them that French was waived when guests were present. Mademoiselle looked as if she were in for one of her fainting fits.

The Chief Commissioner finished his curry, laid down his spoon and fork and said with an affability unusual to him: 'So you're taking the children to the durbar?'

'I hope to,' said Arthur. 'If I'm up to it,' he added by force of habit.

'Upon my word, these children go everywhere, do everything and know everything, I suppose. There'll be nothing left for them by the time they're fourteen. They'll be bored stiff, blasé. God knows what you'll do with them then!'

'There is no God,' said Lucy automatically.

'And all Godth are man made,' Edmund rejoined.

The Chief Commissioner looked from one to the other and suddenly brayed aloud. His laugh was rarely heard.

Lucy and Edmund eyed him with disfavour.

15

Time passed. After two more years some form of schooling became necessary for the two elder children. It was agreed that Arthur should take them to England and put them to school, leaving Isabelle and the three younger children in India with friends. Arthur, Edmund and Lucy arrived in England and set off initially on a round of visits to some of the well-known boarding-schools for girls. It was Arthur's custom to turn to his daughter, after a free interchange of views with the headmistress, to ask her impressions. Headmistresses didn't much care for this. In one study, where Arthur had been politely questioned on India (he had explained at some length that India's troubles could be largely solved by birth control), his eye fell on the scale of charges. 'From this it would seem that some houses are more expensive than others? There are rich houses and poor houses?'

'If you care to put it in those terms.' The head was frigid. She was still reeling under the prospect of birth control for the Indian masses. At that time, the subject was wholly unmentionable.

'I'm afraid it's against my socialist principles that different standards should exist in one and the same institution for the benefit of the privileged . . .' Arthur shook his head and rose to his feet. 'I'm afraid we have been wasting your time . . .'

'Do not worry – we have quite a waiting-list,' said the head coldly.

At another important establishment on the south coast, Arthur was concerned at its exposed position for one reared in the tropics.

'What d'you think, Lucy?'

'Rather windy. With no trees to protect you, I expect you feel the wind a lot here,' she added affably to the headmistress.

'It was as if that child imagined she was interviewing *me*,' the head remarked after their departure.

They settled at last for a rather formidable school in a sheltered position and with a flat scale of charges. Edmund was found a preparatory school on a quiet reach of the Thames. He was a gentle child, afflicted at the thought of parting. Lucy seemed made of tougher stuff. The children satisfactorily settled, Arthur set forth again for India.

Arrived at the familiar Malibar Coast, Arthur stood leaning against the rail. He was not a sentimental man, but it was impossible not to be reminded of former occasions. The first time when he had arrived in the unknown, sustained by high hopes: the second, the third, the fourth, the fifth . . . this time. This time something was wrong. He closed his eyes and tried to think what it was. He could not put his finger on it. Where was the familiar upsurge of the spirit that was his on setting foot on Indian soil? The sights and sounds, the appearance of fevered activity, the very glare had seemed welcome on landing. Not this time. As they approached the Bund, he saw Isabelle standing in a conspicuous position with the Tinies grouped round her and Amma and Fazil Khan a pace behind. He dived below deck to busy himself unnecessarily with his luggage. For the life of him, he couldn't help himself.

'*There* you are! Where *have* you been? The children thought everyone that came off was Father! Dickie and Emmi don't remember what you look like, you see! They've been so excited. Up since dawn!'

Arthur greeted them all hurriedly. 'Confounded steward made a mess of my luggage. One piece missing.' He went off again with

Fazil Khan. They stood waiting, surrounded now by clamouring coolies. He was gone a long time.

When he came back, Isabelle said: 'Arthur, I've got rooms at Wataon's. I asked for the suite we had that time when Eddie was the baby and we've got it! It seems so funny to be there! They've improved it a lot.'

'Good.'

'We've got our same old room,' said Isabelle significantly.

'Did I give you those baggage vouchers in the end?' Arthur was addressing himself to Fazil Khan and the government agent, patting all his pockets in a pantomime of searching.

'Diana and Dickie and Emmi have the room that Lucy and Eddie had,' Isabelle continued. 'It does feel strange!'

'Yes.'

'I'm longing to hear all about them. I found lovely letters waiting here when we got in yesterday.'

'Oh, good.'

That evening after the children were in bed, they sat on the terrace after dinner, waiting for the turbaned, white-robed waiter to bring the coffee. They had split a bottle of tepid hock in the dining-room, which had only succeeded in making Arthur sleepy. As he suppressed his second yawn, Isabelle realized that at any moment she would hear the familiar: 'Well, I think I'll turn in. I'm tired . . .' With a gush of emotion she said: 'It's good to have you back, Arthur. The three little ones are not much company yet. Too young, though Diana has come on. I do miss Eddie and Lucy, though.'

'Me too.'

The waiter arrived with the coffee and Isabelle busied herself pouring it out.

'Not for me, thank you,' Arthur said. 'I don't think I want any. You go ahead.'

'Oh, have this cup. It'll wake you up.'

Arthur noted the approach of familiar symptoms – the enfeebling of the lower limbs until they became incapable of supporting his weight; the little aches and pains that sprang up in

106

his extremities; the insistence of the head for support, as the waves of still distant giddiness grew nearer.

'I'll have to turn in, I'm afraid,' he said and got up to go while the going was good.

'You go! Go!' said Isabelle bitterly. She broke off to smile at a shipboard acquaintance and added in an altogether different tone, 'I'll be up presently.'

When she entered the bedroom, she saw Arthur lying ambushed behind his mosquito netting, absorbed in a problem of mathematical logic. He did not hear her come in.

'Arthur!' she cried, and paused dramatically in the middle of the room. 'What is the matter?'

Arthur slowly made a mark that would show him later on the place he had reached in his calculations. Isabelle watched.

'Feeling very limp, dear. Better lying down.'

'That's not what I mean. I'm not talking about your health. I'm talking about *us*. You know what I mean.'

He knew. All too well he knew.

'And don't say *what* about us?'

The ghost behind the mosquito netting stirred. 'I wasn't going to,' he said feebly, though that of course was what he would have said, to gain time.

'Answer me!' Isabelle said in the voice her mother would have used.

'If there's anything to discuss,' Arthur said at last, mulishly, 'can it not wait till the morning?'

'No. I refuse to be put off any longer.'

Arthur propped himself on his pillows with a show of composure that he was far from feeling.

'You mean . . .' he tried again. 'You mean the prospect of a resumption of sexual relations,' he said at last, in the pompous tone that a great specialist might have used in giving his diagnosis as Isabelle clapped her hands over her mouth to prevent herself from screaming aloud. 'Because if that's it, I'm afraid I'm past it, dear . . .'

'You? Arthur, you're forty-two! That's the prime of life in a man.'

'In some men, perhaps. Not as regards myself.'

'Arthur, are you in love with someone else?'

'No, dear. Of course not.'

'I know you aren't. I don't know why I bothered to ask. You're incapable of love. You don't understand what it means!'

Perhaps he didn't. How explain to her the divorce between passion and intellect? Certainly it was not possible to explain his shrinking from the emotional quagmire of loving Isabelle or his present revulsion at the thought of physical contact. He heard his own voice, tired and flat, coming as if from a distance: 'Fifteen years is a long time . . . Nature has accomplished what she strives after – the reproduction of the race . . . certain species die as soon as reproduction is accomplished . . . and now, tired and worn out by years in the tropics . . .' He was back on safe ground, clinging to the protection of illness.

Isabelle stood staring at him, perplexed, miserable and unnaturally silent. When his incoherencies came to an end, she uttered the one word, 'Rubbish!' Arthur closed his eyes, lifted his hands in a gesture of despair and let them fall again. 'Rubbish!' Isabelle said again, and repeated in a rising crescendo, 'Rubbish! Rubbish! Rubbish!'

'I thought – I always rather thought you hated the carnal approach . . .'

Isabelle ignored this. 'Why don't you speak the truth that you're tired of me? All you ever wanted was to go to bed with me. For years you wanted it, and then you got what you wanted. But you never loved me excepting that way. When you weren't making love to me, it was always your work came first – your work or those stupid problems, or books, or the children – not me. Me, your own wife, whom you've sworn to love till you die. . . . In a hundred letters you've sworn it. And now, you're tired, you say. I'm to be discarded. *You've* had enough. *You* want this or *you* don't want that. It's always *you*, Arthur. And what about me, I want to know? . . .'

Once started, Isabelle found she could not stop. The burden of her grief seemed inexhaustible. It was a bottomless pit from which she dredged up a host of accusations – his quarrel with her mother, his refusal to live a normal social life, her resentment against his family . . . It went on remorselessly. On and on . . .

Arthur lay silent as his discomfort grew. This business of

violent emotions was wholly ridiculous. Why did she have to say these indecent things? Heavens, how ill he felt! He would never be up to the train journey in the morning. On and on, on and on . . . the tortured voice was half a whisper, so as not to wake Amma and the children next door. The meaning of the words escaped him now; there was only the voice like the wind at sea, accompanied by the creakings and groanings of a ship in a storm as she paced about the room. The ghost behind the netting lay very still. Even at this outrageous crisis in his life, Arthur could sleep. Isabelle abandoned herself to her grief.

Henceforth Arthur would not be able to live without illness. What had once seemed to provide a miraculous escape from the unhappy Isabelle of reality to the loving and adorable creature that existed in his dreams was now an escape from Isabelle altogether. When he turned his face to the wall and closed his eyes, he could shut her out from the privileged world of the invalid, where the outsider entered softly with the tempting tray and no voice was ever raised in argument. It was axiomatic – you couldn't argue with the sick. Unable to specify his chronic ill-ness, he invented one to his satisfaction. He settled for a rare tropical microbe with a Latin name, invisible except through a powerful microscope, that featured in an obscure medical dic-tionary and which he referred to as his 'worm'. It seemed to satisfy the current local doctor, who was not ambitious. The symptoms were known to Arthur as 'fatigue poisons'. These manifested themselves with unfailing regularity when anything repugnant was afoot.

Isabelle gave way before the worm. There were times when she raged and other times when she reproached herself and vowed to make allowances for her invalid husband. The children were sorry for their sick father. Amma and the neighbours sympa-thized. All were taken in by the worm, and not least Arthur himself, who had come to believe in his microscopic Frankenstein's monster.

16

Arthur returned to the same post with the same house, but all was changed. With the acknowledged collapse of his marriage, he seemed to lose his zeal. He had always chafed at the life at headquarters. The tours of the outlying districts had grown stale. Perhaps he missed his elder children. He had determined to behave as if nothing had happened that night in Bombay, but Isabelle wore an expression of embittered melancholy. His flippancies were met with stony composure. His withdrawals evoked scenes of passionate resentment. She carried with her the hell of her unhappy marriage. Only when strangers or the children were present did she instantly display all the old vivacity. Now that he had only the worm to fall back upon, Arthur was increasingly ill.

He was on the last lap of his Indian service, approaching the time when he could retire on full pension. It was also the time when big prizes were awarded to the best among the survivors. When, after six months, an official, junior to Arthur and with obviously a long time yet to go, was designated as the future Chief Commissioner, it was clear that he would not be considered for high promotion. He was now a disappointed man. After a painful discussion with Isabelle, during which he stressed his need for a temperate climate and enlarged on the problem of the children's education and their need for a home, it was more or less agreed that they would leave India as soon as his full pension was due.

They sat on the verandah of the Pachmarhi house, half-deafened by a rain that fell in ceaseless torrents, blotting out the familiar, beautiful landscape. They had to raise their voices against the orchestra of sound.

'There's an Austrian archduke been assassinated in the Balkans,' Arthur said loudly above the uproar to distract Isabelle from the threatening tears. 'He's probably better dead anyway.'

'And another reason why it would be better for us if you could put in some more years of service, apart from the money – '

'There's always trouble in the Balkans, of course. Still, it's a long way off. Not as if it was the North-West Frontier . . .'

'Arthur, will you listen to me!'

'Sorry. Can't hear you, dear, with this racket.'

'Let's go in.' They picked their way between the buckets disposed to catch the ceiling-leaks to a dry sofa. Isabelle continued: 'Have you ever thought that Lucy will be old enough to come out in a few years' time and make a good marriage?'

'Have a heart, dear! We abolished child marriage . . .'

'I said "in a few years". Time passes very quickly, you know . . .'

The subject of the passing of time could always be counted on to bring on an upset – especially the landmarks that show the passing of time. In addition to the children's birthdays, Isabelle celebrated also, in a different way, the anniversaries of her father's death, her mother's death, her own engagement day and wedding day. Even in the early years of his ardour, Arthur was incapable of remembering anniversaries of either variety in advance. His brief, 'Sorry dear . . . no good at dates . . .' was exasperating to Isabelle. 'Arthur,' she would say, 'on next Tuesday it *will* be sixteen years since Father died'; or, 'It was exactly at this time, twelve years ago, that first cable came from Archie.' Then Arthur would light his pipe in a cloud of embarrassment and remark fatuously, 'Is it, by Jove! I wonder what he'd have thought of conditions today'; or, 'Is that so? Well . . . well . . .' while Isabelle relived the harrowing scene until the tears put an end to it.

The war came but did not seem to affect India much. Isabelle

111

was very active in collecting money for the Prince of Wales's Fund for the families of war victims, the money rolling in long before the casualties. Arthur had reckoned on six months in which to wind up his job. The war delayed things. At last, however, the horses and pets were disposed of one way and another, furniture sold, belongings packed – it was the end.

A month before Arthur had received an official invitation from Government House to attend a dinner for heads of departments and senior officials – men only. It was in the nature of a command. On the morning of the dinner, he announced that he was feverish; by tea time he was safely in bed with fatigue poisons and dispatched a note excusing himself. Isabelle stormed, threatened and even tried to cajole him into going.

'Arthur, don't you want to say goodbye to everyone.'

'I have already.'

'But this is an occasion you'll remember later with such pleasure.'

'Don't you believe it.'

'Well, you *must* go! You've got to!'

'Nothing doing.'

'I shall go there myself and tell them you're just lying here pretending to be ill.'

'Please yourself.'

'Why must you be so hateful? It's like that awful time of King Edward's funeral when you were ordered to attend the service and you sent word you were ill, and when we all came out of church, there you were playing golf with Eddie and Lucy. I could have died . . .'

'Won't happen this time. We won't be here.'

'Why do you have to behave like this! It's no wonder you haven't got on in the service! No wonder at all!'

'Sorry, dear. I don't feel well enough to attend an official function and sit up late drinking.'

'You're always well enough to do the things you want to do! Sometimes I could kill you!'

The next morning the Chief Commissioner called. Arthur was instructing the Tinies for the last time on the parallel bars he had had erected on the verandah for Swedish exercises.

'Sorry you weren't able to come last night.'

112

'I was seedy. A touch of fever.'

'Too bad. I'm glad you're over it! You missed hearing a lot of complimentary things. We drank a toast in your honour.'

'That's very kind.'

'I wish I had a record for you of the tributes that were paid.'

'Very kind indeed . . .'

'Well, I hear your pension starts as from 12 noon. And you're leaving the Province by the 2.30. Nobody can ever say you blocked promotion.'

The parting with Amma and Fazil Khan took place in the desolate drawing-room, in which were stacked the packing cases that were to follow after. Fazil Khan was transferred to Government House, his future assured. Amma's services were clamoured for and they had selected the family with whom they thought she would be happiest, with a number of young children on whom to lavish her never-ending spring of love. Arthur had decided to pension her so that she could ultimately retire, a woman of substance, to her own people. He was writing on a packing-case, filling up the pension form.

'How old are you, Amma?'

'I forty-five, Sahib.'

'You said that twenty years ago.'

'I forty-five, Sahib,' she smiled through the tears that ran down her face.

'Very well. Can you write your name?'

'No, Sahib.'

'Then make your mark. Here.'

Amma laid down the pen and embraced his feet. Then Isabelle's and Amma's sobs were joined to the howls of the children who recognized emotion when they saw it, though they did not understand the awful finality of the parting. Fazil Khan lifted each in turn shoulder high in the manner they enjoyed. The bushy white eyebrows beneath the turban were in startling contrast to the triumphantly flaming beard. The eyes were infinitely sad.

When they arrived in Bombay, it was to learn that the *Persia* carrying families home to England had been torpedoed in the Mediterranean. She was struck between the soup and the fish

113

course at luncheon and sank in five minutes with the loss of more than two hundred lives. The route to England was closed.

Isabelle had a hard time of it looking after three young children with no Amma, while Arthur besieged the shipping companies' offices. The outlook was gloomy. One morning, he returned with the news that a ship was sailing that evening that would take them as far as Yokohama. From thence they must cross the Pacific, the North American continent and the Atlantic to reach home. It was a roundabout route, but the only one open.

When the moment of departure that meant the final severance from India came, Arthur felt nothing. Nothing at all. He retired to his bunk with no desire to look his last at the familiar scene. He felt like a patient about to undergo a severe operation. Now the fatal step was taken he had no feeling left, no interest even. Positively none. He lay working out his problem while the children ran unheeded over the ship and Isabelle agonized alone. Mr Doongaji, always present at his arrivals and departures, looked in for the last time.

'Take jolly good care of your good self, my dear chap. When our foes are vanquished and this war is at an end, I shall give myself the pleasure of paying you a visit in your future abode. Eh?'

'That'll be very nice.'

'And rest assured I shall never forget to whom I owe . . .'

'How you do harp on a thing! There's the hooter again. You *must* go now.'

'I go, I go. God bless you, my dear Boyne.'

'Good-bye, old man.'

17

The Boynes reached Vancouver only to find the Canadian government had just decreed that no women and children were to cross the Atlantic. Enemy submarines had been increasingly active. The war which they had expected to end soon was obviously settling down for a long run.

They took a large furnished house in Victoria which Isabelle ran with the help of a Chinaman. Arthur had been active on the journey, helping with the children, teaching them and taking them on vigorous sight-seeing tours at every port of call. When they were installed in the new home, with the children settled in schools, he once more fell back on the worm. He could be counted on to descend to meals, however. The worm never affected his appetite, and as he was always considerate in the household and staff was non-existent, he would descend punctually on the stroke of the gong, eat appreciatively all that was set before him and return to bed with his knitting. Arthur was delighted with this new pursuit. It suited the worm and was a welcome change to reading the war news, problems and patience (which was another new interest). He was abominably clumsy with his fingers, and the time taken over his first muffler would have discouraged many an aspirant. But steady application brought proficiency at last and he launched forth on socks for soldiers. The click of his needles, the whispered counting of stitches as he peered myopically at a tricky heel, drove Isabelle to new frenzies.

'It's not a man's job, Arthur.'

'Whyever not?'

'Don't be silly. I simply can't bear to see you lying in bed all day *knitting*.'

'I don't see you've much cause for complaint. You hand them in as yours to your knitting circle and they all say "wonderful little woman! How does she manage it with all she has to do?"'

'I'm serious. Anyway you don't think I'm going to admit that my husband lies in bed all day knitting?'

'That interests me.' Arthur was casting off stitches with the flamboyant satisfaction of a practised hand who has just completed a job. 'It's not as if it's a *shady* occupation – like being a war profiteer, for example. There!' He held the completed sock aloft. '"A poor thing but mine own." So much for the war effort.'

'War effort! Arthur, that's what I want to speak to you about. You ought to be doing something towards the war effort.'

'I am.'

Isabelle stamped her foot in annoyance. 'Don't be so absolutely maddening! You know quite well what I mean. Every day the children come back with stories about their school friends. They've all got fathers or brothers or cousins at the war. Diana's so ashamed, she's made up a story about two cousins fighting in France. And what does her father do? He lies in bed knitting! Oh, it makes me so wild . . .'

Arthur's mood changed to one of depression. 'I'm afraid Diana'll have to stick to her heroic cousins. I'm too old for trench warfare.'

'For fighting? Yes. I'm not suggesting you enlist . . .'

'Thanks very much.'

'But there must be hundreds of other things you could do.'

'I'm too old . . .'

'Nonsense. You're only just forty-four and you haven't a grey hair.'

'I may not look my years, but I feel a great deal older than is perhaps usual for a man of my age. I'm a sick man after years in the tropics . . .'

116

'I know all about that! But you're not in the tropics any more. And you're not ill any more!'

'How do you know that? How does any person know what another is feeling? If I have a pain, can you feel it? I am subjected to a succession of feelings accompanied by a belief of reality. What you may think are illusory perceptions . . .'

'Oh stop! I'm not going to stand here listening to you talking.'

'Then wouldn't you prefer to sit? I won't say any more.' He began to fill his pipe.

'Arthur, this can't go on. I won't have it, d'you hear! The war may last for years. You've *got* to go to England and do your bit.'

'Not as easy as you think. No civilian passages.'

'That only applies to women and children, you know quite well. *Of course* you can get over there, and *of course* you'd be used for something, a man of your experience.'

Arthur puffed at his pipe in silence. He seemed withdrawn, remote, unheeding. His impassivity goaded her to further fury.

'In any case, whatever you decide, this can't go on, d'you hear? Because I won't put up with it any longer! There's a limit to what flesh and blood can stand. D'you see? If it weren't for the children I'd leave you for good!'

Arthur shut his eyes. It was all coming now – the agonizing recital that began with 'married me under false pretences' and would now incorporate 'lying there knitting'. He steeled himself for her to begin, but Isabelle had left the room. Perhaps because she had spared him, he felt a sudden stirring of pity for this hurt and suffering woman. He stretched out his hand in a gesture of affection and let it fall slowly back on the counterpane. The familiar feeling of desolation began to envelop him. Looking round the room, seeking something to distract him from his disturbed and restless thoughts, his eye fell on a used envelope on the dressing-table. With what seemed a great effort of will, moving slowly like an octogenarian, he captured his prize and returned with it to his bed. Once settled on his pillows, he slowly and deliberately unscrewed the cap of his fountain pen and set to work. For these two avenues of escape remained from the ceaseless clash of personality which had wrecked the flow of his life: illness, bringing temporary oblivion – and the beautiful purity, the dignity of mathematics.

The next morning he appeared at the breakfast table dressed for the street instead of in his customary dressing-gown.

'Are you going somewhere?' Isabelle exclaimed in surprise, remembering the conversation of the previous evening.

'Yes, I've got a lot of things to see to. A lot of business. Going to join Diana's cousins in the forefront of battle . . .'

Isabelle, overcome with conflicting emotions, had rushed from the breakfast table.

The journey across the Atlantic, in a crowded troopship travelling in convoy, suited Arthur rather well. He had never required much in the way of comfort. Long days spent in the privacy of his bunk, reading and working on his problems, were precisely to his taste. There was also male company and a game of bridge. He was almost sorry when they landed safely at Liverpool on a cool grey morning.

He went at once to his friends in Hampstead, whose home was open to the children in the school holidays, and thence to visit the children themselves. Edmund, whose school was not too far distant from Lucy's, was given the day off, and Arthur collected the boy and drove in a car hired for the occasion to call for Lucy and take the children out to tea. They sat in a tea-shop wolfing the rather unattractive war-time tea that the waitress set before them. Arthur looked across the table at his offspring with unusual attention. 'You don't seem to grow much.'

'I think I'm stunted,' Lucy said, and Edmund added hopefully that he was a 'late developer'.

Lucy said: 'This is a very special favour for me to be allowed out, you know, I didn't believe my ears when old Rattlesnake sent for me and told me. (I thought I was in for a pi-jaw.) It's because of the war. They expect you to get killed.'

'Not very likely.'

'Heaps of girls *have* lost their fathers and brothers. There's a roll-call – the roll of honour – after prayers when all their names are read out and new ones are added. It's ghastly.'

'Same with us,' Edmund said. 'Will you tell us about Victoria B.C.?'

'Not much to tell. There's a Chinaman called Me-No-Stay. At least I call him that because every day without fail he says "You get another boy. Me no stay." That's all. But he stays. He's quite good.'

'Does Mother like it there?'

'I think so. She's got a lot to do because it's a big place and Me-No-Stay only does the boilers and a bit of polishing.'

'Talking about boilers,' Lucy said, 'the one in our house is cracked, so we never get a hot bath any more. It was only on Tuesdays and Fridays anyway. But do you know, we're supposed to have a cold one every single morning in our hip baths – all the year round!'

'Barbarous!'

'Some people are frightfully hardy and do. I've got a stick with a rag tied round it that makes a splashing noise indistinguishable from me. I keep it at the back of my hanging cupboard.'

'It's a monstrous survival of a spartan age! A cold bath in this temperature – let alone in winter . . . I shall speak to your headmistress.'

'Don't you dare!'

'I most certainly will. A child like yourself reared in the tropics . . .'

'If you dare to butt in, I shall simply disown you, Father!'

'We have this bloater paste at school on Sundays,' Edmund intervened. 'It's good stuff.'

'We have frogspawn on Sunday evenings and hair jam at all times,' Lucy said. 'The food at school's really revolting. Really too, too . . .'. She made as if to vomit.

'Then it's no wonder you don't make much growth. I shall – '

'Do the Tinies like it in Victoria B.C.?' Edmund asked.

'They seem to. But your mother thinks they're getting into rough colonial ways.'

'What are you going to do, Father?'

'I haven't the vaguest idea, dear boy. I shall start by offering my services to the War Office. I don't suppose anyone will regard me as a fighting man but I might get some sort of bottle-washer's job.'

'You know, after the war, they're going to build a chapel,' Lucy said. 'Then we won't have to go all the way to the Parish church on Sundays. The parents are all going to be asked to subscribe.'

'I'll subscribe to a swimming-pool,' Arthur said. He found Lucy rather too absorbed in her school.

The interview at the War Office took place after prolonged delay. Arthur realized he was in the hands of an underling and was not forthcoming.

'Indian Civil Service, you say?'

'That's right.'

'Well, we might be able to use you for clerical work sometime. You've a thorough knowledge of office routine?'

'Er, yes.'

'Any hobbies?'

'Patience. Knitting.'

The interlocutor threw him a suspicious glance. He returned to his questionnaire.

'Any serious illnesses?'

'I've had malaria for about twenty years. Several attacks of dysentery. A dysenteric ulcer. Appendicitis. And I've got a rare worm called *Streptoccocus strongoloides*.'

'How d'you spell it?'

Arthur spelled it out and described his symptoms.

'I see. Look, old man, I've got all the information I need. We have your address. If there's any way in which we can use your services, you'll hear from us.'

Arthur felt depressed as he came out into Whitehall. He walked past the India Office and his spirits sank still further. He decided to try the Red Cross.

The British Red Cross headquarters was besieged by an army of cooks, housemaids and chauffeurs in search of adventure. Arthur waited a whole morning without being seen. He decided to give it up, but the following day found him back in the queue. At last his turn came. Deep in a quadratic equation, he did not realize that he had been summoned.

'Your turn, ducky,' said the fat woman who sat overlapping him on the bench. 'Look sharp now!'

After answering the usual questions, Arthur suddenly said:

120

'I've driven my car for a number of years in India. On all sorts of roads.'

The tired old man whom he had waited so long to see suddenly showed interest. 'How would you like to drive an ambulance?' he asked.

'Very much indeed.'

In a surprisingly short time, Arthur was ordered to proceed as an ambulance driver to the Italian front. There was only a fortnight in which to get his uniform, learn how to handle an ambulance and say goodbye to the children. No one seemed deterred, least of all himself, when he reversed into and knocked down the hospital gatepost on his test assignment. 'No great harm done to the bus,' Arthur said cheerfully. 'You might perhaps take the opportunity to widen the entrance . . . Not a bad idea?'

18

The river Isonzo cut its way southwards from the Julian Alps to the Adriatic marshes. The villa stood a few miles from Gorizia, near the bank of the river. It was an imposing structure approached by a courtyard and flanked by a beautiful grove of sweet chestnuts, the home of a family of Venetian origin whose misfortune it was to live in a region as hideously unstable as Alsace-Lorraine or Schleswig-Holstein. This was the *Irredenta*, Italian by race and feeling, stubbornly dreaming of emancipation from Austrian rule. The villa Chiozza was the home of an Italian patriot. At the outbreak of war, he had been taken to Vienna and thrown into a concentration camp where he died. Only a few hours after his abduction, the villa was in Italian hands. It became the headquarters of a regiment of Sardinian Grenadiers. Their regimental mascot, a wild boar, was housed rather grandly in one of the salones. Arthur could see where the boar's tusks had ripped the golden damask from the base of the walls giving a suggestion of hell's flames.

The British ambulance drivers and mechanics were stationed in the villa sharing a mess with some of the officers. They belonged to the Third Army (commanded by the Duke of Aosta) to whom the British Red Cross unit was attached.

Arthur's room-mate, Miller, was a London bus-driver over military age. His wife had died in the first months of the war.

He was a native of West Ham and childless. Bored with the restrictions of war-time London, he had volunteered for service overseas as a driver and been sent out with the first Red Cross unit. In spite of language difficulties, he got on famously with the Italians and knew all the ropes.

'Thass your bed and thass where you can stow your kit, see? Wait till I get this here paraffin stove going. It's a treat for you special after the journey, see.'

'I didn't expect it to be so cold,' Arthur said, shivering.

'Thass right – cold as ice in winter and hotter'n hell in summer. Healthy, you might say. Mustn't grumble.'

'When does our work start?'

'Whenever a call comes in. The capitano – that's the little Wop with waxed mustachios – he tells us. Nice little chap. He's called Johnny.'

'I understand we collect the wounded at the dressing-stations and take them to the hospitals in the plains?'

'Thass the idear. Only you missed out one stage. You got to take them from the dressing-station to the clearing station first. They get them cleaned up and sorted out there and settle on the hospital they're to go to. Often they don't have no time to do more'n slap a bandage on at the posts.'

'Where's the clearing station?'

'Juss this side of the river.'

'And the dressing-stations?'

'Depends. They move about according to the front.'

'I can hardly believe we're close to the front lines here. It's so quiet.'

'And thass the way we like it. Here, look out of this window. You see them hills, now? Mountains you might say – they're steep.'

'I can see a good deal of cloud.'

'It's on the mountains. Thass where the line is. Right there. It's not more'n a mile away.'

'You don't mean to say so!'

'You'll believe it all right, mate, when they starts squabbling.'

'What's over there?' Arthur asked, pointing to the north.

'Thass worse. Bigger and steeper mountains.'

'And over that way?'

123

'Thass worse still. Over there's the Carso. What they call the worst battleground in Europe.'

'Don't you believe it. Nothing's worse than Flanders.'

'Well, you can take your choice. You'd better have a rest, old man.'

'What time do we eat?'

'You got a couple er hours yet. I'll give you a call.'

'No need thanks. I can wake myself.'

Arthur was proud of his latest accomplishment which was to stand him in good stead. He could not only sleep at will but could wake himself at a stated time as well.

It was dark when he groped his way down to the mess, by the feeble light of a guttering candle which stood in a saucer at the bend of the marble staircase. The smell of spaghetti drew him like a magnet. His room-mate ('Dusty' to Italians and British alike) introduced him first to the officers, who saluted and shook hands ceremoniously, and then to his fellow drivers. The meal was abundant and Arthur ate ravenously. They drank from huge flasks of Chianti. After his second glass, Arthur found himself groping after long-forgotten Latin tags.

Capitano Giovanni Crespi returned the compliment by airing his limited English. He sat at the head of the table with the new recruit on his left.

'Englishe people lika very much Italy. I lika very much English. I *like!*'

'*Res amicos invenit*,' Arthur ventured. 'Plautus, if I remember rightly.'

'You speaka Latino? Isa good. Englishe people helpa Italy. Helpa Mazzini, Garibaldi, Cavour. We fighta together for liberty, no?'

'*Populi Romano res est propria libertas*. Cicero.'

'Good! Very good! You understand very good!' The capitano was delighted. '*Quelle altri barbari non capiscono niente!*' He gave a toast to England. 'You think so England senda armée for helpa Italy?'

'I think so.'

'Now? Damn quicka?'

124

'I hope so. But *Dulce et decorum est . . .*'

'You are my brother,' cried the capitano emotionally, springing from his chair to embrace the new recruit. 'You calla me Johnny. I lika you Arturo!'

The next morning it was still raining and bitterly cold. There had been a little sporadic firing in the night.

'Come along. Johnny says I'm to take you to the posts. Nothing doing at present,' Dusty said.

They drove through the town. There were soldiers about, and Arthur noticed guns mounted in the square. But there were a few civilians about as well, huddled in raincoats. Shutters were going up, cafés being swept.

The roads as they approached the front were deep in mud. The water running off the precipitous slopes ahead transformed them into river beds. The ambulance plunged steadily on. Arthur felt this was the kind of driving that he was cut out for. The road was full of craters now, roughly filled in with crushed stone. The last section was screened by matting and branches.

'Thass to spoil the peep-show for the enemy,' Dusty said. 'Back there, you just got to run for it. Safe as houses under this blinking carpet – I don't fink.'

At the post, the Italian doctor and stretcher-bearers greeted Dusty with cordiality. 'Nothing for you today, *amico*,' the doctor said. He gesticulated with upturned palms denoting regret.

'Not a sausage. I can see that. I'm only doing a bit of sight-seeing with my new mate.'

After visiting several posts, they came to a confluence of two streams, tributaries of the Isonzo. Presently they passed a great cleft in the land, the Vallone, running like a giant trench across the stony uplands on their left. Dusty told tales of the terrible fighting there last autumn. They continued along the Isonzo to Sagrado, a small badly-damaged town at the foot of the Carso plateau.

'I hate this place,' Dusty said. 'Did you hear of the gas attack last June?'

'I don't think so.'

'No? Then I won't spoil your dreams.'

125

Arthur tried to light his pipe, but his hands were numb. He rubbed them in silence. The ambulance turned into a large court-yard with a sodden garden beyond.

'How many men d'you think you could get in here?' Dusty asked.

'Hundreds. Why?'

'Thass right, 'undreds. That time the buggers used gas last June, this place was full up, *and* through there,' he pointed at the garden, 'full up, with men dying. 'Undreds and 'undreds of 'em falling down and twistin' up and dying. We was piling 'em in the cars and coming and going without stopping, but there wasn't nothing you could do for the pore devils. Christ almighty! I hope I never live to see such a thing again. That boy Albert wot you replaced – mind you, I'm not saying young Albert weren't a trial to me at times – he was a bleedin' wonder that night. Only sixteen when he first come out here. Gone in the army now. That's what we are in this business – old men and boys . . . Come on, let's get back to the mess. I'll take you to the hospitals this afternoon.'

'Can I take over now?'

'You're welcome. Watch out for skids in this soup. Blimey, it don't half rain here. Still, musn't grumble.'

The hospitals were at Udine, thirty miles from the front, on a plain of desolating flatness. In spring and summer the orchards and vineyards gave the plain a less forsaken air. Now it seemed to Arthur as depressing as the plains of India in monsoon time. On the long straight road, they passed men, guns, and mules coming towards the mountains through the mud.

'Old men and boys,' Dusty was saying again, 'and I'm one of the old.'

'Same here.'

'I can see I'm going to like havin' you here, Arfur, specially after that young Albert. He were a proper terror. Still, I hope he don't go and get hisself killed and all.'

Every day it rained. They said such rain was without precedent. They said it had brought the battles in France to a standstill.

126

The Isonzo now was a mighty rushing torrent. The engineers working on new roads, bridges and gun emplacements for the spring offensive were held up. The rain stopped suddenly and the *bora* blew, scourging the Carso. Here the men in the front lines lived in shallow trenches blasted out of the rock with virtually no protection against snow and ice. Their sufferings were severe. Arthur was busy taking cases of frost-bite and pneumonia to the hospitals in the plain.

There was depressing news in the mess. Since the autumn Italy had been at war with Germany as well as Austria, their traditional foe. There were daily rumours of German troops arriving at the front. Prisoners taken in trench raids revealed the presence of new Austrian batteries brought from the collapsing Russian front. The newspapers were full of stories of a great Austro-German offensive.

'You think so England senda armée before Germans come, Arturo?'

'I profoundly hope so.'

'And America? When America come in war?'

'Won't be long now. They don't like the U-boats torpedoing their shipping. They've lost four this month.'

'Wanta come quick.'

'America is very big and slow-moving. Takes time. You must be patient.'

'*Patienza! Mamma mia!* Where you learn this *patienza?*'

Arthur shrugged. 'I suppose in India. Anyway, Rome was not built in a day.'

'Indian soldiers very good no?'

'I know men who say there's nothing anywhere to touch their regiments. The Gurkhas, for example. They fight with a curved knife called a kukri . . .'

'Sounds handy for these here trenches,' Dusty said.

'Why you no send us Gurkhas?'

'I will. I'll see to it, Johnny,' Arthur said.

'You are my friend, Arturo. All Englishe people my friends. Italians and English always friends. Garibaldi, he say – England is the friend of poor country. He say if one time England wanta helpa, then he curse the Italian who no want to go to helpa England. I drink to England!'

127

'To Italy!'

Emotional chaps, Arthur thought, but how very pleasant amid the horrors of war to enjoy this affectionate good will in one's daily contacts, this absence of nagging in the home. He felt happier than for a long time, and only faintly tipsy.

When the snow fell, the mule trains passing the villa presented a spectral appearance, the beasts straining silently on the slippery surface. The men's faces were grey with cold. They nevertheless managed a smile and a wave for the passing ambulance. The mountain roads at night, steep, narrow and abounding in sharp bends, became deadly dangerous under the snow. In the plain, the heavy ambulances swayed in the chaos of frozen ruts. Arthur drove his car with loving care, humming to himself as was his habit in moments of concentration.

All through April the weather remained wintry. They watched the preparations for the big attack and sat waiting – apart from the fruits of an occasional trench-mortar raid – listening to the unending rumours, playing auction bridge for small stakes, waiting . . . The hospitals in the plain had been emptied, waiting for the flow of wounded to begin. Every time a gun was fired, the bridge-players paused a moment, listening, wondering if this was it – then slowly went on playing.

With the coming of May, the weather changed almost overnight from cold to hot. The slush melted from the roads. Soon it was very hot. The strain of waiting continued. Arthur was tired of listening to the speculation in the mess. He had set himself to master Italian with his usual diligence. He was half-way through *I Promessi Sposi*. His accent was faulty, but he had acquired a considerable command of the language. It was not like the early days when his strenuous efforts often resulted in Hidustani – or that time when, solicited by a lady of the town, he had finally come out with, '*Io sono antico*.' After that, for a time, he had been affectionately known as Arturo Antico.

19

It was nearly mid-May when the offensive began. The roar of the guns at first light blasted Arthur out of bed and over to the window. The familiar mountains, with the jagged snow-covered ranges towering beyond, rose out of a screen of smoke and destruction. Every battery, he thought, from the Alps to the sea must be in on this.

'Now we're off!' Dusty said. He dressed hurriedly and went downstairs.

He returned as Arthur was finishing shaving. 'Not our pigeon. Second Army. It's heavier in the north.'

All day long the thunder of the guns re-echoed from the mountains. By evening, batches of prisoners were to be seen. Dazed and blackened, they stood or lay in dispirited groups waiting to be marched to captivity. Arthur wondered how human beings could conceivably have survived the bombardment. It continued through the night. The next morning the attack began.

That day they sat in the mess waiting, listening to the reports. The Udine Brigade had won ground at Plava; the bridgehead to the north . . . The Florence Brigade were on Monte Kuk . . . The Campobasso on Monte Santo . . . These were bayonet assaults won at great cost. Ambulances could be seen passing the villa on their way to the hospitals. Still the unit waited.

Arthur stood in the shade of a chestnut leaning against the

trunk, listening to the battle. Then he went up to his room and sent postcards briefly to Isabelle and the children. You never knew. He hadn't written lately, and they'd be reading about the offensive in the papers. Ambulances did get hit sometimes.

The next day was spent listening to news of counter-attacks. After tea, Dusty took a telephone message.

'We're lent to the Second,' he said. 'Two of our ambulances lost from the Sabotino lot. They can't tell me nothing about the drivers. They want four of us up at Plava.'

It wasn't more than ten or twelve miles as the crow flies, but the road skirted the mountains and climbed a pass to drop down into the Isonzo gorge. Italian engineers had constructed a great many hairpin bends over the forested ridge – bends that won Arthur's admiring approval. The ambulances went by the new and returned by the old road – one-way traffic. It was getting dark when they dropped down into the gorge. Arthur found something reassuring in the broad back of Dusty's ambulance in front of him. The road had been shelled at many points, but they could get by. The noise of battle was very near now – the rattle of machine-guns, the whine of tracers, the swish and roar of shells, the echoes coming back from the mountain walls above them. Suddenly his car was exposed to machine-gun fire. It spattered all round. Arthur noted with interest that he felt elated rather than frightened. He drove on slowly, carefully. At the bottom of the gorge, he caught sight of the familiar red cross on a heap of scrap metal. It was one of the ambulances. They were sheltered now by a rocky bluff. It was impossible to approach very near to the dressing-station. He got out of the ambulance and walked through the rows of wounded. Their groans mingled with the sounds of battle. Inside the dressing-station, doctors were operating feverishly by the light of oil lamps. The ambulance drivers were responsible for the loading of their cars. Arthur had always before found his load awaiting him. He stood nonplussed, unable to attract the attention of doctors or stretcher-bearers. When he went outside, some of the wounded seeing his uniform clamoured to him to take them away. Suddenly he saw Dusty.

'Whom am I to take?'

'Take your pick. I'm through. Grab my stretcher-bearers as

soon as they're finished stowing and get on with it. And don't forget – no safety lights till you're over the top.'

Arthur left it to the stretcher-bearers. Unable to face the imploring eyes, he stood, filling and lighting his pipe slowly in embarrassment.

'*Vengono . . . vengono . . . ecco! vengono adesso . . . non ce molto tempo da aspetare . . .*'

Inside the ambulance, he gave brandy to his wounded, pouring it clumsily out of his flask into their mouths. He must remember next time – a tin mug. English cigarettes for the stretcher-bearers. He was off.

He had not gone more than a few yards, the ambulance lurching over the uneven surface, when there was a chorus of groans and cries behind him.

'*Piano! Piano! Per l'amor di Dio! Piano! Piano!*'

'Sorry,' Arthur said between his teeth. It was too dark to see more than the outline of the road. He drove on slowly, concentrating all his powers on trying to avoid jolts. At every bad jolt it was the same –'*Piano! Piano!*'

'*Si, si, io vado piano. Coraggio!*'

'*Ah piano! Madre di Dio . . . Piano!*'

He was glad now of the light from the bursting shells. It took a long time to reach the dressing-station on the other side. The cries behind him were fainter now, despairing.

At the dressing-station, Arthur caught up with Dusty. The wounded were taken out and treated. Their papers were gone through and the drivers told which hospitals they were to go to. Arthur and Dusty found they had each lost a man on the way. The places were quickly filled.

'*Andiamo . . .*'

The familiar drive to Udine had never seemed so long. Now he could use safety lights. At last it was over. He sat for a moment in the hospital entrance, drinking a mug of coffee that someone had brought him, waiting for Dusty who was due to end his round here. Suddenly he saw him.

'Where d'you get that? I could do with some.'

'In there, I think. What now?'

'They wants us to go straight back. Get another coupler loads out before it's light. How about it?'

131

'I'm on,' said Arthur.

The next day they slept through the noise of battle. After supper, they sat in the mess awaiting instructions.

'They got a new bridgehead. At Bodrez.'

'Where's that?'

'It's up beyond yesterday's do. Further up river.'

'Any news of Johnny and the boys?'

'Not yet.'

'They say they got 10,000 prisoners.'

'How do they know? Not had time to count them yet.'

'I wonder how many killed?'

The telephone rang in the office. 'That'll be for us. You go Arfur. Your Italian's better'n mine.'

'Local,' Arthur said when he came back. 'Posts 6 and 7. The rest to stand by for call from Second Army H.Q.'

'Ladies first,' Dusty stood up, 'and old buggers. Seeing as Arfur and me's the oldest here, we'll take 6 and 7. Stand by boys, and don't let the Second Army down with none of your horseplay.'

The fury to the north died down gradually. It was the turn of the Third Army now – the big attack after the feint in the north that was to give them Trieste.

The Carso lay on the east bank of the river, all the way to the marshes at the sea's edge. It was a bleak wind-swept table-land of rock cut by deep gullies and sinister potholes. Limestone boulders were scattered liberally over its surface, with patches of shale and scree. Across this intractable plateau was the deep depression, the Vallone, mainly now in Italian hands after last year's bitter fighting; but at the southernmost end of the Vallone, near the sea, rose the Hermada, honeycombed with tunnels and caverns, bristling with guns, blocking the road to Trieste. The Austrians had spent years converting it into a fortress capable of sheltering whole regiments.

It was dawn, ten days after the beginning of the offensive on the northern sector. The shattering roar of the bombardment on the Carso front made the villa tremble as if in an earthquake. It reached a pitch of hurricane fury that lasted ten hours. The Austrian front-line trenches were blasted out of existence, and by tea-time the Italian infantry crossed their parapets. By evening, the ambulances were working non-stop.

The run along the Vallone, even without a load of tortured wounded, was a great strain on the drivers. For the first couple of miles the road was filled with craters. A slight bend to the east brought Hermada, flashing wickedly, into full view. The road was now non-existent. The end of the Vallone was a shambles. The only cover was the pall of smoke and fumes and powdered rock that lay in the valley like a sulphurous fog.

'Fierce as ten furies, terrible as Hell,' Arthur suddenly said aloud. He had always hated Milton. As a boy he had been made to learn the first two books of *Paradise Lost* by heart. (He could still go from 'Of man's first disobedience . . .' to 'and justify the ways of God to man' without stopping to draw breath.) As he stood half-blinded, wiping his spectacles, he decided in a detached way that Milton could have been describing the Vallone.

> '. . . Yet from those flames
> No light but rather darkness visible
> Served only to discover sights of woe . . .'

He groped his way to the dressing-station, aided by the cries of the damned.

The battle lasted five days. Longer in that stony wilderness was a physical impossibility. (As if to herald the end of battle, the weather broke in a fierce deluge of rain.) The enemy front lines had been pounded to atoms, and the advancing troops had to meet counter-attacks in the open, owing to the lack of cover and the impossibility of constructing trenches hastily in the bald rock. The Italians suffered acutely. Their casualties were terrifying. All night the ambulances worked non-stop. When a halt was called there had been some advances – a few hundred yards here, a couple of miles there – but Hermada remained, obstinately blocking the way to Trieste. The Carso attack had failed.

133

Soon the counter-attacks had faded out and the new line held firm.

It was evening in the mess. Arthur sat reading Pirandello. Johnny had lent him a number of volumes. He read now with ease and enjoyment. Dusty came in.

'I got news at last,' he said. 'It's bad. Johnny got it on the last day.'

'Killed outright?'

'Yes.'

'Oh.'

'And Bruno. Guiseppe's wounded – I don't know how badly. The rest escaped. They're not coming back here. We got a new lot coming. Calabrians.' Arthur sat silent.

'Bad about Johnny. Poor fellow.'

'Terrible. Arfur, you write to his widow from us, will you?'

'Yes.'

'They counted 25,000 prisoners, as near as makes no odds. That's on the whole show. And 100,000 Austrians dead and wounded. Mustn't grumble.'

'It was a famous victoree,' Arthur said.

The summer was another time of waiting. The plain cracked and shrivelled in the scorching heat. The chestnut grove turned silvery under a coat of dust. The leaves wilted on the mulberry trees in the courtyard. Arthur carried several cases of sunstroke. He himself had not known a day's illness since he left England. He thought it very considerate of the worm to remain quiescent. He couldn't have done his bit if the fatigue poisons had been active. It never for a moment occurred to him to question his interpretation of the sequence of events. All of a sudden, however, he was afflicted with toothache. There was an abcess in a back tooth. The Italian doctor, mistrusting the local army dentist, arranged for him to go to Milan for attention. The journey in the circumstances seemed intolerably long and wretched.

Arthur had a poor opinion of dentists. (He always secured the first appointment of the day – 'there's *some* chance then he might have boiled up his instruments and you get them clean'. The same principle applied to barbers.) His approach was unusual. If he were visiting the dentist for the first time, he would say courteously: 'Excuse me. Do you mind if I take a look in your mouth? Yes, in the chair a moment. Thank you. Open . . .'

If inspection revealed a sufficient number of stoppings (for it was no use if the fellow hadn't himself experienced the pain he inflicted) – preferably filled with gold and satisfactorily maintained – he then changed places with the dentist. Whether from surprise or amusement, no dentist had ever yet shown him the door.

On this occasion he dispensed with this opening gambit. The dentist, a surly, harassed-looking man, was uncommunicative. It was all over in a few minutes. Later, when the bleeding had stopped, Arthur descended to the street. A mutinous-looking procession was passing. He took a taxi back to the station and managed by good luck to get a seat on a crowded slow night train to Udine.

Autumn came with gusts of rain that drove down from the mountains. The chestnut grove was bare. One wing of the villa was being got ready for use as a British field hospital of twenty-five beds. An air of depression hung over the town. In the mess, the atmosphere was gloomy, for the Calabrians, though friendly, were homesick.

Arthur sat in the mess, drafting a letter to the *New Statesman*. There had been a correspondence on India in recent weeks in which he had taken part. *The Times* too had published his views. As a moderate progressive, he came somewhere between the two groups. But both sides printed his letters. The conversation went on around him.

'Have you seen the bulletin?'

'Yes. No news.'

'What are you expecting then? Victory?'

'Don't be a fool. There *is* news, but not in the bulletin. The troops have mutinied in Turin. It's been put down. More trouble in Milan, too.'

'Things aren't the same as when I came out here. They're fed up. You can see that.'

'Can you blame them?'

'I'm not blaming. I'm saying how it is. They're all fed up with the war. Had enough.'

'Up at Caporetto they got German shock troops in the front line. They can hear them talking at night.'

'How's a shock trooper talk when he's at home?'

'Listen, they got twenty German divisions up there, straight.'

The wireless operator handed Arthur a telegram. He opened it and read: 'YOU ARE APPOINTED DIRECTOR BUREAU DE SECOURS AUX PRISONNIERS DE GUERRE AND COMMISSIONER BRITISH RED CROSS IN SWITZERLAND STOP HEADQUARTERS FIVE HELVETIASTRASSE BERNE STOP PROCEED BERNE IMMEDIATELY.' Arthur stared at the paper.

'Not bad news Arfur, I hope?' Dusty asked.

'Not bad. No, I don't think so. It means I'm transferred to Switzerland.'

'Switzerland! Go on! Well, it's lucky you had some practice on mountain roads. Switzerland come in the war then?'

'No. I shan't be driving.'

'What then?'

'Well . . . I shall be running it.'

'Go on! Runnin' what?'

'The British Red Cross.'

'Come orf it.' Dusty sounded hurt. 'Here, let's have a look.'

20

The Bureau de Secours aux Prisonniers de Guerre (at Berne, the governmental capital) had started from humble beginnings in the shape of sewing parties among devoted ladies of the legation. As the war progressed and the number of prisoners grew, the bureau secured its own premises with several small packing-shops scattered about the neighbourhood, whence mixed consignments of food and clothing were dispatched to prisoners under the auspices of the Red Cross, in accordance with the Geneva Convention. When this proved inadequate, a packing station was built alongside the railway tracks where the German cars came in, were packed and dispatched the same day. This depot employed about a hundred paid packers while the offices, devoted largely to the tracing of missing prisoners, employed a further fifty or sixty, mostly British subjects long resident in Switzerland.

Arthur now occupied a suite at the Schweitzerhof Hotel. (He had refused a salary, but his expenses were paid by the Red Cross.) On the same floor were a couple of German newspaper correspondents. It seemed odd to find the German military attaché seated at an adjoining table in the dining-room. Arthur found him so much a figure of fun in his resplendent uniform, the Iron Cross dangling large, the haughty face contorted in an effort to keep the eyeglass adjusted to its socket, that he was sorely tempted to engage him in conversation. In addition to the obvious recognizable enemy, the whole place abounded in spies. Arthur found it very stimulating and peered myopically round the potted palms in the hope of seeing a seductive creature bargaining for state secrets.

A few days after his arrival, Arthur went to Geneva for discussions with some international bodies. It was a brilliant autumn evening and he found that he had time to walk to the station before his train left for Berne. At the end of the pont Jean-Jacques Rousseau he stopped to buy a newspaper. The placard caught his eye: '*Armée Italienne en déroute.*' He read: '*Les troupes Allemand-Autrichiennes ont forcé la ligne à Caporetto, dans les Alpes Juliennes . . . avance de dix kilometres . . . descendent dans la plaine . . . ligne ecroulée . . .*' Feeling suddenly giddy, he leaned against the parapet and read slowly to the end, then slowly read it again from start to finish.

'It's a bad business,' he said aloud suddenly. Remembering his train, he hailed a passing taxi. He automatically selected a corner seat on the side that would face the lake with the view he had enjoyed coming to Geneva. He stared intently at the splendid landscape as if lost in admiration, but saw only a more familiar scene. Hill by hill, village by village, farm by farm, he saw it engulfed. He was half-way to Lausanne before it occurred to him that he had got out of Italy just in time.

The most urgent part of Arthur's new job was the sending of food parcels to 40,000 prisoners-of-war stationed in camps mostly in north Germany and East Prussia, where, according to the nature of the camp commandant, conditions varied from very fair to very bad. There were commandants who did what they could for their prisoners: others were disinclined to feed them. In any case, Germany was by then feeling the pinch of the Allied blockade.

Under the Geneva Convention, the Red Cross was empowered to send to each man captured a fortnightly parcel of food and 'comforts'. Of the food, the staple diet was bread (tins of bully beef, condensed milk, cocoa, dripping and cigarettes were strictly limited by weight) – and the bread was the trouble. The deterioration in quality of wartime flour and the time taken in transit (some of the bread was still sent from England) meant that it arrived mildewed and uneatable. It was a heartbreaking state of affairs – and right up Arthur's street. Trained in a hard school where famine, pestilence and cataclysm had taught him to use initiative and resource, and accustomed to a routine of selfless toil, he threw himself into the problems confronting him with his usual zest.

The French had evolved a rusk, only three inches long, two inches wide and an inch thick. It was hard but friable. If a small hole were made in the top, a little water poured in and the rusk baked for a few minutes, it swelled into something very like fresh bread. Arthur placed a contract with the factory at Calais, called on reserve supplies of flour from Canada and urged the Swiss bakers to evolve an improved rusk. The Swiss rusks were smaller and harder – little rocks that had the supreme virtue of lasting more or less indefinitely and transforming themselves into excellent bread. The substitution of rusks for bread began. Within a few months he had over twenty firms engaged in manufacture, so that by the time of the alarming March offensive, when the numbers of prisoners-of-war had doubled, the situation was well in hand.

In 1916, it had been decided to intern prisoners-of-war in Switzerland. The disabled, the very sick, those needing much medical attention and those likely to die on their hands were transferred from German camps to Switzerland, where, at such health resorts as Mürren and Château d'Oex, their improvement was often rapid. Arthur lost no time in starting recreation and training centres for the disabled and sick. Courses in tailoring, carpentry, shoe-repairing, book-binding – even shorthand and art courses – there seemed no limit to what a disabled, ostensibly dying, man could master. In Arthur's office was a huge index of all prisoners. He was in continual correspondence with their families, encouraging and organizing visits of relatives and friends as it became possible, and attending repatriation boards for the very sick.

An even larger field of endeavour was his work in tracing

the missing, the Red Cross being the only organization permitted (in connexion with the Casualty Department at the War Office) to make inquiries for the wounded and missing in enemy territory.

As the prisoners grew in number, the volume of correspondence became vast indeed. In addition, the food parcels sent to all officers and men contained postcards requiring, among other information, their comments on the condition and regularity of the goods sent. Having already added medical comforts, tobacco and tea to the parcels, Arthur set out to cater for the special requirements of Indians, vegetarians and invalids. The system became so efficient that a newly-captured prisoner was able on arrival at camp to communicate direct with Berne. Except where relatives of friends expressed a wish to contribute towards the cost of the parcels, they were sent free. Arthur took precautions to guard against abuse, writing to every officer to ask whether the arrangements met with his approval and whether he wished to contribute through his bankers towards the cost of the parcels.

The new commissioner was now working like one possessed, wearing out his secretaries and rapidly gaining the reputation of a slave-driver. He eschewed the legation, instinctively regarding them with the faint hostility he reserved for officialdom. Not long after his arrival, it occurred to him that it would be a good thing for Lucy to work in his office. He could do with one more secretary. He could not be sure how old she was, but felt it was high time she left school. He wrote a long letter painting an exciting picture of life in a neutral capital, and was nettled to receive a reply impudently declining: 'I've no wish to be done out of my last year here, just when all the privileges are coming my way. I'll come next year, if the war's still on.' Arthur decided not to waste time arguing and wrote to the headmistress withdrawing his daughter at the end of term. It was the first time he had acted high-handedly towards his daughter – an action she was later to approve.

Lucy arrived in the new year after a wearying journey in excessively overcrowded trains and a night spent in an eerily blacked-out Paris. Arthur awaited his daughter impatiently. The express from Paris was many hours late and he could ill spare the time. At last, in the milling crowd, he recognized a grown-up young woman wearing a Red Cross armband.

'There you are, dear girl! Journey all right?'

'Ghastly!'

'You look a bit bedraggled, I must say.'

'I'm filthy. And Father, there was no heating in France and I thought I should die of cold. I sat up all night and never slept a wink.'

'There's a war on, dear girl. Or didn't they tell you at school?'

'Oh Father, shut up! I feel so awful . . .'

'Come on. A hot bath will soon put you right. You'll like the Schweitzerhof.'

When Lucy, revived, entered the dining-room with her father, he lost no time in showing her the sights.

'That's the Dutch minister. (You bow Lucy.) Mynheer Jonk van Beg und Donk mein daughter . . . er . . . h'm . . . Beyond him is the *Daily Mail* – famous correspondent . . . yes, bow. The next two gentlemen are the *Berlinertageblatt* and the *Norddeutscheallgemeinezeitung*. You don't bow . . . Now that table's special – the German military attaché, but he doesn't seem to be here this evening. Lucy, you're not to stare or laugh when you see him . . .'

'Am I *likely* to laugh at a Hun?'

'At this one you are. I wish our waiter'd get a move on. I've a lot of work still to do.'

'At this time of night?'

'Got to. I wasted nearly an hour at the railway station. But I shan't be late. Got to be up early. You go to bed and get a good night's rest. I want you in the office by 8.30 . . . Where's that man got to? . . . Well, you're to learn filing and work on the prisoners' index for the first month. In your spare time, the lunch-hour for instance, you can teach yourself typewriting. In the evenings, you can learn German. I've arranged with the head of the Berlitz school to give you an hour's lesson every evening. (He's a German but he's got a Swiss wife and been here thirty years, so it ought to be considered safe.) With an hour's lesson in the evening and an hour before breakfast going over what you've been taught the night before, you should make reasonable progress.'

'Is that all?'

'You might manage a course of shorthand – our waiter's not usually like this. Just when I'm in a hurry . . .'

'Don't I ever get any exercise, say?' Lucy's tone was aggrieved.

'I've no doubt I can arrange some winter sports at week-ends. My God! That man's disappeared again! Ah, well . . . Lucy, I take it that you know the origin and history of the Red Cross organization? There were some books I told you to get hold of, remember?'

'Sorry, Father.'

'Well, until Napoleon's day, prisoners taken on the battlefield were left to rot – in fearful circumstances. I'll start you on *Un Souvenir de Solferino* by Henri Dunant, a Swiss. It's the germ and origin of the Red Cross. I want you to know how we came about and what our function is now. Ah! *Here* you are! We'll have . . .' and he ordered a meal unbelievably lavish after wartime England. 'We've got to stoke up, you know.'

The 'worm' was never mentioned at this time, not even thought of. Except on one occasion. They were invited to dine at the legation. When it was time to dress, Arthur started complaining of fatigue . . . aches and pains . . .

'I think I'll send word . . .'

'Father, you can't! At the very last minute. You've been quite all right all day.'

'Well, I don't feel up to turning out now, dear girl. I fancy I might have an attack of malaria coming on.'

'Oh Father, *please!* You can't do that at the eleventh hour! I want to go. I want to wear my green evening dress. You haven't seen it yet.'

'Can't you give me that treat some other time? . . .'

'No!' Lucy suddenly looked dangerously like her mother.

Arthur sighed. 'I don't feel up to it at all,' he repeated gloomily. 'Still, I'll make an effort . . .'

The effort did not extend very far. He was uncommunicative at the dinner and left as soon as it was decently possible.

'That's a queer fellow the Red Cross has sent us,' the Minister remarked to his first secretary after Arthur's departure. 'I'm told Dr Gottfried who runs the Berlitz school goes round every evening, ostensibly to give the daughter a German lesson. Now what can that be for?'

142

'He's on the same floor with some enemy war correspondents. He was seen going up in the lift with them the other night.'

'H'm.'

'He was seen at the opening of *Lohengrin* at the Opera House.'

'Better keep an eye on him.'

Lucy took to her new life without hesitation. She relished above all the constant tours of inspection – to the manufacturers of the rusks, scattered about the country, to the little ancient town of Gruyère for the cheese contracts, to the great Swiss chocolate firms where she was invariably presented with five kilos of the best. These gifts, which did not have to be returned as in India, made her think guiltily of schoolfriends suffering chocolate privation at home. The most exciting visits were at the mountain resorts to arrange accommodation for further sick and wounded, more courses in technical training and to inspect the existing camps.

Once Arthur took Lucy with him to meet the prisoners' train from Germany. It arrived at Basle in the middle of the night. As they paced the platform in the icy darkness, they could hear in the distance the screaming and grinding of metal as the long train clanked slowly over the bridge spanning the Rhine that separated neutral from enemy land – a land that had run out of fat and grease for its rolling stock. When the appalling cacophony died in a final exhalation of steam from the engine, there was silence. Heads appeared at the windows. They wore dazed expressions and stared as if unable to understand that their long ordeal was at an end. Soon men were hanging out of the train windows, their arms dangling or feebly waving, still silent. Lucy, who had expected a jubilant cheer, stood disquieted. The station master was unlocking the compartments. Arthur was beckoning to his staff of nurses and orderlies. The prisoners, catching sight of the Red Cross emblem, raised a tentative cheer. Some hardier spirits further along the train started 'Tipperary'. Lucy burst into tears.

'You'd better go to bed now,' Arthur said sternly. 'You're not qualified to deal with these anyway.'

'Oh Father, I can carry cups of tea . . .'

'Then stop crying and get out of the way. Stretcher cases last!'

'How's the German going with the Herr Professor?'

'Quite well, I think. You couldn't call it a *pretty* language.'

'I don't know. It's got some fine open vowel sounds for singing. Anyway, it's going to be very useful to you in the post-war world. Would you like another driving lesson now?'

'*Rather!*'

'I can spare you exactly' – he studied his watch – 'thirty-five minutes. Get your things on.'

Arthur was teaching Lucy to drive the huge office car which he habitually drove – rather dashingly – with the driver (a professional chauffeur) sitting depressed and bored in the back. He nosed his way through the narrow clock-tower gate and made for the open country.

'I should hope you're getting pretty adept at filing by now, dear girl.'

'I'm quicker than Miss Watson, I think. I feel as if I *know* half these prisoners. I love getting the postcards. There's a captain in Karlsruhe this morning who writes: "I did ask for bread and ye did send me a stone!" I imagine him as – '

'Damn and blast!' Arthur exclaimed. 'Some careless fool forgot to enclose the instructions . . . what's one to do with such people? If I could find out who it was, I'd dock them a month's pay. Damned disgraceful inefficiency.'

'Oh do watch out! You nearly had that hen.'

'Not I! I couldn't get one of those if I tried. Now we'll change places. I must remind you to assume that everyone on the road is half-blind, deaf and drunk. Please remember to let in the clutch gently, smoothly. Keep your eyes on the road, dear girl. I don't want any comments on the view.'

The work increased alarmingly as the number of prisoners soared after the March breakthrough. Arthur's working hours now began at 4 a.m. As no shorthand-typist could be got to keep his hours, he started the day with a sheaf of papers in his bed, drafting letters in his neat flowing hand for Lucy to type – letters

144

stepping up production, engaging new firms, expanding in every field to meet the growing contingency. He decided that the regimental system of supply hitherto in existence, with the prisoners of any given unit scattered over different camps, was a great waste of time and material. The War Office agreed to a geographical system by which the camps were divided into two groups, Copenhagen supplying the north and Berne the south, Berne supplying twice as much as Copenhagen. Meanwhile the internment camps and training centres in Switzerland were increasing at a prodigious rate.

'I'm glad to see you're up to reading the newspaper in German.'

'I can't much. Why don't they have a sensible script – this gothic gives me the pip. Father, it says here there's a long-range cannon bombarding Paris every half-hour. It's called *Die dicke Bertha*. I wish it didn't have a funny name. D'you think they're going to take Paris?'

'Who knows? It's a bad business.'

'Isn't it terrible . . . Oh, do you think this is the beginning of the end?'

'Who can tell what's going to happen?'

'I don't feel like my German lesson tonight. I'm sure the Herr Professor is secretly crowing.'

'Nonsense, dear girl. He was through with the Fatherland long ago. All he asks is to live in peace in a neutral country.'

'But he is a German.'

'Not *echtdeutsch*.'

'He *is* German though.'

'And so were some of the pleasantest people I've known. You can't condemn the whole German race on account of the All-Highest and his War Lords. They're not all monsters. The Herr Professor is a decent enough old boy and you're lucky to have a good teacher. You must guard against this tendency to condemn out of hand everything German. You might as well go round kicking dachshunds. Go and get ready for dinner.'

'I couldn't eat any dinner . . .'

'Well, passing up dinner isn't going to help the Allied cause. Now, get yourself ready. I've just time for a ten – no, a nine-minute nap.'

145

The calamitous news that brought smiles to the faces of the enemy newspapermen served only to redouble Arthur's energies. It was naturally not possible to guess that Ludendorff had shot his bolt.

'I'm going on tour tomorrow, Lucy. Want to come?'

'Oh *yes!*'

'I'm starting a class for making hand-carpets at Gunten on the lake of Thun. Then a tailoring class at Meivingen. That new disease that baffled the repatriation board at Mürren last week, by the way – they've discovered the cause. It seems the men were drinking up to thirty or forty cups of black coffee a day – if you can call it coffee – to produce those symptoms. Silly asses, grumbling all day long to get home, when they're getting free what people pay big money for in peacetime. They don't know when they're well off. No sense . . . Of course, they do feel useless and out of it . . . poor devils. That's the root of the trouble. Well, I'm starting new training courses for the disabled at Seeburg – that's on Lake Lucerne. After that to Arosa, where I'm taking over a big new sanatorium for TB cases. On the way back, if we can possibly manage it, there's *Parsifal* in Zürich. It's a chance to hear some really fine artists who'd normally be in Berlin.'

On a blazing day in July, the news came that the French had scored a victory. The German army attacking near Rheims was hurled back across the Marne. The Allied war-communiqués habitually spoke of immense German losses. Arthur was sceptical, but not long after came the news of a great British tank victory, and this time Arthur was jubilant. After four years of ghastly deadlock it had seemed impossible to believe that the German armies would ever be driven back. Switzerland was full of rumours of trouble inside Germany – a mood of despair showing itself in civilian discontent . . . desertions from the army . . . In the hotel dining-room, the smiles were wiped from the faces of the enemy.

Arthur had his own troubles. It was obvious to him that the work involved in making up individual parcels and following the changing addresses of prisoners-of-war was becoming over-

146

whelming. He got the War Office to agree to the sending of unaddressed parcels (three kilos weekly instead of six kilos fortnightly) with a reserve supply sent to parent camps for prisoners-of-war in transit.

'Of course one can't predict an early end, but the enemy would appear to be on the run . . . here and there . . .' Arthur said cautiously. 'There's a lot to do though. I suppose I must have about 150,000 prisoners now where there were a mere 40,000 when I came. But Lucy, it's time to think of your future.'

'Well?'

'I take it you want to go to the university?'

'I think so. Yes.'

'Then you must start in October.'

'But I don't want to leave here before the end of it.'

'You must, dear girl. No sense in waiting for the following year when everywhere will be crowded with men returning from the forces and the men and women deflected from the war effort, on top of those who would be leaving school anyway. Now, I've got some papers here from the London School of Economics. It's a very interesting course and a degree in economics will be useful in all sorts of ways.'

'I don't want to be an economist!'

'Why not? You know nothing about it yet.'

'I'm sure that's one thing I don't want to be.'

'What do you want? What are you interested in?'

'English.'

'What for?'

'I don't know. I just am.'

'D'you want to spend your life teaching English in a school?'

'Er, no. I don't think I do. But I have two friends going to read English at Oxford. I want to learn Anglo-Saxon and Middle English . . .'

'What on earth for?'

'Because it's such exciting stuff. We had a smattering at school, enough to make my mouth water. I'll give you an example. Listen: "Bit his Bone-prison the Blood drank in torrents." Isn't that *gorgeous* Father? Shall I get my *Beowulf* and try to read you a few lines, translating as we go? . . .'

'Another time, dear girl. Lucy, I can't see any point at all in your spending three years studying dead languages, unless it's civilized ones – Greek and Latin. Anglo-Saxon doesn't equip you for anything – except teaching, and you don't show any marked enthusiasm for that profession. The post-war world is going to be full of opportunities for women in all sorts of spheres. With a thorough knowledge of economics, together with some history and modern languages, you ought to have a number of careers open to you. Besides, I fancy you'd find a women's college very restrictive after the kind of life you've led here. Now I want you to look through this syllabus. I must remind you that you were opposed to leaving school, but you don't regret it now.'

'I wouldn't have missed this for the world!'

'Well then, dear girl. I *may* be right again, you know . . .'

After many discussions, Arthur won.

The speed with which events succeeded one another took everyone by surprise. President Wilson's Fourteen Points reverberated to and fro. Each day brought new and astounding developments. Ludendorff was dismissed. The Germany fleet mutinied. The Kaiser finally abdicated. It was the end. The Armistice left men gaping. Arthur was still dazed when he received orders to proceed to Berlin to repatriate British prisoners-of-war in Germany and prepare for the Inter-Allied War Commission that was to follow him there. Exactly a week after the signing of the cease-fire, he landed at the Tempelhof aerodrome (together with his counterpart in Copenhagen), and thus became the first Englishman to fly to Berlin after the war.

21

From his suite at the Adlon, Arthur looked out at the famous linden trees and the Brandenburger Tor beyond. The luxury of the Schweizerhof paled beside the almost Wagnerian grandeur of the Adlon. He had a splendid sitting-room, while from his bed he could press a button that opened the bedroom door and a door in the vestibule beyond, so that a trolley laden with dinner could be wheeled to the bedside – the very thing for a man afflicted with fatigue poisons. It was rather a waste really as the worm continued to leave him alone. Food was abundant and, apart from the ersatz coffee, excellent, after four years of war and a stringent blockade. This was to impress visiting industrialists from neutral countries and international journalists, and for war profiteers. In the streets, particularly in the early morning when Arthur took his constitutional, it was not at all the same. He could not help observing the haggard looks (resulting from a diet of turnip and potato) and the threadbare clothes of the *Lumpenproletariat* – the women and old men who seemed to make up the greater part of the population, as they shuffled noisily along in cracked shoes soled with wood and even scraps of tin. The fearful screaming and clanking of the worn-out tramcars reminded him of the prisoners' train. The men were few and if not old had the furtive air of deserters on the run. Clearly the *Herrenvolk* were in very low water.

149

Arthur's office was in the Wilhelmstrasse in the British Embassy, which had been taken care of by the Netherlands Government throughout the duration. Here he installed himself without delay with the head of the German Red Cross willing and eager to place his staff at his disposal and the *Kriegsministerium* only too delighted to hand over all responsibility for the prisoners-of-war and to transfer to him direct telephone communication with all camps. They lost no time in placing a motor car and an aeroplane at his disposal and providing him with a number of impressive permits authorizing him to receive preferential treatment in every imaginable direction.

It was quiet in Berlin but, while the capital seemed stupefied by shock, indescribable confusion prevailed in the country. The Communist revolution, which had started mildly enough in the fleet, spread rapidly to most provincial cities. These uprisings, basing themselves on the Russian model, set up Workers' Councils (or Soldiers' and Sailors' Councils) whose resentment was directed more against the officer class than against the capitalists. At the same time, so great was their habit of obedience, the Soldiers' Councils, for example, agreed to restrict themselves to welfare while the German war machine carried on. Interested as he was in theory with revolutionary experiments, Arthur was glad not to have to deal with inexperienced revolutionaries. It was, in any case, more of a collapse than a revolution.

The collapse of the transport system was the chief difficulty in moving the men from the camps. Armed with his permits, Arthur commandeered rolling stock that would scarcely roll, coal from unsuspected stocks, army lorries and their petrol, food from his own stockpiles sent from Switzerland and set off on a round of the camps. These he visited mostly by aeroplane, having first managed to telephone instructions as from the German War Office regarding the transfers of men, instructions that met with implicit obedience and were conveyed with the utmost dispatch. In the general chaos, the War Office telephones continued to function.

The camps ranged from Ruhleben (the trotting-horse race course just outside Berlin, where 4,000 prisoners were kept chiefly in wooden horse-boxes – six to a box eleven feet square) to the distant camps in Silesia where conditions were always bad and often terrible and the *Arbeitskommandos* toiled in the salt mines. The prisoners were assembled in special reception camps where they were fed, bathed, clothed, given some pay, and, after usually no more than twenty-four hours, evacuated by the Baltic and later the North Sea ports, where the Royal Navy awaited them. This immense undertaking was complicated by the fact that some commandants at the news of the Armistice had indiscriminately let loose many thousands of prisoners, who ranged the country trying to fend for themselves. In addition, there were the special arrangements to be made for the sick and the badly wounded.

The huge operation went forward smoothly in the face of all difficulties, and by 5 December, less than a month after the cease-fire, the last British prisoners-of-war (apart from the stragglers and missing) left Germany. Arthur had reached the peak of his power.

After the peak, the fall . . .

He was at the big reception camp at Karlsruhe. The bulk supplies of food had, owing to his forethought, arrived in the nick of time; the successful end of the whole operation was in sight. He was in high spirits. It was his habit to address the assembled men, bawling the final instructions through a megaphone.

'We have, as you know, taken some prisoners from each camp every week. Where the whole camp cannot be cleared at one trip, preference is given to those longest in captivity. As any camp is cleared, prisoners will be brought in from the *Arbeitskommandos* to fill the vacancies . . . Take provisions for one day longer than the train journey is expected to last, in case the train be delayed.'

'Go on! De-layed!' came from a cheerful interrupter.

'Such things have been known to happen,' Arthur continued blithely. 'Take plenty of warm clothing for the journey. We have the clothing . . .' His voice was drowned by shrill whistling and good-humoured comments.

'No one will be overlooked or left behind,' Arthur went on above the clamour. 'But I should like to warn you that unauthorized straggling will react to your own disadvantage.' As if he had said something exquisitely funny, there was a roar of laughter and applause. Arthur, encouraged, suddenly found him-

151

self improvising: 'In a very short time you will find yourselves at home.' The uproar halted him again. When he could make himself heard once more he resumed his oration. 'Home is a free country and you will be free men again. I want you to think about what that means. When you get back, you will find England in the throes of a general election. You will be free to vote. Some of your camps here have been subjected recently to a good deal of Bolshevist propaganda. We are well aware that Comrade Radek and other revolutionaries have been disseminating their propaganda in your camps. Don't be taken in. Some countries progress by revolution and violence. Russia and now Germany are having revolutions. Other countries believe in a gradual process of social reform. Think about these things as free men. If you want to see the dawn of a socialist England, then now's your chance. You are free to vote for Ramsay MacDonald – '

The crowd, which had been silent in some astonishment, broke into howls of protest. Arthur tried in vain to return to his theme-song of freedom, but it was impossible to get a hearing and he left the platform. Later that evening he reflected that he had made a mess of things, but, with his usual ability to ignore the disagreeable, he dismissed the episode with a shrug. Anyway, he was far too busy to waste time thinking about a speech that had gone wrong.

The speech, however, was reported unfavourably in high quarters in a garbled version. A few days later the British general on the Inter-Allied War Commission sent for him: 'What's all this, Boyne? You've been telling the men to go home and vote Labour, what!'

'That's not quite what I said.'

'Vote for Ramsay MacDonald you're reported as having said.'

'I was trying to tell them not to be taken in by Bolshevist propaganda, but to vote as free men – Labour, if they felt like it. At least, that's what I meant to say.'

'I see. Rather uncalled for, what?'

'Quite,' Arthur agreed. 'Much better not to have spoken at all.'

'Much.'

'Well, I expect you won't be wanting me any more, general. The job's finished anyway, except for the stragglers and the stores. And there's still a lot to do in tracing the missing . . .'

152

Unquestionably Arthur was disgraced, but his services were far too valuable to be dispensed with, even though he had fallen from grace at home. The British repatriation was from the start carried out so successfully that the German government had requested other nations for similar missions and Arthur was transferred to the repatriation of the French, the Romanians, the Italians and the Russians successively.

The French general in charge of the Inter-Allied Commission was a man after Arthur's heart. He enthusiastically took over Arthur's well-rehearsed organization for the repatriation of his own prisoners. The chief difficulty, apart from the enormous numbers, was the absence of transport to the west. In an agony of impatience to get home, and with customary French independence, the prisoners trekked across Germany in their thousands, ragged and starving, to reach the starving Rhineland, beyond which lay devastation. '*Le pire*,' remarked General Dupont, '*est la liberté absolue dont disposent les prisonniers de se promener en Allemagne*.' But the problem was not insuperable, and one way and another the French got home.

The repatriation of the Italians and Romanians presented difficulties of other kinds, such as the freezing of the Danube and the troubles in Hungary, but it was the Russians whose problems seemed wholly insoluble.

The revolution, however, had meanwhile spread to Berlin. The turbulent atmosphere had become practically a state of civil war. On Christmas Eve the capital awoke to the sound of cannon fire. Sailors quartered in the Marstall (the Imperial Stables) were being shelled on government orders by the soldiers quartered in the Palace opposite. Fearful days had begun. The multiplicity of parties, the absence or incompetence of the leaders and a lack of cohesion in the government added to the complexities of the revolution.

Arthur had enjoyed walking to and from his office in the Embassy. He now found himself held up almost daily by mammoth demonstrations as the Communists of the Spartacus League and the National Socialists denounced each other's terrorism. He learned to avoid passing the newspaper offices as the Spartacists

153

were in the habit of seizing them, mounting their guns on the roof-tops and raking the streets below. Arthur had some narrow escapes, and on one occasion just missed being trampled down by some rather unsavoury Spartacist supporters who rejoiced in the name of the Deserters' Union. Everyone lived in fear of a *putsch*, and it was all very hampering. Driving now to his office, Arthur took his short walks in the Tiergarten, pausing to stare with interest and often with admiration at the great marble groups that were the ex-Kaiser's contribution to *kultur*. The Siegesallée, with its double line of heroes, was a source of amusement, but at the same time he was impressed. After the singularly brutal murders of the Spartacist leaders, Liebknecht and Rosa Luxemburg, in the Tiergarten, Arthur avoided the place. What with the frequent street fighting and the daily bestialities reported from both sides, Berlin was not a pleasant place. Arthur was glad to get down to the problem of the Russians.

These unfortunates, whose number far exceeded any other nationality, had had nothing done for them since the signing of the treaty of Brest-Litovsk. That they were starving was to be expected for they were unpopular with the Germans and somewhat feared after the November uprisings on the Bolshevik pattern. Their remnants of clothing were so tattered as to be funny, if not already so tragic. They were quite literally dying of homesickness. The losses were great before the survivors were herded into the newly vacated camps and fed principally on accumulated Red Cross stores. Arthur was visiting the Russian camps with General Dupont, who was clearly moved by what he saw. '*La détresse épouvantable de ces malheureux . . . C'est absolument navrant . . .*' When Arthur reminded the general of the pitiful plight of some of the French prisoners earlier on, the old man replied: '*Ils avaient l'avantage d'exister.*'

What to do with the Russians? Their overmastering desire to get home took no stock of the fate that might await them, if indeed a home remained. In the meantime, no one would have them at any price: Poland and Romania refused transport, Germany washed its hand by claiming it would have repatriated them long ago if the Allies hadn't won the war, so that they were now Allied responsibility. They had, indeed, been sending them east and throwing them at the Bolshevists, who executed them (as Tsarists) without mercy. Meantime the more reactionary Russian generals clamoured to be armed to return to fight bolshevism. '*Il ne faut pas s'en mêler*,' said the General gloomily.

Arthur had a scheme for the repatriation of the Russians down the Danube and by ship to Odessa. He was absorbed in this complicated project and seemed to be making progress when the revolution broke out in Hungary. At the same time came the news of his recall. He was never to know the fate of the Russians.

Within a few days he had packed up and handed over to his successor. He left Germany with few regrets, having tasted power and authority for the last time. The future held only the life of a retired civil servant, a family man.

22

Isabelle and the younger children were due to arrive in England in the middle of May. Arthur took a room at the Strand Palace. It was, by his own vigorous standards, within easy walking distance of his office in Victoria. Without any thought of renewing contacts with old friends or making new acquaintances, he went to earth like a rabbit to its burrow. He had no interest in the work he was doing, checking over the winding up of the Swiss department and disposing of stores, and realized vaguely (without giving the matter much thought) that he was looked at askance at headquarters since the episode at Karlsruhe. In consequence he was often bored. From that it was but a short step to a return of the worm.

Though not given to brooding, he could not fail to see that the approaching family reunion spelled trouble. Even if Isabelle were now prepared for what he saw as a friendly and reasonable relationship – a joint enterprise to be devoted chiefly to the bringing up of the children – there remained the burning question of accommodation. With every ex-serviceman demanding a home, and homes in desperately short supply (and at exalted prices), what to do for a family that totalled seven? He had managed to rent by a roundabout method a small suburban villa in a decayed district for a few weeks (Isabelle wasn't going to like it) as a base from which to start house-hunting operations.

Meanwhile, Mrs Boyne had required an operation. Nursing-home fees were heavy and the visits to his mother depressed him. Lucy was occupied at college: Edmund away at school. 'It's a bad patch,' Arthur said to himself, 'mustn't grumble, as Dusty used to say. If only I didn't feel so devilish tired. Fact is, I'm getting old. And I'm a sick man, though nobody seems to realize it.' It was in this self-pitying mood that he set out to face the ordeal of reunion with Isabelle.

The ship docked at Tilbury. As they approached the squalid purlieus of Liverpool Street, Isabelle sat, her eyes shining with unshed tears, engaged as was her wont in reliving the past. She saw herself as a bride going out to India, clothed in dewy inno-cence, a lamb to the slaughter. That was the beginning of the long road that had led her to – this. Now she remembered every detail of the fur-trimmed travelling coat she had worn; the matching muff her mother had given her as a parting present (diverse insects in India had soon accounted for that); her mother's attire – the dear mother that she had never seen again because of Arthur's senseless quarrel. The shining eyes were brimful now and ready to overflow. The thought of her mother was guaranteed to bring on a fit of weeping.

'This must be it. Mother, look! We're there!' Diana exclaimed. The facile tears stopped and Isabelle braced herself to meet her husband.

Lucy had taken the day off from college. After due considera-tion, she had decided to doll herself up to kill. The day being fine and warm, she wore a rather low-cut summer frock, very high heels, a lavish amount of lipstick and the conspicuous hair was coiled beneath a floppy transparent hat, better suited for Ascot or Henley. Isabelle stared, appalled by this butterfly that had emerged from the remembered freckled chrysalis. The trans-formation was so disturbing that it served to distract her full attention from the fact that Arthur had not taken the day off to instal her in the suburban house (pleading pressure of work); and, on arrival there, the further fact that he had already secured for himself the smallest bedroom farthest removed from the principal one, a circumstance reported to her by the grim-faced woman who 'went with' the house and corroborated by the presence of a number of books with distasteful titles: *The History of Trade Unionism*; *Das Kapital*. His old friend *The Age of Reason* . . .

Isabelle looked at them with disgust. She could not have been more affronted to come upon a shelf of pornography. Less! That she should be thrown over for *Practical Profit-Sharing as a Cure for Industrial Unrest*, and then this way of reserving his place like a seat on a train; but when at suppertime he arrived, wearing his worried-dog expression and obviously exhausted by the suburban rush-hour battle, she postponed the attack. Later, when Lucy was upstairs seeing to the bedtime preparations of her new brother and sisters (the six intervening years had made strangers of them all), Isabelle spoke of her daughter.

'It was such a shock, Arthur, seeing her looking like that! I couldn't believe it was the little schoolgirl I remember – '

'It wasn't. I mean they grow up. It's a long time.'

'I don't like the way she looks. She doesn't look like a lady, Arthur. She doesn't look quite – well, quite respectable. Don't you mind seeing your daughter with all that rouge on her lips!'

'I mind when it comes off on me.'

'And those ridiculous heels!'

'Mm, yes. I never have seen the point of women's shoes – except in China where malforming the foot had a social value . . . Lucy'll probably end up in surgical boots – still, they're her feet.'

'I don't approve.'

'The only thing I can't seem to get used to is for a respectable young woman to use scent. Ah well, one must learn to move with the times.'

'Anyway, Eddie won't have changed.'

'Won't he? He's six feet tall! Towers over me now.'

'The darling boy! Can I go down and see him at his half-term? Oh, how can I leave the others – '

'That'll be all right. From next week on I'll be here. I'm leaving the Red Cross at the end of the week. My job's finished.'

'Arthur, we've got to get out of this *horrid* little house as soon as possible. It's an appalling district. There's no park anywhere near for the children.'

'I know it isn't very nice. It's all I could get. I wrote you of the difficulties. The hotels are all full with people coming back to England.'

'I thought you'd have a list of houses ready for me to look at.'

'Sorry dear. It's no use my house-hunting. You know your requirements. You're the one who's going to run the home.'

'So the whole responsibility falls on me.' As Arthur had nothing to add, Isabelle continued: 'Well, one thing I know, we're not staying here long. That woman, Mrs Turner, is a beast. We'd hardly set foot in the place before she was telling the children not to kick the paint on the stairs and not to pick the flowers in the garden. They can't stand her. And I can't stand this place.'

From this inauspicious start, worse was to follow. Isabelle set forth on a series of expeditions to Berkhamstead, Bedford, Cheltenham – places renowned for their schools – and returned exhausted and woefully depressed. There were no houses to rent and they would be compelled to buy. But the properties for sale were generally unsuitable and invariably offered at exorbitant prices. ('If you mention the law of supply and demand again, Arthur, I· shall scream!') The schools had long waiting-lists. Isabelle's nerves were shot to pieces by insomnia. The children of the neighbourhood proved unfriendly to the point of throwing stones. Arthur had recourse to his bed and a bad time was had by all.

Someone suggested the Channel Islands as possessing all the answers: schools, a milder climate and a trifling income tax. Isabelle hastened over to Jersey. Here, after many fruitless visits to unsuitable dwellings, just as despair was settling in, she came upon a house that seemed to fulfil all the requirements. All except the price, which was out of all reason. She telegraphed Arthur to come at once, and he arranged to cross over for the weekend.

'I wish I could tell your mother to go ahead. I trust her judgement,' Arthur said to Lucy.

'*You* just don't want to go.'

'I don't. All I need is a room with a bed in it.'

'Well, I could do with a bit more than that. Let's have a decent home while we're about it. Can we afford the price of this one?'

'No. But we'll have to manage it somehow. I'll make an offer . . . Buy on mortgage . . . I'm taking the night boat, so I must get off now. Lucy, I trust you to look after the children properly?'

'Of course. Come on upstairs, you kids. Wash behind the ears and I'll tell you a bedtime story.'

The children were playing with Arthur's medals: French, Italian, Romanian. The Order of St Sava, a particularly resplendent decoration, had arrived that morning. His own country had not recognized his services. A few ill-chosen remarks had probably come between him and a knighthood. Isabelle would have liked that. Not that he cared. He didn't believe in the bestowing of favours. Still, it was funny the way things happened . . .

The house had no architectural merit. Originally two houses, it had a connecting link, the dining-room – a large room with french windows on the garden side and backed by a long, dark passage, very useful for sliding in and greatly appreciated later by the dog for his own purposes when the weather discouraged him from going out. There was a belvedere and two conservatories, in one of which water flowed through a stone basin surrounded by maiden-hair fern. The two upper floors were amply supplied with bedrooms. There was one rather shabby bathroom to serve all. A range of outbuildings included some stabling, a wash-house, fowl-houses, and numerous sheds. While the house itself was shoddy, even ricketty, in respect of doors and windows (which unless securely wedged would carry on a cannonade throughout the gales to which the island was subject), and the surrounding district was uninteresting, the garden was a delight. It contained lawns and flower-beds, a rose pergola, a line of pollarded limes, a stone eagle and some urns, a vegetable and fruit section, a large vinery and other glass-houses given over to nectarines, melons, tomatoes, carnations and chrysanthemums. Though the house had been empty for a year, the garden had been kept up. Secure behind the privacy of its walls, and not so large as to become burdensome, it was a miniature representation of a great garden. In spite of himself Arthur was captivated.

He stood blinking in the sunlight that invaded the large, empty, musty-smelling drawing-room, running his thumb noisily over the stubble on his chin (for the crossing had been too rough for safe shaving). If only he had some money handy – well, no use thinking about that now . . .

'We'll have it,' he said. 'I'd better go to the agents and make an offer straight away. They'll be shutting I expect on a Saturday – '

Isabelle, overcome with relief, precipitated herself on him in an abandonment of joy.

'Don't, dear girl,' he said, disengaging himself from her embrace. 'It's my liver. I can't stand any pressure on it.'

Isabelle shrank back as if from a blow. He knew that he had wounded her. His terror of any step that might lead to a resumption of closer relations was so great that positively he could not act differently. In his embarrassment he continued to administer a cold douche to prevent a scene of affectionate rejoicing.

'. . . have to buy on mortgage . . . you won't be able to spend much on decoration . . . it's going to need a lot of furniture too . . . have to make do as best you can . . .'

When he had gone, Isabelle stood sobbing. There was nothing to sit on.

In a month the house was ready for occupation, with two Breton servants engaged as staff.

The Boynes had a home at last.

23

All went rather well at first. Arthur became a keen gardener. Isabelle was very busy with the new ménage. The children, unrestrained and on the rowdy side (particularly at mealtimes other than breakfast time), enjoyed all that came their way. In the summer holidays, they set forth daily on bicycles to explore the wild north coast with friends old and new. Lucy and Edmund had friends to stay. Edmund and Dickie in particular became adept at high diving. It was an uproarious summer. Isabelle's ingenuous belief that her children were ignorant of the emotional tension between their parents might have been true of those first happy months. After the extreme depression they had just known, they were as if drunk with the joy of liberation.

In the autumn, Edmund went to Cambridge, Lucy returned to college and Diana was sent to the expensive boarding school that Lucy had been to. The two youngest, money being short, were sent to the local schools of which the island was proud. The big house seemed strangely empty as winter stretched before them, punctuated by horrible gales. When the weather was bad and gardening was no longer an agreeable pastime, Arthur, afflicted by ennui, resorted to his usual refuge. He had selected a bedroom in the first house, protected by the presence of the Tinies who occupied adjoining rooms. Lucy and Edmund and any visitors slept in the second house, approached by a separate staircase. Isabelle was over the dining-room in the connecting portion. Here her light could be seen burning in the small hours. In Canada, she had read Havelock Ellis and Marie Stopes with disturbing results. Her mind was obsessed with the problems of sexual maladjustment. She went back continuously over her past life in which she saw herself as the victim of cruel ill-usage, an innocent sacrificed to her husband's egoism and insensitiveness. Sleeping-pills added to her emotional confusion.

Arthur on the other hand refused to think back at all. He had recognized that his life had fallen into disharmony, had failed at several points. Things had gone wrong – sometimes through his own fault. *Tant pis.* He would not consider it further. That was over and done with.

His sex-life (the distasteful term was Isabelle's) was as extinct as the dinosaur, as dead as the dodo. Here he was: a man whose constitution was seriously impaired by years in India, half-dead with tropical diseases, one foot in the grave, asking only to be allowed to spend the evening of his life in peace.

In the sphere of illness alone was he ready for a remembrance of things past. Epidemics of cholera, smallpox and bubonic plague were vividly recalled and began to feature largely in his conversation. He became the true devotee of sickness, interested in every type of ailment, other people's as well as his own. He began to collect the rarer and more distressing forms from a medical dictionary, as a man might collect *objets d'art*.

From time to time doctors were summoned to his bedside. After a searching examination, during which Arthur propounded his views on tropical diseases, they usually made suggestions as to medicine, diets and so forth. Arthur tried diets ranging from starvation to underdone steaks or Bulgarian curds. After a few weeks of subsisting almost exclusively on the recommended food, he would give it up as no good to him. All medicines, he claimed, disagreed with him after the first week. The doctor, baffled, would then suggest cutting out (or at least cutting down) smoking. At that point Arthur changed his doctor.

There were days when he pottered in one of his greenhouses. On other days he lay in bed, offering a stubborn, passive resistance to the atmosphere of domestic explosion that threatened

163

whenever Isabelle's corroding resentment found outlet in violent anger.

When the children returned from the mainland for the Christmas festivities, the house became noisy and lively again, as in the summer. On the last evening Arthur divulged to his two eldest, in separate farewell scenes, that he was a dying man. The next morning early they left the house with stricken hearts. On the boat deck of the wretchedly inadequate-looking ship that was to take them to England, they stood spiritless in the thin driving rain, gazing through their tears at the old fortress which screened their house from view. Not far behind those massive walls their father lay dying.

'I *can't* get over it,' Lucy said in a choking voice. 'I can't believe he's there now, this minute, as we left him, and when we come back perhaps he won't be there any more . . .'

'It's been so terribly sudden,' Edmund said. 'We haven't had time to get used to it. After all, only last summer he was working away in the garden.'

'I know . . .'

'Of course he was ill before, during the house-hunting.'

'He wasn't ever in Switzerland. I can't bear it . . .' Lucy wept aloud.

'We've got to bear it,' Edmund said manfully. 'We've got to think of Mother.'

'I *can't* . . . Oh . . .'

'I say, pull yourself together. There's nothing we can do but try to help when the time comes.'

'To think we've only just settled into a new house. I suppose we shall have to move out ? . . .

'Time enough for that when the time comes.'

'Oh Eddie, don't you wish you'd always done everything he wanted, all our lives – '

'Come on down. It won't help anyone to get washed overboard.'

The ship passed the harbour wall and gave a sudden lurch as she struck the stormy sea raging outside that hurled itself in flying spray against the granite rocks, submerged at one moment and revealed the next in their treacherous, shiny blackness and redness. It was going to be a rough crossing.

At Easter, however, Lucy's forebodings were not realized, for there was their father to meet them on the quay. Hatless in the spring sunshine, he strode up and down with his jaunty step looking, as always, unbelievably young for his years.

'*Oh Father!*'

'Steady, dear girl. How are you, my boy? Had a good term? I want to hear all about everything.'

'But *Father*, you're *better!*'

'It's wonderful to see you up!'

'You didn't *say* you were better!'

'What's done it?'

'I thought you were more or less bedridden,' Lucy concluded.

'So I am,' Arthur answered. He wasn't going to admit to being better ⁓ like that, baldly and blatantly. That was a great deal further than he was prepared to go. Besides, only this morning, he had felt extremely seedy on waking. 'For the moment, I am a shade better,' he qualified. 'I'm a broken-down wreck with one foot in the grave – as you know. But I have my ups and downs. This is one of my rare better moments. Liable to collapse at any time, though . . . Is that all your luggage? Taxi!'

The summer was a repetition of the previous one, but better and longer. There was a succession of visitors, bathing picnics, moonlight expeditions and so on . . . Arthur slaved like a navvy in the garden. His enthusiasm for this pursuit was unbounded. He had taken over nearly the whole of the work. The gardener only came now for heavy digging. Arthur's grapes, Comice pears and chrysanthemums were unrivalled. Visitors on their way to the beach paused to admire the superb displays in the front conservatory. When not on the subject of his health, he was in good spirits. He had also discovered P. G. Wodehouse.

The dear brother, Bertie, was a frequent visitor, beloved by all the children for his light-hearted ways. Isabelle's energies were chiefly devoted to the task of running the expanded household. Though she was often nervy and somewhat exacting as a hostess, things went well enough. But the winter lay ahead, approaching nearer as each glorious summer's day went by. She knew that she could not face another winter there. Something had to be done.

In Canada, Isabelle had been invited one day to speak at a women's luncheon club. It had gone very well. Innumerable societies, thirsting for knowledge and eager to welcome a visiting stranger, had invited her to speak. She found that she had quite a talent for public speaking and prepared a number of subjects ranging from 'The Position of Women in India' to 'Samuel Pepys' and 'City Churches'. She now added 'Wartime Canada' to her list and approached the Women's Institutes for a lecture tour. Their acceptance was gratifying. Now, with an autumn tour and a spring tour to take her away from home, and innumerable outside activities in Jersey itself (for by this time she was an ardent committee woman and devoted much energy to the League of Nations Union, holidays for Welsh miners and other rewarding work), it was possible to survive the winter months. In her absences, Arthur lay in his bed unhindered, bestirring himself now and then to lend a hand with the youngest children's homework, or reading aloud to them if they were on their own. The second winter was tolerable by comparison with the first.

It was their third summer in Jersey. Lucy had finished at the university and was taking up a job abroad in the autumn. Edmund had another year at Cambridge. Lucy got home a week before her brother, who had been climbing in the Lake District. The morning of his arrival found her at the harbour. Arthur couldn't spare time off from his before-breakfast labours in the garden.

'Hullo! It must have been a decent crossing for once.'

'Wonderful! What's the form?'

'Much as usual.'

'Fatigue poisons active?'

'Very. In the intervals of toil that no union would allow.

Dockers and stevedores don't get through the sheer physical labour that Father does.'

'He's the tough and wiry sort.'

'You know, Edmund, it's jolly difficult to feel sympathetic towards hypochondria. I suppose it's because one feels one's being deceived. I'll never forget how he harrowed me. I haven't forgiven him that yet.'

'All the same you should.'

'What?'

'Forgive and feel sympathy.'

'Well, one doesn't, when one's been had for a fool. Nobody likes being had.'

'I say you should, though. It's an illness. A different sort, but illness all the same. How's Mother making out?'

'Jumpy as hell. She'll be all right with you, of course. Dickie and I get it in the neck. I'm glad I'm off soon. Apart from his daftness, I get on with Father.'

'That's a relief to me.'

'Seriously though, why do our parents have to be such crackpots?'

'I don't think they're much different from anybody else's.'

'Rot! You know jolly well they are!'

'I don't think so. You don't know enough about other parents.'

'Just show me a pair of parents as cracked as ours!'

'All parents are difficult, some I dare say much more than ours. And most of the time they're saying the same thing about their children. It's probably only a question of difference in age.'

'Talking of age,' Lucy said, 'now listen. Yesterday, when Mother was at a committee meeting, I borrowed a book from her room. It's called *Married Love*.'

'It's no good to you. You're not married.'

'Listen, ass. It's by a female doctor called Marie Stopes. Well, as far as I could see, the big idea is that you don't just sleep together when you're young and to have children, but go on doing it for fun into extreme old age. She says in it she knew a Scotsman of seventy-five who had satisfactory marital relations with his old wife of seventy and was still going strong. And another of about ninety – yes, ninety!'

'Shut up, Lucy!'

'It's a fact. And if you don't believe me, go and pinch it and read for yourself. You must agree it's a bit off.'

'What's all this to do with Mother?'

'It's obvious, isn't it? If you know a man by his books . . . Oh I do wish our parents were a *little* more normal. Not *quite* so potty . . . By the way, Father's getting a car! That ought to help keep him out of bed.'

'Not enough roads on the island for that.'

Isabelle's chronic insomnia was the household scourge. As the day wore on her condition generally improved, but in the early morning she was dangerous to approach. As she and Arthur preserved the early-morning habits acquired in India, her first encounter of the day was usually with him. At the sound of the gong, one or other of the children would run to summon him from the garden, if it were fine weather, or waylay him in his room. His simple statement: 'Your mother's had a bad night,' with all its sinister implications, was what they most dreaded to hear. With meaning glances, the information was broadcast to the assembled brothers and sisters. The worse Isabelle felt, the more she assumed a tone of desperate brightness. Talkative at all times, her volubility increased under nervous strain. (She always tended to dismiss a silent person, who might be speechless from shyness or, alternatively, immersed in deep thought, as a fool.) After a few opening questions aimed at establishing how each member of the family proposed to spend the day, she would launch forth on a dissertation. Soviet Russia was a favourite topic for a long time. She was infatuated with all things Russian – their abolition of religion, their experiment with free love, their state-run nurseries, farms, cooperative enterprises, broad backs, ready smiles, square jaws and fine teeth – their absolute superiority, in fact.

'If we have Russia again for breakfast,' Lucy declared vehemently, 'I shall *do* something!' But she didn't. Only the younger son dared raise his voice in protest, and then not really audibly, for breakfast was Isabelle's undisputed sphere. Arthur was generally bending over backwards to avoid trouble and no one dared interrupt the flow of that keen, hard, terrible talkativeness, that painful brightness.

The younger son had a somewhat startling originality of mind, which gave rise to a display of eccentricity wholly inexcusable in the young, in Isabelle's opinion. In a brief period of tee-totalism, he had to have a special trifle prepared without sherry, even a special salad without vinegar. Like many another ex-tremist, he tended to vere from pole to pole. There were scan-dalous happenings from time to time – stink-bombs in the headmaster's study; nocturnal breaking-in to neighbouring houses for the apparently innocent purpose of rearranging the drawing-room furniture; and the unaccountable trail of a pair of black footsteps across the newly-painted ceiling of an hotel lounge. (As the ciling was high and far out of reach, this remarkable feat assumed the nature of the miraculous.) It was widely known who was the perpetrator of the outrages: to pin the guilt was another matter. Dickie denied all knowledge with a look of pained inno-cence. His expression ranged from a lowering scowl to a smile as mysterious as the Gioconda's. Isabelle found his antics in-supportable. There came an occasion when she declared flatly to Arthur with her usual intransigence: 'Either Richard leaves this house or I do!' Arthur, looking cornered, lit his pipe to gain time; then, blowing out a cloud of smoke, announced slowly: 'I'm afraid it can't be Richard, dear. He's not yet fifteen . . .'

'So you've decided to take his part against me!'

'On the contrary, I propose to give him a severe talking-to – '

'But you're prepared to turn your own wife out of the house!'

'If you go, it will not be on my initiative. But I hope you'll reconsider the matter.'

It was the best she could get out of him. He was no earthly use to her – as usual.

Isabelle flattered herself on her sense of justice. It was justice for the poor, the underprivileged, the suffering cart-horse, the chained dog that she felt with a burning zeal. She was a born fighter with the ceaseless nervous energy of a child. Had she been in a position to devote herself to a crusade – votes for women, the abolition of capital punishment or cruelty to animals – she would have been in the vanguard, the first to be chained to the railings, forcibly fed or thrown in the cells. As it was, she had nothing on which to grind her teeth. So she took it out on her family. Her sense of justice did not extend to her children. Though she felt a sense of duty towards all, indiscriminately, which showed itself in times of illness, she had marked favourites among them. Edmund, the beloved elder son, and Diana, the vivacious, pretty, companionable daughter who had never left her side in the formative years, were the favourites. Lucy and Dickie incurred her frequent displeasure. Little Emmi, who went her own curious way devoted to animals (and principally to that noble animal the horse), came a long way behind the pair that could do no wrong but ahead of the black sheep.

In Canada Isabelle had been persuaded to join the local theosophical society. She actually thought for a time that she had found consolation. The leading theosophists themselves, when seen on English ground (for they visited England soon after her return), had been a source of disillusion. Isabelle had, however, been carried away by it all and had stuffed theosophy, as she later stuffed Russia, down her children's throats. As she never admitted her error or acknowledged her faults, she merely dropped the subject in question when her infatuation wore off, hoping no one would notice. When Arthur was indiscreet enough to rag her about it, there was trouble. There was no doubt that, in her short time as a believer, she had hoped to approach him through this channel. The theory of reincarnation had seemed to her to account for a number of Arthur's more unsuitable features. Her favourite book at the time bore the title *In Tune with the Infinite*. Arthur called it 'In Gear with the Absolute', flipped over the pages, humming lightheartedly, and returned it with thanks within the hour.

'You've not had time to read it.'

'I've read all I need.'

'Arthur, why are you so blind to the things of the spirit? I see you enclosed in your materialism, as in a coffin. Imprisoned.'

Arthur attempted a couple of smoke-rings and said: 'I think undue importance is attached to human life anyway. Heaven forbid that one should be aware of more than one life.'

'*You* aren't. Only very rare people have that gift.'

'They may think they have, or they may be just humbugging, of course – I wouldn't know about that.'

'Why do you always have to bring fraud into it? One fraudulent medium wouldn't prove that spiritualism was all rubbish.'

Arthur decided not to be side-tracked. 'I can see,' he said, 'that it might be very comforting, if you were dying of cancer, or being tortured by the Inquisition, to console yourself with the idea you've got a good time coming in this world at the next incarnation, or in the next world, casting down your golden crown. But it's pure wishful thinking. We just don't like to think of ourselves as insignificant. That isn't to say that from the point of view of history a man mayn't leave his mark, for good or for bad. Some men are remembered longer than others, but, in the long run, all will be forgotten and the earth will return to primordial slime. The idea of personal survival, of a personal god engaged in supervising the welfare of each one of us, is highly ludicrous. It's the personal aspect that I object to in the Christian religion. And then, again, the whole idea of oblation and intercession is an Oriental notion that I personally find obnoxious.'

'Theosophy's different,' Isabelle intervened. 'It regards man as being body and spirit. The spirit lives on the astral plane – '

'I've been reading about your astral plane,' Arthur said, and chuckled reminiscently. '*A propos*, I should just like to make it plain that if I die shortly (as I well may), it's no use your trying to get in touch with me. I wish to state here and now that if any spirit comes along claiming to be Arthur Boyne, he's an imposter! I positively refuse to haunt you!'

'I wish you'd talk sensibly,' Isabelle snapped. 'You're so steeped in materialism, you can't understand the importance of the spirit, of mind over matter.'

'Mind over matter . . . M'yes. What I'd *really* like to see is a shipload of Christian Scientists in a rough sea . . . Don't misunderstand me, though, when I speak of the insignificance of individuals. I believe that man, while insignificant from the point of view of the cosmos, should be given a chance of leading a happy and useful life. That is why I'm interested in social experiments. Morality changes. Theories of conduct are constantly discredited. But what will make for the greatest

171

happiness of the greatest number is an ideal worth pursuing. The response to favourable circumstances must be greater than the response to unfavourable ones. You might say that's my religion.'

This noble and impersonal goal was apparently not inconsistent with a morbid interest in one's ailments, with a weighing of oneself and a taking of one's temperature – with, in short, an obsessional fear of dying. His horror of flies was so great that he would stand for long periods, poised with a fly-swatter in wait for the single house-fly that had escaped massacre. He waxed eloquent on their habits. He was deeply attached to the dog, but could not stand the friendly mongrel's exuberant displays of affection.

'Don't let him lick you! He's just been licking his fundament. Goodness only knows where his nose was prior to that! Don't let him lick you!'

For a time, Arthur found a winter occupation in translating foreign novels. He was a gifted linguist. With no ear for sound, he could nevertheless master a foreign language with ease. He had a real appreciation for rendering a foreigner's shades of thought into the equivalent English. As always, when committed to some particular work, he became absorbed in it and worked fast and furiously. Starting with a German ex-prisoner-of-war's experiences, he switched to a couple of Spanish novels, a couple of the Tharaud brothers' historical romances and then (in collaboration with Lucy in vacation time) a couple of volumes of Pirandello's short stories. All did very well, and it looked for a time as if he had found a suitable and congenial occupation for his retirement, especially since he could work very easily in his bed. But Lucy went abroad and he seemed to lose interest. What had been enjoyable became laborious. He dropped it and returned to his problems and his Wodehouse.

Einstein published his theory of relativity and Arthur was exhilarated for a week. It was as his excitement was subsiding that his brother-in-law came to stay.

Isabelle had become estranged from Archie after his disastrous marriage and was astonished to receive a letter from him proposing a visit. The letter was brief, suggesting that he would like to stay with his sister for two or three days and call on an old lady living in the island who had at one time been a friend of Mrs Burnett. Isabelle was pleased. For more than twenty years, her correspondence with her brother had been an exchange of Christmas cards without comment. She telegraphed a welcome, but it was with mixed feelings that she greeted the stranger who materialized, feelings that rapidly turned to dismay for the stranger was bald, strangely shrunken and almost stone deaf. He had a curiously furtive air and restless nervous movements. He made no comment on his surroundings and never smiled. Communication was difficult. He produced an old-fashioned ear-trumpet from his pocket, but did not care to use it, preferring to lip-read. This was a technique that Arthur and Isabelle had not mastered, and it was soon evident that Archie disliked being shouted at. He would catch perhaps one word of what was shouted, or an analogous word of different meaning, and set out on a wrong tack. He spoke in the curious booming voice of the deaf, loud and unmelodious.

Arthur had not bargained on a deaf brother-in-law and the fatigue poisons quickly took him in hand. When he had retired, Isabelle gazed at the stranger sitting at the other end of the sofa. For once she was silenced. She hoped that he kept early hours. The French travelling-clock on the chimney-piece chimed the half-hour. Suddenly she remembered that it had been Archie's wedding present to her. She pointed to it as the tears came into her eyes.

'Remember, Archie? It keeps perfect time after all those years in India.' He made no reply, but turned slowly to fix her with his curiously blank stare. 'The clock!' Isabelle screamed. 'Your clock!'

'Stopped?' The stranger slowly produced an old-fashioned gold half-hunter from his waistcoat pocket and checked the time. 'No, that's the right time,' he boomed.

Isabelle recognized the watch as having belonged to her father. Suddenly she saw again the remembered gesture with which her father drew it from his pocket, the seals that used to hang on the gold watchchain.

'Father's watch,' she said with a choking sob.

'Father's,' said the stranger. 'It still goes.' He put it back in his pocket.

At the far end of the room stood a fine boulle cabinet. Isabelle made her way to it across an assortment of tiger and panther skins, interspersed with carved Kashmir tables displaying Indian silver. She stood tapping on the cabinet. When she was sure that she had secured his attention, she returned to close range and said: 'Mother's cabinet. Remember? I suppose it's yours really. It was stored with my things. D'you want it?'

Archie said nothing.

'D'you want it?' Isabelle screamed. She made a gesture as if handing him something. He seemed to consider for a few moments.

'You'd better stick to it,' he said at last.

She resumed her seat in silence. Suddenly she rose again to get the little clock and held it in front of her brother. 'Your clock,' she tried once more. 'You gave it to us.'

Archie nodded without comment. She replaced it in silence, biting her lips to keep back the tears. The harsh voice behind her suddenly asked: 'Are you happy?'

It was the chance of a lifetime – to pour out the long story of her wretchedness, the agony of being married to a man who had thrown her over for his imaginary ailments, wrecking his career and her life by his criminal self-centredness, the chance to lay the burden of her aching heart before a beloved brother: but not this stranger. For where behind the insuperable physical barrier was the Archie who had shared her childhood and youth? She remained standing with her back to him, her arms spread along the mantelpiece, nodding her head in violent pantomime. When she turned round, grimacing miserably, he was looking away from her.

'Yes,' she shrieked. 'Of course.'

She did not repeat his question to him but went round behind the sofa and, resting a hand on his shoulder, addressed the ear for which the trumpet was designed.

'What about bed, Archie. You must be tired out.'

'I've written to her,' was the unexpected reply.

'What?'

'I've written to her to expect me to tea.'

'Oh, Mrs Rideout. I see. Let's go to bed Archie,' she said, mouthing the words carefully.

174

'Right, I'm ready,' Archie boomed with something approaching alacrity and followed her up the stairs.

At breakfast, Isabelle, ill after a sleepless night, noticed that her brother looked wretchedly ill himself. The effort of communication with him was beyond her usual breakfast-flow of speech. The two youngest children (the only ones at home) carried on a conversation of their own, while their uncle threw them curiously suspicious glances. One could guess that he was used to being shut out in his own home and resented it.

Dickie and Emmi left in haste to bicycle to their schools, and Arthur was about to beat a retreat, murmuring something about 'not feeling up to much this morning', when his brother-in-law boomed to him to remain where he was. He then divulged that, at a time of more or less intolerable friction in the early days of his marriage he had had an 'irrevocable clause' inserted in his will to the effect that his wife and issue were to be cut out of his will altogether if the children were brought up in the Roman church. This he had never dared to tell his wife. 'So if anything happened to me, it would go to you, Isabelle – what's left, there's not much. They wouldn't get a *sou*. D'you see? What would you do?'

'Do? Why give it back to them, of course!' Isabelle screeched. 'They're your family.'

'What would you do?' Archie was addressing himself to Arthur.

'I'd see they got it,' Arthur bawled. Then, taking a pencil and an old envelope from his pocket, he put it in writing and passed it across the table.

Archie nodded and seemed satisfied.

'But nothing's going to happen to you Archie! I mean you're not ill?' Isabelle screamed and then followed Arthur's example.

Archie read and slowly shook his head. 'No. Of course not.' He refused a second cup of coffee and sat in silence, directing his blank stare at a bank of daffodils outside the french windows that prostrated themselves in the wind and rain that came driving in from the Atlantic.

Isabelle threshed about feverishly for some point of contact.

175

There were two more days of this ahead. Out of the corner of her eye, she saw Arthur preparing to withdraw upstairs to his lair.

'Do you still play, Archie?' she scribbled hurriedly, foolishly. To make her meaning clear she began to mime a fiddler and a guitarist at play. Archie withdrew his eyes from the garden to study the note before him.

'Yes, in one of the lodges,' he said slowly. 'Long way from the house so they can't hear me. I play out of tune, you see . . . I can't blame them for not liking it,' and he smiled feebly.

Isabelle stifled a groan and drummed nervously on the table.

'I've got some letters to write,' Archie said abruptly and went to his room. In view of the weather, this seemed a reasonable suggestion.

After lunch, he reverted again to the subject of the 'irrevocable clause' and again received their assurances. 'Losing his memory, poor old boy,' Arthur thought. He felt sincerely grieved at the sorry plight of his one-time friend, but that did not mean that he wanted to associate with him. The effort was altogether too great, and for what purpose?

Archie suddenly rose from the table and muttered something about calling on his mother's crony.

'You'll be there too soon,' Isabelle scribbled hastily. 'It's only half an hour's walk. You're going to tea.'

'I'm going for a walk,' Archie said stubbornly, reverting to the booming voice, and left the house.

'Oh, I do hope he's put on his overcoat,' Isabelle moaned, but she was alone. Arthur had beaten a retreat. She glanced out of the window. The rain had stopped and it was quite reasonable to suppose that a man who had spent the morning indoors might feel in need of exercise.

When, by dinner-time, there was no sign of him, Dickie was dispatched to his supposed destination, but returned with the alarming news that he had neither written nor called. Arthur and Isabelle looked at each other in consternation. At this very moment a loud knocking was heard. It was the local constable to say that he had found a body on the beach, who wore, pinned to his overcoat, an envelope with the simple instructions: 'Please remove to mortuary and then be so good as to inform . . .' Here

176

followed their address. He clutched an empty phial of prussic acid in his hand. A woman bicycling to her work along the front had noticed a gentleman propped against a rock, who, in spite of the cold March wind, appeared not to have changed his position at the time of her return. The police had taken the body straight to the mortuary. 'So if I may trouble you to come and identify the remains, sir – '

Isabelle climbed the stairs to her visitor's room, dry-eyed, speechless, numb. Propped on the dressing-table side by side were three letters, one addressed to his wife, another to his sister and Arthur, while the third read simply 'Maid, with thanks' and contained a ten-shilling note.

The dreadful aftermath of coroner's inquest and funeral, attended by the bulky widow, weeping crocodile's tears behind her flowing crêpe (Isabelle's hatred of her sister-in-law was increased by the tragedy) was an ordeal indeed. She who wept so easily could·hardly muster a tear – perhaps because, after all, it was a stranger who had taken his life. But her nerves sustained a further blow and her spirit knew even greater depths of anguish.

And yet time did not drag or stand still, but raced feverishly on as Arthur went his way and Isabelle hers. After astral planes and ectoplasm, the commissars had their long run. The final disenchantment with Russia came slowly. Edmund brought his mother a round-trip ticket (with his first earnings) for an extensive tour, organized by the Society of Cultural Relations, which ranged from the Baltic to the Caspian. Isabelle, at a very low ebb at the time, was touched and overjoyed and set forth to her Mecca with an odd assemblage of dons and other pro-Russians. At Sebastopol, she naively took a snapshot of the harbour (including distant fortifications) from the deck of the ship which had brought the party from Odessa, and found herself gaoled without delay. When released, she returned to find that her soap had been stolen. She suspected the Russian stewardess, who had already shown keen interest in French toilet soap. Whether this episode was the first small crack in the structure of Russia-worship was not certain, but a slow cooling-off was presently noticeable.

177

One by one the children left the nest, and Isabelle, finding life with Arthur wholly intolerable, absented herself more and more. She had exhausted the Women's Institute. From Scotland to Cornwall to East Anglia, in Welsh mountains and Irish bogs, she had delivered her lectures – there was nowhere left for her. Now she went to a Bloomsbury hotel to attend occasional lectures – the Ethical Society, the Fabians – to meet a few old friends, to kill time, brooding miserably in the solitude of her hotel bedroom.

When she left the loneliness of London, her misery went with her, enveloping her like a cloak, gnawing at her vitals, pouring out of her in the ceaseless monologues she addressed to the empty air. There was no escape anywhere. She sat now in her familiar bedroom. (With the children away from home, she never entered the big empty drawing-room.) She was mending household linen, sewing jerkily with a maximum of physical effort, throwing each mended item on to a pile with an air of desperation. *Eleven years*, she was thinking. It was eleven years last month since she had found the house and set to to make it a home. The ramblers in the pergola had been in flower . . . Eleven years in which to shatter her dreams. Rain spattered on the windows, spattered the flowers on the huge magnolia grandiflora that grew against the wall. The windows rattled ceaselessly. The old dog crawled under the bed at the sound of the midday cannon fired from the fort, a sound he hated. She turned to offer him the usual reassurance and caught sight of her reflection in the looking-glass. With a certain perverse satisfaction, she noted her pallor, thinness, the whiteness of her hair. It had been only faintly streaked with grey eleven years ago. As the tears came into her eyes, she turned back to the garden. The rose pergola had been in flower . . . Long new growths and old branches laden with dead roses were threshing to and fro in the wind. It had been all glory then. It had given birth to that favourite dream of her daughters' weddings (brilliant weddings) . . . parties, where bride and groom strolled among their guests in the enchanted garden. But Lucy had married perversely, odiously, in secret. Diana, it is true, had had a fashionable wedding at St Mark's, North Audley Street, only to be widowed within a year in the Sudan. She was engaged to marry again, but not here – no dream party in the garden. Edmund had never disappointed her, but Edmund's nuptials did not feature among the dreams. Now he was far away, in another continent. Dickie, too. What a trouble that boy had been to her . . . Emmi, who was doing a training in horses, was showing an interest in highly unsuitable young men. 'Detrimentals,' Isabelle called them, using an expressive term of her mother's. She looked out again at the dripping garden. It wore an air of neglect. The place *must* be got rid of. When she spoke of it to Arthur he maintained that he was not long for this world and it wasn't worth his while moving.

Isabelle was losing her nerve. She fled again to London.

Lucy came over to deal with Arthur. She was appalled to see his deterioration. The Breton cook told her that her master had not left his room for weeks. She was forbidden to enter there, as he would not expose her to the risk of contagion. She had instructions to leave his tray outside the door, keep his dishes separate and scour her hands after handling them.

Lucy went upstairs and knocked on the bedroom door. There was no answer. She knocked again, and still no answer came. Her heart sank – perhaps she was too late. After the third knock, a hoarse whisper asked who was there.

'It's Lucy, Father. You're expecting me. I wired you.'

The room was dark, the shutters closed.

'Don't come in, dear girl,' Arthur croaked. 'It's not safe for you to come in here. Stay outside in the passage.' But Lucy was already across the room, opening the shutters. A burst of sunshine came in from the balcony. The daylight showed a disordered room, thick in dust. Arthur lay on the bed, blinking at her. He had grown a straggly beard, which gave him the look of an El Greco Christ. His empty breakfast-tray was still on the eiderdown.

'Don't come near! Keep away.' He put up both hands as if to ward off a blow and began to cough. It was not a really convincing cough.

'What's the matter, Father?'

'TB,' came the hoarse croak, 'a very virulent type. Runs in the family. Bertie had it in a less violent form. He got over it.'

179

'Have you had Dr Shone?'

'No. He's no good.'

'Someone else, then.'

None of them's any good. They don't find the TB virus. That isn't to say it isn't there.'

'What's that?' Lucy pointed to a small blue bottle standing on his bedside-table.

'That's my sputum bottle. I'm collecting my sputum to send it away to be analysed. Laboratory in Birmingham – '

'*Father!* Now you get up and have a bath while Angèle and I do this room.'

'Not up to it, dear girl . . .'

'You've got to! D'you hear, Father, you've *got to!*' Lucy was screaming at him now precisely as her mother screamed. 'And shave off that beard because I can't *stand* it – that's why!'

As Arthur protested his weakness, her vehemence increased. In the end he gave way. He allowed her to help him out of bed and into his dressing-gown.

'Be careful . . . I can't raise my arm . . . just put it round me . . . Ouch! Be careful! . . . Never mind the cord . . . My slippers now . . .' Suddenly he straightened up and admonished his daughter, waggling his index finger threateningly. 'Lucy, I absolutely forbid you or Angèle to disturb those papers. You're not to dust that table and you're not to interfere with my books. I insist you leave everything as it is.' His equanimity partly restored by this parting shot, he shuffled off towards the bathroom.

'And if you don't remove that obscene growth, *I* will! And, like as not, cut your throat while I'm about it!' she called after him. Her rancour had subsided.

At long last, bathed, shaved and recognizable, he descended to the dining-room. He forgot to croak. By the end of the meal, it was evident that he was enjoying the change from his self-imposed solitary confinement in darkness. The selling of the house was discussed and agreed on. In the afternoon, Lucy went to the house-agents to strike while the iron was hot. (It was sold for a nursing home.) The deadly disease was never referred to again, though the little blue bottle remained in evidence for a while.

24

Isabelle came back to the island to attend the
dissolution of her home. The wretched business of selling up,
the farewells, the putting down of the old dog, taxed her to the
utmost. She thought and talked continually of following Archie
to a suicide's grave, but though half demented with nervous
confusion, the sheer burden of work kept her going. Together
they left the island and established themselves in a residential
hotel in Bayswater.

It was a bad choice of district for one so given to reminiscence.
She was haunted by memories of her early life, but the hotel
faced the park and a walk in Kensington Gardens kept Arthur
out of bed for a part of each day. Isabelle remained locked in
her hatred towards her husband, though with all her fierce hatred,
there were still times when she found him companionable. She
would die rather than reveal to outsiders that their marriage was
not a happy one. The children, of course, whenever present, got
the whole weight of unrestrained woe poured into their unwilling ears. Three out of five lived abroad now. They came home
periodically and brightened their parents' lives to a greater or
less degree.

Isabelle had talked at times of leaving Arthur, but now that
the need for maintaining a family home had passed, the question
of separation somehow did not arise. The thought that an un-

satisfactory husband was better than none (there were widows in the hotel who actually envied her), the need for a scapegoat on which to vent her spleen, the force of habit and the realization now that it was too late for her to strike out on her own – all made for a continuance of their life together. The deadlock was complete. Sooner or later, one or the other would crack.

The *dénouement* came as a surprise to all.

It occurred to Arthur one day as he strode in Kensington Gardens, Isabelle trudging gloomily at his side, that the financial burdens which had dogged him so long had ceased to exist. His mother who, ever since her operation, had required a nurse-companion to look after her, had recently died at a ripe age, and that drain on his income had come to an end. The children, whose education had been crippling, needed no further financial help. The overdrafts were paid off. Isabelle and he lived modestly enough, and now, for the first time in his life, there was money to spare. (That morning, in a moment of exhilaration, he had sent a large cheque to the Fabian Society. . . .) It came to him suddenly: why not travel, escape from another London winter and head south? Isabelle, whose feet were numb with cold, threw a glance at the bare trees against the leaden sky and welcomed the suggestion. Arthur, always precipitate when a plan of action was decided on, set forth in the afternoon to visit motor-car showrooms, having cut down his siesta to half an hour. He returned to discuss with enthusiasm the rival merits of touring cars, their suitability for continental roads, their petrol consumption, difficulties in regard to spare parts . . . In a very short time he had invested delightedly in a capacious, high-powered Ford tourer. It was now a question of maps, guide-books and the planning of routes. The scheme had materialized. They were off!

Arthur now revealed a hitherto unexpected side of his nature. He turned out to be that rare animal – the born traveller: one who genuinely preferred travelling to remaining in one place. He had always been drawn towards the unfamiliar and had never much minded discomfort. Now at last he could indulge his excessive curiosity, his love of collecting promiscuous information, his insatiable interest in the bizarre. He had the bird's-eye view of the countries through which he ranged. All was a perpetual

182

source of diversion. Not for him were the smart places, nor could he become one of the earnest gang of sightseers thronging the museums, picture galleries, places of pilgrimage and romantic ruins. It was not that he took no delight in romantic ruins. He might pause briefly to reconstruct some scene from the past out of the present-day setting, but only briefly. He was no culture-vulture, but a bird of passage, here today and gone tomorrow, travelling for travelling's sake.

He was enchanted, too, with the casual social contacts provided along the way. A few sentences exchanged with a fellow wayfarer, a few stumbling words (dictionary in hand) with a native did not tax his powers in the way that sustained intercourse did. He need make no effort to get to know the object of his curiosity. What he would have discovered at close range he never knew, for they were no sooner known than lost. They remained a mysterious and diverting memory. He did not want to know more. Isabelle had no chance to protest at his reluctance for closer acquaintance, for they must be moving on again, lest he take to his bed.

The pace he set was terrific. Isabelle was wonderfully game at keeping up with him. Though she had no active occupation beyond packing and unpacking the suitcases (as he did all the driving), she was often afflicted with sheer physical exhaustion. Arthur, too, at the end of a long drive was genuinely weary. He could not then be grudged his bed. But the next morning found him ready for an early start. Isabelle would often have liked to stay at some particular beauty spot, but it did not do. The ominous threat of 'fatigue poisons' moved them on. Arthur at the wheel of a car was impervious to the ills of the flesh.

At the wheel of a car –

Though normally gentle and courteous in all his dealings, at the wheel of a car (particularly a 40-horsepower V8) he was transformed. A passion to overtake and a horror of being overtaken possessed all his being.

'Ah-ha! You would, would you?' he would snarl, pulling out into the centre of the road to check the overtaking offender behind, who protested vigorously on his horn. 'So you thought you'd get by that time? You keep your place, my good man.' After several such noisy and even dangerous exchanges, Isabelle's agonized remonstrances would finally carry weight. Arthur would draw to the side, ordering his enemy to pass with a contemptuous wave of the hand. 'Road-hog!' he would call insultingly after him. Sometimes it was '*Schweinhund*', '*cochon*', '*cretino*' or '*specie di animale*', according to his geographical location. The mild and considerate Arthur was unrecognizable.

Where the traffic was heavy, he would carry on a sarcastic running commentary on other road-users. His minor brushes involving scratched mud-guards and bent bumpers (with all the accompanying hullabaloo) were not infrequent. They would pause on their route for a slight hammering out and a touch of paint. 'Lucky escape,' Arthur would say, 'it might have been a nasty accident. You've just got to assume there's a deaf and blind lunatic on the wrong side of the road coming round every bend.' By extraordinary good fortune, he was never involved in a major accident.

The first expedition was to Italy to revisit the Isonzo front. It was a curious feeling to drive freely where enemy guns had threatened, to see the new houses that had risen from the ruins of the old. Many former acquaintances, however, recognized and welcomed him and he looked with pleasure at each familiar landmark. But the familiar walls were often disfigured by highly displeasing slogans: '*Mussolini ha sempre ragione*'.

'It's a bit thick', Arthur said. 'This fellow Mussolini's getting too big for his boots. Let's get on. I'd like to see Trieste that we were trying to take. Then Fiume and on to Yugoslavia.'

'Oh, no! Now we're in Italy we must go to Venice and Florence and Rome and Naples. Oh no, Arthur!'

'All right. As you wish, dear.'

The pensione at Fiesole was charming, with a view of Florence. Isabelle, determined to halt their progress at this wonderful spot, was pleased when Arthur said: 'There's a picture I want to see here.'

'Oh, Arthur, which one?'

'It's a Buster Keaton. I noticed it on the hoardings as we drove in. They've got Charlie Chaplin next week, but we can't hang about waiting for that. Pity.'

Florence could not hold him, nor Rome, nor Venice for long, nor Naples at all, though in Sorrento, a bridge four halted his progress for a time.

Italy, Yugoslavia, Romania, Hungary, Austria, Switzerland, Germany, the Low Countries, France, Spain, Portugal – most of them luckily well supplied with roads. At intervals, they returned to the hotel in Lancaster Gate for a summer visit, or when one of the children was home on leave, but never for very long, for Arthur's health required the stimulus of fairly constant motoring. On the whole, Isabelle endured the rigours of travel remarkably well. There were times when sheer fatigue or the approach of an anniversary plunged her in gloom. There were times when a hotel proprietor, deceived by Arthur's springy step and lively eye, his total absence of grey hairs and embonpoint, would say: '*Parfaitement: une chambre au premier pour Madame and une chambre voisine pour Monsieur votre fils.*' She would muster a sickly smile while raging inwardly – taken for her *son* when he was always complaining of being too old . . . a broken-down crock . . . one foot in the grave . . . how *dare* he complain . . . how *dare* he look so young! He was five years older than she was anyway! What suffering she had endured to bring her to this . . . old before her time. To be taken for his mother! The cruelty of it . . .

Arthur, devoid of personal vanity, was equally devoid of tact. 'Silly ass,' he would say, chuckling at the hotel-keeper's gaffe. 'Needs to have his eyes examined.'

These were relatively happy years. It was not a serene happiness, for they pursued a policy of sheer escapism as a substitute for thought. It was indeed a kind of lunacy, but the travel-maniac was for the most part a gay, often frivolous, companion, very different from the sick man of the Jersey days who lay with his face to the wall awaiting the end. In addition to the beauties of landscape (the breathtaking views that rewarded a long and often tedious approach), the simplest and oddest things enchanted him. There were the curious habits and remnants of local saints (the 'tribal gods'), the strange and delightful encounters with foreign dogs, the range and variety of fish, flesh and fowl. There was the great pillar of dust seen from far across the Hungarian plain that resolved itself into a herd of long-haired swine, lolloping along towards the approaching car, their flowing tresses haloed by the setting sun. There was the village in the Apennines where, turning back the bed-clothes, fleas were seen to be ironed in to the linen sheets, flattened, preserved like miniature flowers. 'What a crop!' Arthur exclaimed admiringly as he scattered his Keatings against the millions who must have survived the ironing and would presently be making their appearance. 'What a rich harvest and how wonderfully preserved!' There was the toilet in the squalid and desolate village that only saw one newspaper weekly, where Arthur complained that the paper appeared to have been used already. 'But only on one side,' the innkeeper pointed out. Arthur could have hugged the man.

One day, at the end of a picnic by the roadside, high in the French Alps, as Isabelle gathered the remains of the meal together and Arthur sucked his pipe, it occurred to him that the adjoining rock, on which his eyes were resting, had moved.

'Do you see what I see?'

'What, Arthur?'

'It looks to me like a man hiding behind that bush on the right. Against that rock, see?'

'Oh, Arthur! There is someone there!'

'Better not take any notice. We'll move on when you're ready.' He began to hum a tune.

Isabelle was nervous. They had often been warned against giving lifts to strangers. Her hands shook as she packed the picnic basket. Suddenly the stranger spoke: '*Zind wir in Frankreich?*'

'*Jawohl*,' Arthur answered cheerfully. To their surprise, the stranger burst into tears. When he could speak again, Arthur and Isabelle found themselves comforting him like a long-lost child. He was indeed hardly more than a child – an eighteen-year-old deserter from the Italian army. Conscripted by Mussolini from the South Tyrol (a district now Italian, following a further reshuffling by the Treaty of Versailles) he had been drafted into the Italian army, where he appeared to have no complaints, beyond home-sickness, until the order came that his regiment was being sent to Abyssinia. He bolted the night the order came and headed straight for the Alps and then westward for France, after leaving a suicide note attached to his rifle on the bank of

186

the river Po. A mountaineer by birth, he had progressed well over terrible going, until enfeebled by lack of food. For the last few days, he had had nothing but occasional handfuls of snow to stop his thirst.

'We've got to help this boy,' Arthur said. 'I'm all for doing Mussolini out of some of his cannon-fodder! Give him what's left in the basket and we'll find out the form for Italian deserters and get him some clothes. Here you, Andreas! *Wir kommen zurück, mit kleiden.* Cheer up, boy! *Warten sie hier. Wir kommen zurück.*'

At the next village on the road to Grenoble, while Isabelle brought food and peasants' clothes, Arthur went straight to the police station. Here he discovered that there was strong anti-Italian feeling (sanctions were being applied, gingerly, against the Abyssinian war), and the hospitable gendarmerie offered a bed for the night and a permit to pass through France, pointing out that, owing to unemployment, the law forbade the foreigner to remain and work there. Andreas, dismayed at the thought of spending the night in the lock-up, was soon reassured by the kindness shown to him. *Ce sacré Mussolini . . . ah, le pauvre diable . . .* The next day, furnished with a *passe partout* that entitled the boy to travel unmolested through France, Arthur and Isabelle continued north to Luxemburg where they were told there was work to be had, Andreas driving with them by day and sleeping by choice in the open. At Luxemburg, however, his entry was refused and Arthur decided to make for Germany, which would at least overcome the boy's language difficulty. This time they were lucky. After appearing before a magistrate, he was sent to work on the land and Arthur and Isabelle headed south for the Tyrol to reveal in secret to the boy's grieving parents that their deserter son was in safe hands. This was a tricky mission, for inquiries made by visiting foreigners in the tiny Alpine village might have led to the trail of the fugitive. But it was successfully accomplished. Andreas settled happily on a farm and in due course married the farmer's daughter. His grateful Christmas letters became an annual feature that lasted up to the outbreak of war.

On another occasion, in Germany, Arthur fell in with an anti-Nazi who had arranged to visit his son in Canada and fervently hoped never to return to the fatherland. The difficulty, naturally, was getting his money out of the country.

'That's easy!' Arthur said impetuously. 'Give it me in portable form and I'll come and see you off at Hamburg. They'll never suspect me.'

His new friend took him at his word. Arthur was a man who was clearly suffering from corns as he limped past the rows of officials at the dock, for his socks were stuffed with banknotes (and his tobacco pouch contained diamonds). However, all went according to plan. He was elated when he returned to the hotel in the evening.

Isabelle had spent a quiet day of much-needed rest. 'You look very pleased with yourself.'

'I am.' He told her of his successful mission.

'Oh, Arthur, you mustn't, you mustn't do such things! If you were found out, you'd be in terrible trouble. You might never be heard of again!'

'Nonsense, dear.'

'I tell you it's terribly dangerous. It's ridiculous to run such risks for someone you hardly know. You must never do it again!'

'Oh, all right.'

'Arthur, you must swear you won't do anything so stupid again.'

'All right. I've promised. All the same, it's nice to have done that dirty dog Hitler down, even in a small way. D'you know something Joachim told me?'

'What?'

'You have to say "*Heil Hitler*" every time you speak to this upstart. Then d'you know what he says?'

'What?'

'He says "*Heil Hitler*" back! I mean to say . . . really – what!'

So Germany was ruled out, and Italy. Europe was shrinking fast. There remained Scandinavia.

Edmund was transferred from Cairo to San Francisco and arrived suddenly in London.

'Where are the parents?' he asked Lucy.

'They're somewhere in the Arctic Circle. Look, there's a card

188

from Lapland just come. It's a picture of the midnight sun. Father says: "Picnicking is prevented by clouds of the biggest mosquitoes I have yet encountered . . ." Think of that!'

'What did they go there for?'

'Father suddenly heard of a road that's only open for three weeks in the year, so he was off before you could say knife. If you manage this road, which ends apparently at the Arctic Ocean, it entitles you to wear a polar bear badge on your car. That's what he's after.'

'Heavens! Well, it's wonderful how they keep going.'

'It's coming to an end. Father's more or less had Europe.'

'I suppose there's nothing to stop them from going farther afield.'

'Oh, he means to. When they're back, he lies in bed studying maps. It's his favourite indoor sport. I found him poring over Africa the other day. He's planning the Cape to Cairo route.'

'That's a bit much for Mother.'

'She's beginning to kick. In fact she's sick to death of it. His driving scares the pants off her.'

'It's difficult to see the outcome.'

'If only they'd settle down like other people . . .'

'You *know* they can't do that.'

Motoring in Africa was interesting in many respects, but less agreeable than motoring on the Continent. The immense distances, the lonely roads – dirt tracks for the most part, coated with red dust and corrugated by the passing of long-distance lorries – the oppressive heat that preceded alarming storms (for, by escaping the English winter, they came in for the African summer), the sometimes dismal accommodation, all made more for fatigue than for stimulus. When Isabelle, worn out, insisted on staying at a rare delightful spot in the Drakensberg, Arthur inevitably packed up. It could not be counted a very successful tour and no more was heard of the trans-continental trip.

25

Edmund had been sent by his firm to San Francisco. He wrote with enthusiasm of his 'old' (signifying pre-Fire) house on Telegraph Hill, his sailing, polo and the manifold delights of the beautiful city. It was decided that Arthur and Isabelle should motor extensively across the North American continent and pay a visit to their son.

From the moment they landed on American soil, Arthur was constantly stirred by a sense of wonder; from the soaring sky-scrapers of the great cities to the crumbling dereliction of the south, from the friendly interest of the inhabitants with their refreshing lack of servility and vivid flowers of speech (such as 'soft shoulders' meaning no more than the edge of the road), from the antiseptic wonders of the comfort stations and the restaurants that served 'single lamb chop with pineapple ring' on their menus – there was no day but added to his stock of curiosities. The new world was much to his liking. But the distances, as in Africa, were enormous, and the fast-moving traffic, where it was a matter of life and death to stick to the right aisle, proved a fearful strain on Isabelle. By the time they arrived at San Francisco she had reached a state of nervous fretfulness where even Edmund's soothing influence was little help. It was Christmas when, inevitably, the well-known spectres from the past came crowding in upon her.

Arthur was enchanted with the lovely 'old' house on the hill with its stupendous views across the unparalleled bay. He particularly liked the Fillippino servant who arrived daily in his large Buick, whose daughter was training for the concert platform and who, when asked what he would give them to eat, replied unfailingly after deep reflection: 'Libber'n bacon.' Arthur found so much of novelty to please him and was so inured to having at his side a companion chronically on the verge of nervous breakdown that he did not perceive Isabelle's deterioration.

Edmund took a week's leave and engaged a furnished cottage at a resort frequented by artists. Here the central-heating system proved captivating. A switch in the bedroom operated a plant concealed in the surrounding pine-wood which brought the temperature in the cottage from freezing (there was a suspicion of snow among the pines) to sub-tropical in a very short space of time – all without moving more than the fore-arm from the warmth of the bed.

'The Romans managed just this sort of thing or they would never have built their splendid villas in – Northumberland, say . . . But they were catering for the great, not the bourgeosie. The next great civilization will find the means to provide central heating for the proletariat as well.' Arthur sat in an open-necked shirt beside a grating which belched forth a supply of heated air sufficient to make the end of the room dance as in a mirage. Beyond lay the frozen wood, with here and there a glimpse of the blue Pacific showing through the trees. He had been studying a cookery book.

'It says here a junket is a sweetened dish of curds and whey. Now how do we come by "junketing", I wonder . . . I think I should like to become a cook. Some of these processes look very interesting. And the names are fascinating. I should like to make "Angels on Horseback" and a "Toad in the Hole". In Ostend, they used to give us *"Petits Pots de chocolat à la Crème"*. Very nice little poes they were too. I think I shall take up cooking.'

Having had the idea, Arthur was inevitably consumed by a desire to carry it out. It was decided to rent a similar cottage a good deal farther south, where Arthur would be content to remain, engaged in mastering the art of cooking. Isabelle agreed as it would keep him out of bed, little considering that it would deprive her of an occupation.

Edmund returned to his work and his parents motored south, pausing in Pasadena to visit Upton Sinclair (with whom Arthur had corresponded over a number of years), before settling into a bungalow at La Jolla – a small place near the Mexican border and not far from the large naval base and port of San Diego.

They were no sooner arrived than Arthur fairly plunged into cooking. At the outset, he sustained a number of burns and broke a good deal of crockery. ('Only two plates left? I can't have accounted for the rest. There must be a poltergeist in that kitchen . . .') He mistook salt for sugar and sugar for salt and committed innumerable follies. Slowly, as with knitting, he began to get the hang of things. As his enthusiasm grew, he embarked on ambitious dishes, cooking for cooking's sake. He became fussy and meticulous, regarding the kitchen as his sole preserve, and Isabelle's exasperations grew.

The local club had proved less fruitful than in Victoria. It is possible that Isabelle's set, unsmiling face discouraged a friendly approach. Arthur, as always, refused to waste time in what was to him pointless social intercourse. Apart from a brief foraging expedition in the early mornings to procure materials for his new art, and to buy replacements for his breakages, he went from his kitchen to his bed.

For Isabelle, now the victim of acute neurosis, this was a time of almost unrelieved misery. She was corroded from within by a sense of intolerable grievance – grievance against the man who had destroyed her life by neglect and his own by hypochondria. She increased her vexations by ceaselessly dwelling on them. She took long solitary walks on the vast deserted beach in a daily endeavour to reach a state of fatigue that would ensure sleep at night; but when she finally climbed into bed, weary, aching and footsore, sleep eluded her. She consulted a doctor, who prescribed sleeping tablets. She soon found that more than the recognized dose was necessary to induce even a short spell of unconsciousness from the pains that tortured her exhausted mind. As her moral confusion grew, she began to attack her children also, without withdrawing anything from the stock of hatred directed towards her husband. Her feet started to trouble her seriously. Isabelle hobbled on until the pain became agonizing and she was confined to the sofa. There she could only read, and reading had become useless. She would read and re-read a sentence over and over without being able to extract its meaning. One day when Arthur was up to his ears in the manufacturing of a particularly engrossing dish, Isabelle limped into the kitchen and addressed him in a strangely flat voice: 'I want to speak to you.'

'Not now, dear, if you don't mind – '

'Yes, now.'

'Sorry, Belle, this is a very tricky operation. If I leave off now, the whole thing's liable to subside.'

'Arthur, stop that and listen to what I have to say. *I have decided to end it all.*'

Arthur made no reply as her meaning gradually penetrated his consciousness. His actions came slowly to a stop. Then he stood, wiping the steam off his pince-nez. The sickening pain that he remembered from the scenes of his early married life invaded his being. 'I think you should see the doctor, dear,' he said at last.

'I refuse. D'you hear! You're not to send for him! This is my business and no concern of anyone else. And that's that.'

Arthur cleared his throat. He knew that opposition only provoked violent anger. The less she was contradicted the sooner it would end.

'Come and sit down next door,' he said at last. 'You're tired.'

'*Tired!*' Isabelle screamed. 'I'm not tired in the way you understand it with your "fatigue poisons".' She pronounced the words with withering scorn. 'I'm worn out. I'm finished. I'm through.' Refusing his help, she led the way into the living-room. Arthur poured her out a whisky. She waved it away.

'If you want to know why I've reached this decision,' Isabelle said with deadly venom, 'it's because of you. No one could live with you, Arthur. There isn't the woman born who could stand you. You've no understanding, no warmth, no feelings except for your own imaginary ailments – you've nothing.'

Arthur sat huddled like a whipped cur. He was thinking, as the agonized voice went on and on, how long is it going to last and how can I telephone the doctor without her knowing?

193

'And the children to whom I devoted my life – ' Isabelle was saying with resentful vehemence. 'What good are they to me? Lucy is detestable – and the two youngest mean nothing to me. Diana has no use for us – oh, I heard her say so last summer when she stayed with us in Ostend. She's so wrapped up in that spoiled brat and that selfish husband of hers that her own mother doesn't exist for her any more. And as for Edmund – he hasn't said so in so many words, but he was cold and indifferent at Monterey. It hurt terribly. I have nothing left to live for.'

'Edmund has been a very good son to us,' Arthur said feebly.

Isabelle ignored the remark and continued with her theme.

It went on for a long time. When the tears finally came, Arthur felt a sense of relief, for this was generally the prelude to the end. She sat weeping, her face buried in her hands. He looked away from the heaving shoulders. When she finally took a sip of whisky and shuddered, he rose from his armchair almost jocularly.

'I'm going to get you a plate of ragoût, Belle. It's what you need – a poor thing but mine own.'

'I couldn't possibly.' She groaned in revulsion.

'Try a little'.

'*No!* Don't you understand *anything* I've been saying! Don't you *ever* understand . . .'

Arthur shook his head and slumped back in his chair. The convulsive sobbing continued while he sat with his hand over his eyes, in utter impotence before her agony. In the whirlpool of hatred that engulfed her, she was repeatedly aware of something else – the desire to inspire remorse. The storm of tears subsided at last and Isabelle asked in a curiously hollow voice: 'What are you going to do this evening?'

'Would you like me to read to you?'

'No, no, no! What are *you* thinking of doing?'

Arthur racked his brains and said at last: 'I might play a game of patience.'

Isabelle rose without a word and went into her bedroom, groping as if blind.

Arthur remained sunk in dejection. Used as he was to scenes of domestic hysteria, this had been an exceptionally bad one. At last he went to his bed and began to play patience. He laid out the cards slowly and deliberately. It was a complex patience which took a long time and did not often come out, but this time he brought it twice to a successful conclusion. When it was over, he sat shuffling the cards, considering the rival attractions of whisky and tea. He did not feel like any dinner. Having decided in favour of tea, he went to the kitchen. He noticed from the lighted glass panel over her door that Isabelle's light was burning. When he had made the tea, he debated whether to take her a cup. It would inevitably mean a renewal of hostilities . . . He decided she needed it, for she must be awake still. When he knocked, there was no answer and he opened the door carefully, saying: 'A cup of tea for you, Belle.' He then observed that the bedside lamp had fallen on the floor but was still burning, and that Isabelle lay in a curious position with one arm thrown out and was breathing loudly. He could not rouse her. The bottle of sleeping tablets that he had bought for her that morning was nearly empty. Filled with alarm, he telephoned the doctor. Within a very short time she was being removed to a private room in a hospital at San Diego.

Arthur collapsed for two days, during which no one came near him. The doctor telephoned early the next morning to say that his wife was not thought to be in danger, and the following day to say that she could be expected to regain full consciousness shortly. Arthur stirred himself to telegraph to his son, but was scarcely aware of what he was doing. It was impossible for him to think of what had happened. His mind shied away from it like a victim attempting to escape the lash. It was equally impossible to think of any other thing. Mathematical problems, books, patience – all the things that had hitherto provided an unfailing specific had become senseless. He existed in a vacuum. The intellect abhors a vacuum. This was his private hell. Isabelle's was a place of ferment, a ceaseless lashing and striking out – a blind desire to hurt in order to redress her sufferings, a frantic endeavour to pin the guilt on someone or something other than herself. Arthur's was an emptiness, the abomination of desolation – a stink, corruption, dissolution, death.

On the third day, Edmund arrived, having flown the six hundred miles from San Francisco. Arthur met him at the airport. Edmund thought that he looked curiously diminished and moved with a shuffling tread, far removed from his usual buoyancy. He noticed that his father's eyes, that so often had a look of bright, alert expectancy, were curiously opaque, like the eyes of an old dog. He let Edmund drive, handing over the keys of his car without protest.

At the hospital, Isabelle had at last regained consciousness and was suffering a good deal of malaise. The doctor addressed her first and said, somewhat idiotically: 'Well now, Mrs Boyne, you've had a very bad attack of hay fever.'

'Rubbish,' Isabelle retorted with spirit, for she could remember every detail of what had occurred. She looked at her husband and son and noted with satisfaction that Arthur appeared to be crying. He embraced her, clumsy in his tenderness. Edmund in his turn soothed her with loving endearments.

'I'm so sorry . . .' Isabelle murmured brokenly between her sobs. 'All this trouble . . . I've given you so much trouble . . .' Then she made her meaning clear: 'What a mess I made of it . . . Next time I'll do it properly . . . Put out the light first . . .'

26

The next few months were spent at their son's house overlooking the incredible bay. Arthur went to bed for a time with some justification, for he was undoubtedly suffering from shock. Dispirited and ill though he was, he slowly regained his philosophic composure. He overcame his distress by simply not permitting his mind to dwell on it. He worked in the small, precipitous garden and planted the window boxes. Paul, the Fillippino, smiled his enigmatic smile as he listened to Arthur humming unmelodiously at his planting. If only the lady would hum, instead of all that restless fidgeting. Isabelle was supposed to have taken over the housekeeping for an occupation. In the mornings, Paul took her shopping in his Buick.

Her convalescence was wearing in the extreme. There were innumerable topics of conversation to be avoided. Arthur was not clever at this, with the result that he would often in all innocence precipitate a climax of almost insanely violent anger followed by a storm of weeping. There were days when she moved in an extremity of woe. Sleepless nights, and the drugs taken to combat insomnia, induced a mood of depression and peevishness when nothing seemed to appease her. She raged against the brutal interference that had brought her back to life. With the suicide's disregard of the suffering caused to the lives of others, she could not see beyond her own anguish of spirit. In the end, however, an improvement was slowly discernible. Her son's patient devotion, a certain amount of distraction in the form of social life in the hospitable circles in which he moved, outings in the form of motor drives with Edmund through a landscape of exceptional beauty, all combined to make for a gradual improvement. She learned nothing from her experience. Life was more tolerable, so she was prepared to put up with it for the time being. When it became intolerable again, she would get out of it. 'And that's that.' Life at sixty was a losing game anyway and Isabelle had never learned to play a losing game.

It was scarcely believable that two persons who had come into head-on collision in such a grievous way could resume their life together under the same conditions and take up where they had left off: yet they did precisely that. Accordingly, when she was thought to be sufficiently recovered they resumed their travels just as if the dread episode had never occurred. One morning early, Edmund stood waving, the Fillippino bowing. Arthur sneered at a passing limousine and shot away up the precipitous hill. Isabelle, smiling intrepidly, clutched the side of the car. They were off as they had come.

Isabelle was not a cosy travelling companion, but there were many occasions still of shared enjoyment. A visitor to the Mormon Temple in Salt Lake City might have seen an undistinguished-looking couple standing affectionately arm-in-arm before the Sea-Gull monument in Temple Square, reading the inscription: 'In grateful remembrance of the mercy of God . . .' – a monument to the seagulls who devoured the locusts and thereby saved the Mormons from starvation.

'To think that all this has sprung up in less than a hundred years,' Arthur said, surveying the great city in wonder. 'Polygamy practised righteously and with Divine sanction. Wonderful, that! D'you know that fellow Brigham Young, the apostle of the prophet Smith, died leaving 17 wives and 147 children. Not bad. They were a brave lot,' he added ambiguously. 'Now let's see if we can find an hotel run by the Latter-Day Saints. What's the betting on single lamb chop with pineapple ring? . . .' He accosted a passing native: 'Say brother, could you kindly direct us . . .'

The city of Niagara Falls stretched for miles above the cataract. At last they could hear its tremendous booming. They stood side by side on the observation platform, gazing at the great chasm 1,000 feet wide, at the piercing clarity of the water as it slid over the brink to be broken suddenly into the dazzling whiteness of flying spray; transformed again to boiling foam in the churning rapids beneath, where it rushed headlong, between high vertical cliffs, to the great whirlpool beyond. Through the veil of flying spray, they could see Goat Island bisecting the river and the far larger Horseshoe Falls on the Canadian side. They stood for a long time, overawed by the stupendous spectacle, until Isabelle suddenly burst into tears and Arthur led her away. When they had reached a point where the human voice was once more audible she said between her sobs: 'And to think . . . to think that my ancestor went down there in a barrel . . .'

'Not strictly speaking,' Arthur said maddeningly. 'Wasn't he your second cousin once removed – '

'A *barrel*,' Isabelle repeated. She stopped in her tracks and stood weeping uninhibitedly, her hands covering her face. The thought of a human being – even an unrelated human being – enclosed in a dark cylinder, tossed about, falling sickeningly, banged against hideous rocks, sucked under, no escape . . .

'It was suicide, of course,' Arthur said and Isabelle gave a groan. (Now he'd done it.) 'I don't mean intentional,' he added without improving matters, 'I mean – he was trying to demon-strate something, but it was, to say the least, reckless – '

'I can't bear to think of it. Oh . . .'

'Pity he wasn't satisfied with being the first man to swim the Channel.' Arthur racked his brains for a commonsense remark. 'You'd have thought one look at what we've just seen would cure anyone of wanting to go monkeying about in a barrel.'

'Oh Arthur, *don't!* Have you no imagination? No feelings . . .' She was weeping angrily now.

Arthur was saved from answering as he suddenly saw an escape from Niagara. 'I must say, after seeing this, I'm very anxious to see the Victoria Falls!' he exclaimed. 'It's a pity we didn't get there on that African tour. They're quite different, of course. Jungle instead of urban surroundings. Grander, I imagine, with a four-hundred-feet drop as against one hundred and sixty-eight is it here? I believe the Zambezi is a muddy river though. How would it be to go there next winter?'

They sat now in a drugstore, refreshing themselves with coffee. The thunder of the falls still reverberated in their ears.

'I don't mind,' Isabelle said drearily. 'Diana and her baby can spend the summer with us somewhere first. But I thought the idea was for Emmi to do a motor tour with us in Italy . . .'

'Right, if that's the way you want it. I'd be all for Italy if someone would see their way to eliminate Mussolini. Extraordinary how he's got away with Abyssinia. Never a cheep out of us. Not more than a cheep anyway. And now this Spanish business . . . It was a bad day for us all when Hitler seized the Rhineland. He's not going to stop there either. *L'appétit vient en mangeant*. It's a terrible thing when people start thinking they can get all they want by sheer bad faith. They can, too . . .'

Arthur sat plunged in gloom at the European situation on the brink of war, but Isabelle's thoughts were too subjective to wander far from her personal tragedy.

27

'The *gorgeous* old man – I could *eat* him!' Lucy cried. 'Third time lucky, you see! I still simply can't believe it!' She sat with her parents on the terrace of her home in the country. They had just listened to the wireless description of Mr Chamberlain's return from Munich. With a piece of paper in one hand and his umbrella in the other, he had alighted on the soil of his harassed country, brandishing and announcing: 'Peace with honour . . . Peace for our time . . .' In proof of the success of his breathtaking, eleventh-hour mission, he exhibited Hitler's peace pledge to the overwrought crowds gathered anxiously to meet him. The announcer describing the scene had been deeply moved.

Lucy had spent the previous day issuing gas masks to the bewildered peasantry. Arthur and Isabelle had just arrived to discuss their war-time arrangements. They described the guns being mounted and the trenches dug in Hyde Park.

'I really *can't* believe it!' Lucy repeated. 'After the horror of the last few days . . . Tell me, how does the well-dressed beaver wear his gas mask? Whiskers in or out? I had such a row with Farmer Cox. In the end he threw his gas mask on the floor and stamped out shouting: "To hell with the government regulations!" Oh dear, oh dear, it's *too* good to be true . . .'

'No question of that,' Arthur said dismally.

'What?'

'What you said, dear girl – too good to be true.' He fixed his eyes on the middle distance and said slowly: ' "Peace with Honour" – I ask you! If you believe that, you'll believe anything.'

'Oh Father, why do you always have to make the worst of everything? How can Hitler go back on the promise he's just made before the whole world?'

'Why not, dear girl? If you've followed the events of the past five or six years it's a mathematical certainty that he will.'

'Not this time. He can't now . . .'

Arthur sat glum, too depressed even to relight his pipe.

'In India, we shot mad dogs,' he said as if to himself.

Lucy was busy with the drinks. She laughed suddenly. 'I never realized before what a diehard you are! It's all those years in India, of course . . .'

'Funny thing, I used to be considered rather dangerously avant-garde. A sort of a *sans-culotte* . . .'

'Anyway, you've *got* to hand it to Chamberlain . . . Haven't you?' she repeated when he did not answer. He sat with his elbows on the arms of his chair and his finger-tips meeting, withdrawn and meeting again.

'Needs to have his head examined.'

'Father, I resent that! I think he's a hero who snatched us from out the jaws of death.'

'He may be an astute businessman but he's clean out of his range in dealing with thugs. Hopelessly adrift . . . And the funny part is he seems to fancy that he's only got to pay a call on the fellows to secure their good behaviour.'

'Well, we'll soon see who's right,' Lucy said brightly.

'Yes. We'll see. Though I may not live to see it,' he added from force of habit.

'Let's drink to the Joint Peace Declaration!'

'Drink to our complete and ignominious defeat? I can't do that,' Arthur said mulishly.

Lucy was annoyed. Presently, murmuring something to do with dinner, she left them. Isabelle had sat fidgeting in silence.

'You haven't *always* been right about Germany, Arthur, let me remind you. Remember all that talk of faith in the Germans. You sing a different tune now. And you've no business to go

202

upsetting the child in her condition!' Lucy was pregnant and Isabelle held the views of her generation on cosseting and pandering to the whims of pregnancy. He waited for her to finish her lecture.

'I think I'll go and have a rest,' he said when the sound of her voice came to an end.

'You mean you're going to bed? You will *not* Arthur! I refuse to allow you to be a burden on the household.'

That she herself was the far greater burden was a fact which she could not be expected to recognize. With her monumental tactlessness, her unerring instinct for saying the one thing calculated to send her children off like rocketing pheasants, Isabelle's visits were guaranteed to disrupt any of their households within the first forty-eight hours. In addition to the persistent sharp criticism of her children's management of their affairs was the distressingly unreticent harping on her own. Isabelle was determined that her children should be a party to her sufferings. 'I committed suicide while your father played patience in the room next door,' she would say as the tears of self-pity flowed unchecked.

At the time of the Munich scare, Isabelle had already joined an ARP class and was hoping to pass the VAD nursing examinations at St Mary's Hospital which would qualify her for work as a shelter nurse in the forthcoming air-raids. The whole nightmare business of impending war was for her compounded in equal parts of genuine distress and welcome distraction and stimulus.

The question was – what to do with Arthur? Isabelle urged him, with his knowledge of languages, to apply for work among the many organizations dealing with the flood of refugees pouring into the country – Austrian, Bohemian, Spanish . . . But Arthur pointed out that twenty-three years had passed since he had last offered his services, and he was definitely not up to it this time. As the other four children, though often in England for visits, were widely dispersed, it was suggested that he should go and live with Lucy for the duration. 'It's the duty of those who aren't able to contribute to the war effort to get out of London,' Isabelle urged and Arthur agreed. Lucy also agreed. Her husband, who was over military age, had been offered a

203

high government appointment in the event of war and would be mostly away from home.

Lucy's baby was born in London between the crises that punctuated the anxious winter months – halfway between the nightmare of Munich and the rape of Czechoslovakia. The baby was a girl – Frances. Arthur, running true to form, retired to his bed for several days. When he emerged, he found that his daughter, afflicted by the family neuroses, was given over to insomnia and emotionalism.

His granddaughter, however, unlike his own children in infancy, interested him from the start. He found that he had quite got over his aversion to babies. Removing his pince-nez for close inspection, he would peer with interest at the miniature perfection of ear and eyelid. The diminutive hand, so exquisitely formed, that grasped his little finger with a fierce surprising strength, delighted him. When the nurse finally decided that he could be trusted, he carried the swaddled bundle to and fro, the little nuzzling head soft against his chin. He was soon seized with a desire to give bottles and change napkins, but the idea was frowned on by the nurse and not much favoured by Lucy. However, he hung round the nursery on his daily visits and was often allowed to push the pram in the park. This outing filled him with a singular pride. He who had never before observed a perambulator except as an object to avoid when motoring, found himself scrutinizing rival prams and their occupants with a derogatory eye. When he handed back his charge, he would give a report on her behaviour. 'Quite satisfactory, I think. Let me see: no cries or howls, six smiles (excluding wind), one belch, or it could have been a hiccough. And nurse, she's probably wet now – '

'I'll see to it, Mr Boyne. There's a lovely girlie!'

'Would you like me to change her?'

'No, thank you. There's my boofies girlie, then!'

'You'll attend to it promptly, won't you, nurse. I rather fancy she relieved herself quite early on. Couldn't be sure, of course.'

'I'll *see* to it, Mr Boyne.'

'I'll look in for a moment before I go, if I may. Won't disturb

her. And nurse, what's for lunch today? The two-o'clock feed,
I mean: Cow & Gate or my daughter?'

Lucy's home in the country was better suited as a romantic
setting for week-end parties than as a wartime retreat. Its isolation in a little-known, unspoiled countryside cut both ways. It
was ideal in respect of air-raids, but severe petrol rationing and
the burden in winter of getting to the nearest town (Oxford)
made living there difficult. It was the gatehouse of an early
fourteenth-century castle which had figured heroically in the Civil
War, after which the greater part had been blown up on Cromwell's orders. The gatehouse was left intact. It was approached
by a fixed bridge over the moat. The gatehouse itself was a perfect miniature castle, the top floor being one wholly magnificent
room approached by spiral stone staircases. A modern wing had
been added unobtrusively. Stepping over the bridge and through
what had been an arched entrance and was now the dining-room,
one emerged upon a stone terrace leading to a wide lawn, surrounded by a beautiful garden on different levels, surrounded
again by the moat. In winter, there was ice on the moat. In a
really hard winter, it froze solid so that the house literally stood
in ice. The deep stone walls pierced by arrowslit windows could
enclose a degree of cold that, enhanced by the war-time fuel
restrictions, would have killed off a less hardy Indian veteran.
     Lucy and her husband, Francis, had gone to the country at
Easter for the first time in several months, leaving their daughter
in London. On Good Friday, Mussolini, reckoning on English
week-end habits, proceeded to devour Albania before anyone
was aware of it. To Francis, hearing the news on the early-
morning broadcast, the moment had come to put into operation
their war-time plans. While his wife still slept, he motored to
London to collect his daughter, who was to spend the next five
years of her life in the old fortress.
     For a year, a succession of nannies came and went. They
were known (to distinguish them one from another) as Big
Nanny, Little Nanny, Old Nanny, Young Nanny, Nice Nanny,
Nasty Nanny and finally Dirty Nanny. In spite of the range and
diversity of their characters, they had some common ground.

They were concerned solely with the welfare of the infant, and all other matters, even in times of wartime emergency, were outside their province. They all disliked solitude and had no hesitation in ringing their bells for service. What they succeeded in summoning up the stone turret stairs that led to the nurseries might have been one of the village women (who came in at odd hours to help out), a demoralized foreigner, or Lucy herself, often the worse for wear. They rang anyway.

The foreign element in the house was represented by two Viennese sisters of singularly low morale and gargantuan appetites. They spoke a great deal of the former glories they had known at the Vienna State Opera, which was possibly not without foundation in fact, as they had the authentic shape of old-time divas. They ate almost ceaselessly, to keep their spirits up. They were supplied by a refugee agency to replace the cook and house-parlourmaid, who, once war was inevitable, were eager to get into war-work and see life. The Viennese were a mistake.

Another foreigner, a potential enemy alien, was the Italian gardener who went with the place – a man of uncertain temper and undisputed talents.

Into this curious assortment Arthur arrived when the first wave of evacuees had passed over the countryside. He had not been back since the time of the ill-fated rejoicings that had followed the Munich crisis the year before. (He was, however, not one to say 'I told you so'.)

Lucy's evacuees were a part of a convent school for dockers' daughters which, owing to its being far too large a unit to remain intact, and on account of the geographical nature of the evacuation scheme, found itself distributed over widely separated villages and hamlets whose names chanced to begin with the same letter. It took some weeks to withdraw the components to suitably large premises in another county, and by then the nuns and girls, overcoming local prejudice, had made themselves greatly liked. Thus it came about that Arthur, bicycling the twenty miles to Oxford and back to procure stores for the many extra mouths, found himself accompanied by a young Irish nun – her habit hitched up by a system of interior loops, bowling along gaily at his side – for whom he soon conceded an unwilling admiration.

But if the loss of the convent was deplored, the loss of the Austrian sisters was a longed-for goal that seemed impossible to attain. From the first bleat of the air-raid warning that followed dramatically on Mr Chamberlain's broadcast announcing that England was at war, they entrenched themselves in their room and refused to emerge. Arthur, stationing himself on a bathroom stool in the passage outside their door, attempted to reason with them in their own tongue. It was of no avail. They answered in a hysterical duet and remained obstinately locked and barricaded. As the local police refused to allow them to go outside a radius of five miles without a special pass bearing their recent photographs, and as no photographer existed within that radius, the deadlock appeared complete.

'They're here for the duration,' Arthur said, 'unless I can succeed in capturing one of them when they sally forth in the middle of the night. We're not very evenly matched as regards weight . . .'

In the course of time, however, the Home Office caught up with these unwelcome visitors and they were finally removed – in poor form but good voice. When Arthur moved into their quarters he found that the war stores, which had filled a large locked cupboard running the length of one wall, were sadly diminished. Here, looking out on the moat, he established himself with his books, playing-cards and a powerful new wireless set to spend his Second World War. His only other possession was a new bicycle, for he had hastened to present his treasured touring-car to the government.

With the passing of the evacuees and the household staff, autumn gave way to the gloom of winter. The old house was lonely now. It was a time of suspense and inertia. It was the Phoney War – 'une drôle de guerre' – nothing happened. The armies faced each other across the Maginot Line. The dreaded heavy air raids didn't materialize. Morale in the village was low. In spite of their distance from the centres of population, some villagers slept nightly beneath their kitchen tables, wearing their gas masks.

On his good days, Arthur worked in the garden with Lucy, at the disposal of the Italian, who, being also a trained chef, had

207

been conscripted to the kitchen – and resented it. (It had still not occurred to Lucy to learn to cook.) Arthur divided his time between gardening, bicycling to Oxford for provisions and lying on his bed listening to the wireless bulletins. The destruction of Poland had filled him with deep melancholy. 'Horses against tanks,' he kept repeating, shaking his head in despair as he studied the map. But perhaps the severest blow was that he had at long last fallen out of love with the Germans. The First World War had not shaken his esteem. He had felt a sentimental and indulgent attachment for them (more commonly felt by his compatriots towards the French) – an attachment made up of holiday memories and a love of their *Kultur* combined with a fervent admiration for their cleanliness, industry, honesty and friendliness. The apogee of human beauty was not for him to be found in Praxiteles or Michelangelo, but in the memory of a line of German sailors, stripped to the waist, once seen on the deck of a destroyer lying in the Kiel Canal as he drove past. From the night when, as an undergraduate, he had seen his first *Tristan* from a seat in the gods at Covent Garden, he had been in love with Germany. Now he had watched the beloved, the superior race, 'the natural friend of England', led by a maniac into the paths of criminal lunacy. It was not a subject that he cared to dwell on. Instead, he began once more to indulge the worm, held in check during the full-time occupations of the first weeks of war. He spent more and more time in bed nursing his fatigue poisons, sometimes playing patience and interminably listening to the wireless bulletins: first the B.B.C., then the German version. In the middle of the night he would get America on his powerful short-wave set. He discounted ninety per cent of what he heard as propaganda and made a gloomy synthesis of the rest. Rallying temporarily with the stirring battle of the River Plate as it came over the air in instalments, and the dramatic boarding of the *Altmark* in a Norwegian fjord, he lapsed again into a miasma of depression. 'Muddle and incompetence . . . hopeless ineptitude . . . apathy and sloth . . .' He had formed the habit of addressing his strictures to the apparatus as he switched off. 'Bet you we haven't got a single armoured division . . .' Lucy heard him reproaching the instrument. 'Lord Haw-Haw' had ceased to amuse. His views all too often seemed to reflect Arthur's own.

208

His only solace now was playing with his granddaughter, but the current nannie always objected to her being brought down to his north-facing room that reeked of tobacco smoke, and there were times when he couldn't face leaving his bed for the cold trek up to the nursery.

Lucy stood at his window, looking out at the dark water where slivers of ice floated. Arthur lay in bed wearing several layers of wool and an expression of dismal bewilderment. The wireless announcer had just told of the Finns, whose heroic resistance had astounded the watching world, being cut to pieces in the Karelian Isthmus.

'Well, at least we haven't blackened our face by giving a guarantee to the Finns, poor devils. But I expect Chamberlain just didn't happen to think of it . . .'

'I do think you're beastly.'

'Sorry, dear girl.' He folded his atlas with a sigh and groped for the matches. 'It's always been the same at the start of every war. Duds at the top.'

'According to you, everyone's dud.'

'Not to the same degree. No, not everyone.'

'Whom do you favour?'

'I should say Churchill's the man. Competent chap. Very sound on India, I remember. But there's not a hope, of course . . .'

'Father, I do wish you'd stop spreading alarm and despondency.'

'What is there to rejoice over, dear girl? You tell me.'

'Well it's not nearly as bad as we expected.'

'You mustn't be impatient.'

'Oh *Father* – '

'You can't win a war with leaflet raids you know.'

'No . . . I don't know what to do about Nannie,' Lucy said, pursuing her own trend of thought. 'She grumbles so maddeningly.'

'Scrap her.'

'I wish I could.'

'You scrap her. She's a most officious woman. She'll be getting the baby into bad ways. Better without her. Tell you what: I'm perfectly capable of being a nannie. I'm an early riser and it's not beyond my powers to wash and dress and feed – I could do all except washing the nappies and yet I don't really see why I shouldn't . . .'

But Lucy recoiled from the idea. The nannies continued to come and go.

The Italian chef, Antonio, had mastered his art by being sent by his former employer – an ambassadorial gourmet – to Larue's for training. His talents, both as a chef and as a prize-winning exhibitor in the world of flower-shows, amounted to something approaching genius. In neither sphere could he bear to be crossed: he had to be sustained by ceaseless praise. He tended to regard the stringency of war-time rations as a personal affront.

'I don't know what to do about him,' Lucy wailed. 'I fairly dread his rages. I keep telling him *I* didn't fix the ration at two ounces per head per week . . .'

'It's no wonder the fellow's disaffected,' Arthur said, 'with all the poison he absorbs from his wireless. I could hear a Fascist broadcast he had on *fortissimo* while I was doing that row of celery near his cottage. Pure poison. We'll be lucky if some of it doesn't get into the soup.'

'Oh, I'm so tired of it.'

'I'll tell you what,' Arthur said after a pause, 'let me take over in the kitchen. I used to be quite keen on cooking before your mother . . . I've got my recipe book somewhere.'

But Lucy thwarted him again. How much it was due to the prospect of heavy breakages of irreplaceable china, and how much a resolve not to allow her father free rein in her household, it was difficult to tell.

And so the dismal first winter of war passed with its quota of colds and minor discords. 'We certainly didn't know when we were well off,' Lucy used to think later, remembering the early days.

28

The knocking continued. Lucy dragged herself painfully out of the depths. (She had formed the habit of sleeping-pills.)

'What is it?'

'I've brought you a cup of tea, dear girl, so that you can wake up and listen to the news. It's begun. Holland and Belgium and France attacked.' Lucy struggled up in bed groaning.

'I got it on the six o'clock. They started pouring across the frontiers of Belgium and Holland at four a.m. Tanks and aircraft on a huge scale.'

'Oh, how ghastly . . .'

He drew back the heavy curtains and the early-morning sun-shine flooded the room, which seemed suddenly filled with the singing of birds and the scent of may blossom from across the moat. Arthur, striding about the room, cannoning into furniture, had reverted to his old buoyant manner. For weeks past, his anxiety and perturbation had turned to acute distress of mind over the fiasco in Norway. Lucy resented his pessimism. Since the Prime Minister's unfortunate speech in which he claimed that Hitler had 'missed the bus', father and daughter had not trusted themselves to refer to the situation. Now that the dreaded in-vasion of the Low Countries had begun, Arthur seemed almost jubilant. All day long he remained glued to the wireless. By nine p.m., when the Prime Minister broadcast his resignation and called for support for Mr Churchill, Arthur was in high spirits.

'You join me in a whisky, dear girl? I really ought to get registered for my quota of this stuff. Remind me to send a line to the Stores and Whiteley's in the morning. We want to drink to Winston.'

'It's too frightful to think of what's happening in Holland . . . And poor Belgium all over again.'

'These neutral countries are all the same,' Arthur said, measuring out the drinks. 'Won't have anything to do with us beforehand. Mustn't do anything to annoy Hitler. With the examples of Austria, Czechoslovakia, Poland, Norway and Denmark in front of them, they prefer to trust to his word. Then scream like blazes when they're attacked. I say: Blow the neutrals!'

'How *can* you talk like that?'

'Well, it's not *quite* fair. I'm very sorry for their sufferings, which they brought on themselves. And of course we couldn't have seemed very impressive: the Chamberlain government didn't inspire respect . . .'

'Can't you lay off Chamberlain now – '

'I promise never to mention the name again, cross my heart!' Arthur exclaimed gaily. 'And Churchill reigned in his stead. It's an ill wind all right, all right . . . It remains to be seen now if France will hold.'

'Of course France will hold.'

It took five days for Holland to capitulate and a week for the last of the nannies to take her departure. This event, once dreaded by Lucy, had ceased to have much significance for, by now, the French front had been pierced and the fearful news overshadowed all else.

Lucy and Frances moved down to the guest-room adjoining Arthur's quarters. She and her father shared the care of the infant, who, having passed through many hands, raised no objection to the new regime.

The weather was never so lovely. The thousands of tulips bordering the lawn were the most splendid ever seen. The quince trees in the orchard, usually so niggardly of blossom, flowered with a tropical exuberance. The lilac broke all records. Frances, actively crawling already, resembled a golden cherub. The com-

212

bination of idyllic beauty and agonizing bad news was too poignant to bear, Lucy thought. *Blow winds and crack your cheeks* . . . If only it would rain, snow and hail – she would have liked to see all that loveliness destroyed, in keeping with the horror across the Channel.

'They've reached Abbeville,' Arthur said, emerging from his room. His face was haggard.

'Where's that?'

'Between Calais and Dieppe. Not far from the sea . . .'

'My God!'

'Only a few armoured columns so far. Still, it's unbelievable . . . They've reached in ten days what they never did in four years last time. It means of course our army's cut off now . . .'

Lucy, speechless, gathered up the tray and left the room – Arthur sat down on the floor beside the play-pen where the infant was engaged in a vigorous game with stuffed animals. She smiled and held them up to him in turn, waiting while he made the appropriate sound for each and named them to her, a performance which she repeated after him.

'Come on, girlie,' he said with a sigh after a couple of rounds of this, 'I'll take you for a little ride in your pram.'

'Pam-pam.'

'Have it your own way. In your pam-pam.'

'In your pam-pam.'

Arthur let it pass. Usually, he liked nothing better than to instruct his granddaughter. It was a process that often irritated Lucy who held that the child, unquestionably precocious, was being crammed with information and brought on too rapidly. Today he couldn't bring himself to explain the proper use of the possessive adjective.

'They've reached Boulogne.'

'Oh God, oh God . . . It's terrifying, Father . . .'

'Your grandfather had a house there. I remember your mother pointing it out to me once when we went on a bicycle tour. A nice place . . . It must have been a nice place for a holiday . . .'

213

After a pause, Lucy said in an anguished voice: 'Everything's happening so fast. What's going to become of our army?'

Arthur made a gesture signifying despair. 'They're fighting their way back. I was listening to an eye-witness account just now of the state of the roads. The appalling congestion . . . crammed with refugees . . . being dive-bombed . . .'

'I simply can't stand thinking of it. I *can't* . . .'

'In the Great War, there was the same trouble in Italy after Caporetto, I remember. The civilian population obstructing the military. No doubt Napoleon had similar difficulties in his retreat from Moscow . . . I expect Hannibal found the populace obstructing his elephants . . .'

'I'd back the elephants against the populace,' Lucy said tearfully.

'I'd back tanks. But I don't imagine we've got any tanks – yet. We merely invented the things . . .'

'Belgium's packed up. King Leopold's capitulated, all on his own.'

Lucy put down her mending and sighed. There was nothing left to say.

'It wouldn't matter so much,' Arthur continued bitterly, 'if he hadn't bawled for help, got our armies to rush in after it was too late, then ratted without warning, leaving us exposed . . . cut off . . . But I was forgetting, Churchill, announcing this, asked us not to pass judgement at this time – I'll say no more.'

'Goodness, you certainly like Churchill, don't you, Father?'

'If anyone can get us out of our mess, he can. For years now he's been a voice crying in the wilderness. No one's paid any attention. And he's always been right.'

'What about over the abdication?'

'I mean important things,' Arthur said. It was a legacy from his early socialist days that he always regarded crowned heads as slightly subhuman. Lucy hadn't the heart to argue. After a pause he said: 'I'll ride into Oxford tomorrow to see if I can buy a tricycle for Frances.'

'She's not yet eighteen months – '

'She's very active. Soon be getting about. I wish it were possible

214

to net the moat . . . On the assumption that we continue to exist, I want to make sure of a good tricycle – with a good bicycle to follow. When the bombing starts it may not be so easy.'

'So the B.E.F.'s trapped.'

'Looks like it. Yes.'

'Oh Father . . . oh Father . . .'

'There's always the sea.'

'I can remember the time the Germans broke through in 1918.'

'Yes. We had the French fighting then. Don't cry, dear girl. We're seeing history in the making . . .'

'Antonio's just been bloody insolent,' Lucy said, entering the room with an armful of mending. She had formed the habit of listening to the nine o'clock news at Arthur's bedside.

'They've begun evacuating from Dunkirk.'

'He says he's not going to cook tomorrow because there's nothing in the larder. And there's two days to go before we can get our rations.'

'Tell him to give us some vegetables *à l'eau*. Lucy, the evacuation's started. The Admiralty's sent out a call for ships – any kind of small boat. They're taking the men off from Dunkirk and the beaches. It's to be hoped this weather lasts. The sea should be calm – that's something.'

'Oh Father . . . it must, it must go on! It's been perfect for so long now . . .'

'One minute to 9. So Antonio's been rude again, has he? Comes of listening to Radio Milano. He probably imagines he'll be giving the orders soon. There's a lot to be said for jamming.'

'Nearly 50,000,' he said when the announcer's voice had ceased. 'That's better than one could have dared to hope.'

'What's the latest figure?' Lucy asked as Arthur entered the nursery.

'180,000. The bridgehead's reduced. Very heavy air attacks and shelling. We must have lost a lot of shipping. Here, let me do that. Crying won't help.'

'It looks like keeping fine still,' Lucy said looking out at the sunlit garden, while he fixed the side of the cot. 'Thank God.'

'Goodnight, girlie,' Arthur addressed the cot. 'Now you just shut peepers and go bye-byes.'

'All over,' Arthur said. 'Grand total 330-odd thousand. Who would have thought it possible a week ago . . .'

'It's like a miracle!'

'330-odd thousand without their arms and equipment, remember. Barely the rags they stand up in. Don't be misled into thinking of it as a victory.'

'It's a miraculous deliverance.'

'It'll be our turn next,' Arthur said gloomily. 'Talking of arms, does this village boast more than a few hay-forks, if they start dropping these parachutists we've heard so much about?'

'Farmer White's got a rook rifle.'

'Splendid! Churchill's speaking to the House at the moment. Don't be late for the nine o'clock.'

'It *was* a miracle, because look! The weather's going to break. That's the first cloud we've seen for weeks and there's a wind getting up. I never saw such delphiniums – '

The voice had come over the air: 'If necessary for years, if necessary alone, we shall go on to the end . . . We shall fight on the beaches, we shall fight on the landing-grounds, we shall fight in the fields and in the streets, we shall fight in the hills; we shall never surrender . . .'

'You do see what I mean about Churchill,' Arthur said.

The intoxicating feeling of relief that was born with the Dunkirk deliverance could not last long. The spectacle of the French agony haunted everyone who loved France, every tripper who had ever made the day-trip to Boulogne. Within a week, Mussolini had joined in to administer the *coup de grâce*. 'Why, the trait'rous no-good bastard – saving your presence ma'am. That there Tony had ought to be hangin' his head for shame . . .'

Antonio was not hanging his head. He was excited but cagey, his temper *molto nervoso*.

216

Very early on the following morning, Arthur woke Lucy with the news that Antonio had been arrested and carted off in the middle of the night, leaving his unfortunate wife, who was a local girl, in a state of collapse. No one knew what had become of him. The local and county police were ignorant of his whereabouts. The Home Office had other things to think about. He had vanished without a trace. After some weeks, a postcard arrived with a Liverpool postmark stating merely that he was leaving for a destination unknown. When, within forty-eight hours of this, the *Arandora Star* was torpedoed soon after leaving Liverpool, carrying German prisoners-of-war and Italian civilian internees to Canada for safe-keeping, it was natural to conclude that Antonio was among the thousand wretches drowned.

He was sincerely mourned – his virtues extolled, his vices pardoned. The village was shaken by the news.

'He was rather a bad hat,' Arthur said, 'but I don't suppose he knew any better, poor fellow.'

'He was always sweet with Frances – even when he was playing me up.'

'Yes. One really shouldn't judge other people by one's own standards of behaviour.'

'I suppose it's all a matter of upbringing . . .'

'So's cannibalism . . . Well, he was very able. You're going to miss him, Lucy.' This was an understatement. As Arthur threw himself heart and soul into the task of maintaining the garden, while Lucy struggled for mastery with the charcoal-burning range (which was the only medium that Larue's had allowed for *haute cuisine*), news came through at last, through Francis's endeavours, that the lamented one was safe in the Isle of Man. Here, with his compatriots for company, he settled down to enjoy his war.

Meanwhile, it was a time of anguish. After the death, the decomposition of France . . . News of enemy landings and parachute descents were expected hourly. At either end of the village, a felled tree barricaded the road. Here a member of the newly formed Home Guard stood in a shallow trench protected by sand-bags. Sign-posts that might have directed the invaders were everywhere removed. (Travellers without a map or knowledge of the countryside wandered lost, their questions usually unanswered by the suspicious rustics, who sometimes went so far as to misdirect them.) The great bell in the tower which had sounded the hours and rung out across the fields for the past three hundred years was silenced, to ring again only to announce invasion – or victory. This was not the dim vague waiting of the Phoney War, but a sense of keyed-up expectancy, a time of acute emotion.

'Terrible news of the French,' Arthur said.

'What's left?' Lucy asked bitterly. 'What more can there be after what's happened?'

'We've sunk the French fleet.'

'Oh God! In battle?'

'No. In harbour. We bombarded them after due notice. Had to, or they'd be used against us.'

'How utterly horrible. How *unnatural*. Where?'

'Oran. Alexandria . . . Dakar . . . We had to.'

They sat for a few moments in silence. Then Lucy got up, shaking herself like a dog.

'Farmer White's lent his rook-gun to the road block this end.'

Arthur smiled. 'Then it's to be hoped they'll come by the Reading road. He mustn't shoot till he sees the whites of their eyes.' He began packing his pipe. 'You know, dear girl, I think I'll take a day off and run up to London to get a bicycle for Frances.'

'She can't manage the tricycle yet.'

'She soon will and then she'll outgrow it. With all the national effort being devoted to munitions, children's bicycles are going to be in short supply.'

'You're looking a long way ahead, Father.'

'Got to. And then I'll drop in and see your mother. Kill two birds with one stone.'

One of the village women who came to do the washing-up burst into the room.

'Oh, ma'am, they do say as them there parachutists is landing on the Oxford road. Mrs Johnson's youngest had it from that Gloria as works in the Pressed Steel. Comin' down like a cloud they was. Dressed like nuns.'

'Go on, Mrs Barton,' Arthur said. 'Don't you believe a word of it.'

218

'It's very wrong to go spreading stories,' Lucy added. 'It's a punishable offence. And you know what a story-teller Gloria is – '

'Oh I know, ma'am, as how the girl's not to be trusted. Still I thought as I'd come early so's I could get home early. These do be turrible times as we're livin' in.'

'They do. They are. Yes.'

Daylight raids over the Kent and Sussex air-fields were constant. Sometimes the London area was mentioned. Arthur proclaimed the figures given for air losses, the enemy's and the RAF's, as if he were announcing cricket scores. He was always sceptical of these figures.

'Thirty-two for nine – don't believe it. Don't believe a word of it.'

'Why on earth not?'

'Propaganda is a powerful weapon on both sides.'

'Perhaps you'd rather believe the Germans.'

'By no means. I discount all claims. In any case, one plane may be claimed by several pilots in genuine good faith.'

'By the way, did I tell you that rifles have arrived for the Home Guard.'

'Good-oh. How many?'

'Two.'

'Any cartridges?'

'Ten.'

'Between them?'

'No. Each.'

'Jolly good-oh. Doesn't leave much for target practice perhaps.'

Lucy bent to her mending while Arthur puffed at his pipe in silence. Presently he asked: 'How's the petrol situation?'

'All right.'

'If I could possibly take the car tomorrow I could collect those tins I couldn't manage on my bicycle, and there's a message from old Arnott to say he's got a boiling fowl for us. That's big news.'

'Sorry, I'm afraid you can't.'

'Why not?'

'I've lost the distributor arm.'

'What, again?'

'Yes, again. This time I can't find it anywhere. I think someone's stolen it.'

'I don't. You'll just have to try to remember where you put it, dear girl.'

'That's what I've been doing for *hours*, haven't I! And I searched until it was too dark to see in the garage and the sheds. This business of hiding things drives me absolutely insane.'

'It's only a matter of immobilizing the car, dear girl. Not a question of hiding a vital part in a different place every time.'

'Why don't *you* do it then, if you're so clever about it?'

'I will, gladly. Bring it to bed with me every night. They'd never think of looking there.'

'Yes. And invasion night you'll be having an off-day and forget all about it.'

Lucy knew the reproach was unjustified. Arthur's fatigue poisons didn't function in times like these. He ignored her implication and said: 'I'll have a good hunt in the morning. It's bound to be somewhere. And after that I'll see to it. There were instructions again today about locking up bicycles – and food. One can't be bothered locking up the food, and as for the rest, they'd probably bring their own transport.' He turned on one elbow to switch on the wireless. 'Time for the German programme.'

'I don't want to hear it, please.'

'Pity. They've got a new song.'

'Not tonight Father.'

'All right. It's a very jolly tune. Lot of verses and they end – it goes something like this:

> '*Und wir fahren,*
> *Und wir fahren,*
> *Und wir fahren gegen Eng-e-land!*
> *Whew! Whew! Whew!*'

Lucy grunted.

'D'you remember the *Hassengesang* in the last war?' Arthur asked.

'I've still got it. I was always going to have it framed to hang in the lu.'

'They're a rum lot,' Arthur said ruefully.

29

The face of the land was changing. Arthur returned from a walk with the pram.

'There's an excrescence gone up overnight at the junction with the main road. Put up by the soldiery. Two lorry loads of them.'

'What would that be?'

'Blockhouse? I don't know.'

'I was talking to Sheila on the telephone. There's a row of dragon's teeth been sown across her fields. What *could* she mean?'

'Anti-tank obstacle? Who knows . . . One mustn't ask. There've been tremendous air battles all day in the south.'

'London, too?'

'London, too. You know Frances enjoys watching the bombing practice on Otmoor. She says "Oh hairypin!" and, "Bomb-bomb goes bang-bang." I hope it's not going to affect her later on.'

'It won't unless you start putting ideas in her head.' After a pause, Lucy said: 'D'you think it will come next week? It's full moon next week.'

'It doesn't follow they want a full moon.'

'Oh *Father* . . . The awful news . . . this waiting and expecting, the wondering what's happening to them in London – I don't know how to stand it!'

'Since you've no alternative . . .' Arthur said.

The heavy, nightly bombing of London had begun and Isabelle had come in to her own. For nearly a year she attended classes, conducting a desultory feud with the personnel at the First Aid Post. Now she was working on a shift at the busy casualty station, and two or three times a week sent as nurse in ambulances taking air-raid victims to hospitals in the country. 'Nurse!' they would cry out to her, full of confidence in the starched uniform, or sometimes, more intimately, 'Gran!' Lucy thought of her mother, so long a problem and a burden, suddenly, improbably, in the firing-line of all places and, what was more, useful there. There was no doubt that the suffering and devastation which surrounded her brought out the best in Isabelle. The sad chaos of her married life was forgotten for the time being.

As the glorious autumn weather turned to gales, the glaring menace of invasion began to recede and the extreme tension gave way to an agonizing over the nightly destruction of London, a ceaseless speculation as to what had been hit. The wireless revealed very little. Francis got home rarely and in a state of exhaustion, sometimes falling asleep where he sat. Isabelle's letters complained of noisy nights and the absence of water or electricity or gas – or all three. Shaken and worn, she survived the ordeals of the blitz. She was working now twice a week as a shelter nurse in the Praed Street Tube Station. Here conditions were primitive – a bucket behind a curtain of sacking provided the sanitation, while sleeping accommodation was no more than the concrete platform. Here whole families sprawled inert as in a Hogarthian orgy, dead to the thunder of the bombs and the barrage overhead, dead to the approach of the 5 a.m. train as Isabelle struggled to lift their heavy limbs across a line drawn on the platform. With the contempt of the insomniac for the natural sleeper, she regarded them as animals but discharged her onerous duties with true constancy. The raiders came with absolute punctuality – two hundred or more heavy bombers every night without fail. The strain was colossal.

*

Arthur lay in bed, wondering if it were cold enough to warrant the second hot-water bottle that he had in reserve for the winter proper. Lucy entered for the evening session with the wireless.

'It's a wonderful moon outside. Put out the light and I'll shew it you – reflected in the moat. Would you like to see?'

'No thanks, dear girl.'

'Listen!'

The thump, thump, thump, peculiar to enemy machines was heard overhead.

'The Luftwaffe's out visiting,' Arthur said.

'Where are they going?'

'They didn't tell me. Birmingham, Coventry, who knows?' The sound of the machines went on for a long time. At last there was silence.

'I'd better go out and take a look at that damned greenhouse stove again,' Arthur sighed. 'I think it's freezing pretty hard.'

'Can I?'

'No thanks, dear girl. I've got lots of lovely stuff I can't afford to run a risk with. And I can only use the minimum of fuel.' He put on his overcoat over his dressing-gown, pulled on his socks and gumboots and made his way to the moonlit terrace and across the icy garden to the one greenhouse fire that he kept stoked, mainly for the sake of Antonio. Francis had been working for the Italian's liberation, pointing out that he was over military age and of pre-fascist vintage, and there were hopes now of his return.

Antonio returned in time for the new year. A haggard ex-prisoner of war had been expected. Instead he arrived plump and rosy, with soft uncalloused hands and a jaunty, almost truculent, bearing. It was clear at once that he had expected to see the garden laid waste, ravaged by weeds, a desert where he would be hailed as a saviour. He was by no means pleased at the impressive orderliness which was the result of Arthur's unceasing labours.

'*Ho fatto il meglio possibile*,' Arthur said modestly, expecting a word of appreciation. 'Ungrateful devil,' he murmured when Antonio merely glared about him and stalked away.

224

His revenge was simple. Arthur, venturing early to the greenhouse, came upon all his boxes of precious little plants laid out on the frozen path, hopelessly exposed to the heavy frost. He stood staring, unable to believe his eyes, then turned and went slowly back to his bed.

When he had not appeared to breakfast, Lucy went to find him. She was in a black mood. Last thing at night she had chanced to see the eastern sky a fiery red. For a long time she stood staring at this unaccustomed sight. London was burning. Sleep was impossible. How to sleep with the knowledge of that hideously beautiful, glowing curtain hanging outside in the still night. At intervals, she crept shivering to the east window in the turret room adjoining the bedroom. The roseate glow was still there. It was the great incendiary raid that destroyed Wren's churches. Arthur's injury seemed small beer compared with this calamity.

'The beast, oh the brute!' Lucy exclaimed when he told her of his discovery. 'Father, there must have been a mammoth raid last night – the sky was red. I nearly came to wake you to see it. What did they say on the six o'clock?'

'Bad raid.'

'Oh God, oh *God!* . . . Come and have breakfast.'

'I don't want any.'

'Why not?'

'No thanks.'

As he offered no explanation but turned over and settled down to sleep again, Lucy grew exasperated. 'For heaven's sake! You aren't going to be ill just because Toni's been a stinking beast! Father, listen to me!'

'There's nothing to discuss. I don't feel at all well.'

'Have your breakfast and then go over and give him hell.'

'I've no wish to have any further dealings with him.'

'You mean *everything's* killed off?'

'The whole fruit of my labours has been destroyed. It's an act of sabotage. I refuse to have anything further to do with him – or the garden.'

'Oh hell!' Lucy began losing her temper. 'What's it matter anyway! London burns and you carry on like this! What does it *matter*, I say? Damn Antonio . . . damn the bloody garden! . . .'

225

Her father's expression of dejection enraged her. 'I've got more than I can cope with without you adding to it. I can't stand here arguing with Frances loose in the dining-room. I've no time for carrying trays either. If you want your breakfast you can come for it.' Her exit was noisy. Arthur closed his eyes. He quite genuinely did not want his breakfast.

Arthur, usually lenient towards human iniquity, could not bring himself to forgive the perfidious Italian. Perhaps only a gardener could appreciate the extent of the injury he had suffered. Recoiling from the blow, and further wounded by Lucy's lack of sympathy, he turned as it were to the arms of the worm. A severe bout of fatigue poisons set in immediately. He refused all nourishment and lay with the blackout curtains drawn, seeking oblivion in sleep.

The terrible winter wore on. There were times when the old stone house seemed almost uninhabitable. In the morning there were little banks of snow inside the windows which the icy winds forced through the leaded panes. 'They said that last winter was the worst for a hundred years, but this is worse still,' Lucy complained fretfully. 'We had famine two years running in India,' Arthur responded gloomily.

The raids continued. Arthur's chronic pessimism lifted only at the hour of the inimitable Free French broadcasts: '*Les Français parlent aux français*' – and in his granddaughter's company. The war news was generally bad and often distressing. The now familiar names of Arab towns and villages that had spelled the hilarious victories of the first desert campaign featured once more in the news – in reverse. (Only Tobruk held.)

'I dislike the dishonest way the BBC try to pass it off as wholly unimportant,' Arthur complained. 'When we take a place, it's a victory all right: when we lose it, it's referred to in an aside as something of no account.'

'All *right*,' Lucy said peevishly. 'I can hear the beastly news too! I've got ears. Your harping and carping doesn't help, Father.' Their squabbles had become frequent. The trouble was not only her father's pessimism, Lucy thought, it was his in-

226

fluence over Frances. He loved the child with a doting indulgence that he had never shown towards his own children, and the attachment was mutual. It is possible that, in his granddaughter, Arthur found the most satisfying relationship he was to experience. She was the perfect listener, never tired of hearing him talk, as eager to learn as he was to instruct, ever ready to drop what she was doing to go to him when he called, never resentful of his correction. The trouble was, of course, that Lucy did not share his views on what was suitable for a two-year-old. When it was his turn to put her to bed he would stand poised with a pot of ointment in one hand and a tin of antiseptic dressings in the other, checking her over for cuts, bites and abrasions.

'Any sore places?'

'No, I don't fink so.'

'Think carefully now. Were you playing with the cat today? Has he scratched you at all?'

'For goodness sake!' Lucy exclaimed. She had come in to say good night.

'A cat's scratch can be very poisonous,' Arthur persisted.

'But she hasn't *got* a scratch.'

'I'm not saying she has. I'm just asking. Or a small cut, say, with garden dirt in it can soon turn nasty. In India, lockjaw was very common.'

'*Mais, mon Dieu, nous ne sommes pas aux Indes!*'

'*Mieux vaux prendre des précautions que regretter trop tard.*'

'*Tu me rendras folle!*'

'Sorry, dear girl.'

Frances, who had been scrutinizing her anatomy, had decided that a pinkish patch on one knee would qualify for treatment.

'I got a sore place!'

'Let me look at it,' Arthur said, removing his glasses for close inspection. Lucy left the room.

She resolved to have it out with her father. A hypochondriac father was one thing. A hypochondriac only child was something else again.

Seeing all too clearly Arthur's absurdities, she was nevertheless quite unaware of how much the insidious poison accounted for her own behaviour, for she was constantly complaining of minor ailments and insomnia.

227

But that evening there was a gala programme in '*Les Français parlent aux français*', celebrating the ignominious defeat of the Italian navy in the battle of Matapan. To the tune of the French nursery rhyme, they sang:

> '*Il était une flot-te craintiv-e*
> *Il était une flot-te craintiv-e*
> *Qui restait enfer-fermée dans ses ports.*
> *Qui restait enfer-fermée dans ses ports. Ohé! Ohé!*
>
> *Hitler sa patience épuisé – e*
> *Hitler sa patience épuisé – e . . .*'

When the glorious ballad had ended, father and daughter remained giggling harmoniously, their differences forgotten.

The next morning Francis telephoned that he was able to take a couple of days off.

'Come on, girlie,' Arthur said. 'We're going with mummy in the car-car to meet daddy.'

'Where my lickle mot'ring coatee?'

'Here it is,' Arthur cried gaily. 'Now put your handie through there . . . now the other one.'

'S'all I wear my glub-glubs?'

'You'd better wear your glub-glubs. It'll be cold in the car-car.'

'Where my shoe-shoes, Ganfer?'

'I've got them. Now sit down and give me your footies.'

'Blimey,' Lucy said, 'if I'd talked like that you'd have crowned me. You didn't hold with baby talk with us. You insisted on being called father before we could manage dad-dad.' Arthur was surprised. He paused a moment in his valeting, trying to recall his daughter's infancy. 'At that age, as far as I recollect, you jabbered in Hindustani. Now this child, apart from the usual infantilisms, contributes some very interesting words of her own invention. Take the case of her word *bolius*, for example. It has a derogatory significance I can see, though the meaning is not yet precise. It can be used as an adjective or as an adverb and seems to me to fill a long-felt want in the English language. Of course the repetitive doubling of the one-syllable word is a hall-mark of peoples at a primitive level of civilization, as I

228

remember with certain tribes in India. The word tom-tom, for example – '

'Come *on*, Ganfer,' Frances said, tugging at his sleeve. 'S'all we see moo-cows in the car-car.'

'Oh rather!' Arthur exclaimed, 'but not *in*, *from* the car-car. And piggy-wigs and bow-wows if we're lucky.'

'And sheeps?'

'Lots of sheep, I expect.'

'I love sheeps,' Frances said, taking his hand as he led the way out of the room. 'I love all sheeps but I love lickle, clean, baby sheeps better'n big, dirty, bolius, mummy sheeps.'

'So do I,' Arthur agreed, 'definitely.'

'So do I, daffantly, Ganfer.'

The cruel north-easters that blew throughout April gave way to a freezing May as the heartbreaking British campaign in Greece was followed by the savage disaster of Crete. At home, the air-raids were heavier than ever. In North Africa, the presence of the Afrika Korps had already made itself felt. The immense scale of the air-borne landings that overwhelmed Crete were regarded by the local wiseacres as a dress rehearsal for England. Villagers got out their gas-masks again, a sure sign of agitation. A native son had been shot down in an air battle and feelings ran high. One night, a German bomber was intercepted on a Midland raid and brought down in a neighbouring field where it exploded with its full load of bombs. Lucy lay awake after the explosions that rocked the old house had died away. As soon as it was light, she hurried to the scene of the crash. An RAF officer was inspecting two piles of butcher's meat where the fragments of five corpses had been gathered. An indescribable object at her feet suddenly revealed itself as a human eye, glazed but un-mistakably blue. As she fled back the way she had come, she trod on a finger wearing a signet ring that she had missed on the way there.

Arthur was looking forward to taking Frances to the scene. As he finished her toilette, he regaled her with tales of famous crashes: 'Now I'll tell you about the R101. You must imagine a giant sausage – '

'*Faut pas y aller. Il y a des restes humains –* '

'*Mais puisqu'ils ne sont plus vivants –* '

'*Je te défends!*'

'Not educational? All right, as you say. One less over Birmingham anyhow. Poor devils.'

'Can I see the hairypin in Mr White's field?'

'Not now, darling. It's all in pieces, anyway.'

'Can I see the pieces?'

'Presently,' Arthur said with surprising tact. 'We'll go and call on Bessie first and see if her pussy-cat's had kittens.'

' "N" see if her poosy-cat's had kittens,' came his echo.

'If I live to be a hundred, I don't think I shall ever enjoy May again,' Lucy said.

'If you live to a hundred you're not likely to enjoy anything.'

'This time last year it was France, and now – '

'This time last year, we were sunbathing – that's the main difference. There may be many bad Mays before the end's in sight. It's the campaigning season. Except in Africa. I'll switch on for the news.'

'The battleship *Hood*,' the announcer's voice came over the air, 'has been sunk in an engagement with the *Bismarck* off Greenland . . . direct hit on the magazine . . . survivors are not expected . . .'

'Then Philip's drowned!' Lucy cried, referring to a cousin who was serving in *Hood*. She burst into tears. (She was not to know that her cousin was on shore leave and another fate was in store for him.)

The cruel tragedy of Crete continued. The news was unbearable, but there was no escaping it.

'Why haven't we got any air cover?' Arthur asked miserably. 'Why couldn't we hold the aerodrome, after all the months we've had in which to prepare? Why didn't we destroy it, if we couldn't?'

'Don't ask me, Father,' Lucy groaned. They sat at the lunch table waiting for the one o'clock news. There was a long pause after the time signal.

'The *Bismarck* has been sunk,' Lucy said in a BBC voice.

''s been sunk,' Frances echoed.

'The *Bismarck* has been sunk,' came the announcer's voice. It was a moment of indescribable emotion.

'The *Hood*'s avenged,' Arthur said. 'Furthermore, she must have been about thirty while the *Bismarck* was only four days old. The beginner's luck didn't hold. It's a good bag . . .'

And still the bloody massacre in Crete went on . . .

'Breakfast's ready,' Lucy said, 'on the terrace. I do believe it's a heat-wave starting. Any news?'

'One of those everlasting last strongholds has fallen somewhere in Abyssinia.'

'Good.'

'Wavell's sent an ultimatum to Djibouti to break with Vichy. (They won't.) Damascus has fallen.'

'*That's* good.'

'Oh, and Germany invaded Russia at three-thirty a.m.'

'*Father!*'

'Without ultimatum or any kind of previous warning – '

'Oh – '

'The whole length from Finland to the Black Sea.'

'Oh good heavens, who'd have believed it! Why didn't you tell me that first? How maddening of you!'

'It's too soon to make a song and dance about it.'

'But we're not alone any more! We've got an ally! Father, it's *wonderful* news!'

'Won't do us much good if it's another walkover.'

'Well, you can't assume that yet. What's the reason given for attacking?'

'Oh, Hitler's issued a proclamation accusing them of aggression . . . Jewish-Bolshevist conspiracy . . . the usual stuff. Winston's speaking this evening.'

At nine o'clock, the well-loved voice, strong, rasping, sardonic came over the air: '. . . All his usual formalities of perfidy were observed with scrupulous technique . . .' When the Prime Minister had finished speaking, they remained silent, full of inward excitement at the mere fact of living at another moment of history.

But immense disasters followed and the sense of exhilaration gave way once more to depression and dismay.

Another winter. Lucy shrank from the thought.

The war had spread to the Middle East. The campaign in the desert was disquieting. The sinkings at sea continued. Air-raids continued. In Russia, the degree of human misery stunned the spectator. The enemy had advanced half a thousand miles in a series of bloody battles – Smolensk and Kiev fallen, Moscow and Leningrad invested, the government and industry removed to the Urals – the end seemed not far off.

Arthur lay in his bed, finding solace in the company of his granddaughter. His patience cards were spread on a tray across his knees. Frances nestled against him, supported by his left arm, her eyes fixed intently on the play. When the game ended, she gathered up the cards. It was her prerogative.

'Anozzer one Ganfer?'

'Must have a pipe first.'

'Must have a pipe first.'

She watched the fascinating, familiar process of filling and lighting up and sniffed the smoke appreciatively. Suddenly, through the blue cloud, she stretched out a finger and touched him on the cheek.

'Ganfer got a lovely m'stache,' she said.

'Nice of you to say so.'

'Mummy hasn't got,' Frances continued. 'Daddy hasn't got. Toto hasn't got, but Ganfer got! Ganfer got a m'stache. Ganfer lovely.'

Arthur laughed. 'I'm no oil painting. Never have been.'

'Never have been.'

'I remember once I went into a hall of mirrors – it was a looking-glass room, you see – with your mummy and Uncle Edmund when they were little. It was at Brighton. I suddenly noticed a man in there and I remember thinking: that's an ugly chap – and then I saw it was myself. I've never had any illusions about my appearance since. Not many before either.'

'Not many before eiver.'

'Beauty's only skin deep, remember. What shall we do now?'

'S'all you sing Ganfer p'ease? Sing a song.'

'What shall I sing?'

Arthur had a repertoire of music-hall songs dating from his early youth, frowned on by Lucy but cherished by the infant. He cleared his throat and began:

'The old man he came home drunk, as drunk as drunk could be.
He saw a coat on his coat-peg where his coat ought to be.
"Dear wife, loving wife, what is that I see?
Whose coat is that coat on my coat-peg where my coat ought
to be?"
"Oh you fool, you silly old fool, really can't you see?
It's only just a blanket that grannie's lent to me."
"I've travelled far, I've travelled wide, ten thousand miles or more,
Buttons on a blanket I never saw before!"

The old man he came home, drunk as drunk as drunk could be
He saw a form in his armchair where his form ought to be.
"Dear wife, loving wife, what is that I see?
Whose form is that form in my armchair where my form ought
to be?"
"Oh you fool, you silly old fool, really can't you see?
It's only just a chambermaid that grannie's lent to me."
"I've travelled far, I've travelled wide, ten thousand miles or more,
Whiskers on a chamber-maid I never saw before!"'

'That's all I remember unfortunately.'

'S'all we have young man taiken in 'n' done for now?'

This was a ballad that dealt with misfortune. The refrain was simple:

'Young man taiken in 'n' done for,
Oh I never thought as she,
The gal I lef' me 'appy 'ome for
Would er taiken in 'n' done for me?'

'*Ah ça alors!*' Lucy exclaimed entering on the final chorus.
'*Je n'aime pas ces sales chansons!*'

'*Pourtant la petite les aime bien.*'

233

'They're so beastly inappropriate. What's the matter with nursery rhymes? Frances can sing "Ding Dong Dell", can't you, darling?'

'I don't like poosie's in er well.' Frances, sensing trouble afoot, weighed in on Arthur's side.

'Well, "Little Miss Muffet" then.'

'I hate er big spoider.'

'I rather agree,' Arthur said, 'nursery rhymes are often distinctly macabre.'

'But adult indecencies are all right? I do wish you'd try to cooperate, Father.' Lucy, annoyed with herself for quarrelling in front of the child, left the room again. As she went down the passage, she could hear Arthur's voice raised once more in song:

'Mary had a little lamb, its fleece was white as snow
Shouting out the battle-cry of Freedom!
And everywhere that Mary went the lamb was sure to go
Shouting out the battle-cry of Freedom!'

Snow came early that year. In the first week of December, the lovely familiar landscape was lightly powdered over. Arthur took to bed – the only warm place. The electrifying news of the Japanese attack on Pearl Harbor, which broke on 7 December, would have roused a dying man.

It was Sunday evening. They had just listened to the announcement of Japanese air attacks on American ships at Hawaii and British ones in the Dutch East Indies.

'Good God! Then America's in!' Lucy cried, her sewing slipping from her lap.

'Undoubtedly! Where's that medicinal whisky got to?'

'But it's incredible! With all those negotiations going on at the White House! The treachery of it!'

'More mad dogs,' Arthur said. 'I've always thought them a deluded lot. It's all that ancestor-worship . . . Now they're dirty dogs, too!'

'But Father, I can't grasp it! America in at last! It's wonderful surely, isn't it?'

'In the long run, yes, it must be. Meantime the war's spread right across the globe, which is horrible enough to be going on with.'

'What a good thing we've sent the *Prince of Wales* and the *Repulse* to Singapore just in time. For once you can't say too little and too late.'

'It's another historical moment all right,' Arthur said. 'Have a drink, dear girl. I'll see if I can get America on the short wave later on. So far, we only seem to have had the Japanese version.'

Once more, personal considerations were lost sight of in the overwhelming drama. Arthur could not be parted from his wireless. Pearl Harbor . . . enormous damage and casualties . . . Japanese landings in Malaya and Siam and on countless islands . . . Singapore bombed . . . He stared out at the red sunrise on the glittering snow, while his granddaughter breakfasted her toy animals, with a long admonitory monologue, and he thought of the friendly bowing, hissing people he had once encountered – the Japanese race, now to be killed off . . . The news took half an hour to read, owing to the vast extension of the theatres of war. In the evening they listened to Roosevelt, brisk, confident and scathing, and Churchill, grim and tired.

'So they've declared war without waiting for Congress,' Lucy said.

'Yes.'

'So have Nicaragua and Guatemala.'

'Good-oh!'

'I wonder if that's where Tom's been sent? Singapore, I mean.'

'Depends if he was issued with an ice-axe and woollies or a solar topee and shorts. If the latter, he's probably been sent to Greenland.'

'Ha. Ha.'

'Oh, they do things like that to bamboozle enemy spies. It's a good thing we've got reinforcements to Singapore.'

The next day Arthur, usually so punctual, was late for lunch.

'Too bad you're late today,' Lucy said, 'your chop's congealed. Considering it's a windfall I bicycled four miles to fetch, you ought to do it justice.'

'Appalling catastrophe,' Arthur said, sinking into his chair. 'The *Prince of Wales* and the *Repulse* have been sunk.'

'Have been sunk,' Frances agreed.

'It isn't possible,' Lucy said dully.

'Churchill went to the house to announce it. Japanese air attack. That's all we know.'

'Oh God *no!* It can't be! The *Prince of Wales* – no *bomb* could sink her . . .'

'They're both at the bottom.'

Lucy sat with her hands over her face while Arthur fidgeted with his knife and fork and Frances looked questioningly from one to the other. Presently Lucy said: 'I know it isn't the same, but it feels to me like after the fall of France . . . just as bad . . . or anyway nearly . . .'

'It probably alters the whole course of the war in the Pacific. What with the American fleet being sunk – '

'Oh, not the whole fleet – what are you talking about!'

'I was listening to one of their war correspondents just now and he says they've lost more ships in the one raid than we have in the whole course of the war.'

'He was probably tight.'

'Of course, he didn't know about today's item – '

'Why don't you eat your lunch!' Lucy exclaimed irritably and went out to look at the melting snow on the terrace.

Arthur slipped his chop to the hopeful dog. It was not often his appetite failed him; even when the worm was active. Frances scrambled on to his knee.

'What a week for news, girlie . . . Never a dull moment, eh?'

'Nevra dull moment, eh?'

30

That was a terrible year. There was scarcely a week but brought news of fresh, inglorious losses. Sometimes the announcement was disguised to soften the blow, arousing Arthur's scorn. Sometimes it was a recital of stark tragedy. Hong Kong, Singapore, Rangoon, Tobruk, Dieppe were names in a catalogue of grief. With Burma gone, the Philippines gone, the Dutch East Indies gone, the Japanese ready to attack India, Rommel on the edge of the Delta, the U-boats having it their own way and the Russians bleeding at Stalingrad, it was not easy to be light-hearted. Arthur did not attempt it. He gave free rein to his pessimism. This was a different kind of desperation from the bad old days of invasion threat and heavy air-raids. It was a feeling of dismay and disgruntled criticism and a feeble, uninformed wailing for the Second Front.

'It'll take years,' Arthur said, '*years* to reconquer all the ground that's been lost, if the tide were to turn now – an unlikely supposition. I don't suppose for a moment that I'll live to see the end of it.'

Lucy saw the darkened years stretching fearfully ahead. 'Nonsense,' she said roughly. 'I wish I had your strength! The way you scorn to dismount on Headington Hill – it kills me to catch up with you. Even errand boys don't ride up those hills.'

'I shan't last much longer, dear girl.'

237

'Father, you told me that twenty years ago. And while on the subject of your demise, I wish you'd cut out the horrors talk with Frances, especially at bedtime.'

Arthur looked baffled. 'I don't know to what you refer – '

'Yes you do. All those cholera epidemics and plague epidemics and famines in India. And man-eating tigers and crocodiles biting legs off and that sort of beastliness. You'll give her nightmares.'

He was wounded now. 'I'm sorry you think I'm such an undesirable companion for the child,' he said stiffly. (There was, however, no resentment in his tone.)

Oh, I do! I do! Lucy exclaimed inwardly, but she looked at his hurt expression and relented. 'It's not that. You're a wonderful nannie and Frances adores you, as you very well know. She hangs on your every word – that's just it! *Couldn't* you keep off such macabre subjects? It's frightening, and anyway, I don't want her to grow up freakish. If only she could have some companionship of her own age.'

'I don't think any of you grew up very freakish.'

Lucy snorted. 'I do!' She looked across the gulf that separated them.

'As for being frightened,' Arthur went on, 'nature isn't really frightening. Disagreeable perhaps. The thing to avoid is hell-fire and a sense of guilt. I remember being badly frightened for the state of my soul at an early age. *We* suffered from a morbid upbringing, if you like.'

'Well, without indulging in a puritan conscience, I'm determined to give Frances a Christian upbringing. Sorry to disappoint you.'

'Oh well. *A chacun son goût.* To think that a daughter of mine . . .'

'Yes. And I'm introducing her gradually to church. Already she loves helping me to do the flowers.'

'The last time I went to church was in Simla. I remember I started to light my pipe during the sermon – without thinking what I was doing, of course – and was forcibly ejected.'

'And Father, no cracks about God, please.'

'What do you mean?'

'Well, what was that you were telling her when I came in to say good night?'

238

'Ah yes – I was saying the Christians eat their god – and the natives beat their god. If the rains fail or something goes wrong, they turn it upside down and spank it . . . You want to read your Frazer – '

'I give up.'

'Sorry, dear girl. So you've decided on a Christian upbringing and you want me to back you up?'

Lucy nodded glumly, dimly aware of new pitfalls ahead. At any rate the discussion had been amicable. All too often she was impatient and irritable with him. But nothing was settled. Nothing was ever settled in this unending tug-of-war. She sighed as Arthur returned to his crossword.

Spirits rose with the victory of Alamein. For twelve days, as the issue hung in the balance, Arthur remained subdued and sceptical. Battles were no longer settled in a few hours: they were long-drawn-out campaigns whose bulletins kept the waiting world in agonized suspense. Now with Rommel unquestionably in retreat, there came the rousing news of the Anglo-American landings. Not long after, the German army was trapped at Stalingrad. There was no denying that things were looking up.

Arthur celebrated these happenings with a feast of song. The nursery rang with his Hallelujahs as he dug up hymns remembered from his school-days:

> 'They have come from tribulation,
> They have washed their robes in blood,
> Washed them in the blood of Jesus,
> Tiddly om pom, pom, pom, pud.'

His voice soared uncertainly with the jaunty tune:

> 'Mocked, imprisoned, stoned, tormented,
> Sawn asunder, slain with sword,
> They have conquered death and Satan
> Tiddly om pom, Christ the Lord.'

'You'll be the death of me, Father. Trust you to find a hymn like that.'

239

'What's the matter, dear girl? It's All Saints' Day. I've been listening to the Radio Parson. As one who professes and calls herself Christian, you should know about these things. By the way, d'you know the one about the "lion's gory mane"? There's good stuff in that one. Now how does it go? I thought I might borrow an *Ancient and Modern* from the church to refresh my memory. For example, there's the charming "Just as I am . . .".'
He burst into song again:

> 'Just as I am, without one flea
> Save only the one Thou gavest me-e,
> And that I will return to thee-ee,
> Oh pompetty-pom, pom-pom.'

'Will you kindly lay off hymn-singing Father.' Lucy was not amused.
'I thought you'd prefer it to my usual repertoire. I'm only trying to back you up, as you said the other night.'
'You're undermining me, that's all. Shall we play a game with your animals, darling?' The child had been following their colloquy with interest.
'I'm going to play gin wummy with Ganfer,' she said.
'That's right. We were just going to have a game.'
'Very well. You've got half an hour and then I'm coming to give you your bath.'
'Oh quickly Ganfer. I get the cards.'

It was always the way: things no sooner seemed better than they were worse again. Invasion was now officially 'out' and signposts returned to the roads – but the U-boat menace grew. The Eighth Army's triumphant Marathon had ground to a halt at the Mareth Line. There were setbacks in Tunisia. Only on the Eastern front, after the prodigious victory of Stalingrad, the improbable Russian names continued to resound in special communiqués proclaiming the spectacular advances of the Red Armies. 'If we don't look out, the Russians will win this war for us and then we'll be in the soup proper,' Arthur said.
The winter passed. On a blustery March day, the old house

found itself once more in the line of battle – in a rehearsal for the Second Front. The inhabitants were confined indoors. The dog Mincer especially resented it. A series of heavy tank engagements raged for a week. There was a field gun mounted on the terrace and trench mortars outside the greenhouses. Hedges and fields were torn up, trees and telegraph poles torn down and a tank remained stuck in the stew-pond. At last, the victorious army withdrew to the west in a twenty-four-hour stream of motor transport.

'Like the Brighton road on bank holiday,' Arthur said as he returned spattered with mud from posting a letter. 'You'll be relieved to hear the Canadians have won. Now I'll just have a clean-up and give Frances her lesson.'

'What lesson?'

'She's started on her alphabet – largely words of her own composition.'

'Sorry, Father. I *don't* want you to teach her to read and write.' Lucy spoke emphatically.

Arthur's face fell. 'Whyever not? I taught all of you.'

'Because I'm going to teach her myself and it's no use for two people – '

'You've got far more to do than I have.' There was a pleading note in his voice.

'Father, the method's changed since your day. It's not a question of learning the ABC by heart but of learning sounds and combining them into words.'

Arthur looked sceptical. 'Well, I suppose I could master it, if that's the way you want her taught.'

'Father, don't you understand, I *want* to do it myself. You had five of us to amuse yourself instructing. I've only got one child and I insist, I absolutely insist on doing it my way and I won't have her muddled up.'

'Very well,' Arthur spoke resignedly. 'Say no more. I suppose you've no objection to a little simple arithmetic?'

'None. It's beyond me anyhow. But don't overdo it. If only she could play more and learn less . . .'

'This *is* playing. We do it at cards. I've already inculcated the golden rule: never play cards for love – in other words, always play your best. For money at the moment we are using hazel

241

nuts, beech nuts and conkers as I'm very short of small change – '

'Well don't overdo it,' Lucy repeated frowning.

'No fear of that! She'd soon chuck it when she'd had enough, but she's never had enough yet.'

At last it was spring. Spirits rose with the final conquest of the North African coast, the capture of Sicily, the dramatic fall of Mussolini, the Italian armistice – and sank again when it became evident that prolonged bitter fighting was in store.

'Soft underbelly of the Axis,' Arthur murmured. 'H'm.' He pictured the remembered terrain. Suddenly he saw again the Carso front, a lifetime ago. 'Query soft,' he said.

Frances's fifth birthday came at a dark time. Lucy looked back at the bleak years they had spent there. The child had known no other life, had never known what it was to play with other children. Her chosen companion was an eccentric septuagenarian. Lucy raged at the unsuitability of it all . . . But Arthur did not see it in the same light. It was a source of great satisfaction to him – and life held few satisfactions at that time – that his granddaughter was so bright and responsive and so *gemütlich*. It was a pity that Lucy was growing rather like Isabelle. She'd inherited her mother's bad nerves . . . the curse of his wife's family. The child, anyway, was coming on satisfactorily.

He lay in bed playing a game of patience. Frances, pickled in pipe-smoke, huddled against him, her eyes fixed intently on the playing-cards.

'Come on, I'll take you for a walk,' Lucy said to her daughter.

'Ganfer's just going to teach me to play bwidge. S'called double dummy.'

'Well, you've got to have some fresh air now.'

'No, I don't want to. It's raining and winding outside.'

'Winding is good,' Arthur said, 'and perfectly logical. If raining, why not winding?'

'Come and get your things on.'

'No.'

'Go on, girlie. You do as Mummy tells you.'

'I'm going to stay here.'

'You come this instant! And Father, I do wish you wouldn't

242

smoke all over her. It's awful in here. I'm going to open your window.'

'I like thmoke,' Frances declared. 'I like thmoke vewy much.'

'You go with Mummy.' Arthur spoke severely but he was smiling to himself.

It was a miserable spring. There were occasional raids still. The war in the Far East looked as if it would prolong itself indefinitely. The Italian campaign had reached deadlock. There was no end in sight. *But we can't go on here*, Lucy cried in despair.

The miserable spring became a miserable summer. It was decided in the village that this was Hitler's Secret Weapon – control of the elements. There had been no such June, they claimed, in living memory. Cold, blustery winds raged ceaselessly, badly affecting Antonio's unstable temper, already upset by the Italian campaign. Bad temper was not confined to the Italian. Invasion of the Continent was in the air. There was a feeling of intense anxiety: Dunkirk in reverse, with the weather also reversed. Arthur tapped his barometer and shook his head gloomily.

'Mean seasonal average for December. They'll never attempt it in this.'

'All right, they won't.'

'It's a bad business.'

'I do think your teeth are so undecorative lying there,' Lucy said crossly, eyeing a pair of dentures that faced each other snappishly on the mantelpiece. They were far from complete dentures, for Arthur had retained most of his teeth, but here a molar and there a sharp incisor jutted from orange-coloured bases. 'Why on earth don't you wear them?'

'The question of whether I wear them or don't wear them is a matter for me to decide,' Arthur replied pompously. 'At the moment, I'm giving them a rest.'

'Then for heaven's sake put them away. They're not ornamental.'

'That's a matter of opinion. To me they represent the marvels of modern dentistry. When I remember George Washington's teeth at Mount Vernon – two complete sets of sheeps' teeth joined together by hinges (that accounts for the look in some of the portraits of course), I realize how fortunate I am with mine. And I must say that I regard it as an infringement of elementary human rights that you should come dictating to me where I should keep my teeth.'

Arthur's unusual combativeness was an indication of the tension in which they lived.

Suddenly everything happened at once.

'Rome has fallen!' Arthur bellowed, erupting joyfully from his room to the nursery where Lucy was giving Frances a reading lesson.

'Oh how *wonderful!* At last!'

'After heavy fighting in the suburbs – but the centre's not damaged, the monuments are all right, apparently. Tonight we're to hear recordings from Rome itself.'

'Only think! Edmund's in Rome tonight.'

'That's just what I'm thinking.'

Edmund was in Allied Military Government, attached to the Fifth Army as a Chief of Staff to General Mark Clark. His war career was highly distinguished.

'How *wonderful!*' Lucy repeated. 'Poor Toto. He was looking so forlorn just now. And tomorrow he'll be worse, pretending to rejoice. One can't help feeling sorry for him.'

'I'm prepared to surrender what's left of my medicinal whisky to him as a consolation prize.'

'That's big of you, Father.'

'As long as I don't have to make the presentation. This calls for celebration all round.'

It seemed to Lucy that she had only just fallen asleep when her father wakened her. 'It must have started, dear girl – the Second Front. This has been going on for some time. Look!' He drew the curtains. A vast air armada was flying low against the dark, scurrying clouds. Tug aircraft towing the huge tank-carrying Hamilcars and trains of striped transport gliders filled the sky, heading south. They gazed awestruck at the stupendous spectacle. The eight o'clock news was devoted to the fall of Rome and made no mention of the invasion. It was impossible to settle to anything in the prevailing atmosphere of excitement and apprehension and Lucy took Frances for a walk while Arthur remained with his wireless awaiting a special announcement. At noon he was rewarded. 'Somewhere between Cherbourg and Havre!' he called excitedly to Lucy as he heard them returning.

'In this weather!' Lucy cried in dismay. 'It's blowing a gale out and it's terribly cold. Only think of the sea . . .'

'Yes, poor devils. They'll be appallingly sea-sick. At any rate they couldn't be expected in weather like this. They ought to achieve the element of surprise – if they can get ashore. Can we lunch early so that we can hear the one o'clock undisturbed?'

The one o'clock news gave the Prime Minister's announcement to the House: '. . . over four thousand ships . . . eleven thousand first-line aircraft . . . all under Montgomery . . .' Now they waited hour by hour in sick suspense, hanging on the news of the battle on which everything hung.

At the end of a week it was clear that the Allied armies, contesting every inch of ground, were not going to be dislodged. The beachhead was extended. Lucy was filled with insane optimism, daily expecting news of the Nazi collapse.

'I'm old enough to remember the last war and how suddenly the armistice came. We must make arrangements at once to go back to London. Francis is going to look for a house.'

'Two simple words make all the difference this time,' Arthur said gloomily.

'What d'you mean?'

'*Unconditional surrender*. They'll go on to the last ditch.'

'Anyway, the air-raids are finished. There's no reason now for *us* not to return.'

'There can still be a flare-up.'

'Frances is five and *has* to go to school.'

'I should take it easy, dear girl.' Apart from the matter of air-raids, London meant Isabelle and problems that Arthur simply did not care to consider.

Isabelle's letter describing a night made hideous by a hitherto unfamiliar buzzing sound (to the accompaniment of heavy gunfire and nearby explosions) arrived soon after the official announcement acknowledging the arrival of the famous Secret Weapon. This was an ordeal that she was singularly unsuited to bear.

It was one thing to be one of a crowd braving it out with nightly regularity in squalid conditions underground: it was quite another matter to stand up (often alone) to the sheer suspense of this bombardment – the terror that flieth by night and in the noonday and all round the clock. This frightful object, buzzing along (often it seemed scarcely more than chimney-pot height), trailing its long red tail by night, filled her with horror. Her heart stood still at the sickening moment when the engine cut out and she flung herself on her face (in accordance with government instructions), counting the seconds to the moment of explosion – all this was too much for a life-long hater of shocks and surprises. It was particularly diabolical, Isabelle thought, that the thing was a piece of uninhabited machinery, with no one inside it to be destroyed.

After two terrible nights, which brought a good deal of destruction uncomfortably near, though few casualties to her First Aid Post, she set out alone for a walk in the parks, since she could neither rest nor relax. It was her Sunday off. Two of the flying bombs buzzed overhead unscathed through the anti-aircraft fire and pieces of shell fell close to her. She went on raging, perhaps not so much against Hitler as against her husband and daughter, who had not even troubled to telephone, who sat in their safe corner, not caring whether she lived or died. When she was half-wat round St James's Park, the Guards Chapel went up with a full congregation. Isabelle fled the way she had come, trembling with shock and despair.

Arthur and Lucy were indeed slow to waken to full realization of the new menace. The wireless was reticent, referring discreetly to Southern England.

'Have you seen any smoke to the east?' Arthur asked.

'No. Why?' Lucy spoke dully.

'I've been listening to Berlin. They informed me that London's laid in ruins. Smoke can be seen from *Rouen*. Quite hysterical they sounded, and singing '*Wir fahren gegen Engeland*' all over again. Very rum . . .'

246

'Francis has just rung. He's been up all of the last two nights and his glass has gone again. These things come over at any time apparently and this ghastly gale that's prevented all our flying doesn't affect them. Oh Father, isn't it horrible!'

'Well, it's not perhaps the moment for investing in house property in London.'

'Oh stop it,' Lucy groaned. 'Just when I was beginning to see daylight at last. It's like 1940 over again . . .'

'I don't know, dear girl. It all seems rather pointless at this stage of the war. And hysteria in the Fatherland is a most healthy sign. All the roads from London are choked with refugees, they said. Well, I didn't notice any traffic on the Oxford road – '

'Just when everything looked so hopeful . . . Oh *God!*'

'Cheer up, dear girl. This gale will have to drop one day and the Americans have cut the Cherbourg peninsula . . .'

Suddenly their rôles were reversed.

At the end of a fortnight of the pilotless bombing, Isabelle was at her wits' end. She didn't hesitate when Lucy's offer of asylum arrived, but frantically packed a suitcase and took the first train from Paddington. She arrived looking incredibly fragile, white-faced with fatigue. Sleepless nights and unbearable shocks had deranged her meagre equilibrium. Her keyed-up nerves made it impossible for her to rest in the still safety of the countryside. Large doses of sedatives turned her into a virago. In her present state of inflamed feelings she seemed to take an active pleasure in scourging her husband, the child, Lucy's methods of running the household – anything and everything. Arthur withdrew from the fray, taking Frances with him, while Isabelle fought pitched battles with her daughter. After only two days she announced: 'Since I am very evidently not wanted here, I shall find myself another lodging.'

This she succeeded in doing at a neighbouring farm, and moved out on the third day after her arrival. An uneasy truce now followed and Isabelle slowly began to calm down in her relations with her own family, but it was not long before she was at war with the farmer's wife who was no easy character herself. At the end of six weeks, they quarrelled irretrievably and

Isabelle returned to London and the bombs. Even as the train stopped, she could hear the familiar howl of the air-raid warning. Her interior organs leapt from their moorings, formed certain recognized convolutions and slowly subsided.

'Crikey! We 'aven't wasted no time, 'ave we!' the soldier opposite exclaimed, as he lowered her suitcase from the rack. Laden as he was, he insisted on carrying it for her to the taxi-rank. She had to queue for a long time, but she was cheered by her encounter with the young fighting-man – a mere beardless youth seeing the metropolis and bombing for the first time. She, with her experience of war-time London, was delighted at his deference to her *savoir-faire*. She felt like a war-horse roused by the sound of the bugle. It was better by far to have left that forlorn solitude behind her. Within a few hours of her return, she had a narrow escape as her room was blasted. Immediately, however, she was an object for sympathy and concern. Yes, definitely, rather danger, violence and abundant human contacts than the quiet countryside with the close proximity of her loved ones and one uncouth rustic for company. Isabelle, after a slow start, was beginning (like everyone else) to get used to the new bomb.

During the six stormy weeks of his wife's visit, Arthur added a new disability to his store. Abruptly and without warning he was stricken with deafness. It did not need a psychiatrist to discover that once deaf he could not hear his wife's strictures. This sudden affliction, far from arousing sympathy in his wife and daughter, was infuriating to both of them. Arthur advancing across a room, holding a hand behind each ear and wearing the look of a worried bloodhound, goaded them to extremes of irritability. (He never seemed to have any difficulty in hearing his granddaughter.)

'But one can't go deaf overnight,' Lucy protested.

'What's that you said?'

'I said ONE CAN'T GO DEAF OVERNIGHT – unless you've been in an explosion or something.'

'It's been coming on for a long time. I'm breaking up.' He assumed a look of semi-imbecility.

'You'd better go to Oxford and get your ears syringed.'

'Wouldn't do any good, I'm afraid . . .'

'There! You heard me perfectly.'

'I can at present hear you when you raise your voice and speak very clearly.' He seemed to imply that this would soon no longer be the case.

'Oh *Father* . . .' Lucy gave a despairing shrug.

'*You* may find it a trial, but I can assure you it is a far greater trial to me. I was trying to point that out to your mother when she said it would drive her mad.'

'She already is.'

'What did you say?'

'Never mind.'

With her mother's departure Lucy's wishful thinking got the better of her again. The enemy was retreating everywhere. (Edmund was now military commander of Florence.) The flying bomb launching-sites would soon be overrun. They must buy a house in London to move to at the earliest opportunity, taking a chance on its survival. Her thoughts ran feverishly along these lines. It was impossible to face another winter here, especially since her father had decided to become stone-deaf.

It was not always easy to find suitable food for the animals. The cat hardly ever tasted fish but had a penchant for lentil soup laced with Bovril. Arthur had given him a plateful of this and placed it on the scullery floor before coming to the dining room for the evening meal. Suddenly he laid down his soup-spoon with a clatter, bounded from his chair and rushed from the room, uttering a Hindustani oath.

'Aha!' he exclaimed as he returned, leading the culprit, Mincer, by the collar. 'So you thought you'd do poor Hodge out of his soup! And you've *had* your dinner. Shame on you!'

'What d'you mean?' Lucy asked with sudden indignation.

'He was eating the cat's soup.'

'How did you know?'

'I could hear him lapping it up.'

'You're telling me you could hear the difference between the dog eating and the cat eating at that distance – a passage and two rooms away! Don't ever let me hear another word about your deafness, Father! You can hear a damned sight better than I can.'

'I'm rapidly losing my hearing,' Arthur maintained. 'It makes a difference if you know what to listen for. I've been suspecting this thieving for some time past – '

'Oh rot, Father. Either one *can* hear or one *can't* hear. You're not in the least deaf and you can't fool me again. I couldn't hear an elephant sucking up food at that distance – not if I had a trumpet, not if there was an amplifier in the scullery . . .' Lucy was overplaying her hand as usual, but the charge went home and nothing more was heard of Arthur's deafness.

The relief at the removal of Isabelle (and the disappearance of Arthur's deafness) outweighed for a time their consuming anxieties. Frances was playful and happy again, Arthur cheerful, Lucy filled with hope as the armies raced on and the great names from the past, synonymous with battle, familiar in their mouths as household words, featured once again in the news.

'Look at what Monty says!' Lucy cried, brandishing the daily paper that had just arrived.

'Don't tell me. Let me guess: "The Lord God of Hosts be with us. Yoicks and Talley-ho!" Anything about the cat's whiskers – or pyjamas perhaps?'

'No, listen to what Monty says,' Lucy cried. ' "The Lord mighty in battle has given us the victory etc. . . . etc. . . . etc. . . . The end of the war is in sight!" Oh Father *think* of it! Only *think!*'

'In sight, yes,' Arthur said, 'if you're very long-sighted. But the Germans can't be counted out yet. And what about Japan?' He was wiser than he knew. There was a whole long year to go before all fighting ceased.

Francis had found a house facing Regent's Park. The breakthrough in Normandy was going magnificently. Paris was liberated. On a rare fine Sunday morning with optimism in the air, Arthur was putting the finishing touches to his granddaughter's church-going attire. 'There. Don't keep Mummy waiting. There'll be time for a game of double dummy when you come out for the sermon.'

'Oh goody!'

'Mincer and I will be waiting for you outside. Now what was the rule you mastered yesterday?'

'When in doubt lead trumps.'

'Right. Now here's another for you to commit to memory. When you're playing no trumps lead the fourth best of your longest suit. I'll explain later.'

'The fourth best of my longest suit.'

'That's right. Thought for the day. Now run along.'

'G'bye Ganfer.' She raced away repeating to herself, 'The fourth best of my longest suit'.

As the V1s began to decline, the V2s were launched and the whole issue of the return to London seemed to be in doubt once more. As nothing was said concerning Arthur's future, he assumed that he would be going with them. But Lucy was deciding otherwise.

The new house was blasted. It was doubtful now if the workmen could get it ready in time for occupation. Francis had telephoned the news.

'It's too *frightful* to think that another few yards and the place would be a heap of rubble by now!' Lucy cried. Arthur made commiserating sounds. 'Luckily it spent itself in the water. It fell on the edge of the canal. On the very brim.'

Arthur said unexpectedly:

> 'A rocket by the river's brim
> A simple rocket was to him
> And it was nothing more . . .'

'Lord! If you think it's funny – '

'I don't, dear girl. I don't think Wordsworth's very funny either. And I don't think it would be at all funny to go back just in time – ' But Lucy had left the room.

There was a great deal of work involved in moving house, even in favourable circumstances. And the war was not going to be over by Christmas. The Führer continued to escape assassination . . . the agony of Arnhem was on . . . Immersed in the task of packing and sorting, Lucy left Frances exclusively to her grandfather's care.

They lay in his bed enjoying a session together (though they were thought to be out getting fresh air and exercise). From a half-hour devoted to the sufferings of survivors in a shark-infested sea, Arthur switched to a description of a python he had once come upon that had swallowed a goat. He drew a diagram of the goat's horns protruding from a bulge in the reptile.

'Go on, Ganfer. What did you do?'

'There was nothing much you could do for either of them. The goat had had it and the snake's skin was split.'

'Well, but go on Ganfer.'

'Must have a pipe first.'

'Yes, and tell me another one.'

He launched into an old abandoned favourite – the cholera epidemic of '98.

'. . . Well, by that time, I was covered from head to foot in his vomit – '

Lucy, who had been looking for them, suddenly stood in the doorway: '*Father!*' She turned and went away again unexpectedly. Arthur realized that he had erred, but not that he had, as it were, signed his death warrant.

'What's vomit, Ganfer?'

'What you call *guk*,' he answered absently.

'Oh how *bolius!* Well go on.'

'Another time . . .'

'I want you to finish the story.'

'No. Let's have a game now.'

'All right. Let's. It's not nearly lunch-time is it, Ganfer? Shall we play a wubber of double dummy? If you deal, I'll get my money.'

'You've *got* to speak to him,' Lucy said to her husband, invoking woman's immemorial right to shelter behind her husband's authority when the going was hard.

'All right. It won't make any difference . . .'

'Frances has had nightmares several times lately, and can you wonder? Father *can't* go on living with us . . .'

'Well, if that's how you feel about it – '

'But don't you agree?'

'If it were your mother I should agree emphatically. She's such a bundle of nerves that one can't sit in the same room with her. But Father – well, I don't see how he's going to live with your mother.'

'I've known this problem all my life, and it's *their* problem. Other people's parents don't do this to their children, even if they don't get on.'

'But this is a real mis-mating, a miscegenation.'

'Thanks. What does that make me?'

'I admit Father's a bit eccentric, but Frances seems devoted to him.'

'That's the trouble. Can't you see it's very bad for her to listen to him talking all the time about horrors and illnesses, and *his* illnesses, harping on all the gruesome symptoms and . . . and *horrors* . . .'

'It's difficult to know what effect these things have on a child's mind. She'll be going to school – '

'When I was a child, I remember him telling us never to lick stamps because the gum was collected by lepers in the Andaman Islands. I've never been able to lick a stamp since. I always have to spit on the envelope. Haven't you noticed? I remember him reading a story where a pair of mutilated hands were caught sight of under the heroine's bed. For years I used to take a running jump into bed, fairly gibbering with terror. You must agree it's very bad for her to listen to these things. I've argued with him, I've implored him, I've nagged him – nothing makes any difference. I just can't endure it.'

'Well, if that's the way you feel, it's your opportunity to make the break when we move. It's a big house and there are no servants to be had. You can say you simply can't manage it.'

'I will,' Lucy said, but, when it came to the point, she said nothing to her father, who continued to take it for granted that he would go on living with them to help with the care of the child. The house in Regent's Park was spacious, and he assumed that he would occupy an unwanted room in it and be able to take Frances to school and fetch her home.

253

31

The move was accomplished in instalments.
Arthur went to Isabelle's hotel and Lucy moved with the child
to her husband's flat to supervise the furnishing from there.
Arthur called daily to take his granddaughter on sight-seeing
tours, inspecting bomb damage and walking in the parks. When
the home was, roughly speaking, installed, the family moved in.
Arthur arrived now daily on his bicycle to take Frances on
bicycling trips ranging far afield. Lucy, harassed and making
heavy going of her labours, was glad to have the child taken care
of, and Arthur patiently awaited his summons.

After a few days, the glass went again as a rocket descended
somewhere in the neighbourhood. There was a crash as a newly-
painted ceiling came away. Lucy and the Irish help were grimly
sweeping up the mess when Arthur called.

'Here, let me, dear girl. Where's another brush?'

'No. You'll only cut yourself.'

'It's a damned shame but lucky it's no worse.'

'The workmen haven't been out a week,' Lucy said savagely.

'It's a shame. You'd better let me doss upstairs. You've got
too much to get through. It'll be one more pair of hands.'

'Father, no. It's no good. You can't move in here. I can
scarcely cope as it is, and with one more to cook for . . . and
then you'd have your off-days in bed. No, I can't manage it.'

'I see,' Arthur said. 'I see . . . Well, I'd better be getting back if I can't help . . . Where's Frances?'

'She's at Moira's, and they're bringing her back after tea. I was going to telephone you and then this happened . . .'

'I see. Well, I'll push off then. So sorry about this. It's bad luck . . . I'll be off then . . .' But he remained standing there, confused. Lucy continued sweeping, rattling the glass fragments noisily in the dust-pan.

'Shall I call tomorrow and take Frances out?'

'Yes, do Father, do. Take her for a ride in the park.' She could afford to be generous now that he was vanquished.

'Right. Good-bye then, dear girl. I hope you don't get any more of these . . .'

'Thanks. Good-bye.'

'Good-bye, dear girl.' It was, in a sense, a parting. Lucy, overwhelmed with conflicting emotions, sat down and wept. 'A dhrop of tay is what we are both needing,' said the Irish help who had an eye on the tea caddy containing the ration. She wandered off to make it.

Once outside the front door, Arthur felt his knees giving way. He stood leaning against the wall of the house. So he was not wanted. It was as simple as that. Lucy didn't want him. Slowly he groped for his pipe, filled it and lighted it. After all, why should he have assumed she'd want him to go on living with them, he asked himself in humility. It was unreasonable to feel hurt. She had a perfect right to do as she wished. It was quite true that he was often ill. In fact, come to think of it, he could feel the approach of an attack of fatigue poisons at this very minute. He must get back to the hotel. He began gingerly wheeling his bicycle along the pavement. Lucy was quite right – with his poor health he was often a burden. It was strange how swiftly this accursed illness struck at him sometimes. If he didn't get a move on, he'd never reach Bayswater. He mounted swervingly. After all, he'd still be seeing quite a lot of the child, even when she'd started school. The great thing was to get to bed at once, or he wouldn't be up to it tomorrow . . .

He did not, however, return for nearly a week as a severe attack of fatigue poisons set in.

'It's a good thing you haven't moved to 56,' Isabelle said. 'Lucy's got enough on her hands without nursing you.' As Arthur did not reply, she asked: 'When are you thinking of moving?'

'I'm not.'

'You mean you're not going at all?'

'No.'

'Why? I thought you were going as soon as they'd settled in? I thought Lucy couldn't get on without you – after all this time you've been helping with the child.'

'Frances will be going to school.'

'Only a little kindergarten in the mornings. Has Lucy said she doesn't want you?'

'Well, it amounts to that. She's got too much to do. I quite understand – '

'*I* don't! I thought you were supposed to be indispensable! You don't need to tell *me* . . . She's thrown you out! I know Lucy. She was always hard and selfish, ever since she went to boarding-school. She's just made use of you while it suited her . . .'

Arthur shaded his eyes and said no more.

There was no choice of schools. Only one had scorned evacuation. It was a wretched little dame-school, some way off. Here, at the first wail of the siren, the children were shepherded down to the basement to enjoy the protection of a wall, one brick thick (the cost of whose erection in the early days of bombing still featured term by term in the school fees). Here they remained untaught and unorganized, sharpening their little wits in the best ways they could devise. Frances showed the greatest reluctance to attend. For the first week, on arrival there, she clung stubbornly to the lamp-post outside the front door, howling piteously, while Lucy in consternation and dismay struggled to unwind the clinging arms and induce her to enter. She was shy of other children and did not make friends easily. Arthur after a hurried siesta would call to take her out on her bicycle, when weather and daylight permitted. On Saturday mornings they went far afield.

'It's lovely today. You'd better get ready. Ganfer'll be here soon.'

'Oh jolly D.!'

'Isn't it nice for you to have a park so near!'

'I like it better outside the park.'

Lucy had misgivings. 'You're not riding through traffic, I hope?'

'Oh Mummy, it's super!'

'What funny talk you learn at school – '

'There's the bell! It's Ganfer! Whacko!' Frances cried and rushed away, just as Lucy was called to the telephone.

'Where have you been?' she asked her daughter later when Arthur had delivered her home.

'We went to see the rabbits in the dell at Hyde Park.'

'What fun! Were there lots of them?'

'I think so. But Mummy, it was smashing at Marble Arch! Ganfer rides in front, you see, and I follow him. And there were buses on this side and buses on the other side and I thought we'd get squashed! Oh, it was *smashing!* So we went round and round and Ganfer says Hyde Park Corner's better still . . .'

It was one more prohibition that had to be enforced. Lucy was outraged to learn of this new threat to her child's life. Arthur argued a little feebly, but submitted to his daughter's weak nerves. He was bitterly disappointed. There was nothing to be alarmed about and it was depriving the child of outdoor enjoyment . . . He continued to ride to and from the house unscathed. A merciful providence once more protected him as, hampered by poor vision, with one hand on the handlebars, the other serenely proclaiming his intention to the oncoming vehicles, he plunged unhurt through the traffic. Soon the winter weather made bicycling lose its pleasure.

In addition to the usual miasma of emotionalism, the morbid recollections of her past life that Christmas always evoked in Isabelle, the war news took a distressing turn.

'The Americans have taken a nasty knock in the Ardennes,' Arthur said miserably. 'It's a bad setback. We've a long way to go yet . . . We're in the sixth year of war . . .' Isabelle was roused to anger by his pessimism, and he took evasive action in bed for a week. So it was that Isabelle came alone to her daughter's to feast on the turkey (the first they had seen for a long time).

'I don't know how you can stand that horrible thing on the wall, Lucy!' she exclaimed angrily, at a moment when her son-in-law was busying himself preparing drinks in the dining-room. 'It's disgusting! It's disgraceful that the child should be allowed to see such a thing! I can't sit here looking at it. I shall sit with my back to it. It's *corrupting!*' She referred to a magnificent Sickert of the Camden Town period that hung in the drawing-room. It showed an opulent female nude, back-view, standing before a wash-stand (there was a chamber-pot in evidence on the bottom of the stand) and a beautiful, stippled, peacock-coloured curtain for background. On the bed which occupied the other half of the dingy room sat a small, depressed-looking man in his shirt-sleeves. Everything about it offended Isabelle's susceptibilities and, so great was the tyranny she exercised, there was nothing for it but to remove the painting from view whenever she called.

'Jasus, Mary and Joseph, it's the grand-mohther!' the Irish help would give the warning cry when she peeped from a window to see who had rung the front-door bell, and Lucy would fly to replace the offending masterpiece with an unexceptionable landscape before Isabelle was let in.

Arthur did not react to the rockets (which continued in a desultory way almost to the very end) as his wife would have wished. It was one more proof of his self-centred insensitiveness, she felt, that he who took such a morbid interest in his most trifling ailments should pay so little attention to the bangs that made her heart stand still. 'If you've had it, you don't know it,' he would say. 'It's a great advantage to have no preliminary warning.' If the bang were near enough, he would rise from his bed and sally forth to inspect the damage.

They met mainly for meals, as Isabelle still attended her First Aid Post and Arthur still paid regular visits to his grandchild.

Spring brought some beautiful days and the park was filled with blossom and bird-song and warm sunshine – in Holland

258

they were subsisting on tulip bulbs. Arthur put in a new plea for bicycling excursions at the week-end. 'If we made a really early start we'd miss all the traffic.' He wanted suddenly to show Frances the Royal Holloway building at Egham. He had a curiously flamboyant taste in architecture: the cathedral of St Stephen at Warsaw; ex-King Manuel's florid palace at Busacco; and now this enormous, red-brick pile, bristling with white towers had drawn his fervent admiration. It seemed an incongruous taste in one whose other tastes were modest and unassuming. Perhaps the fabulous buildings touched a long-forgotten romantic chord in him, a buried memory of faerie palaces in an age of chivalry inhabited by romantic beings who moved to an echo of the *Venusberg* music, beings who lived at another level – the kind of level where a man might fall hopelessly in love with a photograph and spend half a life-time in patient waiting . . .

'Oh no, Father. No! It's *much* too far anyway.'

'We could stop the night with my brother Bertie.'

'No *honestly!*' Lucy refused to countenance the idea. 'Couldn't you make do with St Pancras? There's a bus goes all the way. Frances loves the top of a bus.' How like him, she was thinking, to start up again when she'd had it all out with him once. He simply never took 'no' for an answer.

The end of the war came in a series of shocks. The armies raced to meet across the heart of Germany: the Russians were fighting in Berlin. Arthur lay studying the atlas open on the patience-tray across his knees. He often found himself back in the closing stages of the previous war. Soon he would be watching as an arm-chair spectator what he had known at first hand – the collapse of Germany.

'It's essential that Montgomery should reach the Baltic,' he repeated, tracing a line on the map with his finger.

'Why?' Isabelle asked.

'Save a lot of trouble later on. It's a thousand pities it couldn't have been Berlin . . .'

'But the Russians are there.'

'Precisely so.'

'I don't understand you.'

'There's trouble enough now,' Arthur said. 'Only need to look at Poland, Yugoslavia, Austria . . . Look at the way they're not allowing us into Vienna. If that isn't enough to give us a taste of things to come . . . Read your Karl Marx, dear girl. Read your Lenin, if you prefer to, I'm sure you've heard of the class war . . .'

Isabelle, though long since out of love with the Commissars, was affronted by his cynicism. 'I should just like to know where we'd have been without the Russians!' she exclaimed indignantly.

'So should I.'

'We've been fighting the same enemy for years – '

'That's my whole point,' Arthur said. 'After the honeymoon's over – what then?'

Isabelle didn't care for his tone or the reference to honeymoons or anything about the conversation.

The news of Mussolini's sordid death brought him little satisfaction. He had personally never fancied the fellow – but what an end! *Sic transit gloria* . . .

Two nights later, he kept himself awake beyond his usual hour for sleep, listening to Hamburg, who had told listeners to stand by for an announcement. They were playing selections from Wagner. On and on and on . . . What was all the build-up for? It was not that Arthur was not enjoying it, but he kept nodding, then waking again to the distant thunder of the *Gütterdämmerung*. As he was about to switch off, it came: '*Unser Führer, Adolf Hitler, ist heute Nachmittag auf dem Kommandposten in der Reichskantzlerei gefallen, kämpfend bis zum letzen Atennzug gegen das Bolshevismus und für Deutschland.*'

'Whew,' Arthur said. 'Well blow me down . . .' and he switched off the light.

Now the fighting in Europe had stopped. There couldn't be so many families, Arthur thought, whose members had been involved and come through totally unscathed. If there were a god, it would be a moment for giving thanks. Isabelle rejoiced after her fashion. She was fully aware though of the fact that the shutting down of the First Aid Post deprived her of her occupation. An immense depression invaded her being as general rejoicing broke out around her.

There were so many sudden reminders that the war was over: the end of the black-out, the return of street-lighting, the return of weather forecasts, the rush for holiday enjoyment – river trips, seaside holidays, Ascot . . . It was a mad, heady stampede back to pre-war fun. Naturally food rationing continued, together with petrol and clothing coupons.

Arthur was always a shabby dresser. He could make a new suit look as if he'd slept in it after a couple of days' wear. And he had no new suits. His clothes were years old and disgracefully threadbare. Isabelle was sick and tired of mending them. She was very vexed when she found that he'd given his clothing coupons away to one of the hotel maids who was getting married.

'It's just stupid when you're in rags, absolute rags, yourself! You may not mind looking like a down-and-out tramp, but *I* mind! I'm ashamed to be seen with you. You should consider my feelings.'

'Sorry, Belle. I see Monty's complaining the clearing up is more work than the battle. I can well believe it. From what I remember the chaos will be colossal. Famine was the spectre then and will be now. Now take a look at the map. He's got to feed the Ruhr for a start, and ruined Essen, and get them going from almost total destruction. What with? The Russians have bagged the corn-lands and the Poles have got the Silesian coal-fields.' (He was back again in that former ruined Germany.)

'Arthur, I cannot mend this pullover any more, I tell you. It's only held together by my darns.'

'Sorry, dear girl. Haven't I got another one?'

'No! That's what I've been saying. The other one's worse. And why are you wearing your bicycle clips indoors?'

'Got a hole in my trouser pocket. Catch the coins that way.'

'God give me patience!' Isabelle screamed. 'You take them off at once!' The flippant rejoinder died on Arthur's lips as he perceived she was really angry. He shrivelled before her blast.

She was not at all well – there was no question of that. For some time past she had been plagued by dyspepsia which was finally diagnosed as an incipient duodenal ulcer. To this was now added a new affliction: a nervous eczema which attacked her limbs. On top of the sometimes acute physical discomfort, she was overwhelmed by repugnance. It was altogether shameful and degrading to her to be suffering from the itch – an unmentionable state of affairs, not as bad as venereal disease but about in the same class as piles. She suffered in agonized silence. Ointments seemed to do no good.

In the hope of cheering her, Arthur put their names down for passages to Africa to visit the other children in Nairobi, Johannesburg and Cape Town. But there was a long waiting-list already. Edmund, when released, would be returning to London with his family (he had married in South Africa in the early days of the war), and Arthur pointed this out as something to look forward to. When Isabelle remained gloomy he packed up. They were back in the old vicious circle. He was intensely depressed anyway as the conditions of the concentration camps, uncovered by the advancing armies, were revealed to a horrified world. It was perhaps remarkable that one with a taste for horror stories should feel annihilated by the concentration camps. Perhaps it was an ache in that old wound – the ruin of his early love for the Germans – that added to his feeling of moral debasement.

The atom bomb on Hiroshima jerked every one out of his usual state of mind. There was general satisfaction at the end of the war – rather than exultation. All were awe-struck at the immensity of the implications. Arthur, shocked, retired to his usual refuge. After three days, Isabelle telephoned to Lucy to come and deal with him. She sounded fretful and was just off to see the doctor on her own account.

Lucy found her father in bed, listening to a description of the second bomb, just dropped on Nagasaki. The Russians had declared war on Japan the same day. ('Ha! Ha! to that,' Arthur said wearily.)

'Father! Are you better?'

'No.'

'Father, I haven't seen you since the A-bomb! What d'you think?' She drew a chair up to his bedside.

'It's the end of civilized life on this planet.'

'You might well have said that if the Germans had got it first!'

'At present, *we* have the atomic bomb. It's just a matter of time before it falls into the hands of the enemies of society.'

'Surely you'd rather it had been used to end the war?'

'Oh rather! Far better than the Samurai going on and on to commit *hara-kiri* in the last ditch. Bound to pack up any minute now. No, it's the future one thinks of, naturally.'

'The future. Yes.'

'One bomb,' Arthur said slowly, 'the equivalent of twenty thousand tons of TNT. It's inconceivable. All former terms are now obsolete. It's a revolution in human development – like the discovery of fire, the wheel, steam, electricity. But where does this advance lead us? To total annihilation, dear girl.'

'As I understand it, it means the power of the universe can now be harnessed to man's bidding. I was thinking of that when I was scraping up the last of the coal-dust for the boiler.'

'Not a hope . . . In my day,' he went on, 'it was held that direct proof of the existence of atoms was beyond human scope. Now they know all about them, their interior structure, how to split them – a process whereby the very elements are transformed. There will be no defence possible against the new destructive energy released. There's no answer but world-wide cooperation, universal goodwill. *Which is a contradiction in terms.*'

'Oh Father, even if you're convinced of what you're saying, couldn't you just not *talk* like that . . .'

'Certainly. If you've no wish to face the facts . . . We as individuals are of no importance anyway – '

'Let's take one thing at a time. The war's as good as over. The fighting's as good as stopped. It's time to celebrate – '

'You celebrate, dear girl. I'll have a little nap.' He turned over as if to put his threat into immediate action and Lucy left him. She felt disquieted for her mother – disquieted certainly, but hardly more than usual. The problem was so long-standing. There was no cure for it . . . and she had problems of her own.

It was indeed the same old story. Isabelle lived in a world of black despair. She saw now only herself – herself condemned to live out her remaining days with the cranky hypochondriac who had wrecked her life. Her drugged mind told her that she had reached the very limits of human endurance. Dispensing with a preliminary scene and laying her plans carefully, she made a second attempt on her life. This time she locked herself in the bathroom, lay down in the warm bath in which she intended to drown, swallowed her pills and opened the veins in her wrists with a sharp penknife bought for the purpose. She was making very sure. Only a chance telephone call which instituted a search for her caused her plans to miscarry.

When Lucy saw her mother in the mental ward of the hospital – the white shocked face, the blank staring eyes, the poor bandaged arms – she was overcome with terror and compassion. She could tell that her mother knew her, but had no wish to communicate with her. Only when Lucy mentioned her father and asked if she could bring him, the unseeing eyes suddenly focused fiercely and Isabelle shook her head with surprising violence.

After two days, she was transferred to a mental home. Here she maintained her frozen silence among the madwomen, but spoke to her daughter: 'I believe in euthanasia . . . I have a perfect right to take my own life if I choose . . . I am in advance of my time – that's all.' Lucy recognized with a pang an echo of Arthur's teaching. She knew that her mother was not astray in her wits in the sense in which her companions were, but soon would be, if she were to remain there. She and her husband moved heaven and earth to rescue her, and after a few weeks, Isabelle was transferred to a nursing-home within easy visiting distance, where her painful convalescence began. As she progressed she became vehement with anguished protestations against her husband, attributing to him all her unmerited suffering. Who at this time could possibly have imagined that this tormented creature would one day come into calm waters? Who could picture that cosy, attractive old lady, gay, alert and stimulating, whose children and grandchildren would actually take pleasure in visiting?

But that lay far in the future.

Arthur found himself almost as much alone as after that first disaster in California. Most of the time he lay like a man in a coma. Lucy, occupied with her mother and her household, resorted to telephone messages and hasty notes. It was some days

264

before she came to him. Shocked though she was at his ghastly appearance, she hardened her heart at the prospect of removing him to her home. The extra burden would be beyond her. Here he had only to ring the bell . . . It is doubtful if Arthur would have gone, if invited, for he was fully conscious of the nuisance he would be, if he couldn't pull his weight. He was unquestionably a sick man as he lay hour after hour facing the wall in listless vacancy, a 'Do not disturb' sign hung on his bedroom door. As at La Jolla, he could not face the fearful thing that had occurred. He tried his utmost not to think of it, but everything else, even the Bomb, was irrelevant.

At what point would his wife come to an attitude of acceptance of himself as the poor thing that he was – an attitude of resignation? The answer was *never* – this side senility. But he was presupposing that she would choose to return to him, like last time . . . Perhaps she never would? He was nearly finished anyway . . .

He lifted his ash-tray and blew the ash off his bedside table. In the remaining dust, he slowly traced a rhomboid with his forefinger as he lay lost in thought.

His children in Africa, appalled by the news, telegraphed, urging him to visit them. Miraculously, Francis secured an air passage. Things were suddenly settled for him and he was not too ill to attend to his packing. Suddenly, there was a lot to do. He called at the house in Regent's Park on his way to having his passport photograph taken. Lucy was visiting Isabelle. The child went to a better school now and was out all day. He had been looking forward to helping her with her homework – when she was given any homework. Children did nothing but play nowadays. At that age surely he'd begun Latin . . . A good education was sound and valid then, on account of the future. The future . . . Well, let them play now! He hurried on his way.

It was a tedious business going through his few possessions. There was a trunk containing his books and old letters methodically filed. A few photographs – his first tiger, wedding pictures – that kind of thing. At the very bottom he came on a quotation (from the Venerable Bede, he claimed) that he had always liked, that Lucy had painted for him in illuminated letters at a time when she had a craze for old manuscripts. 'A little thing is a little thing but faithfulness in little things is a great thing.' Yes, he'd always liked that. Had it framed and hung it on his wall. It could be said to have been his motto. But Isabelle had detested it, objecting fiercely to the emphasis on 'little things' and he'd put it away.

He disposed of everything – his wireless, his bicycle, everything. He would travel light like an old campaigner, with only his clothes, such as they were. That would make less trouble for whoever had to clear up after him.

When he went to say good-bye to Lucy he was business-like, wary of emotion.

'I'm in rather a hurry – '

'But you'll stay to tea?'

'No, dear girl. A lot to do.' He cleared his throat in embarrassment. 'I should dearly have liked to give Frances her first car – and to teach her to drive it.'

'Oh Father,' Lucy was distressed.

'I have not much money, as you know, but what I have I want to leave towards her first car.'

'But please don't, Father. We're so much richer than you are. Keep it. You'll need it.'

'My pension is adequate to our needs. Don't argue, dear girl. One can't see far ahead, and anyway I shall be gone long before she's old enough to get a licence.'

'You've said that as long as I can remember. I'm beginning to think you're immortal!'

'And the Lord only knows what the value of money will be by then,' he went on, 'it'll probably only be worth a spare wheel or a couple of headlamps if inflation comes, but for what it's worth, I've opened a post office account for her with my savings.'

'Father, I *wish* you'd keep it.' She was crying now.

'Good-bye, dear girl. Keep me posted about your mother, and please let me know when you think I can write to her . . . Good-bye, girlie. I'll be sending you some tins of those asparagus tips you like and some sweets. No rationing where I'm going. Good-bye my girlie. Good-bye.'

He was in a fever of anxiety. It might have been his first trip

266

abroad. He fussed about – checking the small essentials over and over – passport, ticket, money, his pipe-and-baccy, his Wodehouse. The luggage was there – would the taxi-cab let him down? . . . As when he had left for good his beloved India, he didn't spare a thought for farewell to the land of his birth. His aircraft left at an ungodly hour. Nobody saw him off.

32

It did not do. His daughters were fond of him and determined to welcome him, his daughters-in-law beautiful and well-disposed, their husbands kind, the grandchildren lively and friendly – but it just didn't work. He did not fit into their households. The hours he kept were a source of continual friction, for his misanthropic ways now involved getting up at one in the morning and retiring to bed for the day (theoretically with fatigue poisons) immediately after breakfast. A wakeful member of the family might hear him unobtrusively turning night into day – the stealthy, restrained running of a bath, the occasional muffled thuds as he did his Müller's exercises: for he still kept to these as rigorously as when he had installed the parallel bars for his children in India in an endeavour to inculcate in them his life-long habit of Swedish drill.

His grandchildren naturally did not replace the one he had known from birth and in whose making he had had a hand. His only approach to children was through the method of instruction, but these had no wish to be instructed. They were little girls, for the most part, acutely conscious of their own undoubted attractions and already taking a keen interest in members of the opposite sex – but obviously not if he were in his late seventies.

In an attempt to break his valetudinarian habits, he would be pressed to join in sociabilities. 'Your father's never about,' friends would say (dropping in in the hospitable manner that had ceased to exist in England). 'We think he's a myth!' When finally prevailed upon to meet them, his almost morbid dislike of small talk made for a strained atmosphere. He would sit in silence, belching forth pipe-smoke, or come out suddenly with inappropriate stories. Unquestionably, his presence was a source of embarrassment. The pattern was always the same. When the strain on one household became too great, the time limit was up and Arthur was passed on to the next.

There were not generally rows, for he was never anxious to give battle if it could be avoided. He was simply not wanted, anywhere. He did not consciously consider this fact. He drove it from his thoughts as he drove away thoughts of Isabelle. (He corresponded with his wife now – friendly, impersonal letters on both sides.) She did not want him back. Neither, of course, did Lucy. After all, why should anyone want a useless old hulk like himself about the place . . .

He was dimly aware of an emptiness, a general sense of futility. Perhaps this emptiness had always been there? For years, his outstanding capacity for work had kept him too busy to consider it. Then his devouring curiosity had filled the gap. He had held the acquiring of knowledge to be a boundless enriching of human life. He could be happy with a page of the encyclopedia. Now, *he no longer wanted to know*. He had lost interest. He who had lived from day to day, and even hour to hour, following the sequence of world events, had cut himself off from all that. He had simply ceased to care about it. The dreary complexities of South African politics bored him. He was too tired now, and too bored to take the trouble to find out.

He was beginning to age rapidly.

His son's household in a prosperous suburb of Johannesburg could not accommodate him. Though equipped with the usual swimming-pool and charming garden, it was short of bedroom-space, since, in addition to the presence there of three little girls, a spare room was an absolute prerequisite. He lodged in a residential hotel, just outside the limits of the fantastic city that soared from the veld. The place was adequate to his needs. Here, in the calm of an assumed serenity, a disguised resignation, he settled down to await death. On his better days, he set off along Jan Smuts Avenue to walk to his son's home. It was his sole recreation.

For the most part, his world had shrunk to the space contained by the walls of his bedroom. Ah well, it was not a bad room. There were many things to be thankful for. The jacaranda tree that he could see from his window for one . . . the climate for another – he had always set great store by a good climate. Here it was bright and dry in winter, just about ideal for human comfort. He lay in bed knitting a combined scarf and hood for Frances. It would be cold in England now. Knitting was an effort though. Funny, he once used to turn out socks by the dozen . . .

He rolled up his knitting and put it on the hired wireless set that stood on the table beside him. The wireless was out of order, but he hadn't bothered to get it attended to. Nothing he wanted to hear anyway. He looked at the travelling-clock and noted that it wanted twenty minutes to his sleep-time. If he went to sleep before nine, he wakened before one. That was too long a wait for breakfast, no matter how many brews of tea he made on his little primus stove.

He lay for a time examining his hands, turning them this way and that. He noted with interest the patches of brown that had appeared on the backs of them. He wondered again if that pain he had felt earlier on were the beginning of an early carcinoma. It had gone now. He hoped he wasn't going to die of cancer. It was such a long, lingering end. Ah well, the end of life was generally a painful affair . . . Two minutes to go. Good. There was a crossword waiting for the small hours. It helped to pass the time. Also a problem, if he could manage to get round to it. Sleep now – that was the best thing he knew – the peerless moment of sinking into unconsciousness . . .

When Dickie told his father that he had been lent a cottage at Plettenburg Bay, a beautiful, new, fast-developing resort on the Indian Ocean, and invited him to come, Arthur refused.

'Not up to it, dear boy.'

'Come on, Father! It'll do you good. Buck you up. Just what you need! It's a glorious place.'

'I'm sure it is. It's very kind of you to suggest it, but I'm not well enough – '

'I'll drive you there. It's a fine drive. You'll enjoy it. And I know you're going to like it when you get there.'

'How far is it?' Arthur asked tentatively.

'About seven hundred.'

'Too far. I couldn't manage it. It's really very good of you, dear boy, but – '

'That's nothing in the Mercedes! You won't notice it. South Africans think nothing of driving from here to Cape Town, which is much farther. Look, here's a snap of the house. Here's your room, see, with two big windows looking on to about the finest beach you ever saw.'

Arthur continued to refuse, but he was tempted, sorely tempted. After Dickie had left, he surprised himself by humming a tune. Though he continued to insist that he was not well enough for such a strenuous trip, the fact of being invited, being wanted, being pressed to go, produced a strange metamorphosis. A mysterious alchemy took place in his being which drove him forth in the morning along the long avenue that led out to his son's house, to ask for further particulars. He accepted the invitation.

As he walked back, the rather unattractive-looking groups of Africans with sullen faces that he passed on his way began to assume a new interest. He wondered why he hadn't attempted to master their languages. Some of these tongues had strange sounds – clicks and so forth that would be fun to attempt. The trouble with the Afrikaaners, he decided, was that they lived in contact with peoples at such low levels of civilization that it gave them an innate sense of superiority. Very understandable. He must study these things . . .

There was a week to go. As the days passed, Arthur grew absurdly excited. He wouldn't need much in the way of clothes. His bathing-trunks, now – where were they? He bought himself some Penguins, old favourites mostly, and laid in a store of sweets for the children.

In his newly acquired energy he managed to walk daily to the suburb to discuss preparations. He wondered whether his son would allow him to take the wheel on the open road. Well, *he* wouldn't be the one to suggest it. It was arranged that the eldest child should travel with them in the car, while his daughter-in-law and the two youngest children went by train.

'FRANCES DARLING,' he wrote in laborious capitals:

I hope you will like your cap-scarf or scarf-cap that I posted you yesterday. I had to make it in a deep coral colour, as it was the only suitable wool the shop had in stock. I am going tomorrow for a holiday with your Uncle Dickie and his family to a beautiful unspoilt bay 700 miles away. I wish you were coming too.

Fond love from
Your devoted Ganfer,
A. Boyne

He always signed himself thus formally, with the flowing signature with which he had signed thousands of official letters. When he went out to the post, he was annoyed to find that the stores were shut. It was careless of him . . . His monthly parcel to his granddaughter would fall due while he was away. He made a note to write to the grocer from Pettenburg.

The city was hushed in the dim light of very early morning. The mine-dumps – man-made mountains of pale sand that had once held gold – were mysterious and beautiful as they drove past them. The highway across the high veld was empty. They made good time. Arthur was enjoying himself.

Towards noon he began to feel ill.

Dickie was unsympathetic. If his father was going to have a go of fatigue poisons, well, it was just too bad. On top of the long hard drive, he had to open up the cottage, see to the boiler and hurry away to the nearest railway – a long way off – to collect his family.

The great car devoured the miles, streaking across the immense wilderness as the hours passed. Arthur dozed and woke and dozed again. When they had travelled a long way, he saw the rugged outlines of mountain ranges far to the east – the great

Dragon mountains . . . Somewhere over there he had stayed with Isabelle on that first trip when, with Europe beginning to taste nasty, they had set forth for pastures new . . . He gazed out at the vast melancholy of the African scene and, filled with a strange disquiet, settled down to sleep.

He woke to an acute sense of discomfort to which was added a pain in his lower regions. He called on his son to stop that he might attend to the wants of nature. He returned just as his son was about to sound the horn impatiently to summon him. He looked curiously crushed and dejected, like an old dog who's been roughly handled. 'Waterworks seized up,' he muttered as he slumped into his seat.

After only a few miles he stopped the car again, holding up his right hand, conveying his meaning by an imperious gesture as if a verbal request were too much trouble. Dickie pulled to the side with a bad grace, pointing out it was not long since they had stopped and they had to get on – there was the devil of a way to go yet . . . Arthur returned in speechless dejection. Not for a moment did Dickie consider that his father was seriously ill. All his life he could remember him fussing over his imaginary ailments. It was only natural that he, who had cried 'Wolf!' so often, should be disbelieved when the hour struck.

The agonizing drive went on. It was night when they arrived. Dickie helped his father up to his room. He threw wide the magic casements opening on the foam. Arthur collapsed on the bed unheeding.

'I want a doctor.'

'Not now. I've got to get the boiler started for the hot water and then there's only just time to get to the station.'

'Get a doctor.'

'You have a rest and have some more whisky. You'll feel better presently.'

'Get a doctor.'

'Father, there *isn't* one here! There are only a few houses and the hotel.'

'Telephone for a doctor.'

'All *right!* When I get back. You stay quiet now.'

'Doctor – ' Dickie left the room. He took his tired little daughter with him on the further drive.

Arthur drank from his flask till he emptied it. He grew befuddled and then unconscious. He did not hear the family arrive. Dickie looked into his room and saw him sleeping.

'Thank God he's asleep! You can't imagine the dance he led me – '

When Arthur woke, he realized that the pain was back and worse than before. He called for a long time before his son, engulfed in the sleep of the very tired, came to him. He stood in the doorway, blinking at his father.

'I've told you to go for a doctor,' Arthur found the strength to shout.

A retired Afrikaans doctor lived up the hill. He didn't like being disturbed in the middle of the night and came reluctantly. Recognizing Arthur's collapsed state, he ordered him to be taken to hospital immediately and gave an injection of morphia. The nearest hospital was at Port Elizabeth, 150 miles away.

The moon was high in the night sky.

Dickie drove like a man in a trance – he seemed hardly to know what he was doing. Now and then he was aware of the savage beauty of the scene – the great moonlit waves crashing in the depths of precipitous chasms that the road skirted at a high level, by miracles of Italian (prisoner-of-war) engineering. Father would have liked that, would like, will like – strike out what's not applicable . . . And the long white lines of the gigantic surf, as high as houses, with a white canopy of flying spray floating above, clearly visible even in the moonlight – that too he would? would have? will? like very much. Spray that looked like a shroud . . . Perhaps Father was dead? As he slowed up, however, Arthur asked his son to assist him to the verge to be sick. (It was the morphia.) Even in his dying, he was precise and scrupulous. ('A little thing is a little thing . . .')

At long last, the nightmare drive ended as the lights of Port Elizabeth, back-clothed by the promise of dawn, came in sight.

Arthur had not spoken. He had only groaned at intervals. He summoned his strength for a final word directed at the night-superintendent. There were forms to be filled in.

274

'Religion?' she asked sleepily and repeated to Dickie, 'Religion?'

'*Atheist!*' Arthur suddenly shouted.

'Look, you can be C. of E., Dutch Reformed, R.C., Baptist, Methodist . . .'

'Atheist,' Arthur whispered. It was an echo of his former assertion. Dickie wrote 'C. of E.' in the space indicated.

The hospital was full. As there was no private ward, room was made for Arthur in a general ward. In a bed in the corner a patient was groaning alarmingly. Arthur's groans were added to the night noises of the ward.

'What about the new patient?' the houseman on night-duty asked the nurse as she handed him the papers.

'Raving. He's asking for tinned asparagus and boiled sweets!'

'I'll give him an injection . . .'

In the morning an operation was performed. Arthur never recovered consciousness – consciousness of his normal waking state, that is. He lay for some hours talking in a clear voice, but was unaware of being moved to a private ward, of all that was done for him. He had retreated now from the torture of the present to a long-forgotten past. The past too had its pain. '*Mother!*' he cried suddenly, starting up with surprising strength, so that the nurse had to push him back onto the pillows, 'Mother, what's that coming under the door? Mother, it's *blood!* . . . Who said the Blood of the Lamb? . . . That's my pater in there . . .'

After a time he grew composed, wearing the alert, gentle, inquiring look that always seemed to be on the point of smiling and was habitual to him. He was back now in the India he had loved, in the days before Isabelle came to cloud the scene. For two long hours he babbled of hills and plains, river, jungle, bazaar . . . on and on clearly and with evident pleasure. At times, he seemed like a man enjoying a private showing of a well-loved film, when he would point and exclaim in pleased recognition at something once loved and long forgotten. 'Fazil Khan,' he said suddenly, giving the nurse an affectionate pat. 'You're to come with me. That's right. That's right. Before it gets too hot. We'll be off now . . .'

275

His speech died away slowly. 'Time for a nap,' he said distinctly. 'Call me in ten minutes – no, I can spare twelve minutes, I think . . .' After that, there was an occasional confused murmur until the moment when he suddenly heaved an enormous sigh as he felt, invading his being, the delicious familiar symptoms of sinking into sleep.

When Dickie arrived in the morning, his father had not known him. When he returned, he was dead.

He stood numbed, agreeing automatically to the necessary formalities. They handed him a box containing the last pathetic reminders – his father's watch, fountain-pen, wallet, teeth . . . (The clothing would do for a needy black.) He walked out on to the entrance porch and remained there for some time, seeing and hearing nothing. He was filled with savage thoughts about his father. 'Cause of death . . . euraemia.' It was his own bloody fault. Why the hell hadn't he had the operation years ago? . . . *How could I have known?* . . . The end was terrible. He had been crazed with pain then . . .

All his life he had been gentle, timorous even. There had never been a trace of malice in him. He had been incapable of crooked dealing.

All his life he had broken the two great commandments: he had loved neither God nor his neighbour. But who would dare to assert that his place was not among the pure in heart?

With a sudden violent gesture, Dickie threw his father's teeth into the bushes that bordered the drive. (Novel playthings for a Kaffir child.)

Then he got into his car and started on the long drive back to the fabulous bay.